DARK PURSUIT

APOCALYPTIC URBAN FANTASY

ANN GIMPEL

Edited by

K. R. SHIELDS

Illustrated by

FIONA JAYDE

CONTENTS

Dark Pursuit   v
Copyright Page   vii
Acknowledgments   xi
Book Description: Dark Pursuit   xiii

Chapter 1   1
Chapter 2   15
Chapter 3   27
Chapter 4   39
Chapter 5   53
Chapter 6   71
Chapter 7   83
Chapter 8   97
Chapter 9   107
Chapter 10   121
Chapter 11   137
Chapter 12   149
Chapter 13   161
Chapter 14   173
Chapter 15   185
Chapter 16   197
Chapter 17   207
Chapter 18   217
Chapter 19   229
Chapter 20   241
Chapter 21   255
Chapter 22   265
Chapter 23   277
Chapter 24   287

About the Author   297
Dark Promise—Prologue   299
Dark Promise, Chapter One   303

DARK PURSUIT

SOUL STORM, BOOK TWO

Apocalyptic Urban Fantasy
By
Ann Gimpel

Old blood and ancient power defy evil so dark, deep, and menacing, it
destroys everything in its path

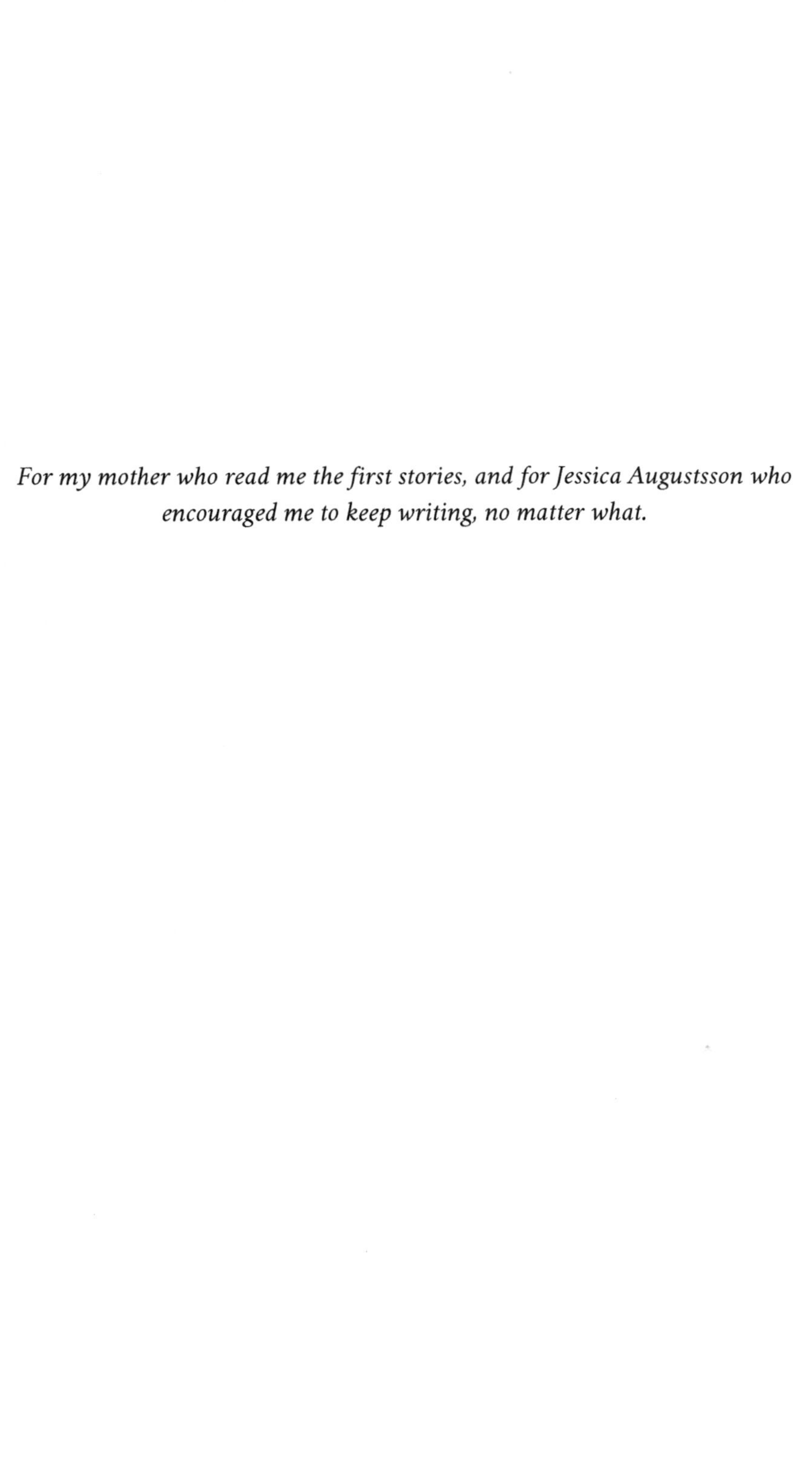

For my mother who read me the first stories, and for Jessica Augustsson who encouraged me to keep writing, no matter what.

ACKNOWLEDGMENTS

I'd like to send warm hugs and thanks to the wonderful women who beta read this book for me. Karen Mikhael, Bridgette Thoroughman, Holli Greer, Missie Kurr, Niki Driscoll, and Cherri-Anne Boitson. I'd also like to send warm thoughts to Fiona Jayde, best cover artist ever. And then there are my author friends who helped with editing. It truly takes a village, and I'm eternally grateful for every single person who's jumped in to support my writing career. Authors are a warm and wonderful bunch, and so are our readers!

BOOK DESCRIPTION: DARK PURSUIT

Widespread rioting, plus shortages of fuel, food, and electricity lure demons across the veil to invade Earth. Drawn by anarchy, they're out of control, drunk on their own power, and growing stronger by the day.

With her life crumbling around her, Lara McInnis is reluctantly roped into channeling her psychic talents to locate a missing teen. Her lack of skill strands her in the murky underbelly of a world inhabited by dark forces.

Trevor Denoble's Celtic blood yields unexpected gifts. After years of uncertainty, Lara is really and truly finally his, and he's determined to keep her by his side. No stranger to violence, more blood on his hands is a small price to pay to keep the woman he loves safe.

CHAPTER 1

*D*r. Lara McInnis began the day clinging to a slender island of solace. Hours later, waves of patients, errands, and phone calls had pounded against that island until it was nothing but a rubble heap.

Rubbing wearily at her eyes, Lara finally gave up and closed them. For a moment or two she thought she might get away with it, but then an image of Arabel, her long time receptionist, lying in a pool of her own blood rose out of some subterranean reservoir. The grizzly scene was so real, Lara's stomach clenched. Like an unwelcome tape loop, it played again. And again. Opening her eyes didn't help one whit. Arabel was just as bloody and just as dead. Over a week had passed, but the raw edges of her grief still cut deep.

Lara collapsed into the chair generally reserved for her patients. Outside her western window a scarlet sunset streaked the Seattle skyline, adding its bloody motif to the one already playing in her head. Disgusted with herself, she got to her feet and paced the length of her spacious office, burning a track in the Oriental rug. She should be boxing up client files, but couldn't force herself back to a task she was ambivalent about—at least not until she wrestled her emotions under better control.

The doorknob rattled. It startled her, and her heart jumped into overdrive. In her current state, the familiar sound was like a reproach. "How could I not have locked it with everything that's going on?" she muttered as she rushed into the outer office. Arabel's desk, another Oriental rug, and ornate Victorian furniture with floral upholstery flashed past the edges of her vision, but she focused on the door as she watched the knob slowly turning.

This is ridiculous. It's probably a pharmaceutical salesman thinking I'm a psychiatrist.

Or that Demon that's been dogging me, a darker inner voice insinuated.

Since the only other option was throwing herself out a second story window and hoping for the best, Lara crossed the few feet to the door and yanked it open. A decidedly overweight woman jerked her hand away from the knob and eyed Lara balefully out of rheumy, blue eyes. Pale brown hair, going gray, was gathered into an untidy bun, and fat rolls bulged over too-tight jeans and under an inadequate T-shirt.

"Mrs. Stone." Lara tried to smile as she coaxed her heart back to a normal rhythm.

"Humph, surprised you remember me."

"Of course I do." Lara stepped aside, gesturing for the woman to enter. The last thing she wanted was another patient visit, but it would verge on the unethical—never mind the rude—to ask Myra Stone to go away without at least finding out what she wanted.

Lara waited while Myra stalked past her, looked inside the inner office, and circled back to stand in front of Lara, hands on her hips. "Guess she's not here," Myra snapped.

"If you're looking for Caren, no, she's not," Lara agreed, mystified. "Is your stepdaughter missing?"

The woman grunted. She still had an expression on her face that could curdle milk, but she knotted her fingers together and said, "How about if we sit down, and you and me can have a little talk?"

"Okay." Lara kept her voice as neutral as she could, pulled the office door shut—taking care to lock it this time—and rolled Arabel's chair out. Her butt had barely grazed the seat cushion when the woman started talking.

"I don't think spending time here is helping Caren. Nope, not at all," Myra complained in an unpleasant, nasal twang. "I never know where she is. She's still taking what doesn't belong to her and that father of hers, well he's not any help at all. So it's just me." Accusatory eyes drilled into Lara. "All my *real* kids turned out fine. This one, she's just a bad seed." Rooting around in a battered handbag, Myra pulled out a cigarette. "Do you mind?"

"Uh, yes, I'd prefer you didn't smoke," Lara managed, struck by the gall of the woman and offended to hear her belittle her stepdaughter so blatantly. Caren had said Myra hated her, but Lara assumed it was just teenaged hyperbole.

Myra stuffed the cigarette into her T-shirt pocket and pushed her bulk upright. "Not much reason for me to stay," she muttered. "Really thought she'd be here. You're the only one she ever says anything good about."

If she felt like one of your real *kids, maybe she'd say good things about you—or feel safe enough to love you.* Discouraged by the woman's callousness—after all, Caren had been through hell in her sixteen years—Lara stood too. Trying for a positive spin, she said, "You must be concerned or you wouldn't have come looking for Caren. Would you like to make an appointment, Mrs. Stone? I already told you on the phone that I'm closing my practice, but I'd be glad to find a time slot for you in the next couple weeks. We could talk about some of the challenges of step-parenting and how hard it is for abused children to learn to trust—"

"Nah." Myra waved her to silence. "Hell, my uncle did me, and I didn't turn out like her. I didn't cut school or steal stuff. Or carve on myself." Shuffling to the door, she pulled it open and stalked out into the hall, the tiny chink in her armor replaced by a brittle, defensive anger.

"At least consider it," Lara persisted, addressing the woman's back as Myra headed for a stairwell. Lara drew the door shut, thinking Myra could do with a smattering of psychotherapy herself. *Yeah, like about ten years' worth.* Crimson from the sunset bled through stained-glass windows, casting her familiar furniture in an eerie light. Lara wrapped her arms around herself, seeking the warmth of her own body for comfort.

That poor child. From abusive kin to a stepmother who doesn't want her. Sorrow for Caren replaced the Arabel tape loop as color faded from the room. Lara decided it was an improvement, all in all, and she kicked a box over a few inches so she could open the lower drawer of her filing cabinet.

Lara pushed her long, red hair behind her shoulders and dumped banded files into the banker's box without any particular regard for order. The outer door of her office rattled again. This time, though, it was a key sound.

"Lara?"

"In here, Trev," she called and straightened to greet her longtime boyfriend.

Trevor, his usually buoyant mood notably subdued, held out his arms. "'Lo, Lara. Sorry I'm a bit late but… Well, never mind, it'll keep." He scanned the room with his intensely blue eyes, taking in her half-finished packing job. "How much more?" he asked tentatively.

Shooting him a pain-laced look, she shook her head. "I don't know. I'm doing this as fast as I can in between seeing patients who want a last session or two. Thank God Arabel started calling all of them before…" She walked into his arms and buried her head against his shoulder.

He closed his arms around her, holding her close. "Doesn't matter, love. It'll be done eventually." Blond curls brushing against her face, he kneaded her shoulders with both hands. "Bloody hell, you're wound tighter than a spring."

The familiar clipped tones of his British accent washed over her, easing her anguish. "Feels heavenly," she breathed. "I didn't realize how tense I was…" Her voice trailed off. "Well, maybe I did, but I've been forcing myself not to pay attention." She pulled away and flopped onto the floral couch spanning part of one wall. Exhaustion dragged at her.

Trevor pushed boxes out of the way and joined her. "I miss Arabel too, you know." His voice cracked with emotion, and he cleared his throat. "Any of those ready to take home?" he asked, pointing at the half dozen boxes littering the floor.

"Yeah, those three." She jabbed her index finger at a corner of the room. "They're records from patients I haven't seen in at least a couple years."

"What are you going to do with the others?" His tone was gentle, but he placed a finger under her chin, forcing her to look at him. "What are you saving them for?"

"Guess I can't very well keep any of them," she muttered. "It's not like we're even going to be here after a little while."

"No," he agreed solemnly. "It's not. And we're not."

Lara set her lips into a thin line and got to her feet. "Okay, then," she snapped, angry with a universe that was intent on stealing her life away. Pulling open file drawers, she grabbed a few charts and dumped them on her desk. "I need these since all of them have appointments, but the rest can go."

Nodding, Trevor joined her in front of the twin horizontal files, and together they began to move twenty years of Lara's psychology practice into the waiting cartons. "You'll need more boxes," he noted after a few minutes. "Lots more."

"Thought we could fill these, dump them at home, and then I'd just bring the empties back tomorrow and begin all over."

"Ah, brilliant. Of course that's the obvious thing to do." Grunting, he shouldered a box and headed for the door. "I'll be back directly for another."

"Right behind you," she said, picking up a box. "I feel better when I'm doing something other than wallowing in my own misery."

"That's my girl," he shot back over his shoulder.

The minute Trevor opened the door of his old Mercedes

convertible, Gunter, their twelve-week-old German Shepherd lunged out of the car headed straight for Lara. The awkward black puppy yipped, whined, and launched himself at her, pulling at her wool skirt with his claws. "There, there, little man," she cooed and set her box down so she could unhook his feet from the fabric of her skirt. "Yes, I've missed you too."

As she fondled the puppy, she glanced at Trevor. Dressed in faded blue jeans, a green chambray shirt, and a tan corduroy blazer, his tall, lanky frame exuded its usual casual elegance. "How'd your day go?" she asked.

"Not bad," he replied, shoving his box of files into the car's small trunk and reaching for the one she'd set on the sidewalk. "We'll have to put the rest in your car, love. No more room in here." He slammed the car's boot. "I started really taking stock of what's in our house and making lists. Went down to the waterfront too." His lips curved wryly. "Didn't find much in the way of antique farm equipment, but I did get some leads. Bloke at the flea market looked at me as if I were daft."

She flashed him a weak smile. "Well, dear, I suppose it's not every day they get customers hunting for scythes, or whatever it was you asked for."

"Let's get those other boxes down here. Then we can walk the pup before we go home."

Lara inclined her head and turned to go back into her building *Lucky for us the electricity's not on the fritz. It's almost dark.* Power outages had been hit-and-miss. More often than not, she'd had to use a flashlight to find her way out of her building. Back in the office, she continued throwing files willy-nilly into the boxes. An orderly part of her rebelled when she looked at the files, no longer alphabetized, lying on their sides like beached whales. "It doesn't matter," she muttered fiercely. "All we're going to do is burn them."

She remembered something Raven had told her. *Your thought patterns are still trapped in your old life. That is what's brought modern civilization to the brink of extinction: an intransigent unwillingness to change anything.*

As she thought about Raven, a vision of the tall, broad-shouldered mage with his flowing black hair filled her mind. The amulet Lillian had given her, nestled between her breasts on its golden chain, thrummed approvingly. Lara grasped the moonstone through the fabric of her teal silk blouse, enjoying its warmth.

Raven and Lillian. Two ancient creatures, somehow alive and well in the early years of the twenty-first century. *Doesn't matter why or how, I'm just glad they're here, helping us.*

Trevor strode back into her inner office. "Got another box ready?" he asked.

"Uh-huh." She pointed. "There. I'll just finish this one and cart it out. Then there'll only be two more to fill and we can head home."

❧

"UGH," Trevor grunted as he shoved the last of the boxes into Lara's silver BMW. "Glad you only got six boxes. I don't think we could have crammed any more in with a shoehorn, since all that outdoor clothing we bought is still in there."

"Brrrr." She wrapped her arms around her upper body. "It's getting cold. Why don't you start for home? I'll be along soon."

"Right, then." He gathered her close. "No wonder you're cold, love." He fingered the silky fabric of her blouse. "Be sure to put your jumper on before you leave."

"Yes, Daddy." She smiled into the folds of his blazer, thinking how good it felt to be cared about.

He ruffled her hair, spun her round, and gave her a friendly swat on the butt. "Off with you, love. I'll have something started for supper by the time you get there. You *are* leaving directly behind me?"

"Right after I lock up."

Lara ran up the broad front steps of her Victorian office building, knowing she'd miss the old place with its unique stained glass windows. Pulling the front door shut and taking care to spin the deadbolt, she padded up the carpeted stairs to her office, opened the door, and stopped short.

Caren sat on the floor in the darkened reception area and shot a defiant glance Lara's way, but didn't say anything.

"Caren! How on earth did you get in here?"

"Back door was open." The teenager's voice was barely audible.

"I don't think so," Lara said and looked closely at her young client. "I distinctly remember locking it earlier."

"So I helped it along a little," the girl said, her voice rising in unspoken challenge.

"It's okay," Lara murmured. "However you managed to get in, it must've been important for you to find me."

"Yeah. I—I didn't believe what my stepmother told me. I thought she was just being mean. But it…it's true." Caren's voice broke and a low, keening moan escaped her. "I looked in there." She jerked a thumb toward the inner office where Lara saw her clients. "You're really leaving, aren't you? Just like everyone else has left me. You're leaving too." Reproachful blue eyes vilified Lara.

"Oh, sweetie—" Lara began.

"Don't *sweetie* me," the girl snarled. "You really had me going there, Doc. I thought you actually cared about me. But it was just a job, wasn't it? Just a fucking job, and now you're…you're…" Her face twisted into a rictus, and Caren began to cry. Soft little animal sounds tore out of her, as she turned her face to the wall.

Ach, what can I tell her that she'll believe? "Do you mind if I sit down?" Lara asked and drew the outer door of her office closed.

"I don't fucking care what you do," the girl choked out between sobs.

Nodding, Lara sank to the floor, but not too close to Caren. "I can see why you'd think I'm abandoning you." Lara reached toward her psychic side for help. Caren's aura reflected the girl's misery. Instead of lively colors, it had reverted to an opaque gray.

"You are."

"Well, I *am* leaving," Lara agreed, "but I'm not leaving to get away from you." Caren was silent, so Lara forged ahead, hoping against hope the girl would listen for long enough to not simply pigeonhole what was happening now into the long cavalcade of adults who'd let her down.

"My receptionist, Arabel, was murdered during the riots last week. She…" Lara swallowed hard. "She was like a mother to me, since my own mother died when I was very young. I— Well, Caren, I can't stand to be here without her. I know it's abrupt, and I would've liked to have had at least a month to tell all my patients goodbye, but…"

A tear dripped down her face, and Lara brushed it away. "I don't think I can keep on seeing people without Arabel's help. What I do is hard work. I can't do it if I'm empty inside."

"Oh." The girl's voice was small and wounded. "You didn't have a good mother, either?"

"Uh-uh. Not after mine died." Fishing around in her skirt pockets for a tissue, Lara wiped her eyes.

"That's why you understood. About me."

"Yes, dear. That's part of it." Lara glanced at her patient. Caren had straightened slightly from her slumped position, where she'd looked like a discarded rag doll. Her aura seemed a bit better too.

"But I don't want you to leave." The words tore out of the girl like shards of glass, painful to hear.

Lara held out her arms. "Come here," she invited. "Let me hold you. You look like you could use a hug. And I know I could." Figuring it was the last phrase that did it, Lara took a deep breath and closed her arms around the distraught teen, who'd scuttled across the floor, flinging herself into the offered embrace.

"This is so hard," Caren snuffled. "You're the first one I've trusted in years. Now you won't be here anymore."

"You'll carry the knowledge in your heart that you *can* trust someone," Lara murmured, stroking Caren's soft, dark hair. "And I'll carry you with me as well."

"You won't forget about me."

"Oh, sweetie, how could I?" Lara closed her eyes. Disclosing personal information ran against her professional grain, but what possible difference could the truth make at this point? Disentangling herself slightly from the trembling girl, Lara said, "Look at me. I want to tell you something."

When the girl's troubled eyes met hers, Lara let out a breath. "I could never forget you because you remind me so much of me when I was young."

Caren's eyes filled with tears. "You aren't just saying that. You really mean it."

"Yes, I really mean it. Now, when I called your stepmother, I asked her to find out if you wanted to come in for a last session or two. Did she tell you?" Caren shook her head. "How about tomorrow after school?"

"I—I'd like that."

"Okay, let me take a peek at my schedule." Lara heaved herself to her feet, even more drained than when she'd been packing boxes. Silent fury at Myra Stone soured her stomach. Her cell phone trilled. Picking it up, she glanced at the number and then pushed the answer key. "Hi, Trev—" she began.

"Where in the bloody blazes are you?" he snapped. "Please, please tell me you've got a good reason for not being home."

"I'm almost out of here," she replied carefully, aware Caren was listening. "I'll call you from the car once I'm on my way. Don't worry. I'm okay."

His breath whistled through the cellular system. "Righto." His accent was very crisp, betraying his anxiety. "I'll wait for you to ring me back."

Of course he'd be worried after the riots and Arabel, never mind that patient of mine who tried to kill me. With her lips pursed together, Lara pulled up the calendar on her phone.

"Is your husband mad at you?" Caren asked tremulously.

"No dear, just worried. Would three-thirty work?" Lara looked questioningly at the teenager. After she nodded, Lara tapped buttons. "There," she said. "You're in. Do you have a ride home?"

"Yeah, I brought my car. It's in the, uh, alley."

"Next to my back door?"

Caren dropped her gaze to her hands. "Yeah."

"Give me a sec, and I'll walk you out."

Lara slipped on a gray tweed wool jacket, grabbed her phone, pager, and purse, and shepherded Caren out of the office, down the stairs, and around to the back. "Is that it?" Lara asked, pointing to a yellow Volkswagen.

"Uh-huh."

"Are you better?"

Caren looked at her, bit her lower lip, and said, "Some. But I still wish you weren't going."

I wish I wasn't either. "Bye, dear. Drive safe." Locking up, she marveled that the unruly teen had managed to defeat a locking mechanism designed to stymie professional burglars. After setting the building alarm, she hit the speed dial digit on her phone that would connect her to Trevor. He picked up on the first ring.

"Well?" he said, still sounding half-sick with fear.

"It was one of my younger patients," she said as she walked to her car, "needing reassurance. She snuck in the back while we were loading boxes." Lara blew out a tense breath. "Anyway, she looked around the office, put two and two together, and panicked. I'm heading home now. Can I tell you the rest when I get there? I'm tapped out, and I don't want to talk and drive at the same time."

"Sure, love." His voice softened. "See you soon."

"I love you." She hit the end call button and engaged the ignition.

Lara shut her eyes for a few seconds to rest them before dealing with the glare from other cars' headlamps. She grimaced. Her eyes felt gritty, and she was so tired her bones ached.

Nothing's going to get better with me sitting here.

As she guided the car through light traffic on her way to the freeway, Lara thought about the last three weeks. Hard to believe it had only taken that short amount of time for life to collapse.

"Get a grip," she hissed and clenched the leather-clad wheel until her fingers hurt. "It's not like Trev hasn't been warning me for months there wasn't enough gasoline or food, but I did my usual ostrich routine and didn't pay attention."

Her mind drifted to Lillian. After years of a love-hate relationship with her own psychic abilities, Lara had finally made an effort to find someone who could teach her about her magical side. "Heh! I got a tad more than I bargained for," she mumbled, finding enough energy to laugh ruefully.

Lara creased her forehead in thought. Everything that had happened since Ken Beauchamp accosted her on the front porch of her office, threatening her because she tried to help his abused wife, merged into a confusing maelstrom.

I can't think anymore. Maybe I could just do some breathing.

When she finally turned the car onto her street on Queen Anne Hill, she was painfully close to the end of her emotional tether. Relaxation breathing hadn't helped much, and she still felt like she was running on fumes. Her head throbbed dully. As she scanned the street for parking spots, she spotted one fairly close to the twenty-five stairs leading to their house and maneuvered into it. Shutting off the engine, she folded her hands together over the top of the steering wheel and rested her forehead on them. A sharp tap on her window made her jump.

"Lara?" Trevor's voice, muted by the thick safety glass, still sounded worried.

"Yeah, yeah. I'm coming." She pushed the door open and stumbled into the chill damp of a Seattle evening. He threaded his arms around her. "Bring what you need, love. Or I can get it for you."

"Bag, phone, pager." She drew in a shuddery breath. "Hell, I'm not that bad off. Nothing wrong with my body. I'm just emotionally drained, and my head hurts. If you hand that stuff to me, maybe you could haul one of those boxes upstairs."

He extracted the BMW's keys from her hand, then reached inside to gather her things. While he did that, Lara moved to the back of the car.

Got to stop feeling sorry for myself.

She straightened her shoulders and called, "Hit the hatch release, would you, since you've got my keys?" Once it was open, she reached inside and grasped one of the banker's boxes by its built-in handles.

Lara walked to the side of the car where Trevor stood, holding her things. "Just drop them on top of this box."

"Bloody bollocks, Lara. When you got out of the car, you looked like you could barely stand."

"Being home helps. Come on, dear. Please don't fight with me."

With an exasperated sigh, Trevor clipped her phone and pager to her bag, then laid all three atop the box she was carrying. "See you inside."

"No, you'll see me back out here in a couple minutes. We can eat after all those boxes are in the house. I can't leave them out here. They're confidential patient files. Burning them is one thing. Leaving them, even in a locked car, is quite another." Turning, she started up the steps to the front porch of their five story home.

"We could try one of those shredding services," he called after her.

Balancing the box carefully on a step, she trotted back over to him. "No, we couldn't," she said in a low voice. "Raven said it'd be dangerous for us if people know we're leaving. If we give hundreds of pounds of files to the shredders, someone's bound to get suspicious. Especially since they, of all people, would know I'm supposed to hang onto things for at least seven years."

Pulling the hatch closed, Trevor picked up two boxes, one atop the other. "Hmm, hadn't thought about it in quite that light, but they'd have to glance through the lot to search for dates, and that doesn't seem likely."

She tugged a back door open and got another box. "Maybe I'm overreacting."

"No worries, love. Lead on, then. I'm just behind you."

CHAPTER 2

*L*ara laid down her fork. They'd made small talk through the fettucini-esque dish Trevor had whipped up out of leftovers. After a mad dash for Lara when she was finally in the kitchen on his side of the puppy gate, Gunter had subsided into a sleepy heap next to his food dish.

"Thanks." Reaching across the glass-topped table, Lara placed a hand over Trevor's. "Part of my problem was I hadn't eaten since breakfast. I feel better, and my headache's mostly gone." She laid a hand over her stomach. "I know I'm too thin, so please don't lecture me about not taking care of myself."

As he grinned at her, Trevor's boyish good looks resurfaced for the first time since she'd arrived home. "Sorry I was short with you," he said sheepishly. "As unsettled as things are right now, it's hard not to worry when I think you're right behind me, and nearly an hour goes by and you don't show up."

"I'm sorry too. Didn't mean to worry you. I got so caught up with Caren, I wasn't thinking. Of course you would've been apprehensive." She offered him a weak smile, and then added, "Things do seem to have calmed down since last week's riots, though." She blew him a kiss that he mimed catching.

"Appearances can be deceiving," he said thoughtfully. "I spent more time out and about today than you did. Everybody was edgy."

"Mmph. Guess I'm still playing the Pollyanna. And doing a damned good job avoiding the truth of things." She cleared her throat. "Since you always manage to have food on the table, the shortages don't seem all that real to me. How's that for denial?" She berated herself for her own foolishness, and heat spread upward from her open neckline.

"Ah yes, haven't said much, but it takes me a bit longer each week to hunt down groceries." He looked pointedly at her. "Only reason we're still eating reasonably well is I've been willing to pay the market rate for food. It's gotten to where a lot of folk can't afford much anymore. That riot a few days ago may have been the first one here in Seattle, but I'll bet you it won't be the last."

"You said in the office you had things to tell me." Lara changed the subject. In spite of everything that had happened, Trevor's blatant dissection of an imploding society was unsettling. "What'd you do today, besides searching for farm equipment that doesn't require gasoline?"

"Sure you're up for it?" He looked intently at her. "Because it'll keep until tomorrow."

"Yeah, I'm sure." Standing, she picked dishes up from the table. "Let's get these in the washer. If we're lucky, they'll run through a full cycle before we lose the power again. Then we can sit in the living room and talk. Or we could go upstairs to bed."

"I'd vote for the living room so we can incinerate a few files. Here, Lara, I'll do the washing up." He made a grab for the dishrag. "Why don't you see to the pup? One of us needs to check the woodstove at some point. We won't even come close to destroying the files we brought home before we go to bed, but we can at least get those boxes emptied, so you can bring another load home tomorrow."

~

SHE WAS SITTING on the hardwood floor in front of the stove, a file open on her lap when Trevor entered their spacious living room. Gunter was busy chasing a green rubber ball.

"Seems to be quite proficient at entertaining himself," Trevor observed as he walked across the room to join her.

"Yes, only children learn that pretty young," she agreed, her gaze on the papers in her lap.

"What are you doing?"

"Probably something I shouldn't," she admitted. "I'm rereading my clinical notes, and some of my dream analyses. Guess I got sidetracked." Resolutely, she gathered charts and loose papers, opened the door of the woodstove, and shoved an armful onto the bed of coals. "There." She shut the stove with a *clang*. "Next batch." Reaching over, she pulled another clump of paper out of one of the boxes.

"I can do that tomorrow," he said quietly. "That way you won't have to say goodbye to each of your patients."

Her gaze skittered away from him and dropped to the woolen folds of her skirt. "I suppose that is what I'm doing," she acknowledged, looking uncomfortable. "Maybe you should have been the analyst."

"I know you pretty well," he said. Taking a measured breath, he added, "Raven stopped by today."

"What! Why didn't you tell me?" Eyes wide, she stopped sorting charts and stared at Trevor. "What'd he want?"

"Which question do you want an answer to?"

"Both."

He laughed. "Okay. I was going to tell you at your office. That's actually why I was later than I'd planned coming by to pick up those boxes. But you just looked so, oh I don't know, so desolate, I wasn't sure I should broach anything."

Lara tossed another armload of paper into the stove. "That answers one question. Now what did he want?" While Raven fascinated her, he frightened her too. She could still remember looking at him with her third eye, the aspect she used to read auras, and seeing light pouring through him. And then there'd been his transition into something like Wôden as he'd joined the Wild Hunt on Halloween Eve.

Nodding, Trevor said, "How about if we go upstairs? I'd like to be in bed holding you before we have *that* conversation. I'll bring the puppy along."

Recognizing he wasn't going to tell her anything until it felt right to him, Lara eyed the stove and judged how much more she could cram in there. She yanked rubber bands off long-closed files and placed them carefully into the flames, watching the fire flare up as she closed the glass door.

"Okay." Steadying herself on a nearby coffee table, she pushed to her feet. "I'll get the lights and set the alarm." Even though Ken Beauchamp—the patient who'd tried to kill her—was dead, murdered in jail by some of his fellow gang members from the Mexican Mafia, she still felt safer with their alarm engaged.

Lillian warded the house, she reminded herself. *Surely that counts for something.* As if in agreement, the moonstone amulet thrummed pleasantly against her skin.

She plucked her phone and pager off the antique armoire in the entry hall and checked for messages as she climbed the two flights to their bedroom. Trevor and Gunter were already there, nestled in the king-sized bed. "I'll just be a minute," she murmured, as she shucked her clothes onto a chair, pulled an old nightshirt over her head, and went into the adjoining bathroom to wash her face and brush her teeth.

When she came back out, Trevor was putting her clothes on hangers and placing them in her perpetually-disorganized closet.

"Er, thanks." She reddened. While she liked having a tidy office, her bedroom had always been another story. Trevor had given up on sharing a closet with her years ago. All his things were hanging in neat rows two floors up in his study.

"You won't be needing these much longer," he said as he picked up her flat-heeled pumps, nesting them under a dresser. "May as well keep them decent. We can drop them at the Goodwill or a women's shelter before we leave town. Someone will be able to get some use out of them."

She climbed into her side of the bed. "Tell me about Raven."

"He was disappointed both of us weren't here," Trevor began, gently moving Gunter off to one side, so he could cradle Lara without having the puppy between them. "I told him you'd be home in a couple hours, but he said he couldn't wait.

"He wanted to let us know he's moved a fair number of livestock to the farm. Half a dozen more goats, a bunch of chickens, and another horse."

"That would make two horses. Guess we'll have to learn to ride. Once we figure out how to take care of them, that is." Worry tugged at her. What they were about to do was radically different from anything either of them had ever undertaken before.

"The horses will likely spend most of their time hooked to a plow." He smiled at her. "So if you had a girlhood dream of learning to ride—"

"No, seriously." Lara met his gaze. "Who's going to take care of all of all those animals until we move out there?"

"I asked the same thing." Trevor settled her more firmly against him. "I know you're worried, love. So am I. There's a whole lot about living like this that we don't know. At least the livestock should be safe. Raven doubled up the warding around the house. He's planning on me dropping by nearly every day. Betwixt the two, he seemed to think there wouldn't be any problems."

Trevor paused, "But the more important thing is that he and Lillian are leaving for a while. They're going back to the Old Country for some sort of Sidhe gathering."

"How are they going to get there?" Lara's voice was muffled against Trevor's shoulder. "The planes quit flying weeks ago, didn't they?"

"You're not thinking, love. They scarcely need planes." He sounded uncomfortable. "Anyhow, Lillian wanted us—or at least you—to come along, but Raven didn't. He prevailed. Mostly he wanted us to not be looking for them for a spot of time. He did make a point of it, though, that you had to study. Every day, he said." Trevor laughed nervously. "He nailed me with those gray eyes of his and made me promise I'd make sure you did some reading out of that book every single day. And that you'd go through it a second time—and even a third—if you finished."

Lara was silent as she digested Trevor's words. Disentangling herself, she flipped on a reading light that was recessed into their headboard. "I'm not sure I like it that they're leaving," she said, looking worriedly at Trevor. "What happens if we need some sort of help?"

"Probably why Lillian wanted to keep you close," he ventured. "Because of Himmelschaun, or whatever his other name is."

"Gradoxst," Lara muttered and thought about the Demon masquerading as an analyst at the Jung Institute in Zurich. "That's his real name."

"Uh-huh." Trevor cleared his throat. "Don't want you to think I'm being pushy, love, but how much longer do you need to be here? The sooner we're out at Raven's, the safer we'll be."

"But Gradoxst intrudes into my visions," she objected, frowning. "Surely he'll be just as likely to do that wherever we are."

Trevor turned her to face him. "The riots are going to worsen as supplies dwindle. Eventually they'll ration petrol, and there'll likely be some sort of martial law. You may still have that madman in your visions, but at least we'll garner a wee bit of control over the rest."

Lara recognized the stubborn note in his voice all too well. "You usually have good instincts," she murmured and picked up her phone to check her calendar. After consulting it, she looked at him. "I have people scheduled through the end of next week. I referred everybody else. So there's your answer." Counting on her fingers, she said, "Eleven days."

"That might be too long," he said quietly.

"But I can't just disappear," she pleaded. "I've cut over a hundred patients down to twelve. They need me, especially now with the world turning upside down. I've seen each of them for a long time. Well, maybe not Caren, but she's different."

"They're all special to you," he countered crisply. "It's why you're such a good therapist. But if it makes the difference between us being able to get out of here or not, I say we go before then, if we can."

"What else did Raven tell you?" she asked, intuition flooding her as she studied his face.

"Never could hide much from you, could I?"

"You managed to do a pretty good job on that front," she said. "For over twenty years, mind you."

He looked sad and chagrined, the corners of his mouth twisted into a bitter expression. "That, my love took a huge effort. I was sure any day you'd ferret my dirty secrets out of me and be gone."

"Well, I didn't and I'm not." She reached for him. "I love you, Trev. We belong together. Now what else did our friendly neighborhood demigod have to say?"

"I still can't believe I can have a normal conversation about what happened when I was growing up," he murmured. "Never thought I'd be able to talk about it at all."

Lara considered saying, *I told you so*, but decided against it. "Raven?" she pressed. "It's getting late and I want to know what else he said."

"Relentless wench." Trevor settled into her embrace. "He predicted a rapid escalation in last week's violence. Said the sooner we're gone, the better.

"I know you'll mostly be working, but I can manage the bulk of moving by myself. Except for the farm equipment. Thought I'd buy an old pickup truck off one of the lots out on Aurora Avenue. That way I'll have something I can use to transport things easily, and with fewer trips. I'll drape a tarpaulin over whatever I've got in the truck's bed. Shouldn't attract too much attention if I get a vehicle with lots of dents and damage."

"So we're going to lock up this house and walk away from it."

"That's about the size of it, Lara. We're between a rock and a hard place. No choice, really."

She nodded somberly. "I don't have anyone until ten tomorrow. I'll set the phone's alarm for six. That'll give me time to sort out which books I want from my upstairs study and which clothes I want to take."

His hold on her tightened, and she knew he'd been afraid she was going to put up an argument against leaving even sooner than they'd planned. "Thanks, Lara. That'd be a great help."

"Speaking of books," she said, "when are we going to have time to look through the ones we bought about farming? If I'm supposed to be spending all my time reading up on magic and you're packing and moving…" Her voice trailed off. Worry about all the things they needed to learn before they could transition to an agrarian existence ate at her.

"We can only do so much, love." His voice rumbled against her hair. "There may not be time to learn anything until we're actually out at Raven's farm."

TREVOR WAITED until Lara's breathing settled into its usual sleepy pattern of catches and half snores. Not quite suppressing his jealousy that she could fall asleep so easily, he gently maneuvered his arm out from under her and slid into his faded blue robe. At a muted whine from the puppy, he picked up the young Shepherd and carried him. The open-architecture spiral staircase that spanned the five stories of their home frightened the young dog.

Setting Gunter behind the kitchen puppy gate, Trevor went up half a flight of stairs to the library to retrieve the lists he'd begun making earlier in the day. Back in the kitchen, puppy at his heels, he continued his inventory of cupboards and drawers.

Guess we really don't need any of this. He set his pen down. The cook in him rebelled as he looked at his knives. *Well, okay, maybe we could bring a few things. There weren't really any decent knives at Raven's when I made supper on Halloween.*

Lips drawn into a straight line, he rested his chin on an upraised hand. The less they dragged from their house to Raven's small farm, located several miles outside of Skykomish on winding dirt roads, the better off they'd be. Every trip ferrying goods upped their level of risk. Once resources became scarcer, the remote farm could easily become a target for hungry mobs in search of provisions.

An image of Raven, with his long black hair caught up in a leather thong, filled Trevor's mind. The mage's directions had been explicit. No one was to know they were leaving or where they were going. Trevor had soft-soaped what he told Lara; Raven had been adamant that they ditch everything and relocate immediately. He'd even told Trevor not to worry about farm equipment, that he'd make sure they had what they needed in time for next year's planting.

When Trevor pressed for reasons, the mage, or Wôden, or whoever he really was, hadn't been particularly informative. He'd just muttered something about humans needing to do what they were told, without asking gratuitous questions.

Raised in rural northern England in a village with Druids and wise-women, Trevor was no stranger to the pagan religions. It had been a relief, though, to move first to London, then Amsterdam, and finally the States, where most people didn't believe in such things.

He walked into the library, puppy shadowing him, to continue his inventory. He and Lara had thousands of books, and there were hundreds more in Raven's library. Trevor wasn't certain who'd accumulated the volumes located in the cozy study of the old farmhouse, but judging from the number dealing with arcane subjects, it was a good bet Raven had something to do with the collection.

Trevor's thoughts moved to Lara as he scanned titles in their library, trying to decide which books they couldn't live without. He raked his fingers through his perpetually untidy hair, worried about the woman he loved.

Only a couple inches shorter than he was, Lara was right when she'd said she was too thin. Between a naturally slender build, and what he'd always seen as a compulsive workout schedule, maintaining her weight was a struggle. Though he'd hidden it, he'd been alarmed when she confessed to going the entire day without eating. She'd looked worn down when she staggered out of her car a few hours earlier. Sure she had a hectic schedule, but she'd always done a decent job balancing work, exercise, and quiet time at home with him.

Arabel's death. That's the difference, he realized with heartbreaking clarity. Arabel was such a kind soul. What happened to her was random and chilling, just pure, blind, bloody bad luck. He wondered if she'd still be alive if she hadn't threatened her assailants with the gun she'd taken to carrying. Arabel was stubborn and self-reliant. She wouldn't have sat back and told crooks to help themselves.

For a moment, he pretended time might have a salutary effect, but then anger rose from his guts, viscous and burning. *How could I be so daft? I may want to get over it, but I never will. Not really. It's like with Lizzie and Dad. I'll carry a picture of my sister hanging from that rafter in the barn to my dying day.*

Burying his face in his hands, Trevor swallowed hard. "I'll never be able to sleep at this rate," he muttered. He'd told Lara sleep was elusive because of his many years as a flight attendant on red-eye trans-Atlantic jaunts, but the truth was he hadn't slept well since finding his sister's lifeless body when he was not quite sixteen. *Don't forget running Father through with that pitchfork,* a nasty inner voice chimed in. Those had been the secrets he'd kept from Lara—just like he'd kept them from everyone—bottled deep inside.

Go through the books. That's pretty bloody mindless.

He circled the library again and again, but an iron bar of tension settled between his shoulders, and he couldn't concentrate. Gunter opened one eye, looked at his master, and then closed it again. Clearly, the dog understood nighttime hours were for sleep. After a time, Trevor's heart rate slowed and when he shut his eyes, he found darkness instead of his dead sister's ghost.

Starting with the history section of their library, he selected volumes, piling them on the edge of an Oriental rug. As he worked, he replayed Raven's visit. The mage had made a cryptic comment about there being others like Lara: humans resulting from a blend of extraterrestrial and Sidhe matings. Raven intimated part of the reason he and Lillian were leaving was to launch a campaign to locate Lara's distant—and maybe not-so-distant—relatives.

The piles of books grew until Trevor finally felt drowsy. Fearing a trip up the stairs would push sleep away again, he turned out the lights, snagged a quilt off the top of the sofa, and rolled himself up in it.

CHAPTER 3

*L*ara was never certain if the gradually escalating chirp of her pager or her chiming cell phone dragged her from sleep. The bedroom was pitch black as she felt around in the headboard for at least one of the electronic devices to find out who needed her. She squinted at the pager's tiny display, but didn't recognize the number. Further blind grappling located her phone, and she looked at the time. Five forty-five. *Ugh.* She shook sleep from her muzzy head and patted Trevor's side of the bed surprised, but not alarmed, to find him gone. He really did keep weird hours. Always had.

She went through an abbreviated version of her usual morning ritual in the bathroom. That done, she climbed back under the warmth of the duvet to interrogate her phone, flipping on a light in the headboard and readying a small notebook and pen. Worry sluiced through her as she accessed her voice mail. Lara listened to the single message and felt even worse. It wasn't so much the words, but their tone that alarmed her.

"Why the hell would Brad Archer call so early?" she mumbled and wrote down his phone number.

Fingers hesitant on the keypad—the last thing she needed was another snag in a life that already felt way too complicated—Lara entered the number. Seconds later, Detective Brad Archer's familiar voice answered, "Archer here. That you, Lara?"

"Yes," she replied. Normally, she'd have asked what he needed, but a part of her didn't want to know. Detective Archer had shot and wounded Ken Beauchamp, setting a string of events into play that led to the man's eventual capture. Since Beauchamp was dead, Lara assumed Archer must want something from her—and pretty badly to call at such an ungodly hour.

There was a pause, typical of what law enforcement officers did when they thought they might have a reluctant recruit on the other end of the phone. Lara's stomach tightened, and she relaxed her grip on the phone because her hand was cramping.

"I—I'm calling to ask a favor, Dr. McInnis," he began formally.

She girded herself for whatever the request might be. *Trev and I owe him big time. If it's a favor, I'll have to at least try to help, even though I'm so overwhelmed with everything else I'm drowning.*

"It's my daughter, Adriana," Brad choked out, anguish blasting through the phone lines. "Lara—she's missing."

"That's terrible! What happened?" Shocked by his revelation, she sat up straighter in bed. More than that, though, she was confused why he was calling her. "Don't you have an entire fleet of officers who hunt for missing persons?"

"Yes, we do. Even a couple psychics. That's the problem, Doctor, uh, Lara. Even with all that, they've been hunting for her for almost a week and haven't found a single lead."

"How old is she?" Lara asked. Warnings rained from her psychic side, but she ignored them.

"Seventeen." Archer's voice was about an octave too high and strained.

"Maybe it's not as bad as you think," Lara suggested gently. "After all, teenagers are notorious for this sort of thing. Are you certain she didn't run off with some boy? Or that she's not holed up with a girlfriend? Did you or your wife have a fight with her?"

"No fights, but I'm not sure about either of the other two," Brad admitted. "Look, Lara, I know you're busy, but I could really use your, ah, special abilities to help me." He sighed heavily, and his breath whistled from between what sounded like clenched teeth. "There's not even a fucking clue, Doctor. Not one. My men have worked this thing to within an inch of its life."

Tormented words tore out of him. "Her car's disappeared, which isn't all that unusual in kidnapping cases, but so have her motor vehicle and school records. Whatever happened to her, it wiped her off the face of the Earth. Christ, her hospital birth records don't even exist anymore. And my wife…" He stopped, obviously struggling for control. "She's been sedated for the past three days. When she wakes up, she starts screaming. Adriana was…is our only child."

Lara closed her eyes. The amulet hanging around her neck pricked unpleasantly. *So there's magic involved here.*

"Doctor?"

"Yes, I'm still here. I'm thinking."

"Please." The single word held all the angst of a man caught in an ever-tightening web.

"Okay, I'll meet you wherever you want around noon."

"I'll come to you," he said quickly. "Your office?"

"Yes," she replied. "If you brought lunch, we could eat while we work."

"No problem," Archer replied. "Thanks, Lara." Before he rang off, she heard him crying, sobbing actually, in great, gulping gasps. More than anything, that gave her pause. He was tough, a twenty year veteran of the police force. Her fears about what she'd just agreed to skyrocketed when the amulet—with its uncanny sensitivity to psychic events—radiated disapproval by sending waves of bitter cold against her skin.

Throwing on a pair of sweats and some slippers, she trooped downstairs in search of Trevor. *He's not going to be happy about this,* she thought and followed the excited sound of Gunter's yips to their library. Trevor was just rolling over from his bed on the couch when she came into the room. "I'll take the pup," she told him. "Try to get a couple more minutes of sleep. I may not eat enough, but you don't get nearly enough rest."

As she stood out on the back porch, watching rain drizzle in the darkness of the new day, Lara thought about Adriana and what might have happened to her. Over the years, she'd had several runaway teens in her practice. They left home for a few days, scared their parents half to death, and then, having exercised a bit of adult power, returned to the fold. This didn't feel like that, though.

There's something he's not telling me, she decided. After giving the pup's oversized feet a lick and a promise with a handy towel, she ushered him inside. When she skirted the corner leading to the kitchen, she caught a glimpse of Trevor, his bare feet huddled on a rug as he made coffee, to avoid the chilly tile floor.

"Come on, boy," she invited, closing the puppy gate behind Gunter. "Here," she told Trevor, "I'll finish that. Go get something warmer on."

"'Kay. Cheers, Lara." He stopped long enough to hug her, and she was shocked by how cold he felt. When she drew his face down to kiss, the smudges under his clear, blue eyes were even deeper than they'd been.

"Couldn't sleep?"

"Not very well," he admitted, shivering slightly. "I am cold. Be back directly."

By the time she heard the clop-clop of his sheepskin slippers returning to the kitchen, she had the coffee ready to go. Shoving a steaming mug into his hands, she said, "Let's sit in the living room. It's warmer in there."

"What happened?" he asked as he eased himself into one of the overstuffed chairs in their front room.

"What do you mean?" she countered, buying time.

"Don't play games with me. Something happened. Tell me what it is." His normally open expression became guarded. "Come on, Lara. Spill it."

"Archer called a little bit ago."

Trevor gazed at her, his head cocked to one side. When she didn't say anything else, he gestured impatiently with the hand that wasn't holding his coffee.

"Seems his daughter is missing."

"No, Lara. You are *not* going to help. We've got too much on our plates as it is. You're so knackered you have circles under your eyes."

Pot calling the kettle black. "I have to at least try to help him," she argued. "He did us a huge favor by staying here that night. He even got shot protecting us. How can I possibly refuse?"

Laying down his mug, Trevor shook his head and the line of his jaw tightened. When he finally looked at her, he said evenly, "If these were normal times, you couldn't. But they aren't."

"Does that mean simple human decency left along with the dregs of the oil?" Anger flashed from her guts, making them burn. "Look, I don't really want to help him. Jesus, it was feeling like all I could do to finish up with my patients and give you a little help sorting things. But I didn't see how I could say no. Geez, Trev, he was crying."

"If I cry and ask you not to, would that help?" His sarcasm sparred with her anger.

"Not fair."

He threw his hands in the air. "You're right. It's not. None of this is. Come here," he patted the lounge chair next to him and drew back the quilt he'd brought from the library.

She joined him, fitting her body against his. "Mmm… You're a lot warmer than you were in the kitchen."

"Got cold sleeping on the couch," he murmured.

"Why didn't you come to bed?"

"I was afraid the trip up the stairs would wake me enough, I wouldn't be able to fall asleep."

"That bad, huh?" She felt him nod, chin bobbing against the top of her head. "Poor baby. Were you thinking about Arabel?"

"That and Raven's visit. This whole thing has me spooked. I'm not psychic like you, but something inside me is predicting terrible consequences if we don't get ourselves out of here."

She stroked his back, breathing in the mingled scents of his aftershave and the lavender shampoo they both used. "The amulet doesn't like this thing with Archer one little bit," she said at last.

"How can you tell?" Despite his discomfort, he sounded curious.

"Hard to describe, but it sort of pricks me, or sends obnoxious waves of cold as a warning."

"Humph," he grunted and repositioned himself. "When did you agree to meet the detective?"

Lara edged up so she could meet his gaze. "Noon today at my office. I made him promise to bring me a sandwich."

"That does *not* make me feel better."

"I'll see if there's anything I can do in the time before we leave. Unfortunately, the girl's been missing for almost a week."

"She's probably dead," Trevor said flatly.

"Yeah, that thought crossed my mind too. And Brad's. He didn't say anything about her being dead, but he didn't have to. He sounded wrecked. Way worse than any of the other parents I've helped whose kids went missing." She shut her eyes, realizing she really did *not* want to hunt for a corpse.

"You may as well tell me everything he said."

Lara relayed an abbreviated version of her earlier conversation while they shared Trevor's rapidly cooling coffee. Once they'd polished it, she left the warmth of the quilt to retrieve her cup.

"Long as you're up," he motioned toward the library. "Take a quick gander in there. I need to know which books you want."

For the next hour, they culled through their shelves, plucking a volume here and another there. Stacks proliferated like some exotic plant on the Oriental rug.

"I'm about done in here," she informed him, wiping grimy dust smears off her hands onto the sides of her sweat pants. "I'll run up and start sorting clothes. I've got just enough time to work my way through the dressers before I have to get ready to leave."

"Take a bowl of cereal with you," he suggested. "I'll get one together with the rest of that pear I had left over from yesterday."

Armed with granola and a refill on her coffee, Lara tackled both her antique oak dressers. Trevor suggested she dump what she wanted on the floor, so she picked her way around a growing mound of warm, serviceable pants, tops, sweaters, underclothes, and socks. She'd just shoved the last drawer shut when a muted chime from her phone told her she'd run out of time.

She stepped into the deep tub, aware how drained she felt. The hot water jets helped, though, and by the time she pulled a green corduroy jumper on over one of her favorite striped sweaters, she felt marginally human. Phone and pager in hand, she slid her stocking-clad feet into a pair of low-heeled pumps and clumped down the steps.

Trevor was still in the kitchen tossing some of his favorite cooking utensils into a smallish box. "Couldn't stand to leave it all behind." He grinned wryly at her, while Gunter made a shameless bid for petting.

"Join the club." She smiled back sadly as she ruffled the puppy's ears. "I left a pretty big pile in the middle of our bedroom. Don't be mad at me, but I did toss in a couple of my favorite dresses, even though it's unlikely I'll ever wear them again."

"I'm off to get us that truck this morning," he informed her. "Once I have it, I'll get a load together to take to Raven's later on today. Don't worry, I'll get whatever you sorted out upstairs bagged up, dresses and all."

"Thanks. Sorry I'm not more help," she murmured, feeling guilty. "Doesn't seem fair somehow, to stick you with all this." With a final pat for the puppy, she straightened. "Once you have the truck, maybe it won't take too many trips." She extended her arms for a hug.

"That's what I'm hoping." He moved into her arms and held on tight. "I love you, Lara. Do try to be careful today. And call me when you know more about this Archer thing, will you?"

She inclined her head awkwardly. "Sure, Trev. Of course I'll do that. I'm sorry about yesterday, but I got caught up with my patient and lost track of things. I promise I'll do better at checking in today."

"When do you expect you'll be home?"

"I'm done with patients at four-thirty. Aw, shit!" She clapped a hand to her forehead. "We need to get those boxes back down to my car. And I'm almost late now." Frantic, she started for the living room at a fast trot.

"Already done," he called after her, a more genuine smile in place this time. "Finished with that whilst you were sorting clothes. It's raining like hell. You need a better coat than what you have on."

"You're such a dear." She ran back for one more quick hug, pulling a woolen cape off the hallway coat tree along the way. "Walk with me." She tugged at his arm, ignoring piteous howls from Gunter, locked on the wrong side of the puppy gate.

"I'll try to get those boxes filled with more files over the course of today. With luck," she smiled brightly as they walked down the front steps, "I should be heading home by five."

He eyed her hopefully. "If you're not too tired, maybe you could come with me when I run the first truckload out to Raven's. We can catch supper along the way and if it gets too late, you can curl up on the seat and sleep on the way back."

"I'd like that," she replied. "There's something about the old farmhouse that feeds my soul. Bye." Blowing him a kiss, she settled herself in her car, tapped the ignition, and backed out onto the rain-slick street.

BRAD ARCHER WAS fifteen minutes early, which was fine since Lara's eleven o'clock hadn't shown up. Eleanor Smathers had called earlier that morning, the message waiting in voice mail when Lara arrived at the office. Her patient said she couldn't get fuel for her car, but Lara suspected it was likely more than that. Whenever a therapist closed their practice, most patients quit coming, including the ones who said they wanted a few last visits. For some reason, it seemed easier for them to leave than to be left.

Human nature. Always better to be the dumper than the dumpee. That's good, though. Maybe I'll have time to finish with those boxes before Brad gets here.

She glanced up from her packing as soon as she heard a knock on the door. "Brad?" she called. "That you?" Once she heard his voice, she added, "Be right there." Scooting to her feet, she walked into the outer office to unlock the door.

Brad Archer stood in the hall, illuminated by light filtering in from stained glass panels a few feet away. Almost as an afterthought, he stuck out his hand, but the gesture seemed oddly automatic. He inclined his head. "Morning, Doctor."

As she extended her hand to grasp his, Lara was so shocked it was a challenge to maintain a neutral expression. He'd aged ten years since she'd last seen him, with blackened splotches beneath his eyes and new lines etched into his austere features. His neatly pressed brown suit jacket had been thrown on over a rumpled white shirt. Both garments hung on his tall, gangly frame, and his close-cropped blond hair looked greasy. She caught a whiff of stale sweat and wondered how long it had been since he showered.

"I'm a bit early," he said apologetically, releasing her hand as he pushed past her into her office. "Do you want me to wait here?" He gestured toward her waiting room.

"No, not at all," she replied and ginned up a welcoming smile. "Come on in. I'm not expecting anyone until one-thirty, so we'll have plenty of time."

Relief radiated from him. For a moment, he looked like the old Brad. "I'll run down and get your...well, our lunches. They're in the cooler in the back of my cruiser. Got something for myself too, but don't know if I'll be able to eat it."

By the time he returned a few minutes later, she'd stacked the four boxes she'd filled in a corner to get them out of the way and was in the process of dragging a small table in front of the couch and clearing a space for lunch. "Hey, thanks. Just set those down." She pointed at the table.

Brad dropped the deli boxes and lowered himself to the couch.

When his knees jammed against the table, he muttered, "Ouch!" before settling himself on the floor where he stretched his long legs out straight and popped the tab on a Coke. "Are you moving?" he asked abruptly and gestured at the boxes.

"Not exactly. I'm closing my practice."

"That seems like good news," he said in guarded tones. "Does that mean you might have more time for police work?"

"What it means," she replied evenly, "is I can't stand to be here and do this work without Arabel." Turning away from him, she went to the outer office to shut and lock the door. She dragged a chair to the other side of the table and sat. "Why don't you start at the beginning?" she suggested, cracking open her white Styrofoam container. "Looks like tuna. Thanks again."

The detective opened his white box as well, stared at it contents, and closed the lid again. "Haven't been very hungry," he mumbled. "And I'm not sure what the beginning is."

Lara chewed and swallowed. "How about if you just start talking, and let me sort out the parts I need."

Nodding wearily, Brad tilted his head back and closed his eyes. After a moment, he brought his hands up and folded them behind his head to support it. "That's just it. I don't know what to say or where to start. I thought we—Barbara, Adriana and I—were a normal family. We had our usual number of spats, sure. But we talked and went on trips, and the wife and I, we went to all Adie's school events." He paused to take a swallow from his Coke. "Adie was really good at soccer and baseball. And she loved drama. Never missed a school play. She could sing too."

Brad set his soda down and grappled with the thick weave of her rug before clasping his hands in his lap so hard the knuckles whitened.

"Go on," she urged, as she continued to work on her sandwich, although she felt less and less like eating. Brad was saying the right words, but something about him felt strange, and whatever was unfolding in her office made her skin pebble with goose bumps.

"Two or three months ago— No, it was a little longer than that, Adie began to fight more with Barbara. I wasn't home all that much, so I missed most of the fireworks. When I was her age, I picked a lot of fights at home to make it easier for me to leave."

He opened bloodshot blue eyes and looked hard at Lara. "So I told Barbara not to worry. That it was normal. Fuck!" He grimaced, looking absolutely miserable. "This is my fault. Maybe if I'd paid closer attention. Maybe…" His voice trailed off, after cracking on his last words.

A chill marched down Lara's spine, and she put the sandwich she'd been holding back into its box. Brad's eyes were glassy and unfocussed, and there was something eerie about the way he was staring at her. She wiped her fingers on a napkin, considering how to ease him out of her office, when he reached inside his suit jacket and pulled out a photo. Lara expected him to lay it on the table, but he just sat there, having switched his focus from her to the picture.

"Can I see?" she asked gently and kicked herself. She didn't want to see; what she wanted was him gone.

Reluctantly, almost as if the picture were a physical link and by relinquishing it he'd lose his only connection with his lost child, Brad held out the dog-eared print. Lara gave her hands one more swipe with the napkin and grasped the photo by its edge. When she turned it to face her, it shimmered. Blinking to help herself focus, she decided she must be more tired than she thought.

Once she realized what was on the small square of photographic paper, her hand started to shake.

The detective, who'd been watching her, said sharply, "What? Do you know her?"

"She's very pretty," Lara managed, not wanting to reveal much more until she controlled her tumbling thoughts.

"No, Doctor." Brad's voice was rough. "You may be a shrink, but I'm a cop. You saw something when you looked at Adie's picture. What was it?"

Okay, I can't smooth my way out of this one. May as well try the truth.

"Your daughter looks so much like someone I know that I was startled. That combination of red hair, green eyes, and porcelain skin with freckles is somewhat unusual."

Probably doesn't mean a thing that Adriana's a dead ringer for Lillian. People have doppelgangers all the time.

Lara smiled a shade too brightly. "Your wife must have that wonderful hair too."

"No. She's dark." Brad's hands writhed in his lap, creating red blotchy places that stood out vividly against his pale skin. "Adie was adopted," he said flatly. "Barbara and I, we tried and tried, but we never could conceive. Even did some of that fancy stuff where they start the baby out in a Petri dish." He laughed uncomfortably. "But none of it took." He blew out a hollow-sounding breath. "After Barbara's last miscarriage, a friend of hers told her she knew about a young child who needed a home. That's how we got Adie. She was about six when we brought her home."

The amulet thrummed a warning against Lara's breastbone. She laid a hand over it, willing it to do more than vibrate. *If you know something, goddammit, find a way to tell me.*

Lara searched for a question to ask. Something was desperately wrong, and she was certain the detective was lying, but finely honed instincts warned her not to go there. Agreeing to meet him had been a mistake. Confronting him about what she was feeling would be an even bigger one. If she could get him talking, maybe she could move him out of her office—and out of her life.

"You haven't told me about when Adie disappeared. What happened that day? And which day was it, exactly?"

CHAPTER 4

Trevor perched in the cab of the battered old Ford four wheel drive pickup truck he'd just purchased. Its stained Arapahoe seat cover felt rough, even through the fabric of his jeans. Every time he went over a bump in the road, the steering wheel lurched in his hands. *Suspension's shot, but what did I expect for a couple thousand bucks?* He might've been able to get the proprietor down a few hundred dollars more, but hadn't wanted to waste the time. He'd seen the look in the fat little car salesman's eyes when he'd agreed to the asking price and begun shelling out bills.

Bloke probably had me pegged for a drug dealer or something equally nefarious. Trevor snorted, biting back a laugh.

He'd managed to get a few concessions for paying full price though, one of which was leaving his Benz parked in a quiet corner of the used car lot. The other had been full gas tanks. He'd been afraid the fellow might balk at that—after all, petrol wasn't easy to come by these days—but the man had nodded, dragged several gas cans from behind one of the dilapidated buildings on the car lot, and dutifully poured until fuel dribbled out.

The truck's once-proud blue-and-white paint job was peeling, but the engine sounded healthy, the brakes worked, and the tires were good. All in all, Trevor felt pleased. Patting the steering wheel, he mumbled, "There's a good old girl. You've got a few more miles in you."

Gunter, curled on his sheepskin blanket on the seat next to Trevor, yipped his approval. Trevor chuckled. "How's my boy?" he asked, angling his body toward the puppy to riffle his fur. The small dog sat up, tail thumping eagerly as he reached for Trevor's extended fingers.

Trevor considered going by Lara's office. It was just shy of noon, and Detective Archer would be there. Lara was right; they did owe Archer a major favor, but this thing with his daughter had a bad feel. Trevor shuddered as something that felt like a small, panicked animal skittered down his spine.

"That does it," he growled through clenched teeth. "I'll just run by. Maybe I can get some more files. If they want me to leave, they can chase me off." Turning back to Gunter, he said, "Let's go visit Mum, shall we?"

East Avenue wasn't far. In less than five minutes, Trevor had backed the truck into an angled slot, jumped down from the high cab, and come round to let the puppy out. Whistling softly, he took a few moments to walk Gunter past some enticing bushes before running up the steps leading to Lara's office building. Once inside, he climbed the carpeted risers to the second floor and tried her door, but it was locked. Raising a closed fist, he knocked. He waited, listening, before knocking again—louder this time.

Trevor was rewarded by the rustle of footsteps. When Lara cracked the door, a surprised look blossomed on her face. "Awesome!" She pulled the door open wider.

"I was in the neighborhood," he said with a smile. "Thought I'd drop by for a few more boxes." He noticed the photo still clutched in her hand. "Why do you have that picture of Lill—?"

"Ssht," she hissed. Jamming her body against him, she whispered in his ear, "It's not her. Couldn't be. Only looks like her. Remember she told us not to tell anybody about her. No one."

"Got it," he whispered back. "Is Archer here?"

She nodded about the time they both heard the detective call, "Lara, everything okay out there?" Gunter chose that moment to wriggle past Trevor and through the office door. "Trevor, that you?" Archer asked, having obviously been greeted by an effusive puppy.

"May as well come in and say hi," she suggested, waving an arm in the direction of Archer's voice.

Trevor strode toward the inner office. Lacking Lara's years of practicing dispassionate facial expressions, he stopped dead in the doorway while his eyebrows crawled up his forehead. "What in the bloody blazes?" he exclaimed. "You look like hell." Stepping forward, he held out a hand. "Terribly sorry about your daughter and all. I do hope you find her quickly."

Archer scrambled to his feet and grasped Trevor's hand. "Thanks." An awkward pause followed. "Did you come by because you knew I'd be here?" Without waiting for a reply, the detective forged on. "Not that I blame you. It looks as if your, um, wife's shutting up shop. What with everything that's happened, I can understand where you'd rather she didn't do any more work."

"You got me on that one," Trevor admitted sheepishly. "But I did have another reason. I wanted to see if she had a few more client files packaged up. We're, ah…moving them to a storage unit."

"I could help you transfer those boxes in the corner down to your car," Archer offered smoothly.

Trevor pasted a neutral expression on his face before saying, "Sure, Brad, that'd be a big help. And then I'll get out of here and you can finish up your business with Lara." Trevor shot a surreptitious glance her way to see if she was okay with that plan.

Lara, who was on the floor playing with Gunter, looked up. "Hey, why don't I fill those last boxes while you're taking the other ones down? That way I'll have done what I can about the files today. At this rate, I should have all my records out of here by the end of the week." Without waiting for a response from either of them, she stood, grabbed another box, pushed it in front of her filing cabinets, and started dropping charts into it.

Trevor hefted a box. Archer took two and they headed outside.

Archer paused in front of Lara's office building, panting a bit as he shifted the weight of the boxes to an upraised knee, "Which way?" Looking up and down the street, he added, "Where's your Mercedes? Do you really expect all these will fit in it?"

"Follow me. It's that truck over there." Trevor set off at a brisk pace for the old Ford. Since he was only carrying one box to Brad's two, he pulled well ahead of the other man.

"Did you just get this?" Brad looked the rig over carefully, including the DMV paperwork tucked in the front window. "Surely you wouldn't have traded your Benz for it."

"Yeah, I just got it. Don't worry, I didn't sell the Mercedes."

"I would hope not." The detective dropped his boxes into the open bed of the truck up near the cab. "That was a classic and well, this—"

Thinking quickly, Trevor adopted a hangdog look. "Um, I don't exactly like to talk about it." He hesitated, trusting it would have the desired effect of projecting embarrassment, along with a healthy dollop of shame. "I seem to have lost my job with the airlines. Got to have something to do, so I thought I'd pick up old beaters like this, fix 'em up, and try to sell 'em for a bit of a profit. Used to be a pretty fair mechanic growing up. Of course, I don't understand the newer ones very well, but something like this—" He slapped the side of the old truck after placing his box into the open bed. "Well, they're a piece of cake."

"In the meantime, it comes in handy for little moving projects like this one?" The detective's eyes never left Trevor.

No wonder this guy made detective. He's good.

"Certainly does," Trevor agreed with a sunny smile crafted to convey innocent agreement. "Let's see, three down and three to go. Shall we?"

"We don't have a whole lot of time before my next patient," Lara said, leading the way back into her office. Brad seemed so out-of-it, she hoped he wouldn't remember what she'd told him earlier.

"Thought you said you were free until one-thirty." Brad glanced at his watch. "It's only quarter till."

Damn. Guess he's more on the ball than I thought. "Uh, my patient called while you were helping with boxes. Asked if she could come by a bit earlier, and since it seemed we were close to done—" *Please, please, let him take the hint and leave.*

"Stop right there," the detective interrupted. "I don't want to waste time—for either of us." He cleared his throat and looked straight at Lara out of haunted blue eyes. "It's pretty clear your boyfriend—yes, yes, I know you're not married—would just as soon you steered clear of me and anything even remotely related to Adie." He paused. "I had no idea you were closing your practice."

"Would you have called if you'd known?" She looked hard at him, trying to see the man behind the cop. His aura was opaque and misshapen; it contracted against his head and neck as if his spirit were dying.

He dropped his gaze. When he answered, his voice was so low she had to strain to hear him. "Yes, Lara. I would've. You see." Those blue eyes caught at her dark ones again, pleading, and he seemed more like himself. "You're my last hope. There're no more leads to track down. The dogs we brought in just ran in circles, and the two psychics we use say they can't *see* anything. Worse, they were so freaked out, they refused to try again."

"Have you slapped her picture up everywhere you can think of, including the Internet?"

He cleared his throat again, looking uncomfortable, "Certainly. That's standard procedure. But—" More throat clearing. "No one's stepped forward with anything useful."

"Why don't you sit back down?" she suggested gently, her compassion rising to the fore, despite her misgivings. "I still have a few minutes. I don't know if I can help, either. But you haven't told me what you know about the day she disappeared." As Lara took her usual therapy chair, the amulet throbbed a warning.

Either tell me more, or stop that. She grasped the stone through the fabric of her sweater.

Staggering slightly, Brad sat in the one of the padded floral chairs across from her.

"When's the last time you slept?" she asked. "Or ate, for that matter?"

"Days," he admitted, waving a dismissive hand. "But that's not important. Adie disappeared last Friday, two days after all those riots began. I'd been on shift since zero six hundred." He dragged a weary hand down his face, distorting his features. "I started getting calls from her about eleven that morning. She was in school, but she told me she felt odd. I was really busy, so I asked if she'd gone to the school nurse, but she told me she didn't feel sick, just weird…" His voice ran down, and he dropped his head into his hands. The rigid line of his jaw told Lara he was struggling to maintain his composure.

When he finally looked up, tears shone in his eyes. "I was just so swamped that day, I told her to call Barbara. That she'd come get her or take her to the doctor or whatever Adie needed." He fell silent.

After a few moments, Lara prodded, "Then what? Did she call back?"

Brad nodded, "Uh-huh. About half an hour later. I asked if she'd called her mom, but she said she wanted me. That she was afraid. I asked why, but she didn't answer. And then the line went dead. I called my wife. She promised she'd run by the school to check on things."

Lara closed her eyes, psychic senses on alert as she intercepted snatches of what happened that day and fleshed out some of the blank spots in Brad's recitation. As she gathered information, she felt worse and worse. She masked her features to hide her rioting thoughts and groaned inwardly.

That poor girl must be lost on the other side. Where I go in my visions.

But why did all of her vanish? When I end up there, it's only my mind. No wonder Archer can't find her.

To backfill a silence that was becoming far too long, she murmured, "When your wife called you later, she told you Adie was missing."

Brad nodded, opened his mouth, and then closed it again, while he shredded one of the paper lunch napkins.

"Did you interview her friends?" Lara asked to buy herself time. She'd never understood anything about how her psychic side operated. Despite her earlier gut feeling, she wasn't entirely sure why she suspected the girl was trapped somewhere in the odd world where her visions took her.

"Of course we did," the detective snapped. "So rigorously some of their parents complained to the Chief."

"And?"

"None of them had seen her after about quarter to twelve."

"You took dogs to the school?"

He inclined his head. "Yeah. Gave them clothing from home to get a scent before we turned them loose. When that didn't pan out, we used forensic kits in the general area, but didn't find anything."

"You mean, no blood or other evidence she'd been harmed."

He nodded, mutely.

"And the psychics?" She watched him intently, certain he wasn't telling her everything.

"Both of them said there was some sort of wall, or veil or something, impeding their normal view. That make sense to you?"

"Maybe," she answered carefully. "Detective, I'm not trained as a psychic. I've had an ability to read auras and see things—generally about my own future—for as long as I can remember. But I've never had any specialized instruction in how to use my gifts. My aunt could see auras and foretell the future too, but she refused to talk about any of it. Frankly, I'm certain her abilities scared her half to death.

"The reason I had those visions about Ken Beauchamp was because he was threatening Trevor and me. Occasionally, I get wisps of other things, but my ability isn't consistent enough to be much help in a situation like yours."

There. At least I was honest with him.

Brad's face crumpled. Tears spilled over, dripping in a steady stream down his weathered face. He wiped his sleeve across it, and Lara heard the fabric scrape against his unshaven chin. "Would you at least be willing to take something of hers?" He sounded desperate. "That way, maybe something might come to you."

"Sure. Did you want to leave me the picture?"

Why did I say that? I should just let him leave. The amulet wants him to leave. It's been warning me ever since he set foot in here.

He nodded mutely, "And this." He dug a brightly colored scarf out of one of his outer pockets and shoved it toward her.

Lara laid it on a side table and patted one of his hands. When he raised his hollow eyes to hers, she said, "Go home. Take a shower. Eat something, even if it's only a cookie or two, and try to sleep. You won't help Adie a bit unless you're able to take better care of yourself."

"I suppose you're right," he muttered, pulled a handkerchief out of another pocket, and blew his nose.

She rose. "If I come up with anything, even something that seems insignificant to me, I'll call you. I promise. Do you want me to use the number you called me from this morning."

"Yeah, it's my personal cell."

"Okay, now go home and get some rest."

He pushed heavily to his feet, weaving a bit and catching himself on the corner of her desk. "I'll try." His mouth twisted downward into a frown "You don't have children, do you?"

Nope, no children. And until recently, I had no idea what it felt like to be stalked, burglarized, or scared shitless of a Demon masquerading as a Jungian analyst.

"You're correct. I don't have children, but I can imagine the hell you must be going through," she said, trying to infuse enough empathy into her tone to move him out the door.

"I wonder," he said, bitterness creeping under the edges of his voice. "I wonder if you really can understand. I—I'd do just about anything to get her back."

Lara stared at him, her psychic side radiating alarm. Something about what he'd just said froze her heart mid-beat. "You're not telling me everything," she blurted, throwing caution to the winds. "What did you leave out?"

A mask dropped over his features: his cop facade. "Now why would you think that, Doctor?"

Her apprehension ratcheted up a few notches, and her heartbeat accelerated.

"Be sure to call me if you think of anything." He turned to leave.

As soon as the door closed behind him, Lara discarded her therapist's face and clicked the deadbolt into place. Dread shot through her with frosty precision. Scrunching her eyes shut, she scrabbled through a host of fears, trying to force the return of rational thought. The amulet had sounded klaxon warnings for the past fifteen minutes, ever since she'd gotten that intuitive blast telling her Brad's daughter was on the other side of a psychic barrier. Was the amulet responding to that or to Brad? Something was badly wrong with the detective, and it went far beyond his daughter being missing.

"I need Lillian," she muttered.

Not knowing what else to do, she cleared the lunch debris and made a trip downstairs to the backyard dumpster to get the tuna smell out of her office. The sandwich formed an indigestible lump in her stomach, and she was sorry she'd eaten it. She heated water in Arabel's kettle and brewed a cup of strong, black tea.

When she glanced at the clock, it read one forty-five. "What the hell happened to my one thirty?" she snapped, and then realized it had been hours since she'd checked her cell phone, locked on its silent setting.

Hunting down the phone, she blew out an impatient breath when she saw all the messages she'd missed. Resignedly, she dropped into Arabel's chair and sorted through emails and text messages, saving the voice mail for last. "Maybe if the power goes out and stays out," she growled, "the fucking phone will die right along with it." As if on cue, the office lights flickered a couple times, dimming before they failed totally.

"Great." She rolled her eyes, feeling even more out-of-sorts. "I didn't mean right now." As she picked through her messages, there was indeed one from her tardy patient asking for a return phone call. Near the end of the emails, was one from an address labeled *private*. Ever cautious about opening things from unknown sources, Lara let her fingers hover over the message until the amulet began to hum pleasantly. "Oh, so you like this one, do you?" she inquired caustically.

"What the hell," she muttered and clicked the mysterious link. Her pulse quickened as the message furled across her screen.

I hope you'll open this, the missive read. *R and I had to leave. Danger still very real, but in a different form. If you need me, use the amulet to call me. You may need to be persistent if I don't come the first time. L*

Lara wondered what sort of effort it must've taken Lillian, born centuries ago, to learn about any sort of electronic communication tools, but then she shook her head briskly. *Doesn't matter. What does is there may be some way I can actually talk with her. Perhaps the place to try is out at Raven's later tonight.*

On her feet because she couldn't sit still, Lara went back into her therapy office. Adie's scarf was still where she'd dropped it, right next to the young woman's picture. As Lara looked at it, the filmy fabric stared back reproachfully. *That's ridiculous!* she told herself and reached for the scarf and photo, ignoring blasts of admonition pounding from the amulet.

Scarf clutched in one hand and photo in the other, she headed for her purse. Maybe if she kept the items close, something might come to her.

Out of nowhere, the tunnel vision that marked the onset of her psychic sendings battered her in vertiginous waves. She dropped the photo and scarf in an attempt to distance herself from the unseen world, but nothing changed. Fighting terror, she barely had the presence of mind to grip the amulet and call Lillian's name before a vision swept her away.

Still frightened half out of her mind, Lara held her breath as whatever had control of her dumped her on a deserted shoreline. The sky was an unnatural shade of bronze and the sand so white it burned her eyes. As if it hadn't heard it should be anything other than ordinary, the sea was its usual gray-blue, lapping against the weirdly iridescent sand in gentle waves.

A weather-beaten shack sat midway between the shoreline and some odd trees with pointy, orange leaves. The door of the hut opened slowly, but no one came out. Used to the parallel universe where her psychic side sent her, Lara waited while she kept calling for Lillian with her inner voice. It was loud in her mind, but made no sound in the odd, eldritch world surrounding her. Minutes ticked by. Time passed differently in this realm, but impatience gnawed at her. Usually, her visions were quick to reveal their purpose.

Realization dawned that something was grotesquely wrong. For the first time, her body had joined her mind in what Trevor called paranormal-land. The clues were subtle at first, but when her foot cramped and she pulled her shoe off to rub it, her mind rebelled in horror. Dread gripped her, and she let go of her foot to hold even tighter to the amulet.

Am I trapped here? Is that what happened to Adie? No sooner had the young woman's name crossed her thoughts, than an apparition—was it Adriana?—walked slowly from the hut. Her hands stretched in front of her as if she were blind, and she turned her head first in one direction, then another. Brilliant red hair billowed about her slender form.

"Is anyone here?" the girl asked in a high, piping child's voice that sounded bizarre coming from someone who was seventeen. "Anyone?"

What do I do? Lillian, goddammit, help me. Get me out of here, for chrissakes, or at least give me some direction. Should I talk to Adie? Is this some sort of supernatural trap?

The amulet remained stubbornly silent.

What am I missing? Lara's fear was partially yielding to anger, mostly because it was a much easier emotion to manage.

"Well, *Doctor*. Apparently we didn't train you so well as I thought."

Lara whipped her head around. She'd know *that* heavily accented German voice anywhere. *Can I speak in this place? No time like the present to find out.*

"Himmelschaun," she snarled, a quick, bright fury displacing the last of her apprehension. "Where the fuck are you?"

"Dr. McInnis! Shame, shame. At the Institute, we taught our acolytes—that is our *pupils*—to treat the master analysts with more respect. What about this poor girl? She needs your help. You see, she reaches out for you." The mellifluous voice, liberally laced with sarcasm, flowed around her, but try as she might, Lara couldn't identify its source. Lillian had called him a Demon. Were there even such things? Her mind shrank from the implications, and she chided herself for self-indulgence.

Dragging in a lungful of air, Lara's temper flared. "I just bet you taught acolytes at some point in time, but they weren't at the Jung Institute in Zurich, *Gradoxst*." Unleashed, Lara's wrath, born of helplessness, developed a life of its own. "What did you do to Anton Tueller anyway? He saw through you for the fraud that you are. While we're at it—how the hell did you wangle your way back into the Institute after they kicked you out? That was a special place for me. You ruined it, as I'm sure you did for a good many analysts."

"My name is Himmelschaun," he hissed menacingly. "You will not call me by that other name."

Flooded with sudden intuition, she shouted, "Oh yes I will. Gradoxst, Gradoxst, Gradoxst. Release me or I'll call Lillian."

Will it work? He's petrified of her. When she showed up the last time he took over one of my visions, he went up in a puff of smoke.

The dream world dissolved around her and Lara came back to herself crouched on the rug in her reception room next to Arabel's desk. "Shit, aw shit," she whimpered and locked her shaking hands together around her knees.

That was too fucking close. It was a trap, using a projection of Adriana for bait.

She sifted her hands through her hair again and again and forced herself to take slow, deep breaths. As her panic receded, Lara realized she was sitting on Adie's colorful scarf. Reacting as if it had been a scorpion, she shrieked and rolled sharply away.

Don't be stupid. It's only a scarf.

No, it's a conduit to that other world, one powerful enough to drag my body there, right along with my mind. Like the amulet could be if I ever learned how to use it.

Feeling absolutely drained, she pulled herself to her feet, using a combination of chairs and Arabel's desk. Shakily upright, she scrabbled for her phone and hit the speed dial number to connect her to Trevor's twin cell phone.

"Lara?"

"Thank Christ you picked up. Trev, you have to come back by here." She heard his quick intake of breath on the other end.

"Sure. But why? What's happened? Are you all right?"

"Yes…no…Hell, I'm not sure. I mean I'm safe, but I nearly wasn't. Archer left some things from his daughter here. Guess that's how his police psychics work. Anyhow, I was walking them out to the front office to stick them in my bag and got caught in a vision, except my body was with me this time, and…"

"And what?" His voice sounded wary. "What happened then?"

"I'll tell you when we're driving tonight," she said after a long pause, still shaky from too much adrenaline. "I can't stand to talk about it right now. But I don't think it's a good idea for me to touch those things again, and I can't leave them lying on the floor where I dropped them."

"Why not?"

Well, why can't I? "I don't know, Trev. Maybe because I don't think I can work in a place where they're out in plain sight. Not for long, anyway."

"Do you know what happened to Adriana?" Reluctance underscored his words, almost as if he'd asked the question against his better judgment.

"I think so," she said slowly. "But I can't talk about that now, either."

"Can't, or don't want to."

"Both. Oh yeah, and the power just went out. Damnably inconvenient timing, since it's getting dark by late afternoon." She sighed heavily. "You'll come. Right?"

"Right-o, love." The British accent was very pronounced, so she knew he was upset. "Pull your car round the back and lock it up for the night. We'll leave straight away from there. Power's out here too, by the way, so the outage must be pretty widespread."

"Do you think the lights will come back on?"

"This time, yes." He exhaled sharply. "But not for much longer. What time will you be ready to go?"

"I should be done around four-thirty." The line went dead. She winced. Trevor sounded really short-tempered. *Oh hell, I don't blame him.* She sucked in a shaky breath, and then another one.

Don't think about it. I need to call my one-thirty back and get ready for Caren.

Grappling for the phone that had slid from her hand after Trevor hung up, she took a mouthful of cold tea, swallowed resolutely, and hunted for her patient's number.

CHAPTER 5

Trevor stood in the backyard of their Queen Anne home. He'd changed into jeans, well-worn leather work boots, and an old plaid shirt after leaving Lara earlier that day. With the help of some pruning shears, he'd managed to pry both overgrown halves of the gate to the alley apart, yielding an opening big enough to maneuver the truck into the yard.

With his lips set in a hard line, he dropped his phone onto a table. Bending, he picked up a fist-sized rock and flung it hard at the fence. "Bollocks!" he shouted. "Bloody, sodding bollocks." A second rock followed the first. Gunter, who'd been curled in a grassy corner of the yard, shot up with a troubled yip.

"Sorry, sorry," Trevor mumbled, hunkering to comfort the puppy, who'd raced toward him to get away from the airborne missiles. "He's a good pup, yes he is," Trevor crooned. "Daddy's just irritated."

You bet I am. I knew when she agreed to help Archer that it would end up buggering us. And now she's caught up in that...that place she goes where she can't control what happens and doesn't even know enough to find her way back.

Feeling impotent and frustrated, he ripped up tufts of grass next to where he was squatted beside Gunter. The puppy, sensing a new game, batted at the grass with his still-awkward front paws.

Eh, enough of this.

Trevor scrambled to his feet. To divert the adrenaline shooting through him, he dumped boxes and overstuffed garbage bags into the back of the pickup. Earlier that afternoon, he'd gone on a hunt for boxes before deciding lawn-and-leaf bags would come in handy too, especially for their clothes and other soft goods.

He'd stopped by the truck entrance at Safeway and was digging in their dumpster area for boxes, when a haggard-looking store employee yelled at him. Apparently the store had started selling boxes, since heating oil, natural gas, and propane were so expensive. Trevor had peeled off a couple twenties to mollify *R. Stewart, Assistant Store Manager*—according to his badge—and the man had retreated inside the store.

After that unsettling experience, Trevor left the truck tucked behind the store so no one would steal his boxes, before going inside to purchase plastic garbage bags and sturdy tarps.

The eight-foot bed of the truck swallowed everything he'd stacked on the patio, with room to spare. As he worked, hucking bags and boxes into the Ford, he started feeling a tad less peeved. Glancing at his watch, he decided he had time to package up more books from their upstairs studies. As long as they were going to Raven's, they might as well take a full load. Lara had yet to cull through her things, but she'd want her dream journals, her psychology books, and her sewing box.

Trevor strode back into their house, puppy at his heels. On his way past the kitchen, his eye caught their safe, built into an alcove that had once held a linen closet. He'd never be able to move the industrial green monstrosity by himself, but he didn't believe they'd need it at Raven's farm.

Gunter whined next to his puppy gate. As soon as Trevor clicked it open, the little dog raced to his dish and began crunching kibbles.

Figuring the dog would remain occupied, Trevor started up the stairs to their fourth and fifth floor studies.

He was just coming down with his third—and hopefully next-to-last—load of books and journals, when Gunter started barking furiously, his high puppy voice shrill against the silence of the house. Trevor set down his burden at the foot of the circular staircase and glanced out a window to see what had set the dog off.

A delivery truck was parked on the street, and uniformed drivers hauled a dolly stacked high with boxes up the front steps. For a moment, he felt confused, and then he understood these must be the things from his Amsterdam flat that a friend had packed up for him.

Trevor brightened. He'd been worried the things he'd left at the flat in Europe were lost to him forever. Latching the puppy gate to keep Gunter in the kitchen, he let the delivery driver and his helper in.

"Where do you want 'em?" the larger of the two men growled. He was sweating, despite the coolness of the day. Droplets skidded down his bald head and into his bloodshot brown eyes. Both men reeked of tobacco.

"Right there." Trevor pointed to the entry hall floor.

"Really?" The other delivery person, who'd been eying the long circular staircase, sounded relieved and started offloading boxes. "Hey, Jack," he said a few minutes later. "We're done here." He slapped a hand against his end of the dolly. "Let's roll. We've got a lot more deliveries, and the sun's going down. I'd have hated to muscle these up here in the dark."

"Just a minute." The heavyset man thrust a metal clipboard at Trevor. "Sign there," he pointed with a stubby, begrimed finger. "You owe three hundred twenty dollars. Shipping was C.O.D." The other man had started down the steps. "Not so fast, Brent," Jack called over his shoulder. "This guy doesn't pay, we got to take the whole lot back to the truck."

Trevor held up his hands. "Not a problem. Let me get my wallet." Soon he'd pressed the bills, plus an additional twenty for a tip, into

Jack's grubby hand. "Cheers." Trevor smiled and pushed the heavy, ornamental door shut behind the men, locking it.

Gunter had subsided into low growls, but he was plastered against the puppy gate, just in case Trevor needed reinforcements. "Go back and eat," Trevor suggested and picked up the bounty from the study that he'd laid aside to tend to the delivery men. Once that was in the truck, he returned with his own dolly from the laundry room and stacked two of the seven Amsterdam boxes onto it.

Eying his watch, he knew he had to hurry. It would take longer than the usual twenty minutes to get to Lara with the streetlights running off auxiliary power.

THE AFTERNOON SKY, never particularly bright that day, had devolved into a gloomy gray-black. Lara's last session with Caren had been fraught with emotion. The two of them had gone for a long walk while they talked. Sometimes it was easier for young people to talk while they were moving, plus it got Lara away from the scarf and photo, still lying on the floor of her office.

She checked her phone again. It wasn't like Trevor to be late, but maybe the traffic was bad with the power still out. She'd pulled her car through a gate into the small yard of her office building and locked it up tight. After that, she sat on the front steps, unwilling to go back inside.

She pulled her jacket closer to her body. The afternoon air was chilly, and the perpetual damp of the Pacific Northwest sank into her bones. She was just getting ready to call, when the Ford rolled around the corner and pulled up in front of her. "Trev," she called, running to greet him. "I was worried about you."

"My own fault." He jumped out of the truck and pulled her into his arms, holding on tight. "I didn't think to check the headlamps when I bought this truck. Had to stop by an auto parts store to replace one of them. The shopkeeper was very helpful, even loaned me a screwdriver. Come on," he turned her around and steered her toward the truck. "I left Gunter inside. Hope he's not chewing the upholstery to bits." Trevor smiled ruefully. "I'd hoped to be *en route* half an hour ago."

"The scarf." She pointed at her building. "And I need to lock the office."

"Sorry." He clapped a hand to his head. "I forgot about the items that pushed you into that unexpected trip to paranormal-land. After you, love." He gestured grandly, and she ran inside and up the thickly carpeted steps of her building.

"Still mad at me?" she asked as she walked into her gloom-shrouded office.

"A little," he admitted. "Bloody blazes, Lara. It's dark in here. Where are the sodding things so we can get going?"

She scooped a penlight out of her purse and aimed the small circle of light at the floor. "'Kay," he muttered, bending low to retrieve the photo and scarf. "Got 'em. Now where do you want them?"

"I did think about that," she said somberly. "The top file drawer should do nicely, since it's empty now." Gesturing with the light beam, she illuminated an open drawer in her oak horizontal files.

Trevor dropped the scarf and picture inside, shut the drawer, and turned to leave. Once they were in the upstairs hall and Lara was locking the door, he asked, "Why don't we start with why Archer's daughter looks like a younger version of Lillian."

"You'd do better to start with something I know the answer to." Lara smiled tightly as they walked down the steps, and she locked the building's main door and set the alarm. "Let's get rolling, and I'll fill you in. Is there anything to eat?"

"Yeah, there is. I'd just made sandwiches before the power went tits up. So there's gammon and cheddar on rye with a couple satsumas and chocolate for desert. Oh, and a few bottles of lager."

"You *are* an angel." Despite the residual unease from her trip to, well, wherever she'd gone, Lara felt a warm glow deep in her midsection. Trevor was such a kind, considerate soul. "I don't deserve you," she said, standing to one side so he could move the puppy from her seat to the extended cab portion of the Ford.

Gunter, sitting dead center on his faux sheepskin mat, licked enthusiastically at her fingers when she petted him.

"Probably not," he agreed, but there was a light note in his voice, and she knew he was teasing.

"...and so," she broke off another piece of dark Swiss chocolate—a favorite Trevor brought back from Europe on a regular basis—"I'm still not sure how I knew the right thing to do, but as soon as I used the Demon's real name and threatened to sic Lillian on him, he let me go."

Trevor reached across for a square of the chocolate. "Mmm," he murmured, popping it into his mouth. "Enjoy this. It's almost the last bar. You said Lillian sent you an email? Did you try to email her back?"

"Yes, but it bounced back, undeliverable. Didn't surprise me, actually. If she and I could communicate that way, it sure would make things easier." Nibbling on her chocolate, she added, "This was an incredibly bad time for the both of them to just up and leave."

"Stop feeling sorry for yourself." His normally gentle tone held an edge. "You've got to play the ball where it lies. Jesus, you spent most of your adult life without any assistance from the Sidhe."

"You're not really angry with me," she said and brushed her fingertips against his arm. "You're scared something's going to happen to me because of this thing with Archer's daughter."

He caught her hand in his. "Damned right, I'm scared. I don't understand any of this, Lara. And I don't like being dependent on Raven and Lillian either. I—" The truck lurched, and he put his right hand back on the steering wheel. "Need both hands," he murmured. "Alignment's a bit off."

Why shouldn't he be scared? I'm petrified. She took another swallow of beer and peered out the windshield into the darkness. Aiming for a more neutral topic, she asked, "Aren't we getting close to our turnoff? It's right past the bridge here in Skykomish."

He braked harder than he needed to, and tires squealed as the old truck floated around the corner on two wheels. "Sorry," he mumbled. "Not used to driving this behemoth of a vehicle." He set the truck's headlights on high beam to illuminate the beginning of the twenty miles of dirt road between the highway and the cozy homestead Raven had created out of the deserted Garland Mineral Springs complex. Lara gathered up the remains of their meal and stuffed the wrappings into a paper bag. For the next bit of time, they drove in silence.

"Circling back to what we were talking about earlier, I don't actually recall being quite this frightened of anything since the days when Dad used to terrorize me." Trevor's voice cracked, and he cleared his throat. "I don't like any of what you told me about your day. Not Archer's insistence that you help him, not his daughter's things dragging you—body and all—into psychic-land, and not even his snoopy questions about this truck. I tell you, Lara, he's a sharp one. I told him we were moving your files to a storage unit, but I'm practically certain he didn't believe me. Wouldn't put it past him to sic a tail on me to see where I went. If he did do that, and one of his men told him about my packing up, well..." He paused for a beat. "If that weren't bad enough, you're convinced there's something wrong with him. And I tend to agree with you."

"It's not against the law to move," she pointed out. "Besides, I did him a favor. Or tried to. You don't usually sic the police force on someone who's trying to help you, unless—" She sucked in an introspective breath, letting it out in a whoosh. "I wish I had more of a take on that strange vibe rolling off him when he was in my office. His aura was practically unreadable, and he lied to me about some things. I just don't know which ones. He closed up like a clam when I confronted him about it." Lara pulled her long hair behind her head and began to braid it.

"What are you doing?"

"Getting my hair out of the way before I help you unpack. Slow down, dear. We're really close."

Trevor turned hard right over a small bridge that spanned a creek, and then they were on the gravel parking pad in front of the rambling, three-story log house that had once been Garland Mineral Springs. Illuminated in the beams from the truck's lights, it looked welcoming indeed. "I put a flashlight in the glove box," Trevor told her. "Why don't you use it to go get one of those kerosene lanterns from inside? I'll free the pup and start untying the tarps."

"How much kerosene is there, anyway?" she asked, wondering how soon she'd have to learn to make candles.

He laughed. "Best I could see, two twenty gallon drums in the shop, mostly full. And one that's nearly empty."

"Don't laugh." She poked him.

"Didn't Gandalf have some sort of mage light? Maybe Lillian could teach you how to do that."

Lara snorted and hopped down from the truck. She jogged to the broad porch steps, bounded up them, and let herself inside. The homey, herbal smell—lavender, honeysuckle, cinnamon, and jasmine —that she remembered enveloped her immediately and she stopped to inhale the pleasing scent. Grabbing two lanterns, she lit them from a box of matches Raven had left on a table next to the front door. *Nice of him to do that,* she thought, *since he certainly doesn't need them.* She propped open the screen, left a lantern on the porch and one in the large front room, then went to help Trevor who'd begun piling boxes and plastic bags next to the truck.

"Get the bags," he suggested. "They're lighter. I popped a sack truck in to make moving the boxes easier."

"Ooooh, what are these?" she asked, pointing at the Amsterdam boxes.

"What with all of your news," he said sheepishly, "I forgot to tell you. The boxes Angelique packed came today."

"Aw, Trev! You must be thrilled." She gave him a quick hug. Gunter, always proprietary when love was being passed around, pushed between them, nipping at the edges of her skirts.

Trevor held her hard against him for a moment. "Maybe relieved is a better word. I was afraid they'd never get here, even if she did manage to get our things packaged up."

"Oh, did she put my things in too?" Lara was surprised. There'd been so little that was hers in their flat, she scarcely remembered what she had there. Some clothes and a few books, maybe. Not really much else.

"Yeah, I asked her to toss in everything that wasn't tacked down." Trevor shrugged. "It's not like we'll ever be back in Amsterdam again, love."

Feeling sad for him, since Amsterdam had been his home before he met her, she hovered next to the boxes, panning her flashlight over the Dutch words scribbled on them. "What does this say?"

"Angelique labeled the contents. That word," he pointed, "is papers. And that one is knickknacks. This one is clothes. There are actually four more boxes, bigger than these, still in our foyer. They're mostly books and more clothes."

Not for the first time, Lara cursed her close-to-inability to learn any language besides English. Trevor made it look so easy. "Better get started," she said, as she laid the flashlight in the truck's cab and picked up two bulging garbage bags.

"I'll check on the animals." Trevor snapped up the flashlight and sprinted toward the barn.

Lara had nearly everything moved inside by the time he got back. "Why'd it take so long?" she asked over her shoulder as she maneuvered the loaded dolly toward the porch.

"Because I don't know shit about being a farmer," he grumbled, picking up the last of the bags. "I think everyone was fine, but I didn't have all that much light, so I checked the chickens and goats over three or four times. Tried to milk one of the goats, but what I really needed was one of those," he gestured at a kerosene lantern. "No one was *baaing*, so their udders can't be all that full.

"Then I double-checked the horse paddock, but they seemed fine. Lots of grass in there, and Raven spread hay in a feed trough. I found a bin and poured them some oats. Hope it was the right thing to do.

The horses seemed to approve. Started crunching them down straightaway." He followed her up the steps and into the house.

Once they were inside, he dropped the bags and reached carefully into a jacket pocket. "Got these." He brandished two eggs. "Hen pecked me for my trouble."

"Farmer John." Lara laughed. "Or is that Farmer Trevor?"

"Not funny." He set the eggs down carefully in a decorative bowl on one of the tables. "There's an entirely new set of skills we'll have to learn."

"Uh-huh," she nodded, solemn now. "I know." Coming close, she hugged him.

"Thanks, I needed that."

"No point in even trying to put anything away," Lara said, looking around at the mess. "We'll have lots of time for that. It's closing on eight." She sank onto one of the upholstered chairs dotting the substantial room. "Tomorrow's Wednesday. I've got my class to teach at the University, but no patients. In fact, if today's any bellwether, I may not need to stay through next week. Three of the five people I had scheduled didn't show up."

"Do you suppose we could sleep here?" Trevor asked hopefully. "It'd be so much easier than driving home. We could get up early to make sure you'd be back in time for your class, and I could take another crack at the goats in the morning."

"We've been together too long." She smiled warmly. "I was just thinking the same thing, not about the goats, but about staying. Look at him." She pointed at their puppy, already curled in a tight ball on a hooked rug in front of one of the sofas. "He's settled in for the night."

"Yes, mustn't disturb the children. I'll just pop outside and close up the truck."

By the time Trevor came back in, Lara was kneeling on the floor, rooting through a clothes bag. "I need warm pants, slippers, and a top. These," she patted her corduroy jumper and sweater, "aren't quite warm enough. Once I've got better clothes on, I'm going out onto the porch to try to raise Lillian."

"Oh." There was such a sour, disapproving undercurrent in that one word she turned around, hoping for a clue about what had spawned his ill humor.

"It's Lillian. Remember, she's on our side. Maybe she knows something about Adriana, or how I can protect myself from any more impromptu trips to the spirit world." Lara paused, and then motioned for him to sit next to her on the floor. "What about it bothers you the most?" she asked quietly, as she continued to hunt for something warm to wear.

He sat across from her and snorted. "Gee, I'm not sure I can pare it down to just one thing." He blew out an annoyed-sounding breath and waved his hands in the air. "I've never had any comfort level with any of this, starting with the Druids and witches I grew up with. The reason it's been bearable all the years we've been together is you've been rather low-key about that aura-reading thing of yours. Until Beauchamp started harassing us, your visions weren't particularly intrusive, either." He captured one of her hands and pulled it into his lap. "Coming face-to-face with evidence there's something like a parallel universe out there is damnably unnerving."

"You think it doesn't bother me?" she asked incredulously, struggling with burgeoning resentment. "Why the hell do you think I went hunting for a psychic to help me with that side of myself? You were going on earlier about playing the ball from whatever muck it's mired in. Lillian tried to help when she sent me that email. I'm going to take advantage of that."

She repositioned her body so she could look right at him, her gaze auguring into his blue eyes. "I had a perfectly wretched day. I felt terrified and helpless. When I figured out all of me was in that godforsaken place, I was so scared I was nearly paralyzed. If Lillian has some way to protect me from that happening again, I'm all for it. Quite frankly, I don't understand why you wouldn't be too.

"Found what I needed." Standing, she stripped off her clothes and donned a set of multi-colored sweats and some thick slippers.

"I'll keep you company whilst you try to hunt Lillian down." He rested his head against her thigh from his seat on the floor. "I—I'm not sure what else to say. How I feel inside isn't going to go away, but I'll find a way to keep it under wraps."

She reached out a hand to help him up. "May as well get this over with. I'm not even sure we'll be able to find her. She did say it might not work the first time."

"I'll get a fire going. Then I'll join you. That way the house can warm up before we go to bed."

By the time Trevor found her on the porch half an hour later, Lara felt edgy and exasperated. Once he plopped into one of the chairs lining the veranda, she turned to him, frowning. "I don't know what else to do," she said flatly. "I've tried holding the amulet and calling to her, both out loud and just in my head. I've tried ginning up a picture of her in my mind. I've tried chanting her name. Nothing works."

"Humph." He pulled one of her hands between his. "You're cold," he observed, as he rubbed her hand gently. "Since being outside doesn't seem to be working, why don't you come on in? I've got a pretty good blaze going. The old place started to warm up straightaway."

"Maybe you've got a point. I *am* feeling chilled, now that you mention it." Snaking her hand out from under his, she trailed disconsolately inside, with him right behind.

The ambience from the house enveloped her, radiant and soothing, and she began to relax. *This place is a living thing, just like Lillian's tree house.* It was decidedly warmer than it had been when she'd started her vigil on the porch. The front room—really, the entire downstairs was one large room with a kitchen alcove at one end— reached out invisible arms to welcome her.

She turned to Trevor. "What are we going to do when we run out of matches?" *Talk about out of the blue. Where did that question even come from?*

"There're a couple flints in one of the outbuildings." His eyes twinkled. "Maybe by then, though, you'll have figured out how to start fires without them. Come sit down," he invited. "We can watch the fire just like we do at home."

Snuggling close to Trevor on a sofa he'd pulled in front of the large stone fireplace, Lara started to feel sleepy. "Maybe it's time to head upstairs," she murmured.

"I thought of something you, uh I mean we, could do that might help bring Lillian—or maybe Raven—here," he said, sounding uncomfortable.

"What might that be? I already froze my ass off out on the porch. If human sacrifice doesn't do it, I scarcely think—"

"Don't make fun of me." He moved so he could look at her, his expression serious.

"Sorry. You're right. I was being sarcastic. Tell me. I really do want to know." She stroked the side of his face.

"The…ah, when… Oh sod it, anyway." He raked curved fingers through his tousled curls. "Whenever the village witch needed to do something really difficult, she always grabbed one of the men—no matter if he had a wife—and had her way with him. Sex enhanced her powers, somehow." Now that he'd started, words rushed out of him. "And sex was what fueled all those festivals. So…" His last word hung in the air between them.

Lara began to laugh. "That's probably the most unusual pickup line I've ever heard. But sure, if you think it might help, I'm all for it." The amulet that had been like so much dead weight between her breasts all night, began to hum delightedly. "Lillian's gift," she plucked the amulet from under her top and waved it in front of him, "agrees with you. Come on over here, Romeo. Now that you mention it, you're looking pretty hot to me."

Trevor's laughter joined with hers. "Not so fast, love, or would that be Juliet? Ach, I never did like that story." He grimaced. "Too much death. I want to hedge our bets, so bear with a spot of Gaelic." He got off the sofa and stood facing the fire, where he chanted a tuneless mantra that swept through her in seductive waves.

After listening for a few moments, she could have sworn the amulet was crooning along with Trevor's odd, monotonic song. The cumulative effect of the two was like warm, buttery silk tickling all her sensitive spots. Lara's breath caught in her throat, and her nipples hardened into throbbing points of sensation. When moisture slicked her thighs, she stood, shucked her clothes and wrapped her arms around Trevor from behind, pressing her nakedness against him.

"Umm," he breathed and turned to face her, the firelight illuminating half a smile on his face. "I always wondered if that would work. I knew it excited the hell out of me." He flicked a finger over the bulge in his jeans. "I just wasn't sure it was transferable. Here, love, let me help you." She'd begun tugging at his clothing, frantic to feel his body against hers, skin touching skin.

As his clothes joined hers on the floor, he lifted her easily, supporting her with his hands under her buttocks. Reaching down, she drew him inside her, heart hammering like a tripwire. Breath coming fast, she twined her arms around his shoulders and pulled her legs up, wrapping them around his lower back as she pressed herself against him.

"Yes," she moaned, as sensation swirled through her. "Oh God, yes." She rocked against him, reveling in the intoxicating feelings pounding through her.

Waves of heat engulfed her. Between his hardness within and the magical moonstone urging them on, she reached peak after peak, crying his name over and over again. A part of her felt drained, yet a deeper part clamored for more.

His fingers dug into her legs. Hot breath scoured her neck where his teeth grazed her skin. What had been gentle kisses became fierce, and he thrust into her hard and sure. She tightened her legs around him, her passion heightened by his rowdy abandon. This was a side of Trevor she'd never seen before and she loved it. *Once more*, an inner voice whispered. *Soon.*

With a cry like a wild thing, he clutched her to him and the contractions of his climax jolted her over the edge one more time. Legs trembling, she clung to him, moaning softly.

She wasn't sure how long they stood there, locked in one another's arms, but when she felt him slip out of her, she wriggled in his embrace. "Put me down," she murmured, "before your legs give out."

Chuckling warmly, he released her, pulling her down next to him on the rug. "Now, try to find Lillian," he urged, still catching his breath. "Wasn't that why we did all this?"

She cuffed him playfully. "If it didn't work, does that mean we have to do it again?"

"Wanton hussy! Come on," he murmured, more serious now. "You need to take advantage of the energy whilst it's fresh."

"Okay." She pushed herself to a sitting position, legs crossed, but still touching his body. Grasping the amulet, she closed her eyes and visualized the red-haired Sidhe with the glass-green eyes.

"Yes, yes, dear, I'm here."

Lara's eyes flew open. Sure enough, hovering a few feet above the ground, not too far from the stone fireplace, was Lillian. It was an apparition; translucent with light flowing through it, but it was definitely her. Jubilation, almost as intense as her orgasms had been, roiled through Lara. "Oh, thank God," she crowed, stretching out both hands toward the Sidhe.

"No, dear, thank the goddess." Lillian chortled, her warm, honeyed tones like a balm. "Simply removing your clothing would've done it. Not that I don't, eh, appreciate the carnal sacrifice. Takes me back to Beltane and the old days… But that wasn't why you called me. Our time will be short since projections drain me quickly. Tell me what you need."

Lara hastily sketched out what had happened that day with Detective Archer.

"His daughter looks exactly like me?" Lillian asked skeptically. "That seems impossible."

"Wish I'd brought the photo," Lara said. "Even Trevor saw the resemblance right off the bat."

"Your corporeal self was in the in-between?" Even in the translucence of the vision, Lara saw the Sidhe frown.

"Yes, my body was there. What's the in-between?"

"It would take far too long to explain. Not much I can do about that right now. You must read the part of the book Raven set out for you. The part about natural protections. And we cannot wait for the winter solstice for the two of you to wed. Do not touch anything that Archer man gave you. In fact, don't even talk to him until I get back."

"When will that be?" Lara was surprised at how desperately she wanted Lillian closer. There'd been a time not so long ago, when she'd resented the Sidhe and wanted to turn back the clock to get the meddlesome woman out of their lives.

"A few days, dear. A few days. Now, if you inadvertently get swept off to the other side again, call for me through the amulet."

"But I did," Lara protested. Fear rose within her like an acrid tide.

"Really? How odd that I didn't hear." The sending, with Lillian anchored within it, became even more insubstantial. "Time for me to go, dear."

The Sidhe's form broke into wisps that floated upward, before disappearing entirely. "Well, that didn't help much," she said, gazing helplessly after the shards of the sending.

"Sure it did." Trevor grinned. "We figured out how to get her to come to us."

"Speaking of that." Despite her newly kindled fears about Gradoxst and the unseen world that commanded her presence at unpredictable intervals, Lara turned to Trevor. "Tell me about the Gaelic thing you were chanting? What was it?" Lying next to him, she fitted her body to his. "You've been holding out on me. If I'd known you could do whatever it was you did tonight, well…"

"Well, what?" He sounded sleepy. "You'd never have paid a whit of attention to my brilliant mind all these years. Besides, that was an honest statement when I told you I wasn't sure it would even work. Come on, love. Let's go to bed."

"Yes, but first I want to know what *it* is," she persisted, snuggling closer.

"Variations of the Celtic language have been around for a very long time. Elidora, the witch-woman in the village where I grew up, cast all her spells in Celtic. And the book from Lillian that told you your forbearers came from some other galaxy was written in it too. That's the language used for incantations and spells."

"I thought Lillian said it was Gaelic."

"So she did." Trevor smiled. "She's lived so long, she's probably scarcely noticed how the language has changed in the past thousand years. Scots-Gaelic, which was spoken by some in my village, is quite similar. It's why I could read that handwritten book. Other than spelling, the only real differences were the verb conjugations."

"So the reason I could almost see the hills and barrows of Scotland while you read to me from that little book was because the older language is magical."

"Likely, yes. What I tried tonight was something I overheard Elidora selling to the lovelorn of the village. She'd always smile and wink and tell the lads and lassies it would make nigh onto anyone fall into their beds."

"Oooch, fascinating. Tell me more. Since they work so well, did you memorize any of her other—?"

"Later," Trevor said, chuckling. "Come on, Lara. For once I think I can actually fall asleep. Let's take advantage of that."

"You run on up. I'll take the pup out, and then I'll join you." Strangely, she wasn't the least bit sleepy; her earlier fatigue had fled, along with Trevor's curious chanting. She dressed hastily, clucked to the puppy, and followed him down the steps.

As she watched Gunter sniffing at things once he'd squatted, she thought guiltily about the Sidhe book from Raven and Lillian, discarded on the floorboards of her car. She hadn't even thought about it since finding Arabel's twisted body lying in a pool of congealed blood.

I need to do better, she chided herself and opened the door to let both her and the puppy back inside. *Otherwise I put all of us at risk.*

CHAPTER 6

*L*ara propelled herself up the front steps of Denny Hall, the University of Washington's psychology building, her dark blue wool skirt flapping in the stiff breeze. Sometime between when she and Trevor had left Seattle the previous evening and now, the power had lurched back into life. Good thing, since it was gray and gloomy. There'd be no ambient sunlight filtering through the front doors of the old building that housed the campus clock tower and carillon bells, along with the psych department. She tried to concentrate on the lecture she was about to give, but gave it up for a lost cause. Her mind was still reeling from the previous night and the long talk she and Trevor had while driving back.

Don't forget Archer's daughter.

"As if I could," she muttered, still lost in Trevor's unlikely recitation of druidic lore and Celtic love charms. The reason he knew so much about the Carlisle witch-woman and her spells was because he'd hidden in the corn crib behind her house to get away from his brute of an alcoholic father. Trevor had figured—and correctly it turned out —no one would ever even think to hunt for him so close to Elidora's domain. Famous for her unpredictable temper, she was rumored to have turned those who sparked her ire into toads. The villagers left the witch alone until they were desperate for her assistance.

If Trevor hadn't been so disgusted by sex, from living in a house rife with molest, he'd probably have employed some of Elidora's charms to tempt the local girls. As it was, he'd run off to sea.

Lara's mouth twitched into a half smile. *I'm glad he waited for me. Makes what we have so much more special.* He'd been her first lover too. Wary her psychic ability might somehow leak out, making her the butt of jokes or scorn, Lara kept to herself through college and graduate school. A natural tendency toward shyness made her self-imposed isolation not only bearable, but comfortable. She'd often thought during her early years of practice, that if it hadn't been for her patients, she'd have had no one to talk with at all—except Arabel. Lara sighed, missing the old woman desperately.

Lara pulled open the door to the fourth floor faculty lounge where she taught her graduate seminar. She gazed at the empty room and then checked her watch. Was it possible no one would show? Last week, she'd offered—albeit reluctantly—an analysis of a student's dream, one that painted a bizarrely depressing picture of a dying planet. *It wouldn't have been so unnerving,* she realized, *if I hadn't had the same damned dream, right along with Trev and a couple of my patients.*

Oh yes, it would have, a different inner voice cut in.

The door swung open, banging against an adjacent wall, and Natasha, Ryan, Michael, Christina, and Rachel pushed into the room. "We were not sure you would be here," Natasha announced in her pronounced Russian accent. "That is why we are late."

"Where are the others?" Lara craned her neck to look past Michael's body that was both holding the door open and blocking the doorway at the same time.

"Well, you see." Christina stepped forward, splotches of color high on the cheekbones of her translucent Asian skin. "Lots of us have left campus. That last almost-fifteen-hour power outage convinced everyone things really are imploding."

"But you're not feeling that way?" Lara asked, curious.

"We are," Ryan answered. His hazel eyes were clouded with worry, and the dark smudges beneath them had matured into full-blown circles. Looking at the small group, Lara's heart sank. They were awfully young to be facing the enormity of what loomed over them all.

"But we wanted to meet with you at least one last time." Rachel's brown eyes had lost their characteristic sparkle. "I guess I'll keep on showing up until...well, until no one else does. I—I've got nowhere else to go."

"I am glad to see all of you. Truly." Lara looked solemnly at her students. "Would you like to talk, or listen or both?" Lara had grabbed her notes from what was usually a later lecture in the current Dreams and Archetypes series. It hadn't made sense to stick to chronological order. Instead, she'd chosen a lecture about the Ruler and Magician archetypes; working together, the two could craft at least the possibility of deliverance.

And if we ever needed redemption...

Her five students flopped into the upholstered chairs scattered about the room, turning them to face Lara. "Maybe both," Michael replied cautiously. "There's something comforting about listening to you."

"How about the rest of you?" Lara scanned the small group. Seeing nods, she clasped her hands together and started talking, ". . . and so, if we've been successful incorporating the Magician archetype within ourselves, it's a way to integrate what is sacred to each of us. That way, the power inherent in the archetype becomes available in a deeply personal way." She stopped for a moment, marshaling her thoughts. "Last week, one of you asked me about hope. It lies in the Magician archetype. For you see, it holds both power and a body of knowledge we can use to heal ourselves and our surroundings."

"Isn't it a bit late for that?" Christina asked earnestly. "We can be totally evolved, but the planet is still going to hell."

"There'll be something left," Lara said softly. "There has to be. It's going to look really different from the way things are now, though."

"How can we make sure we'll come through to the other end of all of this?" Ryan waved an arm expansively. "Do you have any ideas?" He paused, and then added shyly, "Maybe you could tell us what you're doing?"

"Yes," Natasha chimed in, her blue eyes focused intently on Lara. "You knew what Ryan's dream meant. What are you doing about it?"

"I've been stockpiling food," Lara said lamely, remembering both Lillian's and Raven's exhortations to keep their plans hidden. *They're a bright group. They'll know I'm lying—at least by omission.*

"But mostly." She searched for what she could share that would be candid. "I've been hoping for the best. It's not easy. And it gets harder every time the power goes out, or my husband tells me how difficult it's becoming to find food." *There, at least that part isn't prevarication.* She took a deep breath. "You see," Lara went on, her voice vibrating with emotion, "last week during the riots, a very dear friend of mine was murdered."

A gasp rattled around the room, rising quickly in intensity. Lara held up a hand. "Let me finish. She was like a mother to me. So I've spent a lot of time thinking about what's really important in my life… and what isn't. One of the decisions I made was to close my practice." Shutting her eyes, Lara struggled for composure. When she opened them, they were full of tears.

"I've had a psychology practice for over twenty years. Arabel was there almost from the beginning. I just don't see how I can have an office—and try to help people—without her by my side." Lara paused, swiping a sleeve across her eyes. "The reason I shared that with you was to illustrate that, when you look within, the answer you need emerges. If you're open to seeing it. That's part of the Magician archetype. Sometimes, that answer isn't what you thought it would be. I assumed I'd still be sitting with patients until I was too old to drag myself to the office."

"What are you going to do?" Michael asked. "Not that you have to tell us, but since you kicked the door open to personal stuff, I was just wondering."

"I really don't know," she answered slowly. "For the first time in my life, I'm okay with that for an answer."

"Yeah, we're all pretty driven, huh?" Christina muttered. "Go here, do this, finish that."

"And it is all externals," Natasha added. "So little of what we do makes us look inside ourselves. In fact, we avoid it."

Lara eyed the clock on the back wall. "We've only got a couple minutes left," she noted, one corner of her mouth softening into half a smile. "Do any of you have somewhere you need to be at three o'clock?" A collection of nods answered her question. "Okay, no assignment for next week. I promise I'll try to be here, and we can continue talking."

Lara watched as her students filed out of the room, wondering if any of them would survive the riots that were sure to escalate and the food shortages, never mind no fuel or heat. Clean water would become a problem too, once the power failed for good.

"You didn't tell us everything, Dr. McInnis." Ryan, last to leave, faced her, questions mirrored in his weary eyes.

"You're right, Ryan. I didn't. But maybe it's because I can't." Lara met his gaze evenly, thinking he'd aged years since he'd had that prophetic dream.

"Oh." The word held such a defeated note that Lara's heart went out to him. Shoulders slumping, he turned slowly. The echo of his heavy footsteps clumping down the hallway toward the stairs rang in her ears.

Gathering up her coat and bag, Lara was just locking the door to the faculty lounge when Roxanne Dykstra, another psychology professor, appeared from a nearby stairwell. "Lara," she panted, stopping to catch her breath, a hand laid over the chest of her colorful, flowing caftan. The tiny, older woman had long straight silvery hair. Today it was twisted into an elaborate bun and pinned at the nape of her neck. Her usually merry gray eyes were somber and lacked their normal coating of brightly-hued eye shadow. "I'm so glad I caught you. I'd have popped up earlier, but a couple students stopped by."

"Yes, Roxanne?" Lara felt torn. After what had been an intense emotional exchange with her students, all she wanted was to be alone with her thoughts. But she'd gone to Roxanne for help learning about her psychic abilities. In truth, it had been Roxanne who'd introduced her to Lillian. Now the other faculty member wanted to be friends.

In her heart of hearts, Lara knew only too well one of her biggest failings was her inability to form casual friendships. She'd tried many strategies over the years, but socializing with near-strangers remained excruciatingly difficult.

"There's a gathering tonight. Well, actually, it's been going on all day too," Roxanne confided, looking over her shoulder to assure herself no one would overhear. "It's the end of Samhain week. Do you suppose you might drop by?"

"Thanks for the invitation, but I'm pretty busy for the next few days." Lara let her words trail off as she purposefully headed for the stairs.

The other psychologist clutched at her arm. "We're alone up here. Please don't go down quite yet. I know Lillian's gone, since I've been trying to reach her for a while now. There's not really anyone with any, um, power without her. So I'm afraid we won't be able to accomplish much if you don't help us out."

Lara sighed. Roxanne was a self-styled Wiccan. Apparently, the coven she belonged to was having some sort of a ceremony requiring magic. Resolutely, she turned to face the other woman. "I do appreciate you thinking of me. But Roxanne, you need to know I have little to no control over what I can do. Actually, I don't have much idea how to call up my ability, or how to direct it once I've got it. Lillian says I need years of study, and I suppose she's right. So I don't think I'd do you much good, even if I did come by."

Roxanne's face fell. "Are you sure?" she asked.

Oh, very sure. "It's only been a short time since I met Lillian," Lara reminded her. "It would be hard to develop much skill in such a brief amount of time."

"I suppose you're right." Roxanne looked down. "Things are so very bad right now, though, and we all thought if we could make an offering Gaia would approve of that, well, maybe..."

Gently removing the smaller woman's insistent hand from her arm, Lara made an effort to infuse an encouraging note into her voice. "I think you should go ahead and have your Samhain ritual tonight. Even if no one has real power, Gaia may well hear you anyway. I've been telling my patients for years to conceptualize things they want. This isn't any different."

Roxanne brightened a bit. "Would you like me to walk down with you?"

"If you're leaving anyway, sure," Lara replied, understanding how lonely the other woman must be.

Lara walked out the tall front doors of Denny Hall into a blinding rainstorm. After bidding Roxanne goodbye, she shielded her head from the droplets and made a dash for the BMW parked in Trevor's favorite no-parking spot. He pushed the door open and she dove into the car, twisting around to shake the water out of her hair before slamming the door.

"I was beginning to get worried," he said and reached into the back to hand her a towel.

"Roxanne invited me to a coven meeting tonight," she said dryly.

"The one who told you about Lillian?"

"The same." Lara dabbed at her damp face, folding the soaked ends of her hair in the towel. "Still want to pick up your Benz?'

"We have to. I told the bloke I'd be by for it today. Don't trust him not to sell it off if we don't rescue it."

"Where's Gunter?" It had just dawned on her the puppy wasn't in the hatch area of the car. Worry flickered at the edges of her mind.

"He's fine," Trevor said quickly, attuned to her concerns. "After I dropped you off, I swung back by home. Figured I'd get a few things done. Anyhow, I left him there. He's big enough he can be by himself for a couple hours."

They drove in a companionable silence. It was raining so hard even the BMW's efficient wipers had a hard time keeping the windshield clear enough to see out of. "You couldn't have been home for more than a few minutes," she said at last.

"Long enough for me to finish clearing out the studies. Couldn't pack anything in this downpour, though. I'd have the dickens of a time getting the truck into the back yard. I'm afraid it'd mire up to the axles in mud. Are you going to go?"

"Huh? Go to what?"

"The coven meeting."

"Of course not. It's not like we don't have more than enough to do at home. I'm still not done with sorting clothes, and there are some of my sewing things I want... Ooops, phone's vibrating." She filtered through debris in her shoulder bag until her fingers closed around the cell phone. "Oh-oh, it's Archer."

"Lillian said not to talk to him."

Lara nodded. Staring at the phone, she willed it to stop ringing. "I need to sort through my messages. There're quite a few of them." Scrunching up her face in distaste, she started with her clinic email account. She was still punching buttons and replying to emails when Trevor pulled up alongside his Benz.

"Want me to wait till you're through with your phone?" he asked. "This isn't the best neighborhood."

"Sure. That'd be great."

"Who all did you hear from, anyway?" he asked, after she'd tucked the cell back into its leather case.

She snorted. "Shit! Four emails and two voice messages were from Archer. He's worse than Beauchamp was. The rest are just...messages. Not particularly important."

"What did our boy in blue have to say for himself?" Trevor leaned toward her, his forehead creased with concern.

"First, he wanted to know if I'd gotten any *hits* off Adriana's things. Then he wanted to know why I wasn't calling him back. The last message, the one that came in right before I caught up with my phone, he sounded decidedly aggravated."

"Humph...not good. If he gets too angry, I'm afraid we won't be able to leave the house without one of his officers breathing up our arses. Maybe you need to get back to him, Lara. You know, to placate him a bit."

Nodding, she hit redial on the phone. The detective picked up immediately. "Where've you been?" he growled, and then immediately backed off a few notches. "Sorry, Lara, I didn't mean to sound so...so..."

"Sharp?" she finished for him.

"Yeah, I suppose that's as good as whatever word I might have come up with," he said sullenly.

"Look, Brad, I didn't think I was supposed to check in with you unless I knew something. We went out of town last evening, and today I taught my class at the University." She hesitated, softening her voice. "I'm really sorry, but I don't know anything more than I did yesterday when you left my office. I promised you I'd call if something came to me, and I will."

There was a long silence. So long that she checked the screen of the cell phone to see if they were still connected. What he said next, chilled her. "You, ah, you were correct I'd left something out. How about if I come over to your house tonight to talk with you?"

"Not a good idea," she blurted. "I think I'm coming down with something, and I plan to turn in really early."

"Do you have patients tomorrow?"

She squeezed her eyes shut. Her pulse was racing and sweat formed in her armpits. *I haven't felt this scared since Beauchamp was stalking me.*

"Yes, I do."

"Well, when would be a good time for me to stop by?"

"I need to check my schedule. I'll call you back." When she glanced over at Trevor, he was making chopping motions with one hand.

"Tonight, Doctor. Call me back tonight." The phone went dead in her hand.

"I never should've—" she began.

"Wouldn't have mattered," Trevor interrupted, his voice harsh.

"He'd just have come by if you didn't call. I suppose I could hide all the packing detritus, but what does he want that can't be accomplished by phone?"

"I don't know. I just don't know. Something's really, really wrong here." Now that she wasn't trying to sound nonchalant, Lara's voice trembled. "We have to find out what it is." She snapped her fingers as she thought of something. "Did you ever check the Internet or the papers or the television—well, scratch that since we don't have cable—for information about Adriana?" He shook his head. "Neither did I, but the first thing I'm going to do once we get home is check the net. Maybe…"

Maybe what? Maybe he doesn't have a daughter? Maybe she's not really missing? What the hell is going on here?

"Brilliant plan. See you at home." Having fished his car keys out of a pocket in his rain coat, Trevor pushed open his door and sprinted for the Benz.

Lara thought about walking around the car, but decided to crawl over the console instead. As she was getting situated, her phone, so recently moved off its vibrate setting, began to ring. Fear settled into her guts like a lead shot put, and she peeked at the screen. *Hmm...don't recognize that number. Maybe it's safe to answer my own phone.* "Dr. McInnis," she said tentatively.

"Lara, it's Roxanne."

"Hi. What can I do for you?"

"My, you sound so formal. It's me, dear. You can drop that professional veneer."

"I'm just tired. Really, what do you need? I'm trying to drive home, and the weather is perfectly abysmal."

"Yes, it is, isn't it?" Roxanne sounded absurdly pleased with herself. "I just wanted to let you know you were right. We did get together. In fact, like I told you, some of us have been praying all day. This simply magnificent downpour was the result. Thought you'd want to know. Cheers, dearie. Call me when you're not so grumpy."

"Sure. Will do," Lara said, before disconnecting. She shook her head and began to giggle. *So now we're weather masters, are we?* She dropped the phone into its customary spot in the console, kicked the defroster up to high, and backed out of her parking place, heading for home. She'd barely made it half a dozen blocks when her phone rang again. Pulling it up to eye level, she saw Trevor's number. "Hello?" she pulled her car over to a convenient curb.

"Lara, I've been in an accident. You need to come."

An accident? Her heart started pounding. Trevor was an impeccable driver. So much so, she'd teased him on many occasions about having been a chauffeur in a former life. "Are you all right?"

"Think so, but my car's totaled. I'm at the corner of Queen Anne Avenue and Galer."

"Be there as soon as I can."

"Drive slow. The streets are slick. I'm still not sure quite what happened."

CHAPTER 7

*L*ara clutched the leather-clad steering wheel so hard her hands began to cramp. Flexing first one, then the other, she forced herself to drive the speed limit.

He said he's all right. He sounded all right.

She frantically tried to reassure herself, but still felt nauseated, and her brain shifted into hyper drive, scattering her thoughts in all directions. The amulet didn't care much for the situation, either. It had begun its characteristic warning vibration a few minutes before Trevor called. *I sure wish you could talk,* she muttered, grasping the magical moonstone. All it did was send prickles into her hand.

In spite of the defroster, the windshield was fogging up. Cracking a window, she grabbed the towel she'd used on her hair and cleared a big enough spot so she could see. She didn't want to take the time to pull over. It only took a few minutes before the red sweep of emergency vehicle lights came into view. Parking the BMW, she jumped out of her car and raced to where Trevor was engaged in a heated discussion.

He held out a hand as soon as he saw her, while continuing to argue with a cop and a paramedic, "No! I am *not* going to the bloody hospital. I'm not so banged up I can't take care of myself. I told you my wife was on her way. She's here now, so I'll be leaving."

"But sir." The cop had what looked like a none-too-gentle hand on Trevor's arm. "You might have a concussion. I insist you go with the paramedics."

"Am I under arrest?" Trevor snarled.

The officer, water streaming from the brim of his hat, said, "No, sir. But I'd like it if you stayed until my captain showed up."

"If I'm not under arrest, I'm going home. I gave you a statement. I even called a wrecker for my car, so you could rest easy I'd pay to have it hauled off. There's nothing else for me to do here. I want to get out of my wet clothes and into a hot bath with a strong cuppa. Come on, Lara." Yanking his arm away from the police officer, Trevor limped toward her.

"Are you sure—?" she began.

"Yes, I'm bloody well sure." He draped an arm around her shoulders and hissed, "It's likely some sort of stalling tactic until Archer—or one of his minions—can get here."

"Doesn't feel right to me, either," she murmured and pulled open the passenger door of the BMW. "Shit! Too late." Another car, siren blaring, careened around the corner.

"No, it's not. Don't pay any attention. Just drive off." Trevor maneuvered awkwardly into the car. "Let's go. Hurry." A desperate undertone in his voice alarmed her.

"What happened?" she asked as she drove, surprised the newest cop on the scene hadn't chased them down. "I walked past your poor car. Argggh. God bless the engineers at Mercedes Benz. That you could walk away from a car that's bent up like a pretzel defies credibility." She felt the hot sting of tears. "I don't know what I'd do if something—"

"Not a time to get maudlin. Pull yourself together and leave me off in the alley," he told her, his voice as strained as she'd ever heard it. "That way I won't have to climb the stairs."

By the time she'd locked the BMW and carted her bag up their twenty-five front steps, Lara was soaked to the skin. Gunter leaped on her the moment she came through the front door, and she bent to pet the enthusiastic puppy. "Where's Daddy?" she asked, making a quick tour of the lower two floors. "Hmm…better take you out, and then I'll see if he's in the tub."

Trevor was indeed in their oversized Jacuzzi tub. Purpling bruises were spreading over one leg and the front of his chest, and there were lacerations on his face. "Oh my." Her hand flew to her mouth. "Is there glass in any of those?" She waggled a finger at his face.

"Nah, safety glass held. I took a couple of those codeine tablets left over from something-or-other. Figure I'll be beastly sore tomorrow morning, but I've had worse. This is nothing compared with what my dad dealt out." He smiled crookedly. "At least it didn't knock out any of my caps."

"Maybe you shouldn't have taken those pain pills. If you do have a concussion—"

"Leave it." Despite an abrupt edge, Trevor sounded more like himself. She thought better of saying anything else about the ten-year-old codeine he'd fished out of their medicine cabinet.

"Feel like talking about any of this?" she asked, treading carefully.

"Sure, when I'm out of the tub. Suppose you could heat up the soup? It's in that big tureen in the fridge. I'll come down in a bit. And Lara, get out of those wet clothes."

"Thanks for the reminder. I'd almost forgotten about them." Back in their bedroom, she stripped to the skin and pulled on a thick terrycloth robe and a pair of warm socks. Relief that Trevor wasn't badly hurt made her almost giddy. As an afterthought, she picked up her sodden garments from where she'd let them drop on the floor and draped them over a chair back.

By the time Trevor made his way slowly down the circular staircase, she was just dishing up the split pea and ham soup he'd made earlier in the day. "Found this." She pointed to a plate of cornbread she'd set on the table. "So I zapped it in the wave."

Trevor winced. "Aw, Lara. Not that I'm complaining. Or maybe I am, but the microwave ruins food."

Guess I won't tell him I nuked the soup too.

"Will you be able to sit at the table?" She looked at him and drew her brows together in concern. "Or would you rather we ate in the front room or the library, where you could put your feet up on one of the couches?"

"In here's fine," he replied. "Tomorrow will be much worse than right now. Don't even think about nagging me to take it easy. It's paradoxical, but the more I do, the quicker all this," he ran his hands up and down his battered body, covered in a robe identical to hers, "will normalize."

They ate in silence for a few moments. Lara realized she was famished as soon as she began spooning soup into her mouth. Once she'd worked her way through her first bowl, and gone to get more butter and preserves for the cornbread, she cocked her head to one side and asked, "Well?"

"Guess you want to know what happened."

She nodded emphatically.

Trevor laid down his spoon and took a deep draught from the Cabernet she'd opened. "The reason I've been so quiet is I've been trying to work that out for myself," he admitted, grimly. "I wasn't going all that fast, and from out of nowhere I thought I saw something. It took a few seconds to sort it out since the weather was so beastly, but it was a dark form that looked a lot like a person. Anyway, he—or she, or it—pretty much threw themselves in front of my car. I wasn't thinking when that happened, there wasn't time. I reacted and cramped the wheel hard to avoid hitting whatever it was. That's when things got weird. My car never did hit whatever I'd swerved to avoid. I'd have known if it did, 'cause I'd have felt it. I was straightening out the wheel when it tore through my hands, locked at the stops, and my poor little car started spinning. It stopped when it hit a power pole. Good thing I had the presence of mind to engage the electric window button whilst I was in that spin, or I'd never have gotten out of the car as easily as I did."

"You crawled through your window?"

He nodded, looking the tiniest bit pleased with himself.

Lara felt the blood drain out of her head. The amulet's unpleasant refrain didn't help. "You're lucky you weren't killed," she managed at last out of lips that were set in a hard line. "Damned lucky."

"Yeah, that's sort of how I see it too," he muttered, picking up his spoon to resume eating. "If I'd been going much faster than twenty, I'd be in a box at the morgue."

Her appetite gone, she drained off half her wine, before resting her head on an upraised hand. "You said out there in the rain you thought this was Archer's doing. Why'd you say that?"

He hesitated. "Now that you ask, I'm not really sure. Maybe it was just an intuition, sort of like those psychic insights you get. All I know is when I was standing out in the rain next to my tangled heap of a car, I felt certain if I'd gotten into that ambulance, they'd have killed me on the way to the hospital and trumped up some story that I had internal injuries or something. There was something else too…"

"Jesus Christ, what more could there possibly be? What happened to you is appalling."

"Humph! Well, it does get just a smidgeon worse. See, as soon as I'd slithered out my window, I got up and started looking for whoever had tossed themselves in front of my Benz. A couple of folk standing around saw me start spinning, but when I asked them, neither one had seen anybody else anywhere near my car. They just assumed I lost control on the wet pavement. One chap said it seemed odd to him, since I'd been going so slowly."

The amulet was practically bouncing up and down on her chest. Its endorsement of her concern opened a gateway to terror that all but annihilated her. The world tumbled slowly, end over end.

"Lara?" she heard him as if from a great distance. "Lara!" He clapped his hands an inch in front of her nose. She jumped, but at least the sticky molasses inertia weighting down her limbs receded a little.

"You're white as a sheet. Drop your head betwixt your knees, or I do believe you'll faint. I'm not in any kind of shape to carry you anywhere."

She obligingly pushed her chair back and lowered her head, trying to modulate her ragged breathing. Once her head was down, she stayed that way for several minutes.

She finally straightened, twisting from side to side. "That's better. What with everything that's happened to you, I never did check on the Archer-daughter angle. I'm going to run up and get my laptop. Anything I can get for you while I'm upstairs?"

Shaking his head, he reached for the wine again.

She turned to look back at him from the kitchen doorway. "What happened to you is so dreadful I almost can't bear to think about it. When I do, it sucks me into this hopeless, helpless place."

"There's not much point now, is there? In thinking about it, I mean." Between the wine and the codeine, he was actually smiling at her. "The bastards tried, but they didn't get me. Game over for now."

Yes, an inner voice nattered. *But who are the bastards? And what about next time?* "There just can't be a next time," she muttered half to herself as she clumped up the stairs.

Back at the table with her computer booting up, she finished her dinner, even though she no longer felt the least bit hungry. With relief, she noticed Trevor had drained a second bowl of soup. "'Kay," she mumbled, punching keys on her laptop. "Here we go." For a few moments, the only sound in the kitchen was the muted click of computer keys. "Oh my God," she gasped, clicking faster. "My fucking God."

"What?" In spite of his injuries, Trevor was out of his seat like a shot and bending to look over her shoulder. He let out a long low whistle. "So," he said through clenched teeth. "That bastard knew we didn't have the telly here. He knew because we told him that night he stayed to protect us. He also knew what a news-phobe you are, because we told him that too. Given both those things, I suppose he figured we'd never find out he lied to us."

"Yeah," Lara snapped, filled with sudden fury at being duped as she stared at the picture of Adriana Archer that had probably been posted on every television network and the Internet ever since her disappearance. Adriana looked a lot like her father: blonde and blue-eyed with a dewy Miss America patina.

"What I want to know," Lara spat through gritted teeth, "is how the hell he got a picture of Lillian? And how he—or someone else—managed to do something to it to make her look sixteen."

"Photoshop?" Trevor smiled grimly as he made his way slowly back to his chair.

Gunter suddenly shot up from his puppy bed in the corner, yapping fiercely. "Hah!" Trevor looked angrily in the direction of the front door. "Looks like you'll get an opportunity to ask both those questions if you want to. I may not be psychic, but I'll bet you a hundred quid Archer's on our front stoop." The chime from the front bell pealed softly.

Lara looked questioningly at Trevor. "Go answer it, love," he said smoothly. "I'll just take the pup out back for a second." When she hesitated, he made shooing motions. "He's not going to shoot us in cold blood in our own home, but you might want to power that down," he said, pointing at the computer.

After a few key strokes, Lara gathered her robe more tightly about her, retying the sash, before walking toward the door. When she looked through the security glass she saw Detective Brad Archer, in the same bedraggled clothing he'd worn the previous day, standing with his back to their front door. The rain had let up, and she wondered if Roxanne and her coven had gotten tired. *Try to focus*, she admonished herself as she took a deep breath, unlatched the deadbolt, and opened the door.

"Brad," she gushed warmly. "I'm so sorry I didn't call, but Trev was in an accident, and I got sidetracked." His eyes widened. This was obviously not the greeting he'd been expecting. "Anyway, if you'd like to step in for a few minutes, I can check my schedule and let you know what works for me tomorrow."

"Sure, Lara. That'd be fine." He paused a beat. "Heard about the accident. Glad he wasn't hurt worse, but I still think he should've gone to the hospital."

When Brad stepped into the light of their entry hall, it took all her years of professionalism to hide her shock at his appearance. He looked far worse than he had just thirty hours before. Eyes deeply sunken into his skull, he could have passed for a corpse. And the whiff of stale sweat she'd caught the previous day had become a positive stench.

What the hell? This is far more than even a complicated bereavement would create for anyone.

"Just a sec, let me get my phone. I had Arabel to handle all this for me for so long, I forgot my phone has all that information when you called earlier." She shrugged apologetically as she picked up her bag from its usual spot next to the armoire in the entry hall and rooted around in it until she came up with her cell. "Let's see here," she muttered, scrolling through menus and submenus. "That mid-day spot should work." She stood looking at him, her eyebrows raised expectantly. When he didn't respond, she prodded, "Well, shall I put you down?"

He finally nodded mechanically. "How's Trevor?" he asked, but the question had an odd cadence to it.

"I thought you already knew. A bit banged up, but I'm sure he'll be fine," she said cheerily. "Now, was there anything else you needed tonight?"

"No, guess not," he mumbled, still not moving from where he stood. "What are those?" he asked suddenly, pointing to the boxes that had come from Amsterdam stacked against one wall.

"Things from our flat in Europe. One of Trev's friends packed them up after he lost his job. We thought it'd be tough to try to get over there ourselves, so…" She let the words hang between them.

"Are you planning on going somewhere?" he asked abruptly.

"Look closely, Detective," she said, her voice decidedly cooler than it had been. "Those boxes came from Europe. We had an apartment in Amsterdam. We were lucky to get our things back."

Walking over to the stack of boxes, he gazed intently at them. "Looks as if you're telling the truth," he said dubiously as he turned back to face her, but avoided her eyes.

"If that's all, I really need you to leave, so Trev and I can get some rest."

"Huh?" The vacant look gradually left Brad's blue eyes, and he seemed genuinely surprised to find himself standing in front of her. "Uh, guess I'll talk to you tomorrow, then," he mumbled, finally turning his big body so it faced the door. Afraid manipulating the knob might be beyond him, she extended a hand and pulled the door open.

"Night, Brad," she said, pointing toward the front porch.

Without answering, he walked outside and started down their front steps with jerky, puppet-like movements.

Lara locked the door and set their alarm. The minute Brad turned away from her, her pleasant smile vanished, replaced by pursed lips.

"Brilliant, Lara. Positively brilliant. You missed your calling, love. You could have gone on the stage." Trevor, who'd obviously sequestered himself in the hallway just out of sight, limped into the entry hall.

"Oh, Trev." She looked at him beseechingly. "Did you see him?"

"Yup, smelled him too. Ugh!"

"Not funny," she barked. "I'd never have agreed to meet him, except it seemed to be the only way to get him to leave He's acting like someone having their first schizophrenic break, but he's far too old for that."

"What do you mean?"

She frowned. "Go on upstairs, I'll clear up in the kitchen and bring the pup."

"No." He shuffled to her and placed an arm around her shoulders. "I may not be able to help much, but I will keep you company in the kitchen whilst you straighten up. Explain that schizophrenic thing to me."

"People develop that illness somewhere between their mid-teens and late twenties, never when they're Brad's age."

"Is there anything else it could be?" Trevor limped down the hall to the kitchen.

"An early dementia, but that wouldn't explain the coincident disappearance of his daughter. Plus, the detective wasn't anything like this two weeks ago. Maybe a situational depression with psychotic features." She spread her hands in front of her, and then ran them through her hair, shoving it over her shoulders. "Nah. This just doesn't have the feel of any mental illness I've ever come across. And the amulet keeps clamoring, so that means there's magic mixed up somewhere."

Trevor grunted, resettled himself in his chair, and tipped the wine bottle to pour another jot. "Now that you know how to get to Lillian, why don't you try her again once we're in bed?"

"Now you wait just a minute." Lara, soup tureen clasped in both hands, eyed him with some asperity. "No sex until you're better."

"Who said anything about sex?" he inquired sweetly. "Didn't she say all you had to do was take your clothes off?"

Lighting a cinnamon-vanilla candle for ambience, Lara shucked her robe and her stockings, clasped the amulet, and stood in the center of their bedroom floor. Emptying her mind, she called for the Sidhe. This time it was Raven who appeared, much as Lillian had the previous night.

"Why you and not Lillian?" Lara asked, exquisitely conscious of her nakedness.

"Because I'm stronger and can stay longer. Tell me what I need to know."

Lara was just completing her description of Brad's unsettling appearance, when the mage held up a hand. "I've heard enough. I'm deeply relieved the person missing in the beyond isn't related to Lillian, but I'm troubled by Trevor's accident and the fact this detective is lying to you…something that's likely very out of character for him. Lillian and I will return in two days' time. We can't come before that or our entire journey will have been for naught."

Two days. Lara considered all that had happened in the previous two days and felt deeply frightened.

"Yes, daughter, it's good for you to be afraid." Raven's resonant voice, little changed by the distance over which it was projected, reverberated through her. "If you're afraid, you'll be careful. And you'll study harder."

"But…" Guilt washed against her soul. Despite Lillian's warning from last night, that damned book was still moldering on the floor of her car.

"Listen to the amulet. It can communicate quite succinctly, but you need to pay closer attention. That's why you need the book." His form wavered. "Be sure to summon us if you find out something new. And in the name of the triple goddess, child, finish getting moved."

Lara shivered. Leaving the candle burning, she pulled a flannel nightgown over her head and clambered into bed. "What do you suppose he and Lillian are up to?" she asked. "Didn't you tell me they were meeting up with other magical beings somewhere in the Old Country?"

Trevor nodded from where he was propped on fluffy down pillows. "Who knows what the Sidhe—and whoever else they hobnob with—can do when they're together? I've always assumed Cailleach pulls out her cauldron and they all share boiled babies, whilst hatching up plans to rule the universe."

"Ugh! That's gross."

"You knew it was a rhetorical question when you asked it. What we need to puzzle out is where Archer got a photo of Lillian, and who told him to show it to you, passing it off as his missing daughter. We also have the question of the scarf. I'm sure you're correct it's some sort of conduit to the other side, but it seems to me that it's more connected to whoever wants to lure you over there, than to Adriana."

"Gradoxst?" The amulet jerked against her chest as soon as she uttered the Demon's name. Closing a hand around the moonstone, she murmured, "Maybe he's at the root of all this. After all, he was waiting when the scarf dragged me over. But he was skulking about the other times I ended up in psychic-land too."

An ugly thought shook her. "Maybe he'll be there *every* time from now on, when my psychic side hauls me into a vision." She shuddered.

"Humph." Trevor blew out a weary breath. "We won't solve this one tonight, love. Come on over here. Gently, though. Let's have a hug and try to get some sleep."

After a gingerly embrace, Lara got up to brush her teeth and blow out the candle. She was close to figuring out something important, but cobwebs—lots of them—obscured her normally-sharp thought processes. She stood for a long time at the window, staring out at a quarter moon. Clouds from the earlier storm concealed any stars. Finally, when her cold feet began to complain, she slid them into her slippers, and draped a long coat over her nightgown. "Trev?"

"Mmph?" He opened one eye a slit and looked her way. Then the other eye opened, and he sounded rattled when he said, "Where the hell are you going?" Gunter whined softly from his spot on the duvet next to Trevor.

"Out to my car to get that damned book."

"Wait." Trevor struggled with the sheets as he tried to sit up. "I'll come with you."

She walked to his side of the bed and laid both hands on his shoulders. "Uh-uh. If I'm not back in five minutes, you can come hunting for me. For now, you need to stay put."

"Not sure I like that," he grumbled, as he lay back down.

"Love you," she said softly, kissing the top of his head. "I'll screech like a banshee if I run into problems."

He started to laugh, and then laid both hands over his midsection. "Can't do that. It hurts too much."

"Sleep," she murmured, letting herself out their bedroom door. At the bottom of the spiral staircase she snapped up her keys from the armoire, paused the alarm, and stepped onto their front porch, scanning the street carefully for Archer's cruiser. The last thing she wanted was to run into the policeman again, but their street looked quiet. The usual compliment of cars jammed into every available parking spot had thinned out, and she wondered if some of their neighbors had left town after the last power outage.

A few minutes later, she was back in the house, door locked and alarm reset. The amulet thrummed pleasantly as if it approved of her decision to rescue the book. Slipping silently into the bedroom, she returned to her cozy spot under the duvet and ruffled the puppy's soft fur.

Brow furrowed in concentration, she turned to the place where she'd left off reading and tried to concentrate, but it was a losing battle. Finally, after the lines of print blurred again and again, she laid the volume in the recessed headboard, turned out the light, and shut her eyes. Tired as she felt, sleep was a long time coming.

CHAPTER 8

revor's moans dragged her out of a deeply disturbing dream. She opened her eyes to daylight and determined that the low, gagging sounds were coming from their bathroom. Throwing back the quilts, she raced for the adjoining bath and yanked the door open. Trevor was on his knees on the Italian marble floor in front of the commode being sick.

She plucked a washcloth from the nearest towel rack and flipped on the taps, silently urging the water to warm faster. When she finally had a washcloth saturated with warm water, she wrung it out and handed it to him. "Here," she said softly. "Wipe your face and let me help you back to bed. It was those damned codeine tablets. They always make me sick too. That's why there were so many left over. Don't know why I didn't just chuck them."

"Ooouch," he groaned. "Wasn't doing all that badly till I stood up, and my head went all odd. Actually," he dropped the lid of the toilet, flushed it, and used the commode to push himself to a standing position. "Seems better now. Really. I'll just take a quick shower."

"Are you sure?" she asked worriedly. "Do you want me to stay in here with you?"

He shook his head. "Nope. Better take the pup out. If you could manage something for breakfast, I do think I could eat a bite."

"You got it, sweetie." She wrapped a robe around herself, stuffed her feet into slippers, and took the dog downstairs.

Cook? He wants me to cook? Lara laughed wryly to herself as she stood out in the wet grass of the backyard overseeing Gunter's morning ritual. She was a perfectly abysmal cook, and both of them knew it.

I suppose I could try my hand at scrambled eggs and leftover cornbread. How hard could that be?

When Trevor stumbled into the kitchen, she was just placing two plates on the table. "There," she announced with an edge of triumph in her voice. "Eggs, cheese, and cornbread something-or-other. And coffee. I managed to make that too."

"Ha! You'll oust me right out of a job," he said, looking suspiciously at the eggs. "At least they don't smell burnt," he muttered as he folded his body slowly into his customary seat.

"I never cast aspersions on what you make," she pointed out.

"True, true. Hey there, love, you've got a spot of grease on your nose."

She poured him a cup of French Roast. "No more complaints. I'd like to bask in my glory if it's all right with you."

"Mmm." He sniffed appreciatively at his mug. "Smells wonderful."

"That's better." Pouring herself a cup, and adding cream and sugar, she sat down to what was probably the first meal she'd cooked for them in twenty years. "They say it tastes better if you made it yourself," she laughed, "but I never believed it. On a more serious note —" She picked up her fork. "How are you feeling?"

"Not nauseous anymore," he replied, taking a bite of her egg concoction. "Hey, this is pretty damned good, love. Maybe there's a future for you in the kitchen after all."

"I'm glad your stomach's back to normal, but how's the rest of you?"

He looked down, as if he were taking stock of his body. "Sorest thing is my chest," he said, a couple bites later. "Steering wheel caught me when I hit that pole. My knee's a bit off, but overall I'm mostly unscathed."

"I'm so glad to hear that." She beamed at him over her plate, and then her smile faded. "I had the oddest dream this morning."

"Do you want to tell me?" He looked up expectantly.

"I don't generally talk about my dreams. I think about them and analyze what they might mean, but I don't discuss them casually."

He nodded, continuing to eat and sip his coffee.

"But this one just seems so obvious. I was back on that beach—"

"What beach?"

"Oh, that's right, I didn't tell you about the place where the scarf dragged me. It was a bizarre beach with strange sand and a stranger sky. Anyway, I was back there. Pretty much in the same spot, as far as I could tell. Adriana was there too. But this time, she was the real one.

"She was sitting on a stool outside this primitive hut on the edge of the beach, chained to the side of it. I couldn't see terribly clearly since it was night in the dream, but it looked as if chains looped around her arms and ankles, almost like shackles. She cried out to me, begged me to rescue her."

Lara swallowed hard. "She told me she was afraid she'd die there, and she'd never be able to say goodbye to her family." Sadness welled within Lara as she recounted Adriana's helplessness and fear.

"I tried to talk with her. Asked her who'd kidnapped her, but she didn't know. She'd never seen him before. I described Gradoxst, but she just looked confused. That was about it. I don't know how much more would've played out if I hadn't heard you in the john and gotten up."

"Do you know where she is?" Trevor's voice was deadly quiet. He'd stopped eating as he listened to her describe her dream.

She shook her head. "Uh-uh. I don't even know where the place I go in my visions is. I've always assumed it's out there somewhere." She waved both hands expansively. "But that beach and that sky. I've never seen anything like them before. They looked as if they belonged on some other planet."

He pushed up from his place. "Where are you going?" she asked, worried about how stiff he was. "I can get whatever you need."

"I was going to rescue that bloody Sidhe book," he said, limping toward the kitchen door. "Maybe it explains paranormal land."

"I got it last night, remember? It's upstairs in the headboard." She shouldered past him. "I don't understand what it is that makes me keep forgetting I have to study what's in there, but it must be linked to everything else that's happening. When I tried to read last night, I had the devil's own time concentrating. I didn't make it through more than a handful of pages." She hesitated, thinking. "And I'm damned if I can remember anything about them this morning."

"All right, Lara." He resettled himself in his chair. "Up to the bedroom, get the bloody book, and come back."

Once she had the book in hand, her head began to clear. The spider's webs standing between her and her ability to reason dropped away, and she felt more like herself. Why hadn't the book engendered this sense of peace last night?

Even if I don't read it, maybe I need to keep it and the amulet close to me. Once I'm separated from the book, something seems to intrude. It's almost like there's a spirit or something that doesn't want me reading any more of it. A chill raised goose bumps along both arms. *Aha! A bit too close to the truth there?*

When she came back into the kitchen, Trevor was clearing dishes off the table. "You were finished, weren't you?" he inquired.

"Uh-huh. Do you think you should be up and about?"

"Remember, I asked you not to nag?"

"'Kay." She swallowed down her next words. "What are you going to do today?"

"That's better." Turning away from the sink, he grinned at her, but his expression was a pale reflection of the man she'd known before Beauchamp had come into their lives with his threats. Trevor's mouth might have been smiling, but his eyes looked old and grave. "Thought I'd at least sort out the last of the books from the library."

"You're not planning another trip to Raven's are you?" Clapping a hand over her mouth, she mumbled, "Sorry, that just slipped out."

"Not today," he replied grudgingly. "I will give you that much. But tomorrow I'm going to try for two loads, one early, one late. I'm supposed to be checking on the animals. Hate to miss a day, but I suppose it can't be helped. Anyway, you can help me pack the early load when you get home tonight. If I'm lucky, those two trips should just about do it. How about you?"

"Another six boxes of files, another few patients, and my middle of the day love fest with our favorite detective. Wonder if he managed to work in a shower?" She wrinkled her nose.

Trevor set his mouth in a thin line. "Middle of the day?"

At her nod, he went on, "Maybe I'll drop by. I could do the same thing I did before and haul your file boxes off."

Stilling her mind, she listened to the amulet. It seemed to be doing something like purring. Of course it had help, since she still held tight to the Sidhe book. Lara walked to Trevor's side and laid her head on his shoulder. "Yeah, that would be a good idea. I don't want to spend any more time alone with Brad than I have to." She shrugged. "Wonder what would happen if I called and told him not to come?"

"Not a good idea, love. He'd show up anyway."

"You're probably right." Lara shuddered. "I feel like I stumbled onto the wrong train and can't get off."

Trevor went back to the dishes. "Interesting analogy. I scolded you for wishing Lillian and Raven were here, but I have to admit I'm feeling the same way right about now."

"Maybe I could call and tell Brad I'm sick," Lara persisted.

"Then he'd show up here."

"Never mind." Her fear was getting the better of her, and she reined it in. Striding the length of the downstairs hall, she headed upstairs to get dressed for work."

~

Trevor sat wearily on one of the butter-colored leather recliners in their library. His chest muscles ached every time he breathed. Stacks of books formed neat piles around the room. "There," he told Gunter who was eying him, likely hoping for another lively round of chase-the-ball. "We'll miss having all the rest of these, but I'm sure we'll get by. I could go the rest of my life without reading *Caesar's Commentaries* again or *The Decline and Fall of the Roman Empire.*" The puppy yipped sagely in something Trevor assumed was agreement.

The muted jangle of the land line sent him on a hunt for the handset that had fallen behind a pile of books. "Hullo?"

"Trevor, glad I caught you." Hearty tones sailed through the phone lines along with the echoey satellite delay that sometimes accompanied calls from Europe.

"Smythe?" *Why would my old boss be calling?*

"Of course. I can't believe you don't recognize my voice. It's only been a couple weeks for chrissakes."

Trevor shuffled to a recliner and sat carefully. "What can I do for you?" he asked conversationally, still mystified as to why he'd be hearing from KLM Airlines.

"I've got most excellent news, old boy. Seems the European Union's made a deal with Russia. In any event, we've got fuel again, so I'm calling to entice you to come back to work. You always were one of our best stewards."

"Thanks, but Angelique just finished cleaning out my flat. And I talked the landlord into terminating my lease."

"Not a problem. You could bunk with me until you can come up with another place. Lots of vacancies in Amsterdam. Hell, you could probably re-let your old apartment. Come on, Trevor, please say yes. It hasn't seemed the same without you around the hangars."

Yeah, it hasn't been the same because nobody's been anywhere near the hangars. "I'm really flattered and all, Mr. Smythe, but I'm afraid I've made other plans. Besides, I'd be leery of being stuck over on the continent in case this new arrangement with the Russians didn't quite work out somehow."

After a longish pause, Smythe began talking again, but he didn't sound nearly as friendly. "Since we've offered you your job back and you've refused, there's the matter of your severance pay."

"I still spent twenty-seven years working for KLM—" Trevor began.

"Yes, yes. Nonetheless, I'll need to tell them to reduce the amount substantially."

Trevor chuckled. "You haven't talked to accounting, have you?"

"No. Why?"

"They transferred those funds the day after you gave me the sack."

"We'll simply ask for them back."

"Good luck. That account's been closed. I really am sorry, Smythe, but—" There was a loud click, and Trevor stared at the piece of black plastic in his hand. "Bloody bugger hung up on me," he muttered, wondering if this was some ploy on the part of KLM to avoid the expensive payouts that must've been part and parcel of shutting down their operations.

Maybe it's more of the same malevolent force that shoved my Benz into that spin. Except now it's trying to separate me from Lara.

Moving slowly and painfully, he made his way to the kitchen where Lara's laptop still sat on the table. Booting up, he searched for a news article that might memorialize some sort of trade agreement between the European Union and Russia. "Son of a bloody bitch," he mumbled. "Guess he was telling the truth."

Trevor scanned the article. Apparently the Russians had uncapped wells somewhere in Siberia and were offering petroleum products on the open market for exorbitant fees. "Hmm…wonder what KLM will charge for tickets to cover *those* increases?" he mused, powering down and shutting the computer's lid.

It was only ten thirty. On a whim, he clucked to Gunter, grabbed the truck keys, and locked up the house. Whistling softly, he made his way down the front steps, boosted the puppy into the cab of the Ford, and headed for Magnolia.

I know Lillian's not there, but I wonder if her house will let me in anyway.

As he drove, Trevor pondered why he was making the trek out to Lillian's tree house. The best he could come up with was the incredible sense of peace he'd felt wandering among the primordial tree trunks while Lillian and Lara talked. Traffic was light. Though he kept a sharp eye out for unexpected problems, his twenty minute drive was absolutely uneventful. After what happened to him the night before, he worried driving might provoke so much anxiety he wouldn't want to do it anymore. He felt pleased when his tight muscles began to relax.

Pulling up in front of the tree-filled lot where Lillian lived, he leashed Gunter and headed into the midst of the thick, pungent forest. It only took a few seconds before the house—that, according to Lillian, only appeared to select people—came into view. He wasn't surprised to find the heavy oak front door, with its runic carvings, standing slightly ajar. The puppy leaped forward joyously. There was something about the trees and the Sidhe's home that he absolutely adored. Trevor stopped just past the lintel and craned his neck to look up at the trees filling the dwelling. Their crowns disappeared into unseen rafters a long way above his head. A heady evergreen scent filled his nostrils, and as he sucked the musky smell down greedily, his sore muscles eased a bit.

Wandering through the trees, touching a trunk here and a bough there, Trevor lost all sense of time. The lushly-needled evergreens reached out to him with their boughs, stroking gently at his arms and legs as he passed. A gentle susurrus filled his mind, and he felt linked to the trees' ancient knowledge and power.

Despite letting go of the leash, he sensed the small German Shepherd right at his heels. When he eventually came out near the alcove where he, Lara, and Lillian had shared tea, he understood it was time to leave. Another door stood open off to his right. As before, it wasn't the same door he'd entered.

He smiled and recovered Gunter's leash. The pain from his previous night's accident was gone. Curious, he pulled up his shirt. Sure enough, no evidence remained of the bruising. Finally understanding the intuition that had sent him here, Trevor walked into bright sunlight. Squinting a bit, he started toward his truck, just visible through the trees. As he walked he inhaled deeply, filled with joy at being alive.

He glanced at his watch. Plenty of time to make Lara's office by noon. The last time they'd visited Lillian, hours had passed. This time, he'd only been lost in that ageless place for about thirty minutes. Grinning, he decided the Sidhe's trees must've known he was on a tight schedule.

"How about if you wait here?" he told Gunter as he closed up the truck in front of Lara's office. He scanned the street for Archer's unmarked car, but didn't see it. *Guess I'm a bit early.* Excited to tell Lara about his visit to Lillian's and his miraculous recovery, he sprinted up the steps and into the building. It had been ungodly quiet since Dr. Schneider, the psychiatrist Lara shared the second floor with, was killed in one of Beauchamp's earliest attempts to murder her.

The CPA and the architect, who worked on the first floor were on holiday in Australia—or was it New Zealand?—which meant the building was vacant but for Lara. Taking the carpeted risers two at a time, he rounded the corner past the second floor landing. He tried the outer knob of her office, but the door with its gold placard stating, *"Lara McInnis, Ph.D., Clinical Psychology,"* was locked.

He knocked and waited. And then he knocked louder. After waiting a full five minutes he called out, "Lara?" Ear to the door, he heard nothing. Not a whisper, not a rustle. Trevor plucked a second set of keys out of a jacket pocket, rifled through them and selected the one he was pretty sure would open her door. Gratified he'd picked the correct one, he pushed the door open, stuck his head in, and called her name again.

When there was no answer, he walked inside, looking around. What he saw disturbed him. Her bag, phone, and pager were scattered on Arabel's desk, along with the Sidhe book, but Lara wasn't in her office. Quickly dodging back out into the hall, he tried the door of the women's room. It wasn't locked. After knocking discreetly, he pulled it open far enough to ascertain that it too, lay empty.

Maybe she just ran out to get herself some lunch. Even as the thought crossed his mind, he discarded it. For one thing, her car was parked outside. For another, it was straight up noon, and Lara had never been more than a couple minutes late for an appointment with anyone in her life.

Back in her empty office, he picked up her phone and inspected messages that had come in. When he interrogated her voice mail, the last message was from Archer. It said the detective was coming at eleven thirty. His eyes widened with sudden understanding, and Trevor's heart thudded wildly against his ribcage. He crossed the two rooms in a few short strides and pulled open the filing cabinet where he'd dumped the scarf and photo two days before, but they were right where he'd tossed them.

He waited until twelve thirty, pacing back and forth, knowing she was gone but not wanting to believe it. "What in the bloody hell can I do?" he asked the silence of Lara's office. "I can't call the cops. They wouldn't be any help. I need Lillian or Raven, but they won't be back until sometime tomorrow. By then Lara could be...might be..."

Got to get hold of myself, an inner voice hissed. *I won't do her one whit of good if I lose it.*

Gathering up Lara's purse, phone, and pager, he locked the office. As he headed down the stairs, locking the outer door of the building as well, a plan took shape in his mind.

CHAPTER 9

*L*ara sat at Arabel's desk. She'd seen two patients and packed up three more file boxes. She was just finishing her notes on her morning's patients when her phone began to both ring and vibrate. Glancing at the number, she saw it was Archer and ignored it. *I'll see him soon enough,* she thought consulting the clock. *In about forty-five minutes to be exact. He can talk with me then.*

She stood and walked an armload of files to the inner office, dumping them into an open box. Avoiding the empty drawer where the scarf and photo were, she pulled out the one below it and continued filling her banker's boxes, hoping to have at least this chore complete by the time Trevor showed up.

This is getting easier. Once the first few hundred files went up in smoke, I haven't been quite as attached to the ones that are left. Good thing. If I read through each of them, I'd never finish this.

She was on her knees, getting dust all over her long, gray skirt when she heard the outer office doorknob rattle *What the hell? It can't be twelve already.* Standing she called, "Trev, is that you?"

"No, it's me," Archer's voice answered through the door. "I'm early. I called to tell you I was coming a bit sooner than expected."

Groaning inwardly, she marched to the outer office prepared for...

well, for just about anything. But Brad didn't look any worse than he had the previous night, and at least he'd changed into cleaner clothes, trading his suit for a sports coat and slacks.

"I came early on purpose because I figured you'd have Trevor show up at the same time you were expecting me, just like you did before."

"Trev did that on his own," she said softly. "Without any prompting from me."

"But you *were* expecting him," he persisted. "You just called his name."

"That's true. Um, Brad, why don't you come on in and sit down. You can tell me why it was so important to have me all to yourself." The amulet did *not* approve of her invitation, letting her know in no uncertain terms by sending wave after wave of cold into her skin. Because it was so uncomfortable, she drew it out from beneath her sweater and laid it on the fuzzy black wool to get something between her skin and its chilly emanations.

Trev will be here soon, she promised it.

Brad's eyes narrowed as they settled on the large moonstone. "What's that?"

"A gift from a dear friend. Any new developments about your daughter?" Lara seated herself, hoping the detective would follow suit. He was making her extremely nervous, towering over her. *I can be pleasant for the next few minutes. Soon as Trevor gets here, I'll ask Brad to leave.*

"The reason you came early?" she prodded, back in therapist mode as she pointed to a nearby chair. "You'd probably be more comfortable if you sat." As she talked, she reached out with her psychic side. The detective's aura was even more truncated than it had been two days before. There were places where it didn't exist at all.

He flinched. "Don't do that."

"Don't do what? All I'm doing is sitting here trying to figure out what you want from me."

After circling the chair she'd indicated, he finally lowered himself into it. "When you looked at Adie's picture—" he began.

"Look, Brad," she interrupted. "We'll get a lot further here if we're truthful with each other. I was trying to gather what information I could about your daughter's abduction, so I looked it up on the net." She let the words hang between them, while thinking, *don't go there. Just humor him.*

A different inner voice had other ideas: *This office has always been a place for absolute honesty. Even though I'm closing my practice, there's no reason to sully that track record now.*

"Probably didn't find much," he muttered, looking uncomfortable.

"I found enough to figure out the photo you showed me wasn't Adriana." Lara took a deep breath and blew it out. *In for a penny, in for a pound.* "She looks a lot like you, so I figure that story you told me about her being adopted was a fabrication too." Lara hesitated, giving her words time to sink in. "Who gave you that other photo? And why'd you lie to me?"

"Y—you have no right to talk to me like that," he sputtered. "It's disrespectful. That *was* Adie's picture. In fact, I'd like it back if you're going to treat it so lightly."

"It's in that drawer." She swiveled slightly to point. "If you want it, you'll need to get it yourself. I've found odd things happen when I touch it or the scarf. Things I don't like very much."

His face crumpled, and he twisted his hands together in his lap. When he met her eyes, she saw flickers of the man he'd been before Adriana disappeared. "I don't know how much I can say. How much he'll, uh they'll, let me. But you have to believe me, Lara. All I ever wanted was to get my daughter back. He promised that if I—"

She was watching him closely, so she saw the transformation begin. The light surrounding Brad shifted, and he started turning into something else. Something not very human. Alarm ricocheted through her. She leaped out of her seat intent on escape, but the room went dark around her, dissolving into a jagged vortex, and she fell into blackness. When she landed with a spine-cracking thud, she was back on the beach again.

Wind knocked out of her, she lay on her side, trying to suck air into her lungs and figure out if she'd broken anything. The amulet, still suspended from its golden chain around her neck, lay on the sand next to her. It tried to bounce toward her, so she resettled it beneath her clothing where it sounded unpleasant warnings.

Shit. She rolled onto her back and thence to a cross-legged sit. *Since Psyche didn't drag me here, I bet I have a hell of a time figuring out how to get back.* Last time she'd tricked Gradoxst. She had a niggling hunch she wouldn't be so lucky again.

That thought sent her over the edge. "Trapped? Christ, I can't be trapped here," she shrieked, aware she sounded crazed, but unable to stem the flow of words.

Adie was, her inner voice reminded her, and Lara panicked. She screamed and clawed at the sand until the amulet emitted calming vibrations. *If it can pull itself together, I can too. Besides, I'm being stupid and self-indulgent. That won't get me out of here.*

Once she started thinking again, an image of Archer, morphing into something otherworldly when he'd tried to confide in her, filled her mind. The something had looked like a gray-brown great ape with a black serpent's tail. She wasn't certain of the final product, since she'd been forcibly ejected from her office before the shimmering mess solidified.

Lara wrapped her arms around herself and shivered. The solid feel of her own flesh and pain from her abraded nails confirmed her body was here with her, not back in her office. "Hah! Good thing. Don't think I'd have wanted to spend much time with whatever Archer turned into," she muttered.

She looked around. Was it the same beach? The sand was more sand-colored, not so blindingly white. The sky was more mauve than bronze. Where was the hut? She scanned the horizon, but couldn't locate any structures at all. The trees looked more like pines, firs, and aspens than the orange-leafed ones from her previous trip. *Where am I? Ach, Christ, where the fuck am I?*

Panic built again, narrowing her airway. *Breathe. Just breathe.* In spite of those calm instructions, she clung to sanity by the thinnest of margins. *What happens when you go mad? Do you ever come back?* Something had happened to Brad Archer, and he'd certainly tumbled over that fine edge into madness. The kind, considerate cop who'd helped her and Trevor fight off Ken Beauchamp was nowhere to be found in the strange, shambling creature that had stood in her foyer the previous night. Or in her office a few moments before.

"May as well get up. Maybe if I start walking I'll get some ideas or find a way out of this place." She spoke aloud to steady herself and groaned as pain from multiple body parts assailed her when she dragged herself to her feet.

∾

TREVOR YANKED OPEN the door of the Ford, startling Gunter who'd been asleep. Lifting the puppy down gently, he walked him long enough to squat a few times. "That should do it, my man," Trevor announced, shepherding the dog back to the truck. "Up you go."

His first thought, once he realized Lara was gone, was to head back to Lillian's, hoping the trees would provide hints about how to communicate with the Sidhe. He was sure if Lillian knew Lara was missing, she'd drop everything to try to rescue her. As he walked Gunter, another possibility emerged. *What if I go to Raven's instead? Would that be better?* The only problem with that option was it took a good two hours to get to the isolated farm and only twenty minutes to get back to Lillian's tree house.

Undecided, Trevor sat in the cab of the truck, head buried in his hands. A wrong choice might mean he'd never see Lara again. Time was critical; he had to do something—and bloody, damned fast.

He racked his brain trying to puzzle through what might have happened. Did Archer kidnap her? Was she in the place her visions took her? Or was she back on that beach she'd described? For the briefest of moments, he wondered if there was a way he could follow her, but then knew he couldn't leave the puppy, even if he figured out where to go.

What would I do once I got there? I know less than she does. It'd be like throwing my life away on top of hers. No, I'll do much more good on this side of things.

As he played the choices back and forth in his mind, Trevor finally settled on returning to Lillian's. That had been the idea that came to him first, and the others didn't hold any obvious advantages. First intuitions had rarely failed him, so he sucked in a shaky breath and started the truck.

As he drove, he thought about himself and Lara, linked at a level that plunged far below waking consciousness, and his fears flared into a conflagration. She was in deep trouble. This wasn't his imagination. He started to envision life without her, and then put the brakes down hard on his internal machinations. *Stop that. Just get through this next part.*

When he pulled into his same parking place from a few hours before, uncertainty gripped him. "Get out and get moving," he muttered half aloud. "If there's no help here, I'll find out soon enough."

The puppy, excited to be back, bounced along next to Trevor. The door of the tree house was more than ajar this time. It stood fully open. Trevor wondered if he'd left it that way and then clearly remembered closing it.

Maybe this is where I'm supposed to be, then, he thought as he walked inside.

The trees soughed, branches creaking and brushing against one another. Not sure quite what to do, Trevor stood next to the nearest tree, closed his eyes, and tried his best to empty his mind. As an afterthought, he grasped the tree's trunk with both hands.

He didn't have to wait long. The noise from the trees intensified so much his eyes flew open. *"Who enters my home?"* echoed in his head.

"Lillian?" he croaked, his throat dry as a windswept desert.

"Goddess be damned," she swore. *"Trevor. What are you doing stirring up my trees?"*

"Thank the saints," he breathed. "Lillian, Lara's gone missing.

There's something barmy about Archer. He showed up early at her office, and now she's not there. Bloody bollocks, I think she's in that spirit place where you all congregate. Either that, or Archer kidnapped her."

"Whoa, whoa, slow down." Lillian's voice reverberated around him, not just in his head. Her form flickered into view a few feet away. She wasn't as transparent as she'd been that night at the farmhouse, so maybe the trees lent her more of a material presence. "You were here earlier, weren't you?"

"Yes, but for something different."

"The trees healed you. They told me. This time, though, you were so scattered and distraught they reached out to me. They sensed your desperation before you even set foot on my property. What are you trying to tell me about Lara? Be quick about it, young man. We may not have any time to lose."

"She's gone." Trevor racked his brain for something else to tell the Sidhe. "Not sure if this'll help, especially if Archer has her, but she told me about a place with a beach and an odd-colored sky. Said it looked like some other planet."

Lillian's form wavered. "Wait!" Desperation racked him, turning his muscles to stones.

"What?" she asked, with an undercurrent in her voice that he recognized as fear. "I'm off to hunt for her. Wasn't that why you came to my house? To spur me into action?"

"What should I do?"

Sodding hell, I sound like a ten-year-old.

"Go home and finish getting your things out to Raven's. If you'd been there by now—like he and I both told you—none of this would've happened. And take your hands off my tree. You're upsetting him." Clucking disapprovingly, her sending winked out.

Trevor pulled his hands back and waited until the trees settled back into just being trees. Then he hunted for a way out. A doorway he'd never seen before opened in front of him, and he and Gunter found their way into an afternoon drizzle. He felt empty inside, grateful he'd found help for Lara, but at loose ends.

Go home and pack, huh? Yeah, I could do that. But I'm going to pop by her office on the way, just to make sure she didn't end up back there.

Checking his fuel, he realized he needed to find a station. The old Ford had two gas tanks, but it got something less than ten miles to the gallon. He stopped at three places before he found one with petrol. Even then, it cost him over ten dollars a gallon. As he counted out twenties, handing them to the cashier, he thought of his earlier conversation with Smythe.

Doesn't matter if the planes are flying again. If aviation fuel goes up as much as petrol has, only the very rich will be able to afford to fly—and KLM will end up scaling back so radically, they may as well have stayed shut.

He selected a shockingly overpriced bag of Cheez-Its, some beef jerky, and a Coke at the gas station's convenience store. Back in the truck, he forced himself to eat something, but had absolutely zero appetite. The ambiguity of not knowing anything was the worst part of today. Simply the worst. The sick feeling in his guts didn't improve with the addition of junk food and soda. Gunter, oblivious to the fact his human mother had disappeared, got two of the jerky strips as they drove, chewed happily, and then begged for more.

Trevor maneuvered the long wheelbase of the Ford into a parking place and looked at the puppy. "Maybe I will take you," he said. "You can smell things. Perhaps you'll notice something I don't." Gunter yapped happily, delighted to be included when Trevor opened the door on his side of the truck.

He let them into the silent downstairs hallway, felt an odd sensation, something between an electric shock and a chill, and debated locking the dual-dead-bolt door behind them. In the end he decided not to. If he had to make a hasty exit, he didn't want to be scrabbling around trying to slot a key into the lock.

Something's different. What the bloody fuck happened between when I was here before and now?

The puppy growled low in his throat, and hackles rose along his back. He clung close to Trevor's leg, his tail tucked low. "You sense it too, boy, don't you?" Trevor whispered, seeking an infusion of courage. Every fiber of his being urged him to run like hell. After a few tense seconds, he forced himself to start upward. The insidious sense of wrongness worsened when he moved up the stairs. As he turned the corner into the second floor hall, he saw Lara's door pulsing like an out-of-control video game.

The two-inch thick oak door trembled and made a *whoomping* sound. Trevor felt the fine hairs on the back of his neck tingle unpleasantly. *How the hell can this be happening?* The puppy's growls shifted to low whines. He tugged at the leash, obviously wanting to retreat to a place that felt better than this one to his touchy canine senses. Trevor scooped the puppy into his arms. Gunter immediately buried his nose in Trevor's corduroy blazer, his entire body trembling.

Trevor watched the door with macabre fascination, wondering if he should unlock it or simply wait for it to blow out once the wood couldn't take any more. He carried the puppy to the stained glass windows at the top of the stairwell and put him down. "Stay," he said, pointing, and for once the three-month-old Shepherd paid attention.

I'll stuff the key into the lock, push it a bit, and jump out of the way.

Creeping toward the door, palms damp from sweat, and heart dancing in his chest like a wild thing, he noticed an odd, burnt smell. High-pitched caterwauling assailed him, making him wince. Trevor fumbled with the key with shaking fingers. It didn't take much. He'd no sooner turned the key a tiny bit than the door whooshed open, slamming against the wall with an earsplitting bang.

Staying to one side, he peered into Lara's office and was faced with swirling black nothingness. The light that should've spilled in from Lara's windows wasn't there, nor was anything else familiar. Trevor clawed at the neck of his shirt, hoping for more air. Breath whistled from between his teeth, and sweat gathered, dripping down his face and body.

What the bloody hell is this? Some sort of gateway to wherever Lara went?

He tried to enter, but gave it up for a lost cause after the unnatural wind blew him into the wall on the far side of the hallway, knocking the breath from his lungs. He lurched upright and girded himself to try again, but didn't feel right abandoning Gunter to whatever fate would befall him as an orphaned puppy. Trevor was certain a trip into that hell-spawned hole would be one way only.

He felt something brush against his leg and squawked in surprise, but it was only the young dog that had crept close. "You're scared," Trevor patted the puppy's head. "But not so scared you didn't come to rescue Daddy." He picked Gunter up again. "You're going to be quite the guard dog when you grow up."

Trevor stared into the maelstrom, debating his next move, when the howling wind wound down, dropping by degrees until nothing remained but silence. When he peeked around the corner, Lara's office was normal again, without so much as a paper out of place. In its own way, the stillness was as eerie as the fury preceding it had been.

He walked inside and heard a low groan that made him sprint for the inner office. "Lara, Lara! Bloody fucking Christ." Falling to his knees, he set the puppy aside to gather her into his arms.

Within seconds, Lillian took form. Raven too. Where had they come from? Trevor looked around, thoroughly confused. Gunter headed straight for Lillian, jumping on her legs repeatedly until she pulled the frightened dog into her arms.

"Seal the portal," Lillian hissed, long black skirts swirling round her. "Cast the spell of unmaking so it can never again be used from this location."

Raven, in a white linen shirt and leather breeches, raised his arms and chanted in Celtic Gaelic so old even Trevor couldn't follow it.

Trevor shifted his full attention to Lara and felt ill. Her fingernails were cracked as if she'd been clawing at something, and her hands were scraped and bleeding. Long rips marred her skirt and sweater. One side of her face held lacerations and swollen spots that would turn into hellacious bruises. But she was breathing. Goddammit, she was alive and that was all that mattered.

Trevor let out a shaky breath and tightened his grip on her. Perhaps in response to the increased pressure, she stirred in his arms. When she opened her eyes, they filled with tears and she clung to him as if he were the only solid thing in a world gone mad. Looking past him at Lillian, she asked, "How did you know where to find me?"

"Trevor used my trees to call me. He described a beach that, fortunately, I knew all too well."

"Ach, thank Christ I told you about my dream," Lara murmured to Trevor. "I didn't understand why I did, but the goddess must've been watching over me."

"Well, She's needed more than a little help of late," Raven commented dryly and dropped his arms to his sides. "Are you both well enough to talk?"

"I am." Trevor locked gazes with the mage. "Lara was already gone when I came by here at noon, but the office hadn't turned into that otherworldly wind tunnel. If that was part of what dragged her away, why wasn't it here then?"

"It wasn't essential to moving her into their world," Lillian answered curtly. "Once they'd done that, they used Archer to build a gateway into this world, for purposes that had nothing to do with Lara. There's such turmoil between the shortages and riots. That's what's drawing Demons and their ilk, since they feed off chaos. Convenient for them. Bad for you—and a mixed bag for us.

"Time is different in the contiguous worlds, particularly one that's Demon-spawned. We found that meddlesome detective midway betwixt the worlds, struggling against what should've been indestructible shackles. Likely his reluctance as a participant interrupted the bonds and slowed formation of the gateway as well. Bah! I hope we do not regret freeing him."

"Where is he?" Trevor looked around, curious.

"I didn't want him anywhere near Lara," Lillian rolled her eyes, "so we ensured he'd return to this world in a different place."

"Lara," Raven's gruff voice broke in. "Tell us exactly what happened. Trevor's questions aren't important right now."

"Can't you give her a bit of a break?" Trevor cradled Lara protectively against him. "I'd like to know what happened and where she's been, but she's in pretty rough shape."

Yeah, and she might have been dead if I hadn't guessed right about Lillian and her sodding trees.

"No." Raven's reply was stern and succinct. "I can't."

Lara glanced around her familiar office. "My bag..." she began. "Where's—?"

"I've got it. And your phone and pager as well," Trevor said. "But you'll want the book. That's still on your desk."

"My God!" Lara shot out of Trevor's arms, looking wildly about. "Where's Adriana? I found her. I had her." Switching her focus to Lillian and Raven, she shrieked, "How could you leave her there? How could you?"

"Because she was already bound," Lillian said. "With metal."

"Had we been but a few minutes later, you would've been beyond our reach too—and required a great deal more planning than went into today's effort," Raven added, his ancient eyes sad. "I'm sorry, daughter, we did what we could."

"But she was there with me. Talking to me—" Lara scrunched her eyes shut as if trying to block out Raven's words, before collapsing against Trevor. Her voice muffled against his chest, she asked, "What do you mean bound?"

"This isn't the time..." Lillian fell silent at a piercing glance from Raven. Watching the exchange, Trevor assumed there would never be a time for *that* explanation.

Trevor cleared his throat and gazed at Lillian and Raven. "It'd be good if one of you could have a gander at those things Archer left here."

"What things?" Raven asked and drew his thick brows together.

"Top drawer of the left hand filing cabinet," Trevor replied.

Raven raised a hand, pointed at the drawer, and it slid open. The two items floated to him. When they landed in his hand, he started, lips drawn back into a snarl. Still grimacing, he barked a word, and both scarf and picture disappeared.

Lillian pursed her lips. "You might have waited for me to get a closer look."

"Demon-spelled," he growled. "You didn't need to look. And they didn't need to be here." He nailed Lara with his gray eyes, "Why do you keep returning to this place? Stupid human woman. Haven't you yet learned it holds danger for you?"

"This is where I work," Lara replied, bristling. "It was safe enough for a very long time. Besides, I need to destroy my clients' records if I'm not going to be here anymore."

"The paper in those cabinets?" Raven shot a questioning look her way.

She nodded. "And in those boxes over there. I was at least trying to follow your directions."

Raven wove his hands together and chanted. The storage boxes wavered in pale afternoon light filtering through the windows, and then dispersed into the air, as if they'd never existed.

"I'll take care of the rest," Lillian announced, setting Gunter next to Lara. Muted crackling sounded from the filing cabinets. "There," she said. "That should finish the job. Let's get out of here. We shall have the discussion Raven alluded to at your home, over something to eat."

Rocking back on his heels, Trevor kept firm hands on Lara's arms. "Come on, love," he urged. "I'll help you." In a few moments, she was on her feet, wobbling against him, but standing.

"I really am all right," she protested. "I should drive my car home. That way, we'll truly be done here. After what happened today, I don't think I'd want to come back, whether or not Raven thought it was safe." She glared defensively at the mage and started shakily out the door, picking up Arabel's sweater on the way.

"You forgot something." Lillian's voice cracked like a whip.

"Huh?" Lara looked uncomprehendingly at her. "Trev said he's got my things. And I wanted something of Arabel's, so... Oh."

Understanding creased her battered face. "Trev, could you get the computer? Shouldn't leave that here either."

"Not what I meant. Your book is still on this desk." Lillian tapped the well-creased leather binding with her long-nailed index finger, making a little clicking sound.

"Oh yeah, the book. I don't understand why it keeps slipping out of my mind." Voice fading into nothingness, Lara picked up the Sidhe book and walked unsteadily into the hall with the puppy right behind her.

Trevor had just bent to the task of unhooking wires and cables from the computer when Raven said, "Just go on, son. We'll take care of this."

"Thanks for everything." Straightening, Trevor held out a hand to the mage.

Raven's handclasp was warm and firm. "Now get going," he said, his voice unexpectedly gentle. "See she gets home before something else happens."

"Yes, do move along," Lillian suggested, with her usual asperity. "No need to thank either of us again."

As he turned to leave, Trevor saw a long, anxiety-ridden glance shuttle from Raven to Lillian and back again. Desolation swept through him, gnawing at his soul. *If they're feeling worried, what the bloody blazes does that mean for the rest of us?*

CHAPTER 10

*L*ara stood next to her car, a rumpled looking Trevor hovering by her side. Not quite sure what she was feeling, she pivoted to look at the pale blue Victorian that had housed her psychology practice for as long as she'd had one.

Like Lot's wife, except there's no one to turn me into a pillar of salt.

"Are you certain you're right enough to drive?" The glass-sharp edges of Trevor's voice interrupted her reverie.

"I think so. That's not why I'm standing here, though." She gazed at him, feeling drained and drawn. "I'm saying goodbye to, well, to a lot of things. The building, my practice, Arabel..." Her voice broke on that last word, and she started crying. Tears rolled down both cheeks like indomitable soldiers marching off to fight in an impossible war. Trevor drew her close, stroking her hair.

One of his best traits has always been he knows when to be silent, she thought, grateful he wasn't prodding her or asking questions she wouldn't have answers for.

"Okay," she snuffled after a long five minutes. "I'm ready to leave. Do you think—?" She looked around and drew her eyebrows together in confusion. "I was going to see if they wanted a ride, but they must still be inside."

"Crikey, Lara!" Trevor held her at arm's length before bending to kiss her in the center of her forehead. "The likes of them don't need cars any more than they need planes. I'll follow you. Let's get going."

Her thoughts were a jumble as she drove from Capitol Hill toward Queen Anne. When she tried to make sense of what happened after she'd fallen down Alice's rabbit hole, her mind rebelled. It was like trying to put her fingers into the gas flame on a hot stove. After a while, she stopped trying to dredge any meaning out of her descent into hell. What happened after Lillian and Raven appeared like latter-day warriors wasn't any more explainable.

Fixating on the clock in the BMW, she was shocked to discover only three hours had elapsed since Archer had shown up at her office. It seemed she'd been gone for days.

Lara closed her eyes. They felt heavy and gritty, and it was a relief to not pay attention to the world outside her windshield. A sharp blast from someone's horn brought her out of her semi-trance in a hurry. She caught a glimpse of another driver shaking his fist at her.

She felt horrified by how difficult it was to keep her mind on driving. Blearily, she took in her surroundings. *Only a couple more blocks. Surely I can keep it together for that long.* When she looked in her rearview mirror, she saw Trevor, with Gunter sitting upright in the passenger seat, and she clung to the deep love she held for them both. If it hadn't been for Trevor's stellar ability to reason out what to do, she'd still be trapped in that unspeakable place. And if what Raven said was true, trapped beyond all possibility of rescue.

Cold slid along her limbs, a chill so deep, she imagined herself freezing from the inside out. *What's wrong with me? I don't feel anything like myself.* A clinical cavalcade of the symptoms of acute stress disorder—numbness, hypervigilance, depersonalization, derealization—crowded her mind, until she realized the futility of trying to diagnose herself. In a dim corner of her brain, she noticed she'd turned onto her street. Lara took the first parking place she found; the sooner she got out from behind the wheel of the BMW, the better.

She was dragging herself up the front steps, still feeling as if her limbs were mired in molasses, when Trevor and Gunter caught up with her. "Here you go." Trevor thrust her bag, phone and pager at her. And then he stopped abruptly. "Give me your keys."

"Why?" She settled her purse over her shoulder while digging for the car keys in a pocket of her skirt.

"Because you left the bloody book in your car again."

Looking hard at him out of narrowed eyes, she muttered, "So I did. Good that you noticed."

"Isn't it though. Why do you—?"

"I have no fucking idea," she snapped, and then the quick anger bled out of her, replaced by a weary remorse. "Sorry, sorry. Didn't mean to take any of this out on you. I need to ask Lillian or Raven what it all means. Should've asked them back at my office, but I didn't have the energy. It's like something's wrong with the part of my brain that's linked to that book. I don't understand it any better than you do."

"Why don't you go on in?" he suggested. "Here, take the pup with you." He handed her Gunter's leash.

Nodding slowly, she climbed the last few steps, and then realized her house keys were on the ring she'd given to Trevor. She was just settling herself on a bench to wait for him, when her front door swung open. "Come in, child," Lillian invited.

Lara jumped to her feet. Her head began to spin and she closed her eyes abruptly to regain her equilibrium. "What? How? Oh, never mind." She pried one eye open as an experiment. The dizziness receded a bit.

Gunter was tugging hard at the leash to get to Lillian. His link to the Sidhe both amused and mystified Lara. She let go of the puppy and he launched himself at the Sidhe's skirts.

Lillian held out a hand, and Lara grasped it to steady herself. The moment she touched the other woman, she felt better. "That's right, come on in. We just got here a few minutes before you, that's all," Lillian murmured soothingly.

Lara dropped her purse, phone, and pager in their usual spot in the front hall. When she looked up, her eyes widened. "Oh my," she exclaimed, a hand flying to her mouth. "Who are they?" Standing next to Raven in the hallway leading to the kitchen were two other people, a man and a woman. Their old-fashioned garments, long hair, and an ethereal presence gave them away as being something other than human.

"We'll get to introductions after Trevor gets here," Raven said briskly. "In the meantime, why don't you show us where we might all sit comfortably?"

"Sure. Follow me." Lara went up the half flight of stairs leading to the living room and library.

"Oh, aye, that'll be perfect, lassie," the woman who didn't yet have a name said in a strong Scottish accent, as she settled herself into an upholstered chair. She was dressed in a richly-embroidered, sky blue robe, belted at the waist with a thick leather sash. High top boots that looked handmade peeked from under her skirts. Her long black hair was pinned up in braids similar to the ones Lillian always wore. The strange woman looked at the woodstove with eyes so dark they seemed bottomless, and the remains of the last fire that had burned there began to glow. "Will ye pit a few mair sticks on th' fire?" she asked, looking at her companion.

Pushing cream colored linen sleeves above his elbows, the man bent to comply with her request. His shoulder length, mostly-gray hair fell forward as he did so. When he turned back toward the center of the room, Lara noticed the clear, golden color of his eyes. The man wore cassock-like skirts in unevenly dyed black homespun. A red-gray beard was trimmed tidily, and when he smiled, his teeth gleamed white against it.

This just gets stranger and stranger. But at least that fog around my brain has lifted. The man went to stand next to Raven. Lara sensed something like an energy field emanating from the two men, and she had a hunch they were communicating in some fashion.

"How are you feeling?" Lillian's green eyes drilled into Lara as she stroked the puppy that had curled up in her lap, making himself at home in the folds of her woven skirts.

"Better than I did driving over here. But still really odd. Like I'm standing outside myself, watching." As she talked, Lara shifted from foot to foot, hoping movement might hasten the return of something approximating normalcy.

"Humph!" The newly arrived woman snorted. "Ye 'ave jist journeyed tae th' in-between. 'Tis a tappitless place that would be drainin' anyone."

"But that's where I go in my visions," Lara protested. "And while they do tire me, the feeling's nothing like this."

"They're not the same place, child," Lillian spoke softly. "Not the same place at all."

"Maybe you could explain that to me. There are lots of things I don't understand. How many places could I end up in, anyway?"

Just then Trevor bounded into the room, stopped dead, and exclaimed, "Elidora! What the bloody fuck are you doing here?"

"Aye and 'tis a fine thing t' see you too again, laddie." The strange woman laughed. "Ye always were a bit o' a handful. Sit down, sit down. 'Tis I, by fegs, and glowerin' like a moonstruck bairn willna change that."

Lara stared at Trevor. "This is the witch woman from the village you grew up in?" At Trevor's reluctant nod, she added, "How could she still be alive?" Switching her gaze to Elidora, Lara sputtered, "Trev told me you were old when he was a boy."

Elidora was still chuckling. "Seems I likely look a good deal younger'n I did forty year ago, eh? The simple answer for you, lassie, is I am Baen Sidhe."

"Oh, of course." Lara felt stupid. None of her normal assumptions about people and age fit with any of this. Color stained her freckled cheeks. "Sorry if I offended you. I'm not very quick on the uptake right now."

Elidora waved a hand in Lara's direction, muttering something soothing in Gaelic.

A wave of dizziness washed through her, and Lara reached out to steady herself on a nearby wall. Suddenly realizing she felt hollow inside, she looked wanly at Trevor. "Is there anything we could eat?"

"Haur." The strange man, who had an accent Lara couldn't place, removed a rucksack she'd not even noticed he was wearing. Withdrawing an antique bottle made of wavy, dark green glass, he used a pocket knife to trim wax from the seal. "Micht thaur be a curn quaich?" he inquired.

"Huh?" Lara looked at the stranger, mystified.

Turning to a nearby cabinet, Trevor, who'd obviously understood far more than she, pulled half a dozen glasses out of it and set them on the granite sideboard. The man strode across the room, black cassock-like skirts flapping while his soft soled leather boots made a whispering noise on the hardwood floor. As he poured the gold-hued liquid, a heady aroma filled the living room.

"Smells like your house," Lara mumbled, looking at Lillian as she took a glass from Trevor. "I'm not sure I should drink any wine. It's been hours since I've eaten."

"'Tis mead and it smells of earth an' life," the man, sensitive to her earlier confusion, advised in more understandable English. "Thou wilt find th' drink nourishes thy spirit." Looking right at her, he bowed low from his waist. "I am Gren, Arch Druid of..." He hesitated. "Och, but that were faur back. An' a tale for anither day, mayhap."

Raven had migrated to the center of the room. Twirling in a slow circle, he made eye contact with each of them. "Settle yourselves. We have two tasks to accomplish this evening," he said solemnly. "First, Lara must tell us what happened to her today. When she is done with that, we'll have a wedding."

"What!" Lara, who'd just sat next to Lillian, bolted upright. "Now just a minute here. I'm a filthy mess. My clothing's torn. I know the two of you have been going on about moving up the wedding date from the winter solstice, but I'm exhausted. Can't it wait until—?"

"No," Raven thundered, cutting her off. Lara shrank back in her seat, cowed as always by Raven's quick temper. "You'll begin to do as I instruct, human," he said, biting off the words. "Even within the dim corners of that stubborn brain of yours, you must—"

Lillian moved quickly from her chair to his side. Laying a peremptory hand on his arm, she shook her head and said, "She isn't your child. Times have changed. They no longer listen so closely to us as they once did."

"Isna *that* the truth?" Elidora chimed in, sighing heavily.

"Do you feel up to telling us what happened?" Trevor asked hesitantly. "I almost don't want to hear it, but I have to if I'm going to understand things."

Lara took a sip of the mead. And then another. The fragrant liquid sent warmth all through her, and even a hint of energy. Resolutely, she drained off half the glass, feeling her cheeks flush again, this time from the alcohol.

"May as well get it over with," she murmured. "I was alone in my office when someone knocked on the door. I thought it was Trev, but when I called out, Archer answered. He didn't look as disheveled as he did the night before. We started to talk, and I guess I made a major mistake when I told him I knew the picture he'd shown me wasn't actually his daughter. After that, this wind started blowing through my office and Archer... He changed into this misshapen, unnatural thing. I knew something horrible was about to happen, and I tried to run. Except I couldn't. And then I was just gone, sucked down a funnel to that godforsaken beach.

"All this," she ran her hands up and down her body, gingerly brushing over her bruises and lacerations, "happened when I fell. Felt like someone dropped me a good twenty feet. I sort of lost it at first... Clawed at the sand and started shrieking, but the amulet snapped me out of it." She stretched out her fingers, staring at the broken nails.

"You've skipped a thing or two, I fear." Lillian stared at Lara. "How did you come to find Adriana?"

Lara twined her hands together in her lap, as she girded herself to relive the nightmare she'd escaped from. "I'm not exactly sure," she began. "The amulet urged me to my feet. After that, I started walking up the beach. I remember that part clearly. Then things got weird." Lara dropped her head into her hands, fighting to resurrect her memory.

"Keep going," Lillian urged softly. "You must tell us everything."

Pain lanced through Lara, as if something were tearing in two. She brushed away tears, stood, and began pacing up and down the living room.

Just tell them. There's not so much more.

"This tree, it reared up in front of me from out of nowhere, with Adriana attached to it. That poor girl—" Lara stifled a sob. "She had chains around her, and they were looped round the tree and connected to stakes in the ground. It was almost like in a dream I had. At first, I thought I'd be able to pull up the stakes, but I couldn't get them to budge."

"An' was she a'callin' for you?" Elidora asked curiously.

Lara shook her head. "Aw crap." She looked helplessly at Raven. "Why can't I remember more clearly? What's wrong with me?"

"You have traveled through their lands." His gaze sought hers. "Memory is a struggle because they don't want you to recall anything. It's how they keep their existence a secret."

"And fend their insidious lies," Elidora added.

"How was Archer's appearance altered?" Raven asked pointedly, shifting the conversation away from Adriana.

"Like a gorilla with a serpent's tail." The words had scarcely left the safety of her throat when Gren's sharply drawn breath cut into the quiet of the room.

Lara looked from Gren to Elidora to Raven to Lillian. She set her empty glass down, mildly surprised since she didn't remember finishing its contents, and found her seat again. "What aren't you telling me?"

"It *is* Gradosxt or one of his Goblin henchmen, but we assumed as much when we found what was left of Brad Archer in the conduit," Lillian said, sketching an odd sign in the air with two fingers. "They're truly Demon-spawn. We angered him, you and I, when we cornered him in your vision. He seeks revenge."

"Oh, he was angry enough at me before that for spurning his advances." Lara scowled and pressed her lips together into a thin, bloodless line. "What did you mean, what was left of Brad?" *Ach, do I really want to know?*

"They were working on breaking his mind, child," Raven replied. "That animal form was Gradoxst borrowing Archer's body for long enough to see you trapped."

"I—I'm not sure I understand."

"Wirricowe, or Demons—and Gradoxst is of the Goblin kynd—" Gren explained patiently, "have little enough of thair ain pith. Eh, mayhap, tha' isna alanerly true. One of th' reasons thay're so powerful is thay niver use thair ain resources whene'er thay can tap anither."

"Is that why he stole Adriana?" Lara asked in a small voice. "To use her to get back at me?"

"Mayhap," Elidora answered carefully. "Who's this Adriana?"

"Archer's daughter," Raven answered, frowning deeply. "Lillian and I believe Gradoxst captured her and used her father's love as a tool, forcing him to set a trap for Lara."

"Aye, tha's something very like a Demon would do," Elidora agreed, nodding her head as she blew out a breath through pursed lips. "They pervert the finest o' human emotions intae something they can manipulate and soil."

"Let's back up a bit." Trevor broke in. "This whole thing still feels sketchy to me. Could you start over from when you ended up on the beach?" He glanced at the mead bottle, and then at Gren for permission. After the Druid nodded, Trevor got to his feet and refilled Lara's glass and his own. That done, he sat next to her and clasped one of her hands between his.

"I sat there for a bit," Lara said, "until I was done railing against the fates. And then I got up and started walking." She took another hefty swig from her glass, put it down, and pinched the bridge of her nose between her thumb and forefinger, trying to sort through her jumbled thoughts. When she looked up, her eyes were damp with tears again.

"The first time I was in that place, there was a little hut. It was in a dream I had too. Adriana was in it, or at least a projection of her, so that's what I was looking for. Didn't know what else to do. I tried calling for her, but the roar of the surf was so loud, I don't think she could've heard me.

"After a while the tree line moved closer to the shore, and that tree I told you about reared up in front of me with Adriana bound to it and crying. She was just so glad to see me. I held her, and she clung to me as if she were still a small child. After a bit, she started talking. She was frightened she was already dead, but I convinced her I was very much alive, and if I was, so was she."

Lara's voice ran down. The leaden weariness she'd struggled with while driving home was back in spades. She slumped against the cushions of the couch and closed her eyes.

"Uh-uh, not a good idea." Lillian spoke briskly. Dropping Gunter gently onto the floor, she was beside Lara in an instant, squatting in front of her. Gripping Lara's hands in her own, Lillian chanted in Celtic Gaelic. It took a few minutes, but the bleak fog surrounding Lara finally receded.

"I don't understand." Lara met Lillian's eyes. "Why can't I shake this lethargy?"

"It'll pass. It's a residual from the place you were."

Lara clung to Lillian's hands, trying to suck some vitality back into herself. She hoped the Sidhe would say more because she still felt wretchedly confused. In the meantime, the puppy, after a startled grunt when Lillian displaced him, clawed at Elidora.

"The worlds that Demons inhabit resonate to different frequencies than this one." Lillian spoke softly. "It's not possible for any of us: Demon, Sidhe, or human, to travel directly from this world to any of theirs. The in-between is the stopping-off point where the frequencies neutralize. It often takes many days before a living creature can be moved from there to elsewhere."

"Guid an weel too, aye?" Elidora, more serious now, had picked up the puppy and was stroking him. "We willna have a place akin t' it since we have never been a'wantin' their sort here."

"The longer you stay there, particularly if a Demon uses metal to bind you, the more difficult it is to return," Lillian went on.

"Which is why you left Adriana," Lara muttered.

Lillian closed her eyes; her shoulders slumped and she looked like the ancient being she was.

"There's not much more for me to tell." Lara kept hold of Lillian as she talked. "I tried to undo the chain. Finished off what was left of my hands on it. But I didn't have any tools, so it was impossible. I tried to comfort Adie—to give her some hope. And then you two," she looked from Lillian to Raven, "shimmered into being, did whatever you did, and I was back in my office."

Letting go of the Sidhe, Lara stumbled to her feet. She walked to the woodstove and bent to warm her hands in front of it. When she turned, she'd set her mouth in a determined line. "I want to go back and rescue Adriana," she said. "Even if it kills her to bring her back here, it's not right to leave her to Gradoxst."

"Be reasonable, woman," Raven grunted. "She's likely gone from the beach by now, and we would risk another journey for naught."

"You don't know that," Lara replied, glancing from Raven to Lillian. "Time seems to be different there. And you've brought reinforcements." She gestured at Gren and Elidora. "Surely they could help."

"I'm come to mairy thee," Gren said, a half-smile on his high cheek boned face. "I telled thee earlier. I am a Druid high priest, forby aw ither thing."

"And I came to gi' m'boy away," Elidora added, smiling warmly at Trevor. "Ye 'aveno other kin 'ere. Raven told me he will be givin' the bride, but the groom must be given as well. Ye canna say nae. We 'ave come from faur awa for this."

"But Adriana," Lara protested. "She's suffering."

"You may not be able to return to that place at all, but you cannot return unwed." Getting up, Lillian moved to Lara's side. "Were you to do so, even we could not bring you back. There's something elemental about the marriage bonding. It'll protect the two of you. Surely you're not so naïve as to believe Trevor's accident the other night was simply a mishap? The same energy seeking to destroy you has finally targeted him as well. Gradoxst has assistants. And not only among his own kind—" Lillian blew out a bitter breath and caught her full lower lip with her teeth. "He has co-opted many a human with empty promises of wealth and power."

Lara opened her mouth. She tried to speak, but all that came out was, "Oh." Casting a worried glance at Trevor, she felt worn to shreds. *It's not safe for him—or me, I guess—if we don't do what they say. It's not that I don't want to marry him. I've wanted that for years.*

"Could we, er, would you at least reconsider a conversation about helping Adriana after the ceremony?" Lara asked, unwilling to give up on Brad Archer's daughter.

"We shall discuss it further," Raven replied brusquely. "But no promises. We will reassess how the energy feels to us once the wedding is complete. Now, the both of you must bathe, but separately. Are there two tubs here?" At Trevor's nod, Raven asked, "Where?"

"One's on the third floor where our bedroom is, and the other is off the kitchen," Trevor answered.

Shooing the women away, Raven herded Trevor toward the downstairs bathroom. "Come on, son." He gestured impatiently. "It's not every day you get married."

"What about the pup?" Trevor asked, casting a worried glance at Gunter. "He probably needs to go out."

"I'll tak tent o'im." Gren whistled softly, and the puppy ran to him. "'Twould be best if 'e 'ad a bittie nap. Thare'll be ower mony candles on th' fluir suin to let 'im chase aboot."

BY THE TIME Lara walked slowly down the stairs, flanked by Lillian and Elidora, the living room was ablaze with candles set in a large circle. She wore a simple silk shift and her wet hair hung down her back. The moonstone amulet gleamed warmly against her skin. It was purring, obviously pleased by the turn of events. The men had scared up a tunic and a pair of loose pants for Trevor. All of them had bare feet. When Lara asked about the absence of footwear, Elidora told her she must be in contact with the earth. In fact, someone had scattered dirt and rhododendron petals within the circle.

"I cast the saucrit circle," Gren intoned.

"Aye, and I bless and consecrate it," Elidora replied.

"Let the four directions be honored that power and radiance might enter our circle for the good of all beings," Raven sang and gestured for Lara and Trevor to stand next to one another. Once they were holding hands under the archway leading into the living room, he continued his chant. "With the blessing of the great bear of the starry heavens and the deep and fruitful earth, we call upon the powers of the north. With the blessing of the great stag in the heat of the chase and the inner fire of the sun, we call upon the powers of the south. With the blessing of the salmon of wisdom that dwells in the sacred waters of the pool, we call upon the powers of the west. With the blessing of the hawk of dawn soaring in the clear pure air, we call upon the powers of the east."

"I call on th' great powers and commaund thair presence inower th' circle," Gren said, swinging his arms to each of the four compass points. "Who gie's this wife?"

"I give her," Raven answered and strode to the threshold to offer Lara his arm. "We enter the circle in the name of Brigid, goddess of the bright flame, keeper of peace."

"An' who gie's this man?" Gren went on, his voice rich and low.

"I give him," Elidora replied, walking to take Trevor by the arm. "We enter th' circle in th' name of Angus mac Og, god of love."

As Lara, hand latched beneath Raven's arm took her place next to Trevor and Elidora on the hearth in front of the woodstove, she understood she was taking part in a ceremony that was likely thousands of years old. A shiver ran up her back. This was a true joining, not something that could ever be set aside. *Like the sacred marriages I read about in mythology.*

"Heart o' my heart, body o' my body, bluid o' my bluid." Gren pulled the same small knife out of a pocket. "Trevor, dost thou bind thysel' tae this wife for all eternity?"

"I do so bind myself," Trevor answered. Lara's eyes opened wider as she realized Trevor was no stranger to the Druid ceremony. Gren took Trevor's right hand. Quick as lightning, he made a deep cut with the knife in the meaty part of Trevor's thumb. Rubbing an index finger in the wound, he drew his bloodied finger down Lara's cheeks and across her forehead.

"Heart o' my heart, body o' my body, bluid o' my bluid," Gren went on. "Lara, dost thou bind thysel' tae this man for all eternity?"

"I—I do," she said, feeling shaky.

"I dae sae bind mysel'," Gren prompted.

"I do so bind myself," she murmured. Pulling at her right hand, Gren cut deeply into her thumb, and then used her blood to paint the same arcane symbology on Trevor's face.

"Gie's yer right haunds," Gren instructed. Reaching into another pocket, he withdrew a length of white linen that he wrapped around their hands, joining them. The cloth quickly reddened from their still-welling blood. When the first drop fell onto the floor, Gren began to chant in the melodic, ancient Gaelic Lara had fallen in love with when Trevor read to her about her origins from beyond the stars.

Suddenly she felt Raven's arm hard around her and his lips full on hers. Before she could react, he'd spun her to face Trevor, pushing her into his arms.

Clearly knowing what came next, Trevor swept her up and kissed her long and tenderly.

"Ye're nou man an' wife," Gren continued.

"You are now man and wife," Raven, Lillian, and Elidora chanted as one.

"Honor th' four gates wi' yer lives, and ye'll be gifted wi' baith love an' peace. Micht th' gods sain you." Gren bowed his head.

"Aye, and keep you," Elidora echoed.

Lara felt different somehow. It wasn't anything so obvious she could label it, but lightness radiated from her core. When she pulled back to look at Trevor, he seemed to be glowing as well.

"Thank the gods, it is done," Raven said, a cautious smile on his usually stern face. "And not a moment too soon."

"What do you mean?" Picking up on an undercurrent in his tone, Lara pulled away from Trevor to stare at the mage.

"Never mind, child. Enjoy what you can of your wedding day."

"I brochten a wee thing to hae wi' th' mead," Gren said and pulled a nut-studded cake out of his backpack. The knife appeared again, and he cut chunks of the pastry which he handed round. Lara had just taken a bite when the phone rang.

Taking a few steps backward, she picked up the handset. "Hello?"

"Lara, it's Brad. I've got to talk to you. Be there in five minutes." The line went dead.

"What?" Trevor asked, his eyebrows raised in concern as he shoved a piece of cake into his mouth.

"It's Archer. He's on his way here."

CHAPTER 11

"Should we be takin' our leave, then?" Elidora asked Raven. "'Tis a big house. 'Twould be nary a problem t' lose oursel' on one of th' upper floors."

"I think not," Lillian murmured. "We can tell enough of the truth to avoid suspicion. We're guests from Europe, arrived for the nuptial celebration."

"He knows what you look like," Lara reminded her. "Remember that photo?"

"Scarcely a setback." The Sidhe smiled, and the air around her took on an incandescent look. When it settled, Lillian had turned into a striking blonde. She had the same green eyes, but even Brad Archer's well-attuned cop senses wouldn't have taken her for the woman in the photograph, particularly since Gradoxst—or someone—had altered it to resemble a teenaged girl. Lillian looked ageless, but no one would ever accuse her of still being an adolescent.

"Do we have a plan?" Trevor spoke around a mouthful of cake. "Archer or no, I truly am famished."

Elidora laughed. "Aye, and ye always were. Did ye think I dinna know ye were th' one takin' the offerings th' villagers left for me?"

Blushing to the roots of his hair, Trevor stammered, "I only did that when I was half-starved."

"An', I knew 'at too, so I dinna ever call you out on it. Poor laddie, your life was such hell. 'Twas little enough I could do." Walking to Trevor, she gave him a kiss on each cheek.

"Trevor asked about a plan. I'd like to know if you have one." Lara furled her eyebrows in Raven's direction.

The mage had been gathering his long hair into a queue at the base of his neck and securing it with a leather thong. "Yes. In fact, I have two. First, though, I must determine if this human you call Archer is salvageable."

"And if he's not?" Lara asked with a catch in her voice since she was pretty sure she knew the answer. But Raven just looked sadly at her, grim and resolute at the same time. Gunter, newly wakened from the spell Gren had cast to keep him from hurting himself in the candle flames, barked sleepily from the corner of the room.

"Oh, aye, best t' be puttin' these out," Elidora murmured as she grabbed the nearest candle, blowing gently on the flame. "You could be answerin' th' door." She gave Trevor a gentle push.

"I can do that," Raven announced. "But I'll wait for the bell to sound."

Right on cue, the tones of the front door chime filled the living room. Exchanging a meaningful glance with Lillian, Raven strode across the room. In a moment, Lara heard Brad Archer's agitated voice, "Where's Lara? What have you done with her?"

"It's her wedding day. Calm yourself." Raven replied. "She's inside."

"Wedding? How could anyone be getting married *now?*" Brad burst into the living room and came to an abrupt halt as soon as he saw Lillian, Elidora, Gren, and the circle of partially extinguished candles.

"Congratulations," he mumbled, looking at his feet. "Why didn't you tell me?" He looked accusingly at Lara. "I wouldn't have come."

"You didn't give me a chance," she replied, eying him critically as she tried to assess if he was still bound to Gradoxst. "You seem better than you were earlier. Anyhow, what was so important?"

Brad, dressed in jeans, a plaid cotton shirt, and a denim jacket, looked as if he'd managed to find a shower sometime during the hours since he'd been rescued. He glanced at Trevor, Raven, Lillian, Elidora, and Gren, his gaze settling briefly on each person, before moving to the next.

"Could I talk to you alone?" he asked Lara, sounding exquisitely uncomfortable. "After today, I, ah took a leave from the force. Don't think I'm fit to serve the way I am."

Lara looked at Lillian, who shook her head. Plus, the amulet sounded a clear warning that vibrated against her breastbone. "I'm afraid alone isn't possible," Lara said gently. "These people are like family to me. You can speak plainly in front of them."

Brad's eyes began to roll wildly, and he shook his head from side to side. Stepping forward, Raven grasped his wrist. "Hold yourself here, man," he hissed. "Do not let them enter you again. If they do, you'll be lost."

"How do you know about...?" Brad Archer stammered.

"I just do," Raven grunted. He pressed his lips together and drew his eyebrows into a tense line.

"It's better with you hanging onto me." Brad's blue eyes sought the mage's gray ones, desperation shining from their depths.

Gren thrust a cup of mead into Brad's free hand. "Drink," he said. "'Twill help too."

"Come." Raven gestured toward one of the couches. "Have a sip or two, and tell us what has happened to you since your daughter was taken."

"How do you know about that? If you know something—anything at all—you have to tell me." Brad's voice held a hard edge, and he was instantly back in cop mode.

"We all know quite a bit. We need to hear your version of things." Lillian glided to Brad's side. Between her and Raven, they maneuvered him into a seat, settling themselves on either side. Lara saw the outlines of the spell they wove, and she guessed it was to deny Gradoxst—or whoever wanted entrance to Brad's body—access.

"My version?" Brad sounded mildly bewildered. He dropped his gaze to the floor, as if considering where to begin. "I suppose the weird shit began a couple days after Adie disappeared. I started getting text messages and emails. And a few phone calls too. They all said Lara was the only one who could find my daughter."

Brad looked across the room at Lara. "I remembered what you'd done when Beauchamp was after you, and our police psychics were getting nowhere fast, so I ginned up something I hoped would convince you to help me." He hesitated, gaze back on his shoes. "I'm just so sorry. I can see now it was a trap someone constructed to try to get to you. They never intended to give my Adie back." Color suffused his fair featured face, and Brad looked up. His hollow eyes nailed Lara, imploring her forgiveness.

"Where'd you get the photo and scarf?" Trevor asked roughly.

"The same guy who'd been sending me the texts and emails told me to meet him at a diner late one night. So I did. The place he suggested was a real dive, and it was pretty dark in there. He was sitting in the back at a corner table, just like he said he'd be. I didn't stay long. There was something bizarre and repulsive hanging in the air around him. Like a haze making it impossible to really see him. Anyway, he handed me the photo and scarf and barked that I knew what to do with them."

"Despite the fact that wasn't really Adriana's scarf, and you knew the picture wasn't of her, you gave them to me anyway?" Lara felt a hot, excoriating tide of anger rise in her guts. "How could you do that to me, Brad?"

"If you had children—" he began.

"That's not good enough," she snapped, jumping to her feet. "I'm going to take the dog out." Clucking to Gunter, she stomped toward the door.

"Thou must bide here, lassie. Thou canst leave just yet." Gren's tone was gentle, but it brooked no possibility of disagreement.

Lara stood in the doorway, hands on her hips, as fury swept

through her. She wanted to order Brad out of her house, but ground her teeth together to hold the words in.

"I don't blame you for being pissed," Brad muttered, his gaze on Lara. "I had no right."

"No," Trevor said coldly. "You didn't."

"I'm thinkin' ye might have more t' tell us, laddie," Elidora urged.

Archer nodded slowly. "Things got eerie after the scarf and photo. Like I'd fallen into the *Twilight Zone*, and I felt stranger each day. Caught a glimpse of myself in the mirror one morning, and I felt disgusted. Even though I could see I was filthy, I couldn't force myself into the shower. And then today—" Clapping a hand against his chest, Brad's eyes widened. He tugged hard at the collar of his shirt as if it were choking him, and a frantic look washed over his face.

"Lillian!" Raven's voice held an urgent note. He faced Brad, grasping the detective's head between his large hands. "Help me," he urged as he began to chant. Lillian's voice rose with his and after a moment, Gren and Elidora joined in.

From her spot in the doorway, Lara sidled over to Trevor and asked, "Do you know what's happening?" But he looked as mystified as she felt.

"Seems as if he might have had a heart attack," Trevor said softly. "Except I'm sure it's nothing that prosaic. He was getting ready to tell us something, and I reckon the other side didn't want us having that information."

The Gaelic chant came to a crescendo, before leveling off. Brad opened his eyes and started moaning softly. "Jesus, what's wrong with me? Will this ever end? I thought losing Adie was the most horrible thing that could ever happen to me. But this is worse. I'm losing myself."

"Yes, son, you are." Raven's tone was deadly serious. "You must do exactly as I tell you. Are you ready?"

"How do I know I can trust you?" Brad asked, eyes narrowed. "Shit, this is all so bizarre, I don't know who's wearing the white hats anymore."

"Your *Twilight Zone* analogy was a good one. You might run with it," Lara said brusquely, still angry at him for betraying her.

Lillian waved her to silence and focused on Brad. "We'll give you something to do—a ritual—so they'll never again be able to use your body for a conduit as they did today. That we know they did should be proof enough that we're trustworthy."

"What do I need to do?"

"Dost thou trou in ocht, laddie?" Gren asked.

"S—sorry," Brad stammered. "Could you, ah, repeat that?"

"What he asked," Trevor broke in, "is whether you believe in anything."

"You mean like religion?" At Gren's nod, Brad shook his head. "Nah, no one who's been a cop for very long believes in anything but themselves and their partner."

"This might be hard for you, then," Raven said sternly. "For you must consecrate yourself to the old gods. They're the only ones who can protect you from the Demons hovering around you." Brad glanced upward, searching the air. The mage laughed grimly. "You can't see them, but we can." He gestured around the room.

"Lara?" Brad said nervously. "You have every reason not to answer me, but can you see these Demons too?"

"I can't see them like the Sid...like my friends can, but I sense you aren't the same as you were a couple weeks ago."

Dropping his head heavily into his hands, Brad scrubbed his hands down his face. When he looked up, the desperation in his eyes was pitiful. "Okay. What do I have to do? I'm not any good to anybody the way I am."

"He asked for this of his own free will." Lillian looked pleased. "Elidora, would you assist me?"

"Aye. My pleasure. Come with us, laddie." She stood, hooking a finger at him. "Ye were sayin' ye were hungry." She looked over one shoulder at Trevor. "Might ye come up with a bit o' somethin' we could eat whilst Lillian and I are occupied?"

"What a grand idea," Lillian concurred. "We'll be in the backyard. Trevor, a bottle of red wine, if you please."

Lara watched the two women herd the detective out of the living room, Elidora clutching a bottle of cabernet in one hand. Though curious, Lara found she was just as glad to not witness any more magic quite yet. The residue from her wedding still left a warm glow, and she had a feeling the ceremony about to unfold in her backyard would hold a far darker quality.

$\sim$

IN SPITE of everything that had happened after the wedding, Trevor was happy in a way he didn't ever recall experiencing before. Lara was finally really and truly his—forever. Whistling a poignant Irish folk tune, he headed for the kitchen to try to come up with something to feed all seven of them.

"Want some help?" Raven's voice boomed after Trevor. Footsteps sounded on the wood of the hallway floor.

"Sure, just as soon as I figure out what I can throw together. Doesn't help that I'm so hungry I wouldn't care if the nosh was raw." He sucked in a breath, as he looked into the relatively barren fridge. "Hasn't been all that easy to get much of anything to eat here of late," he said apologetically, switching to the freezer. He'd just pulled a good-sized roast out when the lights flickered and died. "Bloody hell. Guess we won't be having this after all. I was about to compromise my principles and toss it in the 'wave to thaw."

"I'll take care of it." Raven held out one ham-sized hand. "Though I never could figure the advantage of freezing anything. Catch it fresh, eat it fresh, I always say."

Trevor stared at the mage.

He sounds positively chuffed. Rather like he was when Lara and I visited his farm.

Raven cradled the meat between his hands. In a minute or two, he laid the roast on the sideboard. "There, should be ready for whatever you planned for it. What else are we having?" Raven raised a quizzical eyebrow.

"Well, we've got plenty of rice. We could have that, or quinoa or couscous since they cook faster. Can't do much with the oven, but the hob's gas. All I need to do is light it." As he spoke, Trevor pulled open a drawer and peered into it, coming up with a box of matches. Smiling at Raven, he said, "Heh! I forgot. Don't need these, since I've got you."

"Truer words were never spoken, son."

Working together in a companionable silence, they sliced meat for the skillet, got a pot of couscous bubbling, and heated a couple cans of diced tomatoes. When supper was well underway, Trevor turned to the mage. "Do you suppose we could talk about Lara's obsession with rescuing that girl?"

Raven frowned. "That's been in my head as well. Likely why you gave voice to it." He snorted. "If what the women are doing is successful, and I suspect it will be, since they've been out there so long, the next logical thing would be to at least try to bring the daughter back. Wresting the father away from the Demons should improve our chances."

"I thought you said it wouldn't be possible if too much time went by." Trevor felt confused. But then, Raven often engendered those sorts of feelings in him. "Not that I'm trying to be selfish here, or maybe I am," he went on, "but I don't like the idea of Lara going back to that place she described. It gives me the creeps."

"As well it should." Raven sighed. "Unfortunately, blood links are the strongest. That's why there is shared blood as a part of the wedding ceremony, and why there are still blood sacrifices in the old religions. With Archer firmly out of the Demons' clutches, it'll loosen their hold on his daughter."

"I see." Trevor lifted a lid to stir the tomatoes. "But I still don't like it." He hesitated, and then forged ahead. "As long as you're answering my questions, do you know why Gradoxst is after Lara?"

Raven turned to face Trevor, a frown creasing his forehead. He blew out a breath, and for a moment Trevor thought the mage would shake his head and remain silent, as he'd frequently done before.

"I'm not sure I know the whole of things," Raven began, his lips drawn into a bitter expression, like he'd taken a bite of something sour. "But I believe Gradoxst has been feeding off the analysts at the Jung Institute for as long as he's been there. The Jungian practitioners tap into Psyche regularly, and there's unbelievably potent energy tied to Her realm. When Lara called the Institute and ended up talking to Gradoxst for the simple reason that he happened to be there and spoke English, he must've looked up her training records, realized she had power, and decided to usurp it for himself."

"Hence his incessant telephone calls," Trevor muttered. "And his campaign to ingratiate himself into her life."

"Exactly." Raven nodded. "The other ingredient in this mix is what Lillian mentioned right after we rescued Lara from the in-between. Demons are drawn to chaos. Anarchy is like a fine wine to them, and they get drunk on their own power. What's been happening with the shortages of fuel and food, not to mention the riots, is drawing them into this world like pigs to a trough."

"I know I kicked the door open by asking," Trevor grimaced as he continued to nurture dinner along, "but this conversation is unsettling. Can we talk about something else?"

Raven clapped Trevor on the back. "If the gods are good, you'll never be comfortable with *anything* linked to Demons." He shrugged, but his eyes held a warm glint of silver. "Sorry to be the bearer of unpleasant news, but as you noted, you *did* ask.

"I'm going to go see what Gren and your lovely wife are up to. Once we get the Adriana problem under control, mayhap we can finish getting the two of you moved." Raven trotted toward the kitchen door, but he paused and looked over his shoulder, an earnest expression on his face. "One more thing. That chaotic energy is developing vigor as it spreads. Once it reaches critical mass, there'll be no going back. You must be gone by then. People will turn on one another until there's nothing left to salvage."

Touché, Trevor thought wryly, wondering again why he and Lara had been so laggardly following Raven's and Lillian's exhortations to get the hell out of Seattle. He kicked himself for not being more insistent. Grabbing up the matches, he lit a couple candles. He hadn't realized it, but Raven had a glow about him, which illuminated the kitchen's workspace. He glanced at his watch. While not exactly certain of the time he'd begun cooking, he was sure at least an hour had passed since Lillian and Elidora had taken the detective into the back yard.

Trevor looked over what felt like a paltry and uninspired dinner. After putting some muscle into grating a block of hardened parmesan from the back of the fridge, he tossed a few handfuls into the couscous along with a splash of olive oil and some fresh ground black pepper. He tasted the result and smiled as he drizzled tomatoes over the cooked beef slices, adding herbs to the mix. Done with dinner, he turned off the stove. *Too bad we don't have some lovely crusty baguettes.*

Gunter yipped right before the back door opened. Lillian and Elidora swept into the kitchen with Brad between them. Trevor did a double take. The detective looked as close to radiant as a human being could. "I gather it was a success?" Trevor cocked his head to one side.

"Aye, that it was." Elidora smiled. "Need a hand with that supper, lad? Smells delightful in here. Never knew ye could cook."

"I couldn't when I was hiding in your corn crib."

Brad shrugged back into the jacket that had been slung over one arm. When Trevor looked closely, he saw cuts on the backs of both the detective's hands and more lacerations on both sides of his neck. "What did you do to him?" Trevor asked curiously. "I thought bleeding went out with the eighteen hundreds."

"A little of this and a little of that. Blood consecrates all," Lillian answered cryptically. "Seems to me you left some blood at your wedding ceremony, young man."

Yes, if it's one thing I know about, that would be blood, he thought as he recalled the Druidic rituals and ceremonies from his childhood. "Welcome back." He stuck out a hand to Brad.

"Thanks." The detective's smile was genuine. "Good to be back. Also good you made something to eat. I don't think I've had anything since this whole odyssey started. The best thing is, the ladies told me Adie has a better chance of coming back because of what they did. Now, if they'd told me that in the first place, I wouldn't have hesitated for a moment."

"Nay." Elidora held up a hand. "Ye must've wanted this for yoursel', or it wouldna have worked."

"Enough." Raven, followed by Gren and Lara, had crowded into the kitchen. "Let us break bread, and then we shall talk about Adriana."

"Best not to get thy hopes up, laddie," Gren said solemnly. "The odds may have improved, but we're faur from Psyche's domain. We micht need to return to th' *Dreaming* afore we can dae ocht about thy dochter."

Lara latched a hand beneath Trevor's arm. Her long red hair had dried and she looked like a Botticelli angel cloaked in living flame. "We had the most interesting talk," she said excitedly, hugging him. "The Druids have almost the same beliefs the Jungians do about the importance of linkage to the natural world and the truth Psyche brings in dreams."

"Maybe you won't be leaving all your training behind when we finally manage to leave here." Trevor shut his eyes and wrapped his arms around Lara, feeling something indefinable at the pressure of her body against his. It wasn't sexual, not exactly. More a sense they belonged together, had been together throughout space and time, and would be linked through eternity.

Lara snuggled closer to him. "Righto, to borrow one of your phrases. I can still live in my dream world and pay homage to Psyche. Honestly," she bubbled, "it'll truly be the best of both worlds. Especially if we find Adriana. Psyche will help. I know she will."

"Enthusiasm," Lillian sighed, linking arms with Elidora. "My dear, were we ever truly that young?"

"Speak for yoursel', lass," the Carlisle witch sputtered. "I am young as I have ever been."

"Raven mentioned bread a while back." Ever practical when it came to food, Trevor looked from Lillian to Raven. "Do either of you have any ideas? It would be lovely to have some fresh baguettes to go with supper."

"Humans!" Lillian swallowed a snort. "I can do many things," she shot a bemused glance at Trevor, "but manufacturing food out of thin air isn't one of them." She poked Raven playfully in the side. "Do you suppose we've spoiled them?"

"Never mind." Trevor rolled his eyes. "I'll get some crackers out of the cupboard."

CHAPTER 12

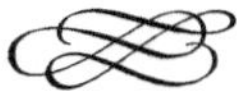

*D*inner was long since over and everyone had moved to the living room where they sat on cushions on the floor watching a fire blaze in the woodstove.

Raven glanced around the group and said, "We cannot put this off any longer—"

A cell phone vibrated, cutting off his words. When Lara looked for hers, she decided it must still be on the armoire in the entry hall.

"It's mine, but I'm almost afraid to look at it." Brad rooted in a jacket pocket.

"Exceptin' thou be doin' somethin' to be biddin' them back, thoo'll 'ave no need t' be afeard," Gren reassured him.

"They could still follow him," Lillian muttered. Gren shook his head and sent a subtle glance her way. If Lara hadn't been watching, she'd have missed it.

Peeking at the screen, Brad let out a loud sigh. "It's the station. Thank God." Punching the answer key, he said, "Archer here." As he listened, his face became more and more troubled. "All three of them, you say. But how? Just a minute..."

"Lara." The detective motioned with an impatient hand. "Flip on the television, would you?" He turned back to his call.

"Don't have one, remember?" she replied. "Plus, there's no power. But I can get my laptop. It was plugged in before the power went out, so it should be good for a few hours." She pushed upright from her cross-legged sit and walked from the room. As she went up the stairs, she caught snatches of Brad's conversation, none of it sounding good.

When she came back with the computer tucked beneath her arm, she stopped long enough to unclip her cell phone from her shoulder bag. A quick glance told her she had work to do. Brad, who'd gotten off his cell, reached for her computer as soon as she walked into the front room. His eyes held a haggard edge.

"Just a sec," she said and sat on the edge of a couch as she flipped open the laptop and booted it up. Once she'd typed in her password, she handed the computer to the detective as the startup menu flared to life. "I've got to catch up with my electronic sidekick," she murmured, tapping keys and scrolling through menus on her phone.

Focused on the cell phone's display, she wasn't paying attention to the drama unfolding in her living room. Brad, staring at Yahoo! News, had started to cry. If he'd been sobbing, she'd likely have noticed. As it was, when she finally looked up, silent tears ran down his cheeks as he clicked the laptop's keys.

"What happened?" she asked, alarmed. Most of the messages on her phone had been inconsequential, except for emails from two patients who'd come for their appointments, only to find her building locked.

Brad turned slowly, his face a study in agony. "The riots started again. Three of my best men are dead. Gunned down in the Wallingford District." He wiped at his face. "I've got to get back on the job. They depend on me. If I hadn't been wallowing in my own shit, hell, Duffy, Smith, and Kasabian might still be alive."

The detective laid the laptop gently onto the floor and lurched to his feet. "Sorry, I've got to go." He'd taken two steps toward the front door when he whirled and stopped. "Christ, I can't leave. There's Adie." He raked his fingers through his short blond hair. "She needs me. My men need me. I—"

"You can go," Lillian said gently. "What we needed most has been accomplished. The dark forces can't use your energy as a crucible any longer."

"In any case," Raven added, "You couldn't have come with us. It's not a place for those without power."

"But Adie doesn't have any sort of magic. And she's there." Tears leaked from Brad's eyes again, but he ignored them.

"They uised fushion reft frae thee for tae capture her an' haud her in th' in-between," Gren said. "Withoot thee as a source, they'll hae a sair fecht transportin' her awa frae th' strand."

"What? Could you try that again, please?" Brad looked at Trevor for assistance, but it was Raven who answered.

"What Gren said is the Demons have been using their link with you to hold your daughter prisoner. Now that you're free, they'll have a more difficult time transporting her from where she is to their world.

"We will do our best," Raven assured him. "We must return to the *Dreaming* afore we can do aught else. We need guidance if we are to have even a sliver of a chance."

The minute Raven mentioned the *Dreaming,* Lara's amulet began to thrum. It had done the same thing earlier in the kitchen when the topic came up. "This," she said, fingering the amulet, "seems excited by the prospect of a trip to the *Dreaming*."

"Aye, and so it should, lass. 'Tis where it was mined," Elidora said. With a half-smile, she pulled a pendant that could have been a twin to Lara's out of the folds of her robes. "Moonstones are my gem, as well," she murmured, answering the question in Lara's eyes.

"Are you sure?" Brad asked, dragging Lara's attention back to where he stood, framed in the living room doorway. "If there's anything I could do… Even something small that might mean the difference between getting Adie back or…or not." His voice cracked, and misery rolled off him in waves.

"No, you'd just be sitting here with Trevor, waiting for us to return," Lillian said grimly. "If you think you can do some good out there in this world before it turns entirely upside down, go and give it your best shot. You can always check back here. Either we'll have returned, or we won't."

The detective stood as if cast from immutable stone, his eyes shut tightly in thought. After a moment, he said, "All right. I'm going to see if I can keep the rest of my men alive. Lara, you've got my cell number. Call me if anything, anything at all—"

"I will," she cut in. "Promise."

The door had no sooner shut when Trevor got up and went to Lara. "I'm not pleased you're going off somewhere without me." He placed a possessive hand on her arm.

"There's no help for this, no other possible path," Raven said, sounding dour. "We need to get going. Besides, someone needs to stay with him." He pointed at Gunter, curled up in a corner of the room.

"But why does Lara have to go with you?" Trevor persisted. "She could stay here and wait, like me."

"Because she spent time with Adriana. So she will be able to help us find her again," Raven answered as he stood and went to gather his knapsack.

Lara pulled Trevor into an embrace. "I'll be safe." She tried to reassure him. "I'll be with Psyche. Not the way she's come to me in my visions, but—"

"How can you know that?" Trevor asked fiercely.

"The amulet, it tells me when things aren't safe, and it's practically dragging me to this *Dreaming* place." Lara reached between them to clasp the moonstone and glanced at her impromptu wedding dress. "Eh, I need to change."

"Yes, child, that would be wise," Lillian murmured. "We'll wait for you, but you must hurry."

Lara ran up the stairs; her bare feet had moved past cold to numb. Once in her bedroom, she rummaged about in the dark to find what she needed, pulling on a thick pair of sweats, woolen socks, and a warm pair of lace up boots. Halfway down the stairs, she doubled back for a knit cap and gloves, thinking it might be cold where they were going.

In spite of everything that had happened that day, she felt excited by the prospect of a visit to the Sidhe's home. If it was anything like Lillian's tree house or Raven's farm, she'd fall in love with the place. She remembered the strong attraction she'd felt the very first time she'd looked at Raven through her third eye. The amulet had been pulling at her then too.

If what Elidora says is true, it wants to go home.

"Ready," she called out from the bottom of the circular staircase.

"They're all in the back garden," Trevor noted glumly, trooping over to her with Gunter at his heels.

"Try not to worry," she said and kissed him firmly. "We'll be back before you know it. Time flows differently whenever I leave here." She started to walk down the hall that led to the laundry room and the backdoor, but noticed he wasn't following her. "Aren't you coming?" she asked over one shoulder.

"No. They told me to stay inside."

Hurrying back to him, she placed a hand on either side of his face, feeling the stubble of his beard rasp against her fingertips. "I do love you, Trev."

"Yes, Lara. I know. Do try to be careful." His accent was very clipped, betraying his anxiety, and he smoothed hair out of her face with gentle fingers.

"I promise." If she lingered in his arms, she'd never leave, so she kissed him again hard, before spinning away and heading outside.

RESISTING a close-to-overpowering urge to sneak to a window so he could watch whatever might be happening with Lara, Trevor forced himself to return to the living room. "By the time I'm done clearing up here," he announced to the empty room, "they should be good and gone." Instead of doing anything, though, he sat on one of the leather upholstered couches and clucked for Gunter, who trotted over. The dog seemed more lethargic than usual, and Trevor assumed it was a byproduct of Gren's spell.

"I don't get it," he said to the puppy. "If the whole reason for us getting married was to protect both of us, then how come the first thing that happens is they whisk her off to God-only-knows where?" Gunter whined and thumped his tail, and Trevor ruffled the fur between his ears.

Time dripped by. Finally, Trevor stood and slowly gathered up the dishes from supper. The food had actually tasted better than he'd hoped. On his first trip to the kitchen, bearing a stack of plates topped with silverware, he stopped in the back garden to give the pup a chance to go out. The yard was empty, but the puppy, apparently smelling something unusual, ran from corner to corner of the enclosure, barking excitedly.

Trevor rekindled the candles and gradually cleaned the residue from supper in water that started out hot, but was barely lukewarm toward the end of things. With the power out, the house was silent as a tomb. Thinking he'd move the Ford into the backyard so he could pack up a load for tomorrow, Trevor went upstairs to change into warmer clothes. He'd just pulled a dark blue flannel work shirt over his head when the unmistakable sound of breaking glass crashed against his ears. Gunter, also in the bedroom since Trevor had carried him up the stairs for company, began barking and growling frantically, his puppy hackles on alert.

"What the bloody fucking hell?" Scowling resolutely, he picked up the shotgun from behind the door, and dropped shells into it. He traded his leather boots for soft-soled shoes that would be quieter and lured the puppy into the bathroom. "Stay here," he said softly. "You'll be safer." He pulled a rubber bowl from under the bathroom sink, filled it with water, and left it in a corner.

Shotgun in hand, Trevor closed the bedroom door behind him as silently as possible. His eyes were close-to-fully dark adapted from the hours the power had been out. Ever so slowly, he crept down the stairs, listening to his heart thud against his ears. He'd just made the bottom step when he heard a noise coming from the living room. And then voices.

"Fuck no, man. No one's here. Let's score some of this stuff, and then we'll split. That dog we heard must be caged up somewhere."

"Hey-hey, there's fucking food in here," another voice called from the kitchen. "Lots of food. Shit. We lucked out."

Shit, indeed, Trevor thought, wondering how many young toughs were in his house. They sounded like teenage boys, with off-key voices still in the process of changing. He debated whether to approach the living room first—or the kitchen.

The intruders saved him the problem of figuring that out. Hearing footsteps from the direction of the living room, Trevor flattened himself against the wall behind the staircase. Two young men darted down the hallway leading toward the kitchen, lured by the siren call of something to eat. Even in the relative gloom, Trevor saw handguns clutched in their fists.

Christ, they're even younger than I thought.

Sparing the briefest of glances at the front door, Trevor noticed that the one remaining Italian glass panel had been smashed in. Ruefully looking at the plywood panel left from Beauchamp's assault on the other stained glass insert, Trevor shrugged pragmatically.

Maybe matching plywood's best. We won't be here that much longer.

Hoping to simply shoo the boys out, Trevor walked softly down the hall to the kitchen, reminding himself he had the advantage, since he knew the layout of the house far better than they. His palms were sweating, and it took a great deal of effort to remain calm.

"Game's up." Trevor infused a ring of authority into his voice. He emerged from the shadows of the hallway, shotgun pumped for action and pointing at the kitchen table where three boys were demolishing the food they'd pulled out of the fridge. "Time to go home."

"We ain't going nowhere," one of the boys said, casually raising a small caliber handgun.

Trevor watched in mystified stupefaction. *Surely he won't shoot me. Children can't do things like that.*

Oh really? I did when I killed Da.

The gun reached the top of its arc. Trevor spun sideways just as the report from the small weapon reached his ears. As he ratcheted his body about, something hot grazed his temple.

Because he had no choice, Trevor fired. The three boys were sitting close enough that the spray from the shotgun got all of them. The one in the middle crumpled off his chair in a geyser of blood. The other two screamed curses as they struggled to train their weapons on Trevor with blood-slick fingers.

I can't think about this now.

With the report from the first blast still ringing in his ears, Trevor pulled the pump action and fired again, killing another of the boys. The third one backed away from the table, his hands held in the air. Blood trickled from a scalp wound and he was limping, but it was too dark for Trevor to see much more than that. Something warm ran down the side of his own face and he pulled one hand off the shotgun long enough to swipe it away.

"I'm leavin', Mister. I'm leavin'," the third boy said, his voice high and scared.

Trevor caught the pungent scent of urine and didn't know if it was from the bladders of the dead or the one who was talking to him. *Can I let him leave? If I do, will he just round up more of his buddies and come back for revenge?* Undecided, Trevor pumped the shotgun and kept it trained warily on the boy.

"Do you have a home?" Trevor asked after a few moments of edgy silence.

"I don't got to talk to you," the boy snarled. "You killed my brother —and my friend. You fucking bastard." His cracking voice rose to a screech.

Trevor reacted to deep intuition and pulled the trigger, firing a third shot. As the boy fell, blood sprayed from what must've been a severed artery. The shotgun slipped from Trevor's fingers. It made a hollow, *plonking* sound as it hit the floor. *Ach, Mary, mother of God, what have I done?* Nausea rose in his gorge, hot and acrid, and he raced for the sink, violently ill.

The spasms were slow to pass. When Trevor straightened, after rinsing his hands and mouth in cold tap water, he ran to find Lara's phone since Archer's number was stored in it. After he'd hit redial with fingers that were shaking so hard it took him a couple tries to land on the right button, he was unspeakably relieved to hear the detective snap, "Archer here."

"Thank bloody fucking God, you're there. Ach, t—thank Christ," Trevor gasped, his head spinning.

"Trevor? What is it? Did something happen to Lara?" Brad asked anxiously. "You're calling me from her phone."

"Lara's fine. But I'm not. You see…" As the story poured out of him, Trevor felt a semblance of sanity return. "…I didn't know what to do. I figured if I left the last one alive he'd just come on back here with someone else and—"

"It's all right," Brad's deep voice soothed. "You did the right thing. They broke into your house. They threatened you. For Christ sakes, they *shot* at you. And from what you just told me, it sounds like they nicked you."

When Archer paused for breath, Trevor fingered the raw spot just above his right temple. *Guess I was damned lucky.*

"Uh, anything particular I should do besides put iodine on the wound?" he asked, suddenly lightheaded, as the truth about how close he'd come to dying filled him.

"Not that I can think of." Brad said tiredly. "I'll send one of the crews over to pick up the bodies."

"Thanks," Trevor croaked feebly, his mouth dry from being sick and talking to Brad for so long. "How soon? There's an ungodly mess in here."

Archer made a grim clucking sound. "Yeah, we've lost hundreds tonight so far. All over the city. Tell you what. Normally we don't like to disturb crime scenes until we can look them over, but it'll take weeks to dredge through what's happened. That's if things level out. It's past eleven, and criminal activity's escalating. If that's even possible. What's gone down tonight has been horrific, even for me." Trevor heard a weary intake of breath. "Just drag the bodies out onto your porch. I'll send the meat wagon by. That way you can at least clean up your house."

"Thanks, Brad. I'm on it."

Trevor lost track of time.

It was hard to see by candlelight, but he did as good a job as he could with cold water and detergent. He threw dozens of buckets of bloody water down the kitchen sink as he mopped and scrubbed. At one point, he heard someone on the porch and went outside to find cops, dressed in riot gear, hauling the bodies away. He tried to talk to them, to thank them, but they waved him back into the house.

Too tired to talk. Yeah, I get that.

He stripped to the skin in the laundry room before going upstairs, not wanting anything with blood on it anywhere near him. Since he wasn't sure when the power would come back on so he could use the washer, he piled his blood-soaked clothing in the utility sink, filled it with stone cold water, and mixed in laundry soap.

The last things he did before falling on his face in bed were letting the puppy out and standing in a bone-chilling shower for as long as he could stand it.

Wrapped in the down comforter, Trevor shivered. Teeth chattering, he watched helplessly as his mind replayed what he'd done, skittering away from the three young lives he'd snuffed out. One of the boys had been a neighbor, but he hadn't realized it until he'd heaved the bodies out onto the porch.

Just like with your dad, an unpleasant inner voice jeered.

"No!" Trevor spoke to the darkness, scarcely recognizing his own voice. "This is nothing like with my dad. Nothing at all. I—I hated him."

Grinding his teeth together to forestall a delayed reaction to shock, Trevor pulled the bedspread over him, his thoughts on Lara. She'd been gone for hours. Worry nagged on top of everything else, and his head pounded, but he was too done in to do anything more. He closed his eyes. Despite his weariness, sleep was a long time coming.

CHAPTER 13

*L*ara looked around her. The journey to the *Dreaming* had been a lot like her travels to where her visions occurred. Not the trips to the beach, but the more usual places where her psychic abilities had led her over the years. To be sure, her body had come along for the ride this time; but it was a pleasant sensation, nothing like her descents to the beach. "Where are we?" she asked, curiously. "This looks a lot like Ireland, or maybe Scotland."

"The hill country," Lillian answered, a faraway look in her clear, green eyes. "The mounds and barrows where we live when we're not on the other side. And our castle. Much of our power is rooted deep within it." She gestured toward a medieval behemoth, complete with turrets and a portcullis, standing on a small rise a few hundred ·yards away.

Lara stared at it, fascinated. "Does it have a moat?" she asked, starting toward the stone structure to get a better look.

"Come!" Raven's tone was curt. "We have much to do here, and you can't stay long, else it'll be difficult for you to return." He spun Lara in the direction he wanted her to go. "The first order of business once we return will be to teach you a few rudimentary spells. You're helpless here, which makes this dangerous for you."

She wanted to ask why, but sensed it wasn't the time. She'd learned to read when Raven would be forthcoming and when questions from her fell on deaf ears. They trotted through a lush, green countryside, thick with heather and gnarled, leafless trees she didn't recognize. As she walked, Lara made out the barest of paths under her boot clad feet.

The patter of running water grew louder. As soon as she crested a small hill, an iridescent waterfall came into view. Gren walked into the cascade and disappeared. "Where—?" she began.

Raven took hold of her arm and said, "Follow him."

Ducking and scrunching her eyes tight, Lara expected a drenching as she trailed after Gren, Elidora, and Lillian into the multi-hued water. Instead, she walked through into a tunnel, shocked to find herself perfectly dry. "How in the hell?" she sputtered, as she hurried after Lillian's rapidly disappearing form.

Glowing lights embedded in dirt walls caught her eye, and she stopped short to stare at them. "This looks like the tunnel in my dream," she exclaimed, reaching out a tentative finger to stroke one of the lighted places. It flickered as she touched it, blazing brightly again when she pulled her hand away.

"Lara! You can't linger." Lillian admonished from twenty feet ahead. Soon the tunnel angled downward, and the similarities to her dream intensified.

She turned to talk to Raven, but he shook his head and made shooing motions with one hand. "Not now. There'll be time once we arrive at our destination."

She walked for a long time before the tunnel widened into a large subterranean chamber. The same little lights studded the walls, and glittering, rose-colored stalagmites grew from the floor at intervals. Water cascaded down the rear wall of the cave into a turquoise pool that was lit from within. Coming closer to inspect the water, she saw strange orange and yellow fish swimming languidly.

"What is this?" Lara asked, keeping her voice low out of a sense of reverence filling her.

"This an' th' castle are th' heart o' th' *Dreamin,*" Elidora answered softly. Her voice tone suggested both were holy places.

Well, maybe they are, Lara thought. *This cave has a sacred feel to it. And a primordial one too.* Gren, Elidora, and Lillian perched on conveniently flattened stalagmites. Lara wasn't quite certain how she knew, but she was sure they'd occupied those same places many times before. Raven guided her to a large, low boulder next to the pool.

"Sit," he said, patting the stone. "Close your eyes and picture Adriana."

Culling up a vision of the blonde teenager, sadness rose in Lara. The guileless girl had been lost and helpless—as if all the fight had been drained from her by whatever her captors had done. With Adie's delicate features splashed across her mind, Lara could almost feel the young woman's hands reaching for her. Stretching out her own hands, she tried for contact.

"It is enough."

Lara heard Raven, but he sounded muted, far away. It was impossible to stop thinking about Adriana and easy to ignore Raven— until his voice ripped through her.

"I said, enough."

Shaken, Lara's eyes flew open. Raven strode toward her, arms folded across his chest, dark hair flying behind him.

"You must do what I say." He spat the words out individually, enunciating each one. "Do you want to get sucked back into that hellhole?"

"Of course I don't," she replied, feeling defensive. "Was that close to happening?"

"Closer than I widae liked," Gren said from a few feet away, an unforgiving edge in his voice.

"I thought once Trev and I were married I'd be safe." As soon as the words were out, they sounded foolish to her, and childish.

Raven laughed hollowly. "Safer. There is no way for any of us to be entirely safe from evil."

"Does the fact I could find her so easily mean Adriana is still in the in-between?" Lara asked hopefully. After a thoughtful moment, she added, "I could feel Psyche's presence within me. She led me straight to Adie."

"Aye, tha' is exactly whit it means, lass," Elidora's soft brogue soothed Lara's frayed nerves.

Looking from one to the other in the dim light of the cave, Lara finally asked, "Can we get her out of there?"

"Aiblins." Gren's usually pleasant voice was still curt.

"Perhaps. At great risk to ourselves," Raven muttered, turning away from her.

"But none of this was her fault." An impotent sadness surged, and Lara's hands balled into fists of their own accord. "We can't just leave her there. It's wrong. She's suffering. She'd be better off if she were dead."

"Lara." Lillian had moved silently behind her. "We may well kill her moving her back to this world. There must be some problem with transporting her out of the in-between, or she would've been gone long since. When we were freeing her father, I assumed Gradoxst—or one of his Goblinesque ilk—would move her as soon as they sensed what we were doing. While they still had access to Brad's blood-linked energies."

"I don't understand. Why'd you tell Brad there was a better chance of bringing Adie back if you didn't think it was true?" Lara looked accusingly at Lillian.

Raven stepped between them. "She was trying to anchor him to Earth," he explained. "His spirit was fragile after the rite she performed, and hope is a potent elixir. Providing him with as much as possible might be the lynchpin that helps us retrieve his daughter."

Lara settled her head on an upraised hand, realizing how bone tired she was, and how little she understood about the complicated, interlocking rules Raven was describing. She looked up from her seat on the boulder and murmured, "If we're done, I'd like to go home to Trevor."

"Soon," Elidora said. "Someone seeks us, so long as we're here."

Almost too weary to feel more than the mildest of interests, Lara glanced about, mystified. The far end of the cave began to glow, and she shaded her eyes with her forearm. "What's that?'

"Hush, lass," Elidora whispered. "'Tis Brigid, keeper of the sacred flame."

Lara struggled to remember Celtic mythology. "The one in my wedding ceremony?" she asked, but no one answered her.

A tall woman, with blonde hair so long it swept the floor of the cave, came into view. Her robes were purple and black, and she carried an old-fashioned lantern that blazed with warming light. A thick golden torc circled her neck, and gold rings adorned her two index fingers. Small cunning creatures in a variety of colors floated about her as she walked. From time to time, one lit on the goddess, and she stroked the fairy, straightening a gossamer wing or a stray lock of hair.

Fascinated, Lara wondered if they could be air sprites. She was also struck by the similarities between Brigid and the shamanistic guide who'd led her beneath the Tree of Life in a dream she'd had. A dream shared by a student, some patients, and Trevor. And if she could believe Gradoxst, by others at the Jung Institute as well.

"You have returned to the *Dreaming*, bringing one whose magic has yet to blossom. Tell me why you have done this?" Brigid's voice reverberated off the walls of the cave. She spoke in Celtic Gaelic, but for once, Lara had no trouble understanding the ancient, mellifluous tongue.

It's as if the language is bypassing my brain and going straight into my heart.

Raven stepped forward, knelt, and bowed low. Still on his knees, he kept his head bent as he told Brigid of Adriana's plight and Lara's link to the unfortunate girl. Once he was done, he touched his forehead to the goddess's feet, before standing. For long minutes, the only sounds in the cave were water rushing into the pool and the muted swooshing of the air sprites as they circled their mistress.

"It has come to this," Brigid said sadly. "We are reduced to rescuing humans from their folly. Humans who have ceased to pay homage to us." Tears gathered in the corners of her eyes and dropped onto the lantern, making a soft, sputtering sound. "If you must do this thing," she said, after a brief pause, "wait until two nights hence at the stroke of midnight. The moon will be full then, and you might hope for Artemis's aid. You'll have but one half turn of the glass. If you have not released the maiden from her prison by then, she must be sacrificed, else the Dark will have their way with her."

Brigid shut her eyes. Nostrils flaring, she stretched out the hand that held the lantern, as if she held a divining rod. The lantern swung first one way, and then the other, until it stopped pointing right at Lara.

"Ah, it is you," Brigid breathed, opening her luminous, golden eyes. "I consecrated your marriage but a few short turns ago. Already it has been fruitful. A perfect time for your powers to flourish, sweet child. There is none better."

Shimmering so brightly Lara couldn't look at her, Brigid turned and left the same way she'd entered, through an entrance cloaked by shadows. Once she was gone, the temperature dropped several degrees.

Shivering, Lara gazed into the pool and forced her tired brain to puzzle through what the goddess said. She moved from Brigid's lament that humans no longer prayed to her to *fruitful* when her mouth fell open. *Fruitful usually means...Oh my God.*

Lara laid a hand over her stomach. "But I can't be," she mumbled. "I mean, I never have been, so why now?" And then she remembered Trevor's incantation at Raven's farm and their lovemaking. That had only been a few days ago. How could the goddess possibly tell something like that so soon? Even pregnancy tests weren't accurate this early.

I'm thinking with my twentieth century mind. Of course she'd have ways to know.

Lillian and Elidora crowded on both sides, laying their hands over her midsection. Because she was looking at Lillian, Lara saw the

Sidhe's lips curve into a broad smile, and she heard Elidora's soft, "Oh, aye. We shall be havin' a bairn. Tha' is byous news. An' your Trevor, he is just a sterling lad. Ye know, I helped him intae this world, an' his puir sister an' brother as well."

"I knew there was some reason—beyond the obvious—I felt such pressure to get them wed," Raven murmured. "It'd be cause for celebration if we had the time, which we most assuredly do not. Come. I must show Lara some landmarks, in case she manages to fall into the *Dreaming* without one of us as a guide."

Following dutifully after the mage, Lara's mind was reeling. *Pregnant! What will Trev think? He never wanted kids, but maybe that'll be different now he's fessed up about his past and isn't trying to hide anything. What if I'm too old? What if I have an impossibly hard time because of that? What if I lose the baby, or die myself?*

"Child!" Lillian's voice was stern. "Stop that. I will be here to help you."

"As will I," Elidora chimed in. "I wouldna miss it for th' world."

Oh yes, they can read my mind. I suppose I keep forgetting that because it feels creepy.

Lara passed back beneath the waterfall and turned to look at Lillian and Elidora. "It's quite uncomfortable that you two can read my thoughts so easily."

"We'll name th' bairn Elizabeth, efter th' sister Trevor lost." Elidora smiled, ignoring Lara's comment. "'Twill help restore a piece o' balance tha' was lost t' th' universe when th' puir lassie took her own life."

"Are you sure it's a girl?" Lara glanced at Elidora, saw her nod, and smiled.

A daughter... Will she be fair like Trev, or redheaded like me? Or maybe something all her own that's not like either one of us.

"Lara." Raven gestured for her to stand next to him. "Look at that oak tree over there. See how it forms a triangle with the waterfall and that distant rock cairn? The castle lays over yonder." He pointed. "Each of these four things is visible from at least a mile distant. Were you to be pulled here, the first thing to do would be to search out one of them…"

As Lara listened, the amulet's song shifted, holding half an extra tone. *Maybe it's singing for both of us now. Or maybe it always was, and I didn't understand what it meant.*

"…we must intensify your studies," Raven was saying. "Brigid was correct in what she told you. This may be exactly the opportunity we were waiting for."

Gren had slipped away from the group while Lara was listening to Raven. Returning, he held two of the unusual green-colored bottles, one in each hand. "Thought I should git us a wee bi' o' sirple sae we micht handsel wi' th' faither-tae-be," he said cheerily, his good humor restored.

Lara wondered about the time. "Feels like we've been gone for hours," she ventured.

"Aye, 'tis past time to return. Your beau will be right worried about you." Raising a hand, Elidora began to chant. The others joined in and the green meadows fell away, dropping Lara into the void between the worlds.

Are they different worlds? Or am I different? How can I move out of modern America to somewhere else so easily? Promising herself she'd try to find answers to all her questions, Lara blinked as the familiar territory of her backyard rose around her.

The eastern horizon was beginning to lighten—pale streaks of the coming dawn a delicate pink against the still-black night sky. "Holy shit, we've been gone all night," Lara cried, her exhaustion momentarily shoved aside. "Trevor must be frantic." She twisted the back door knob, surprised to find it locked. Reaching to the lintel above the door, she found the spare key they kept there for just such occasions.

When she walked into the darkened house, the first thing she noticed was that the power was still off. The second was the utility sink full of clothes soaking in murky looking water. *Why'd Trevor want to wash his clothes? Seems like he could have waited until we got power again.*

A high-pitched puppy bark told her where to look for Trevor. She was just rounding the corner into the hallway off the laundry room when she heard footsteps moving toward her.

"Lara, that you?" Trevor's worried-sounding, sleep-saturated voice rose from the interior of the house.

"Who else would it be, silly?" she called back.

A very bedraggled looking Trevor came into view, with Gunter tucked firmly under one arm. Lara took a careful look at him, and her heart clenched. Something had happened here; whatever it was must've been devastating. She held out her arms to embrace man and puppy. Gunter wriggled and licked her, whining happily. Trevor just held her close with his free arm, his heart thudding against her ear where she pressed close to him.

"Jesus, you're shaking. What the hell happened to your head?" She touched the spot where the bullet had come close enough to shave off a few layers of skin.

"Got to take him out," Trevor said, still sounding half dead to the world. "We can talk after that."

She heard his muted greetings to the others, who were just now coming into the house. Lara backtracked to the kitchen where she found everyone except Trevor milling about. "Here," she said, "Let me get some hot water going on the stove."

Lillian laid a hand on Lara's shoulder, intercepting her on her way to the sink, kettle in hand. "Death visited this room," she said quietly. "And not so very long ago."

Lara peered around the familiar four walls with a morbid curiosity. And then she saw bullet holes and gasped. Moving toward a wall, she traced the uneven sheet rock with a shaking hand. The kettle hung by her side, forgotten. "Even I could sense something unpleasant went on just from looking at Trevor, but death..." She searched the dark kitchen with her third eye, trying to *see* what had alerted the Sidhe.

"I can smell it," Raven muttered. "I suppose we should consider ourselves fortunate Trevor is unharmed. Ah, here he is now. Set yourself down and tell us how you spent your evening, son."

"Gladly. It'll be quite the relief to talk about it." Trevor refilled the puppy's kibble dish from a nearby sack of Puppy Chow. He leaned against the refrigerator, ignoring Raven's invitation to sit. "There were these three young hoodlums who broke out the other Italian glass panel—"

"Oh, no!" Lara exclaimed, as she lit the gas stovetop with a match and settled the kettle over a burner. "So both of them are gone now."

"'Fraid so. Look, love, it doesn't matter. Those things were nothing but a silly indulgence in the first place."

"I suppose you're right," she said, chewing on her lower lip. "It's easier to think about lost stained glass than to think I nearly lost you." She threaded her arms around him, hugging him close. "Come on, dear," she urged. "Sit down. I'll bring you a nice cup of tea once the kettle's boiled."

"Thanks, Lara.

"...and so I did the best I could to clean everything up," Trevor shook his head. "Didn't do the most bang-up job, what with having only cold water. And no light."

As if responding to the reproach in Trevor's tone, the electricity sputtered a couple times, before whirring back into life. "Thank the sodding saints, we'll have hot water soon." Trevor shut his eyes. "That cold shower I had right before bed was the capper. I tell you, I must've shivered for close to an hour afterward.

"But the worst part of all of this, now that I've had a chance to mull it over, is that one of the boys I killed was young Timmy Jenkins. Remember him from a few houses down the street?" He looked at Lara, who nodded, swallowing hard.

"He couldn't have been more than thirteen or so," she muttered, aghast. "He used to help you bring groceries in sometimes, didn't he?"

"Yes, and he trimmed the grass in our front yard and steps. Didn't even have to ask him. Once he knew it was a job that needed doing, he was all over it. Sometimes it was a struggle to pay him. He'd just walk away from me." Trevor shut his eyes. When he opened them, they glistened with tears. "It was just so dark in the kitchen," he said, his voice anguished. "If he'd told me who he was…"

"It wouldn't have mattered." Raven's tone was cold. "I've been trying to tell you. Demons are here. They've broached the veil betwixt this world and several of theirs. Thank the goddess there aren't too many of them yet. After there are, the downhill slide will make this look like child's play."

Lillian wove an arm about Raven's waist. Watching, Lara wondered if it was some sort of signal that, for once, Raven had disclosed too much.

Corroborating her suspicions, Raven deftly shifted topics. "Weren't you listening when the detective told us he'd met one of them in that eating establishment? It doesn't matter how *good* a person is. Once a Demon whispers in their ear, all is lost."

"I just don't know anymore. Goblins. Demons. Other worlds." Trevor's voice shook. He took a sip of tea, slopping some over the edge when he tried to hold the cup steady.

"You must be exhausted," Lara said, struggling to overcome a sick helplessness roiling through her. Trevor's near brush with death was tearing a hole in her guts. Never mind their young neighbor's untimely demise. She was trying really hard not to think about that— or about Raven's proclamation of a Goblin-driven Gotterdammerung.

"I'm pretty wiped out," she went on. "How about if all of us catch a nap for an hour or two?" Seeing nods all around, she waved both arms wide. "Feel free to sleep wherever you want. The heat's back on, so the house should warm up quickly. There are blankets in the laundry room, and more upstairs."

"We'll be fine, child," Lillian murmured. "Don't you want to tell—?"

Casting her professionally-trained eyes over Trevor's shell-shocked demeanor, Lara shook her head. "Later," she said. "Once we're better rested." She glanced in Trevor's direction, but he was so out of it, the words she'd exchanged with Lillian hadn't registered.

"I'll waird th' haudin," Gren offered. "Syne I'll lean an aw."

Lara had been about to ask Trevor to translate, when a harsh, metallic burst sounded in the distance. "What's that?" Lara cocked her head to one side listening. "Gunfire?"

"That's exactly what it is," Trevor said wearily. "It's been going on virtually all night. Every time I woke up, I'd hear it. I was just grateful it wasn't all that close, because I was too wiped-out to do anything more than what I'd already done."

CHAPTER 14

*L*ara wakened to the staccato tattoo of rain hitting the bedroom window. Prying her eyes open, she looked out into another gray day, *de rigueur* for the Pacific Northwest. Turning slightly, she glanced at Trevor. Since he was still sound asleep, she took advantage of the opportunity to really look at him. What she saw broke her heart. Dark smudges rode beneath his eyes, and far more gray strands wove through his hair than she remembered. The fine lines around his eyes had deepened, and even asleep, his forehead was creased into a frown.

Wish I'd have been here, so he wouldn't have had to face a choice like murder all by himself.

Trying to be quiet, she slipped out of bed with the thought of taking a shower, but the puppy began wriggling and making little whining noises, so she knew she'd have to take him out first. She was just snugging a robe around herself when she heard Trevor's sleepy, "I'll take him, love."

She walked to his side of the bed, perched on the edge, and placed her hand on his bare shoulder. "That's okay, Trev. Why don't you see if you can't get a bit more sleep?"

"Humph," he snorted. "Not much chance of that. Never was one for naps."

"Or for sleeping at night, either." She laughed wryly.

"Right you are," he agreed, sounding much more awake. "Seriously, how about if you get us a tub going? I'll join you once I'm back from taking the pup out."

Now that she considered the possibility, a hot bath did sound wonderful. "Sure. That's a great idea."

She'd just bent to flip on the taps when she heard the snick of the bedroom door and the muted clomp of Trevor's slippers on the risers. Rummaging through one of the bathroom cabinets, she found some lavender-scented milk bath and poured a generous amount into the tub.

She settled into the deep tub, luxuriating in the hot water soothing her tight muscles. Trevor cracked the door just far enough to slide into the steamy bathroom.

"Mmm… Smells ambrosial in here. Wonder if we'll be able to find herbs and flowers to recreate those commercial preparations we won't have access to any longer."

Lara chuckled. "We've spent too many years together. I was just debating the same thing. Come on in. As they say, the water's fine."

Trevor's robe puddled around him as it slid to the floor. He toed off his slippers, leaving everything in an untidy heap. "I didn't make a full transit of the house," he said, easing into the warm water. "But I didn't see anyone else."

"Maybe they're all still asleep."

"Or maybe they went off somewhere. Umm, this feels really good. Think I strained a bunch of muscles last night either puking into the sink or dragging the bodies round to the front porch—or maybe even from the kick from the shotgun. Hate to say it, but my ears are still ringing a bit."

She leaned back against him, letting the soothing warmth of the water caress her. She'd had a few doubts about the wisdom of getting such a large tub, but Trevor had pointed out that European tubs were all deep. "Thanks for insisting on this bathtub," she half-turned to smile at him.

"Too bad we can't take it with us, but the one in that upstairs bedroom at Raven's place looked fairly adequate."

"Except we'll have to haul hot water up from the kitchen stove," she pointed out.

"Perhaps by then you'll have figured out a way to bend magic to heat it on the spot."

"Uh, Trev, there's something I have to tell you..." Her voice ran down. *Was this the right time? What if he didn't want the baby? What then?*

"You sound serious. Go ahead, love. Whatever it is can't possibly be worse than what happened here last night."

Well, he told me to go ahead. So just spit the words out. But they clung stubbornly to the roof of her mouth.

"Lara?" A note of concern entered his voice, and he tightened his arms around her under the water. "What is it?"

"I, uh, I mean we... Oh, blast it, Trev. I'm pregnant."

She felt his body stiffen behind her. Where before it had fitted against her, fluid under the hot water, now it felt like hammered steel. "A—are you sure?" he croaked.

"Uh-huh. We didn't tell you about the *Dreaming* when we got back this morning because what you had to tell us was so much more important. But remember Brigid?"

"Who?" He sounded baffled.

"The goddess who blessed our wedding, along with that Celtic god."

"Oh, that Brigid I was trying to think of a person."

His body was relaxing again where it touched hers. Lara thought that might be a good sign, but she wasn't sure. "She showed up in this cave where we were, and she told me our marriage had been fruitful." Turning in his arms, so she could look at him, Lara went on, "Honestly, it took me a minute or two to figure out what she meant. And then Elidora and Lillian started cooing over me, and Elidora even said we should name the baby Elizabeth, after your sister, Lizzie."

"Elidora knows it's a girl?" Trevor's voice had an odd catch in it. As Lara watched him, anxious for cues about how he was feeling, his eyes filled with tears and he pulled her roughly toward him. For a time, they rocked against one another.

"I think it was that Gaelic love spell of yours," she said finally, her voice muffled against his chest.

"Huh?"

"Out at Raven's that night when we were trying to raise Lillian. You did that chanting thing. We need to ask Elidora, but I'm pretty sure if you learned it by eavesdropping on her, it was likely a fertility charm."

He started to chuckle, and then to laugh. "Bloody blazes, I do believe you're spot on with that. She wouldn't have had to sell the villagers charms for sex. God knows they had plenty of that without any assistance at all."

"Are you okay with it?" Lara asked. "I, um, suppose I could try to scare up my friend Helen Morgan in the obstetrics department to try to, er, do something."

The smile fled from his face. "Is that what you want?" he asked abruptly. "Tell me the truth, Lara."

What do I want? "I'm not exactly sure. I am pretty old, closer to fifty than forty, you know. But Lillian says she'll be there to help and Elidora too." *Ach, I'm babbling.* "Back when we first got together, I assumed we'd have children, but you were always so dead set against it, I guess I sort of stopped thinking about it."

"Yes," he interrupted impatiently. "I know all that. What I need to know that you haven't answered is whether you want this baby…our baby."

"Do you?" With her gaze locked onto his, she sought entrance to his secret places—the ones bound up in his sister's molest and subsequent suicide, and his father's murder.

His aura flared in purples and golds. "I don't think I've ever wanted anything quite so much," he said quietly. "Now you tell me."

She let out a breath as relief swooshed through her. "Yes, oh yes, I do want her. I think I've wanted to be a mother all my life. That's what I've been to a lot of my patients. And that's why I wanted a dog when it seemed we wouldn't be having kids."

Her words tumbled out in a rush. "It's what every woman needs to be complete. The triple goddess is the maiden, the mother, and the crone. Mothering is part of how we're made, and there's always been this blank spot inside me that has the possibility of being full now." Tears welled. She brushed them away, and then he wiped tenderly at her wet cheeks with his thumbs.

"There, love. Hush. Everything will work out. Come on. We either need to add more hot water, or we need to get out."

She leaned forward and flipped the hot water tap on, before settling back against him. "We haven't talked much about this," she said, "and maybe there's not much point, since we can't change anything, but I'm appalled that our world is going up in smoke. All those simple little things: driving, listening to CDs, going for a run and grabbing a latté down at the café, researching things on the Internet... All that's going to be gone. And I don't know that I'm quite ready to say goodbye to the way I've lived for forty years." She hesitated, mulling over the thoughts she'd just given voice to. "We'll be bringing our child into a world neither one of us knows very much about."

He pulled her closer. She felt him kiss her hair and heard him sigh. "There's a bittersweet quality," he murmured. "I've not let myself think much about any of this because, as you said, it doesn't matter what we want." He hesitated. "It is a tad difficult to just jump on Raven's bandwagon, though. No matter how much sense it makes."

Nodding, she tilted her face up for a quick kiss, and then turned the water off. "Getting out's a good idea. Regardless of how we feel about any of this, we need to pack what we can to make another run out to Raven's."

"That's what I was planning to do last night before those young ruffians showed up. Here, let me help you." He stepped out of the tub and held out a hand to her, looking curiously at her body.

She scrunched her nose at him. "There's nothing to see, silly. I'm only a few days pregnant. The embryo's probably not even implanted in my uterus yet." She blotted water off him with a handy towel, and then grabbed a dry one to work on herself, wrapping her bedraggled hair up last. When she stepped into the bedroom, she was shocked by the temperature differential. "Brrrrr! It's freezing in here."

"Yes, and it's raining like hell," he said, flicking a finger toward the window, "but at least I don't hear any more gunshots."

She pulled on the clothes she'd shucked the night before. They were thick and cozy, and she felt chilled in spite of the heater blasting away a couple floors down. As they emerged from the bathroom, Gunter greeted them enthusiastically from his nest in the down comforter on their bed. Using his puppy claws, he managed to work his way down to the floor. From there he went to sit by the bedroom door, tail wagging effusively.

"I'll take him down and get some coffee going," Trevor said, pulling her into a hug. "If that's all right. Can you still drink coffee?"

"I'm sure coffee's fine." She smiled warmly. "It's just booze I'll have to stay away from. No more oaky cabernets for me for a while."

"Maybe you should ask Elidora about that," he said thoughtfully. "As I recall, she dosed pregnant women with something decidedly alcoholic. See you downstairs."

After the door swung shut behind him, Lara sat on the edge of the bed, a protective hand over her stomach. Settling the amulet around her neck, she felt its ecstatic song run through her. *Guess it's happy about the baby too. Wonder what it would've had to say about my offer to abort it?*

She considered Trevor's emotional reaction to her news. It finally dawned that he must have some of the same empty places she did. Thinking about how patient and solicitous he was with the puppy, she nodded to herself.

He wants to be a daddy just as much as I want to be a mom. But what kind of world will we be bringing this child into?

~

TREVOR WENT through the process of coffee making on autopilot. All he could think about was Lara and their child, and the cold tongue of fear that had practically paralyzed him at the thought she might not want to keep the bairn…their bairn. He pushed the button to activate the grind-and-brew coffee maker and opened the fridge in search of something to make for breakfast—well, brunch at this point, since it was the middle of the day. Lara was too thin. And now she needed to eat especially well.

He saw smears of blood he'd missed the previous night under the refrigerator door. Cursing, he dampened a dishrag and squatted to wipe the rust-colored stains. As he glanced around the kitchen with a careful eye, he noticed a couple more spots on one of the walls that he hadn't seen in the candlelit kitchen.

"Shit!" Lara's voice preceded her into the kitchen. She clutched her phone. "Damn it. I forgot to call and cancel my other two patients from yesterday. I didn't call this morning's bunch, either. If that's not bad enough, my pager has thirty calls on it." She clapped a hand to her head, then trolled through the contact data in her phone, jotting names and numbers on a kitchen notepad.

"As long as you're calling," Trevor noted, his voice even and precise, "you may as well call anyone you had scheduled for this afternoon and next week, because you are not returning to that office of yours."

For a moment she stared at him, and then she nodded glumly before dredging up a frown. "Unfortunately, you're right. Guess I'll call the ones I owe an apology to before breakfast. I can catch the others later. I could offer them phone sessions if they wanted to close things out."

He grinned at her. "You were about to let me have it. It's easy to recognize that mulish look you get on your face. Thanks for being rational."

"Humph!" She snorted. "You really do know me far too well. I'm not particularly thrilled about the prospect of going back to my office, either. What happened there scared me beyond… well, beyond anything I can even talk about. The only things we need from there are the Oriental rugs. Oh, and I'd like Arabel's teapot too. Should've grabbed it when I got her sweater."

"On a more practical note," he said, turning back to an open cupboard, "how about pancakes? I've got some frozen blueberries to jazz them up, but the bottom line is we're close to out of food. Either we need to go shopping, or we need to get ourselves moved." He grimaced. "Hope Raven has more in the way of provisions than what I saw that one night we spent out there."

"Do you suppose there's anywhere left to shop after last night?"

"Now that you mention it, probably not," he muttered. "Not if what Archer told me is accurate." Clearing his throat, he added, "We've quite the array of canned goods. Should suit you just fine."

"Maybe you'll develop a taste for them," she joked as she walked out of the room. "I'll be back as soon as I'm done."

Trevor picked up a can of chili and stared at it. "Not very bloody likely," he said, reading the ingredients. Lara was content to eat out of cans or the freezer. He far preferred fresh ingredients, skillfully prepared. Mixing up flour, dry milk powder, a touch of sugar, and baking powder, he'd just cut in some shortening and was preparing to dribble water into his pancake mix when the air near him took on a shimmery hue.

Understanding it must be one or more of their magical buddies returning, he kept on with his brunch preparations, pouring frozen blueberries into the mixing bowl and plucking a heavy cast iron skillet from the pot rack.

Raven appeared in a corner of the kitchen. With his brows drawn into a thick, heavy line, he didn't look pleased. "Making breakfast? You're making breakfast? Why in the nine hells aren't you packing?"

"Nice to see you too," Trevor retorted, pouring batter into his skillet.

"Have you looked at the news this morning on that Internet contraption of yours?"

"No. But that would be a grand idea. Silly of me not to think of it. I'll make sure to follow up whilst I'm eating."

He heard Lillian's voice before he saw her, telling Raven to back off a notch or two. Not exactly in those words, but close enough. They spoke Celtic Gaelic, and Trevor didn't have any difficulty understanding her. "Good morning, sweet boy," she cooed as soon as she materialized.

"Yes, yes, you too," she said and bent to scoop up the puppy, who'd made a dash for her long skirts. "Where's Lara?" She looked around, and then answered her own question. "In the living room."

"She's on the phone with patients," Trevor explained, flipping pancakes onto a platter. "Breakfast anyone? There's coffee in the pot."

"Sounds wonderful," Lillian smiled as she picked up a pancake with her fingers and nibbled on it.

"Lillian!" Raven hissed. "Now is not the time to indulge ourselves with food."

"Pregnant women need to eat," she pronounced and clapped a hand over her mouth.

"Don't worry," Trevor informed the Sidhe cheerily. "Lara told me."

"Isn't it just the most thrilling news?" Lillian gushed. "A baby. It's been eons since I've been around an infant. Elidora and I will be the aunts."

Lara made it a few feet past the kitchen door before Trevor noticed she'd returned. "All done?" he inquired.

"Not exactly. All those pager messages? A whole bunch of my patients are panicking. Not surprising, given what's happening, but it could take me hours to call each of them back."

"Why do you have to?" he asked, keeping a close eye on her to judge her reaction.

"Uh..." She bit her lower lip. "Because I'm programmed to be responsible, and it's the proper ethical course."

"That was in our old world," he said. "Maybe the rules have

changed. Ready for breakfast?"

When she nodded, he asked, "What did you do with your laptop? Is it still in the living room?"

"Yeah, I plugged it in, but I can go get it and plug it in here just as easily."

"Never mind," he said. "I'll get it. Help yourself to something to eat."

"Hi." She smiled breezily at Raven and Lillian. And then she looked more closely at them. "Is something wrong?" she asked Raven.

"Is something wrong?" he mimicked in a high, sing-songy voice. "No, nothing much. The city is in a shambles. If you didn't keep your fuel tanks full, I'm not sure how you'll make it back out to the farm. There are bands of misfits and miscreants roaming the streets." As he spoke, Lillian edged to his side and placed an arm around his waist.

"He's just worried," she interpreted unnecessarily. "We knew you were going to get a bit of sleep, so we stopped by my trees. I hadn't been home for a while. Not since Trevor rousted me out of the Old Country to hunt for you. Anyway, it was passing difficult to get from here to there and back again, what with all those troubled dead wandering the spirit paths."

"Sort of like Arabel?" Lara asked.

"Exactly like Arabel," the Sidhe replied, "except these poor souls didn't have the advantage of me singing them to peace in the Summerlands."

"What happened to Elidora and Gren?" Trevor asked as he returned with the laptop under his arm.

"They're still at my house," Lillian replied. "Eli's always loved my trees, and Gren had never met them before."

"Lara—" Trevor set the computer down on the kitchen table, shooting an accusing glance at her. "You haven't eaten anything yet."

"Sorry, sorry," she mumbled, grabbed a plate, and speared a couple pancakes. "Are you going to spend the next nine months nagging me?" Looking around, she added, "By the way, is there any syrup?"

"Yes to the first question," he said grimly. "And no to the second, but you could sprinkle sugar over them. That's what we did when I was a kid."

"Good idea." She stopped by the canister to spoon brown sugar over the contents of her plate. Settled in her customary place, she waited for Trevor to sit down before asking, "What does your fuel tank look like? The BMW's practically full."

"So's the Ford," he replied, around a mouthful of pancake. "Why?"

"Raven says things are bad out there. Let's look at the news." She flipped open the laptop, booted it up, and waited for the Internet. "Oh my God." The fork that had been midway to her mouth dropped back down, clinking against the stoneware plate.

"What?" Trevor asked, alarmed by her reaction. Scooting his chair over next to her, he positioned the computer so both of them could see the screen. In the meantime, Lara managed to get local news from Yahoo!

"Five thousand dead!" he exclaimed. "How could that be? It was only one night. It's hard to have those kinds of losses in twenty-four hours of active combat."

As he read, Trevor felt worse and worse. The National Guard and the Army from Fort Lewis had converged on the worst of the riots, mowing down gun-toting citizens before they could do even more damage. Mobs had trashed supermarkets, carting off whatever food they could carry. Gangs had broken into homes, killing indiscriminately and making off with whatever the homeowners had been hoarding.

"It's not difficult to obtain guns," Raven noted dryly. "It would appear those who had them chose to bring them out for a bit of exercise last night."

"Being hungry does tend to bring out the worst in humans," Lillian concurred with a grim expression.

Trevor thought she looked worried beneath her cynical banter. Much to his immediate relief, Lara was still eating. It looked mechanical, but at least she would finish both her pancakes, along with her coffee. "Do you suppose we'll be able to drive out of here?"

Trevor turned to face Raven. "Mobs have been known to throw themselves at cars, drag the drivers out, and commandeer the vehicles for themselves."

The mage's troubled gray eyes were hooded in thought. When he finally met Trevor's gaze, he shrugged and said, "I don't know."

"Last time this happened," Lara pointed out, "things settled down in a few days. I suppose this might too. We could try to wait it out. As Trev mentioned earlier, there *is* still food here, even if it's not what he'd prefer."

As her words died away, the muted rattle of gunfire reached them.

"I suppose that settles it," Lillian said. The earlier lightness had fled from her tone. "No point in going out there if they're going to shoot at you. Probably better to wait until nighttime. It's going to rain on through until tomorrow, and the clouds will help obscure things when you do leave. Plus, Raven and I will place a protective spell to help things along."

The mage nodded. "Yes, we could do that. We'll spend what's left of the day packing, so you'll be ready to leave as soon as it's full dark." Looking from Trevor to Lara, he went on. "Take everything you want, because this will be a one way trip."

"But—" Lara stopped, probably because of the stern look in Raven's eyes.

Trevor curved an arm across her shoulders, pulling her close. "She'd planned on retrieving a few special things from her office," he explained to Raven.

"Like what?"

"Arabel's teapot and the rugs," Lara mumbled. "I feel foolish wanting those things, but Trev brought those rugs back from Pakistan and Arabel... Never mind. It's okay. I'll get by fine without them."

Relief filled Trevor. He hadn't relished the thought of setting foot in her office again, even for so simple a task as rolling up rugs. Despite no longer being the slightest bit hungry, he pecked dutifully at his pancakes. Since food was scarce, and likely to get even more so, leaving anything uneaten on his plate was unthinkable.

CHAPTER 15

The afternoon fairly sped by. Lara convinced Raven to let her take the BMW, rather than driving with Trevor in the Ford. "Look," she argued. "If we have to get everything into this one load, we need both cars. We'll be leaving lots behind as it is."

Trevor pulled both vehicles into the back yard, and they spent the waning hours of daylight stuffing things into them. The rain didn't help matters. Even though Trevor backed the truck up as far as he could toward the back porch—under the overhang provided by the upper stories of their house—rain still blew under the tarp and got the things they were piling into the truck's bed wet. Lara had wanted to bring their mattress, but decided it was too bulky and would likely be ruined if it became soaked. "If we take it," she told Trevor, "there won't be room for a bunch of other things." Nodding blearily, he went off in search of another load.

They hadn't planned it that way, but she spent the day sorting her things, while he did the same with his. The gold and cash from their safe went into the BMW, along with what foodstuffs they had left. At some point during the afternoon, Lara sat down, preparing to call her remaining patients, but Lillian shook a finger at her. Laying the cell phone aside, Lara asked, "Why not?"

"Because it's better if no one has any idea you're leaving."

Lara chafed at that. It went against her training and ethics to abandon her patients. *Seems like a small thing, what with the world imploding, but damn it anyway, I don't like the way this feels.*

Someone made tuna sandwiches using the crackers left over from their wedding dinner. Lara ate on the fly in between lugging items downstairs. The food could have been cardboard, she wouldn't have noticed. At last, there truly wasn't any more room left in either car. It had been a challenge maintaining enough seat space for the puppy to curl up next to Trevor. As it was, the dog would be half on Trevor's lap for the journey.

"When will we see you next?" Lara asked, making a strong effort to relax her tense muscles. "It's tomorrow night we're supposed to go after Adriana, isn't it."

"Told you she'd remember." Lillian looked meaningfully at Raven.

"I didn't doubt it for a moment," he replied dourly. "If things go well, child, we shall be at the farm when you get there."

"And if they don't?" Trevor quirked an eyebrow at the mage.

"In that case," Lillian answered for Raven, "We shall be there as soon as we can."

"If things seem more settled in the small communities off Highway Two, do you suppose it would be all right if we stopped for more fuel and whatever food we might find?" Bracing herself for his disapproval, Lara walked up to Raven, hands on her hips.

"The wisest course is to not stop for anything," Raven said quietly. "You won't need gasoline. If you remember my earlier instructions, once you're at the farm, you won't be leaving. Everything you need is there. If it isn't, one of us can see to it."

"Even if we did stop, where would we put so much as a tin of cookies?" Trevor threw up his hands, curved his fingers, and pulled them through his disorderly hair. Lara could tell how tired he was by the gesture.

"I should call Brad," Lara said, culling through her memory for loose ends. "It would be good to let him know we're at least trying to bring Adie back."

"No!" Raven thundered. "Not a good idea at all. If the goddess smiles upon us and we have luck, I will tell him then. Other than that, he can't know what we're about."

"But he knows we're going to try to rescue her," Lara protested, feeling bewildered.

"Yes," Raven replied evenly. "But he doesn't know when. And that is where we shall leave this topic."

Lillian walked far enough out from under the porch overhang to peer up at the darkening sky. After a few deep breaths, she raised her arms and began to chant. Lara felt her amulet pick up the pitch and timbre of the Gaelic as it rolled off Lillian's tongue. *Must be the protection spell,* she surmised. *It's the only thing left.*

Standing in the yard of her well-beloved home, Lara felt sad beyond words. Knowing she didn't really want to leave, she felt bereft. She tried telling herself she was being silly. That it was only a house. In her heart of hearts, she knew better. A sudden tat-a-tat of gunfire shocked her out of her spate of self-pity. "Jesus," she muttered. "That sounded awfully close."

"It was," Lillian said, dropping her arms to her sides. "I don't know what you think," she looked at Raven, "but I believe it's far too dangerous for them to leave, at least right now. Whatever charms we cast will only stretch so far."

"I don't like this." He spat in the dirt of the yard and made a curious sign with three fingers of one hand. "But you're correct. We must wait until the worst of this turbulence blows itself out. Or at least until there's a break."

He trudged across the sodden yard to wrap lengths of heavy wire attached to a padlock around the halves of the back gate. Lara tried to do a better job securing the sopping tarp over the back of the pickup, but Trevor shooed her away. "Just lock up your car, Lara, and go inside. Might be best to keep the lights out. We'll be better off if no one thinks there's anybody home."

~

THE FOUR OF them were settled on the floor in the living room in front of the unlit hearth eating cheese and crackers and drinking wine. The house was warm enough, and Raven concurred with Trevor that the less indication anybody might be home, the better.

Earlier, Lillian had pawed through the empty pantry, coming up with a wheel of cheese that had been shoved to the back, and a long-since-forgotten box of Triscuits. Trevor had fished a bottle of merlot out of the wine rack.

Knowing he might not pour any for her, Lara asked Lillian about the advisability of drinking anything alcoholic, and the Sidhe looked at her as if she'd lost her mind. "Back in my youth," she advised confidentially, "if mothers-to-be didn't drink spirits, they'd have had precious little to drink at all. The water in Europe, and what's now the United Kingdom, was far more dangerous than the wine."

"Perspective is everything," Lara muttered, reaching for the glass Trevor poured for her. She was just beginning on her third cracker with a thick slice of half-moldy cheddar when the doorbell rang and the puppy, who'd been begging cheese scraps, barked like mad and raced for the door.

"Pup's getting braver," she noted, adding, "Wonder who that could possibly be?"

Raven, who'd said little during their meal, stopped staring into space for long enough to murmur, "It's the detective."

Trevor pushed himself upright. "I'll go let him in," he said, shooting a questioning glance at Raven and Lillian. "I'd like to, since he pretty much saved my bacon last night."

"Go ahead." Raven made shooing motions with both hands. "Just watch what you say. Both of you."

"I'll go too." Lara got to her feet and trotted after Trevor's retreating form.

After checking through the peephole, Trevor pulled the door open. "You look frightful, old man. Come in, come in. Would you like something to eat? How about a shower? Power's on so we've plenty of hot water."

Brad blinked wearily. "Maybe in a bit. I was close, so I thought I'd stop to make sure the both of you were surviving. Didn't see either of your cars, so I wasn't even sure you were here." He paused, coughing. "Damned smoke," he growled. "Gets into everything. Even with a respirator, it hasn't been particularly easy to breathe in some places."

"Jesus, Brad." Lara narrowed her eyes. "You look like hell." She took in his filthy, ripped clothes with stains that looked like a combination of soot and blood. Black streaks ran down his face, and his blond hair had darkened considerably. One cheekbone was bruised, and his left hand was wrapped in a blood-stained bandage.

The detective smiled crookedly. "Thanks. At least I'm still alive. Lots aren't."

"To answer your question," Trevor said. "I moved the cars into the backyard. Thought they'd be safer off the street."

"Good move." The detective nodded approvingly.

"Would you like a shower?" Lara repeated Trevor's suggestion.

"Not much point, since I don't have anything to change into."

"I've got clothes that would fit you," Trevor offered.

Nodding thoughtfully, the detective said, "Okay, maybe it would perk me up a bit. Technically, I'm still on duty, but there's no one at the station house right now to call me on the radio. Whoever's left is out on patrol to make up for everyone who's been killed. Do you have any coffee?"

"I'll make some while you're cleaning up," Lara said.

Half an hour later, Brad joined them in the living room, a cup of steaming black coffee in hand. "Helped myself." He pointed at the cup with his free hand. "Hope that was all right." Sitting on the edge of one of the sofas, he pulled a cracker out of the open box. "I remember you two from the other night. You in particular." He half-smiled at Lillian. "But I never got either of your names."

Lara glanced at Raven and Lillian. Would they make up names, use their own, or just not answer?

"I am called Raven, and her name is Lillian."

Brad swiveled to look at Lara. "Say, I must've been pretty befuddled not to notice, but you're all banged up. Your face looks worse than mine. Judging from the color of those bruises, they must've been there last night when I was here. What happened to you?"

Heart racing, Lara turned toward Raven, all too aware of her bruised and lacerated face.

I can't answer that. Not honestly. It would be hell for him to think of his daughter in that horrid place.

"What you really want to know," Raven said silkily, as he went to stand next to Brad, "is who else was here last night."

Scarcely missing a beat, Brad asked, "Who was the other woman who took part in what we did outside?"

"Elidora. And the other man who was here, his name is Gren," Lara said, trying to keep her voice steady. Raven—who'd faded back to his seat as soon as Brad began talking again—had obviously done something. The mindless ease with which he could exert control over others was unnerving.

Thrusting about for a different conversational topic, she asked, "Can you tell us anything about the riot? We picked up some information off the Internet, but you've been out in the thick of things. Unless you'd rather not," she finished lamely, realizing too late Brad might want a break from whatever he'd dealt with the past twenty-four hours.

He sighed heavily. "It's far worse than what's come up on the news." He munched another cracker. His forehead crinkled in thought, and the corners of his mouth twisted downward. "The Governor put a gag order on the press around three a.m. People were absolutely panic-stricken, which was making things worse. Hordes of them got it into their heads to run somewhere, so there were impossible traffic snarls on top of everything else, and hundreds more dead from accidents. People got out of their cars and shot other drivers who were in their way."

"Does it seem to be settling down?" Trevor asked, his voice carefully neutral.

Yes, we would like to know that, wouldn't we, Lara thought, watching the detective closely.

"It was for a bit, but there's been a resurgence in the past hour or so. Not sure why, exactly. Smart of you to move the cars and keep the lights out, though. No point in calling attention to the fact you're in here. By the way, where are the other two?" he asked, taking a healthy slug of his coffee. "Elidora and Gren."

"They went to my house before the worst of things began last night," Lillian replied. "I've been anxious about them, but I think they're safer staying there than trying to come back here."

"Have you spoken with them?" Brad asked, sounding concerned.

"Yes, we have." Raven jumped into the conversation. "They're fine."

"I'd be glad to run by and check on them," the detective persisted. "Or I could find a car in that vicinity and have someone else do that."

Lillian glided to where Brad sat and settled next to him. Leaning close, she said softly, "It shouldn't shock you that my house is special. You couldn't find it, even if you looked."

A corner of Brad's mouth twitched. "Why am I not surprised by that?" he asked. Setting down his coffee, he reached for more crackers and a slice of cheese. "You haven't heard anything more about Adie?" he asked.

The question was casual, but Lara heard desperation beneath the simple words, and her heart ached for him. *That's really why he stopped by here. He's still hoping against hope to get his girl back.*

"We did seek information." Raven spoke carefully. "As yet, nothing has surfaced for us to follow up on."

The detective's face fell, and Lara knew he'd been hoping there'd be some news. She practically bit through her tongue to stop herself from telling him that Adie was in a place where they could still conceivably rescue her.

Looking over at Raven, she heard his voice in her mind, *"Be silent, child."* The amulet agreed with the mage, since it sounded a warning where it lay against her skin.

"I do understand what you said, about seeking information." Brad looked plaintively at Raven. "But isn't there anything more we could be doing?"

"Not at the moment," the mage replied. "Please trust we're doing all we can."

"How?" The word burst from Brad. His blue eyes raked mercilessly over each of them in turn. "You're all here, and she's somewhere else. Are there others like you searching for her?"

"Yes." Raven shifted his gray eyes to Brad's blue ones. "There are. I know you would rather it were otherwise, but this is not for you to understand. She's moved beyond where you can reach her."

A tear formed in the corner of one of Brad's eyes and rolled slowly down his stubble-covered cheek. "How's your wife doing?" Lara asked softly.

"A bit better," he said sadly. "At least she's not sedated twenty-four seven anymore. I had a hunch the riots were going to worsen, so yesterday I packed her off in the car to her sister's house in Wenatchee." He hesitated. "She texted me she got there, so at least she's out of the worst of things."

"Is Seattle the hardest hit?" Lara was curious.

Brad nodded. "So far as we can tell, it's the only place in Washington where things are anywhere near this tense. There's still food everywhere else, except Tacoma, but we count that as part of the greater Seattle area." Glancing at his watch, he drained the last of his coffee. "Thanks for the shower and the clothes. I'll bring 'em back once I've had a chance to wash them."

"Don't worry about it." Trevor smiled warmly. "After last night, it's the least I can do."

Brad got to his feet. "I need to push off. I'm worried. My radio hasn't transmitted anything at all in the time I've been here. It runs off satellites in emergencies, and you wouldn't think there'd be anything wrong with them. At least not yet."

Lara plucked her cell off a nearby end table, noting the battery was getting low, but signal strength was good. "Have you checked your phone?" she asked.

He pulled it out from the pocket of one of Trevor's flannel shirts, peering at the screen. "Good idea," he muttered. "I've got messages up the yin yang here. Wonder why it didn't ring?" Pushing buttons, he held the device to his ear. As he listened, his face became grave. After a few more minutes, he did some fiddling, and then dropped the phone back into his pocket.

"Well?" Lara gazed at him.

"The easy part is it didn't ring because I'd inadvertently shut off the alerts. It does seem things are quieter, but there's a real mess on the University campus. I'm headed there now, but I'll check back as soon as I can."

"Try to get some sleep," she said, worried about the black smudges beneath his eyes.

"Hah! Feels like I'll never sleep again. Every time I shut my eyes, all I see is Adie's face."

"I'll call you if I find out anything," Lara said, feeling perfectly rotten she couldn't say more. "Be safe out there."

"Walk you to the door," Trevor offered.

The University, she thought. *My students. None of them live on campus, but I hope they're all safe.* Knowing she'd never see any of them again, she sent up a prayer for someone to watch over them. By the time Trevor came back into the living room, Raven was on his feet and so was Lillian.

"It's time for you two to leave," Raven said. "I can feel it. Lillian—"

"On my way," she cut in and walked toward the back door, probably to restructure her protection spell. Stopping in the doorway, she gestured to Raven. "You should be there too," she reminded him. "I need the masculine half of the energy to make this as strong as I can."

"Just a minute," Lara said from her spot on the floor. "A couple more seconds here shouldn't matter one whit. Why couldn't we tell him where Adriana was?"

"Because he wouldn't have understood," Raven said, more kindly than Lara expected. "He would've assumed that if we knew where his daughter was located, we should be there moving heaven and earth to free her. He wouldn't have accepted Brigid's instruction to wait until tomorrow evening."

"Nor are we supposed to reveal any more than is absolutely necessary to humans about our existence," Lillian added briskly. "Is that enough, dear?"

"I suppose so," Lara said, still unhappy about being less than straightforward with the detective.

"Look, love, I like him too. And I do feel sorry for him. But he came very close to selling you out." Trevor held out both hands to help her to her feet. "Are you sure you have what you want? Looks as if we're almost gone from here."

No, I don't have everything I want. I want to stay here with my books and my familiar things. I want to be able to call my patients back. They reached out to me. I'd like to be able to help them.

"Yeah, Trev. I've pretty much got what I can't live without. Even if I did come up with something else, there's not any space for it." Feeling morose and very, very sorry for herself, she reached for Trevor and let him pull her up.

Once she was on her feet, he gathered the remains of the crackers and cheese. "We'll take this with us," he said, giving her a handful of Triscuits and slicing what was left of the cheese. "Half for you and half for me. Dinner was on the skimpy side."

"What about all the wine we're leaving here?"

He shrugged. "As you said, there's not much more room, and somehow the rest of the wine didn't feel as important as the things we brought. I did toss in better than a dozen bottles—"

"Lara!" Raven's voice thundered through the house.

Hastening outside, with Trevor and Gunter right behind, she noticed someone had opened the back gate. "You have to leave *now*," Lillian said briskly. "The window is closing."

"What window?" Lara asked, mystified.

"No time," Raven snapped. "I will answer that when I see you next. Now, go." He opened her car door and shoved her inside, closing the door firmly as soon as she had both legs in. Out of the corner of her eye, she saw Trevor boost Gunter into the cab of the Ford. Reaching down, she tapped the ignition and guided the car toward the open gate, feeling its tires skid on the rain-soaked grass.

CHAPTER 16

*L*ara waited until Trevor backed the Ford into the alleyway. When she got out of her car to latch the gate, Raven was already there shooing her away. "Goddess blast it, woman. I told you to leave. Lillian and I will close things up here. We'll ward the place too. That should make it more-or-less invisible to marauders."

Knowing it would be pointless to argue, Lara hopped back into the BMW. What she really wanted was to sneak back into the house, curl up on her wonderfully soft bed, and sleep for the next week. The amulet began a variation of its chiding vibration, subsiding into neutrality once she was safely in the car again.

As she drove down the steep, narrow alley, her thoughts turned to what she might find in the world outside the haven of her home. *Humph! House wasn't much of a refuge for Trevor while I was gone.* The muscles in her neck and shoulders tightened almost to the point of spasm, and she forced herself to relax her death grip on the steering wheel.

She and Trevor hadn't discussed a route, so she hit the single digit on her cell to speed dial his phone. He picked up immediately and asked, "Is something wrong?"

"Yes, everything. I didn't like being shoved out of my home."

"If you called to grouse, can it wait until we get out of town?" He sounded exasperated, and she understood he was just as stressed as she. Maybe more, since he hadn't had her respite in the *Dreaming*.

"Never mind. It's not important. Which way we should go?"

"I just turned on the local AM station. They'll have a traffic update momentarily. Unless the roads are blocked, let's take I-5 until we get to State Route Two," he said in a slightly softer tone.

"That's what I thought," she agreed. "Should I listen to the radio too?"

"You don't have to. If anything changes, I'll call you. We'll have cell service until just past Skykomish. Be sure to plug your phone in, though. When I looked at it last, it was close to dead."

"Right you are," she said sheepishly, glancing at her battery indicator. "Be careful, Trev. We don't know what we're going to find out here."

"You too, love."

After manipulating the small charger head into her phone, Lara tried to relax against her multi-position leather seat. She fooled with some of the adjustments before realizing the discomfort she felt wasn't the seat's fault. A glance out the windshield told her she was almost to the freeway onramp.

As she braked for a light, she caught movement at the edge of her vision and realized someone had run up next to her car. A man shouted at her through the glass. When she ignored him, he grasped her door handle and pulled hard on it, rocking the heavy car. Lara's heart thudded in her throat, and it was hard to swallow. Her stomach twisted sourly, shooting bile into her mouth until she was afraid she was going to be sick. A fist banged against her window. She willed the light to change before he exchanged it for a rock or a brick.

Her phone rang, startling her further, and she remembered Trevor right behind her. She'd no sooner pressed the answer key when he shouted, "Gun it, before I have to get out and shoot the bastard. We're the only cars on the road."

She hit the accelerator so hard she was thrown back against her seat. She heard a shriek—or maybe it was a curse—from outside her window. Slowing only enough to check for cross traffic, she ran another light. The last one before the freeway. Remembering Trevor on the cell, she picked up her phone with shaking fingers and asked, "You still there?"

"Uh-huh. Bloody blazes, why'd you just sit there?" His voice was shrill, the accent so broad the words tumbled into one another. "There were three more right behind him, running toward your car for all they were worth. I kept thinking you'd take off, but you sat there like a fucking nitwit."

"I—I was waiting for the light," she finally managed, feeling intimidated and stupid in the face of his anger.

After a long silence, he muttered, "Sorry. Old habits die hard."

She nodded, and then realized he couldn't see her. "Yeah, I'm sorry too. When he grabbed the door handle and started rocking the car, I felt paralyzed."

"Didn't that amulet-thing warn you?"

Reaching up to touch it, she said, "No. It mostly reacts to magic or if I'm in serious trouble because of magic. That man who wanted my car—or me, or both of us—must've been human, not a Demon like Gradoxst."

Trevor blew out an uneasy breath. "We should be all right until we exit near Monroe. The traffic report didn't indicate any closures on our route."

"Are there other places where the roads are closed?"

"Yes, lots." He paused for a beat. "Are you… Do you think you can manage…?"

"If you're asking can I drive from here to Monroe," she said briskly, "the answer is yes. Look, I got rattled. I'm not used to people jumping the car I'm in." *Just like I wasn't used to being accosted on the porch of my office building,* she reflected, thinking of when Ken Beauchamp had lain in wait for her with a gun in one hand and his dick in the other.

"Okay. I'm going to ring off then." Trevor's British accent was very proper this time. "If it seems quiet past Monroe, perhaps we might stop long enough for Gunter to run about for a bit."

"I love you," she said, wanting to lessen the tension between them.

"Love you too, Lara. Next time, if there is one, for Christ's sake, look about you."

She was going to tell him she would, but he'd disconnected. Careful to not dislodge the phone's charger, she slid it into its usual place in the console, set her cruise control for sixty-five, and tried for music on the radio. Unable to find anything she wanted to listen to, she rustled around for a compact disc, settling for Maria Callas clips from various operas.

As she drove, listening to Callas's haunting soprano, Lara thought about what she and Trevor were doing and why. And she thought about Arabel, who was supposed to have come with them. Her heart ached, as she called up an image of the eighty-something-year-old African-American. Arabel had tended far more than her garden. She'd cared for Lara as well, shoring her up after difficult patient sessions and always standing by with just the right piece of pithy advice.

A sharecropper's daughter, she'd made her way out of the Deep South as a young woman, working nights in a fast food outlet so she could attend secretarial school. When Lara had first hung out her shingle, she'd done all her own receptionist work for the first couple years. When it finally seemed she could afford to hire help, she'd dropped an ad in the Seattle Times, and Arabel had called the very next day.

Lara still remembered Arabel's soft southern drawl when she'd offered to *jus run on up an' meet you whenever you'd like.* Lara had hedged, thinking it might be best to schedule several interviews, when Arabel added, "I'm not doin' anythin' right now. How's about if I drop by 'round about five or six? When you done for the day, hon?"

Because it felt right, Lara agreed to meet at seven. The minute Arabel's gnarled, work-hardened hand had gripped hers, Lara knew she and the older woman would be a good match. The business side of her brain urged her to conduct an actual interview, but instead they'd talked of inconsequentials—jus gettin' to know one another, as Arabel would've said—until her phone rang an hour later with Trevor wanting to know where she was.

Lara smiled at the memory. Arabel had shown up at the dot of eight the following morning, taking over the office with all the energy of a doting mother. Once managed care had come into play, the outspoken old woman had become a force to be reckoned with, and Lara had been pleasantly surprised to find she didn't have nearly the issues with collections that many of her colleagues complained of.

"And now all that's over with," Lara murmured as she sped down the mostly-empty freeway. She hadn't exactly been counting, but she was sure she'd seen less than twenty cars since getting on the expressway. "No more office, no more Arabel, no more patients, no more students. Who in the hell am I now?"

Well, an inexorable inner voice offered. *I'm who I've always have been: me.*

"Wonder if that's going to be good enough," she answered herself and considered the shreds of life taking root within her and the unfamiliar path of parenthood stretching out ahead. She shook her head, feeling worried, and braked hard to slide into the right hand exit lane she'd almost missed.

She'd just turned right, when Trevor's name flashed on her ringing phone. "Hi dear," she said more cheerfully than she felt.

"It looks pretty quiet all in all," he observed. "I'm going to take a chance and stop for petrol, if I can find an open station."

"Raven said not to," she protested.

"I know what he said," Trevor cut in. "I also know he told us we shouldn't ever leave the farm once we get there, but that doesn't feel practical to me. So I'd like to at least try to fill the tanks. We may never want to leave, but it's good to have options. What if we need something, and Lillian or Raven haven't stopped by in a while?"

"Do you want to be in front?" she asked, not wanting to debate the advisability of crossing Raven.

"Yes. I'm pulling around you just now. Don't worry. I can keep near as close an eye on you from my side mirrors as I could from the front. Assuming I find an open station, it's best if only one of us gets out of their cars at a time. That way, the other one can make a run for it if something unexpected happens."

Jesus. He sounds wiped out. "Sure, Trev. Whatever you want."

"I have the shotgun." He hesitated. "It's loaded and on the floorboards next to me."

She didn't know what to say, so she just murmured, "Bye," and hung up.

It's come to this, she thought, sadly. *We can't even drive two hours in the middle of the United States without a loaded weapon.*

Trevor found an open Shell station. The only hitch was that gas was more than twelve dollars a gallon. They left over four hundred dollars with the smiling cashier. Lara was just getting back into her car when a dark sedan flashed past, teasing the edges of her vision. She turned to stare, since it was the first car she'd seen since exiting the Interstate, but it was gone before she got a good look at it. Figuring it was safe to have a brief chat with Trevor; she pushed her door back open and walked to the Ford.

Trevor rolled down his window, eyebrows furled. "You've something in mind. What is it?"

"It seems safe enough here, and I see a grocery store about half a block down." She gestured toward a flashing neon sign proclaiming *Buster's Fine Foods.* "Since we managed a fuel stop without incident, do you suppose we might pick up a few things from that store too?"

"You're as bad as I am, love. What if Raven's waiting for us, sees the grocery bags, and turns us both into snails?"

"I'll risk it," she mumbled grimly. Walking toward the roadway, she peered more closely at the market. "Parking lot's well lighted," she announced. "I think we should go for it. Might be the last milk and butter we see that aren't the byproducts of our own labor."

Half an hour later, they crammed a dozen overflowing shopping bags into their cars, cursing and rearranging as they went. Lara walked the puppy while Trevor made the final adjustments that made everything fit well enough to at least close the doors. They hadn't been particularly discriminating, simply tossing things that looked good into their cart as they moved up and down the aisles in the deserted grocery store. They'd bought most of the fresh produce lining the depleted fruit and vegetable displays and more of the same in cans, despite Trevor's protests.

"Well, we can't buy frozen," she'd argued. "No freezer.

"Nice job," she said, handing him the puppy's leash. "I really didn't think there'd even be room for one sack, let alone everything we bought."

"Thanks. I was motivated." Trevor offered her a lopsided smile. "I'm sure we'll work our way through all of it in short order and wish there was more."

"Bye, dear. See you at Raven's in an hour or so." Blowing him a kiss, she returned to her car, hit the clicker to unlock it, and latched her seatbelt. As she nosed onto the highway, she saw another dark-colored car, wondered if it could possibly be the same one she'd seen at the gas station, and then decided she was being ridiculous.

If anyone was following us, they'd have jumped us at the gas station or leaving the market. My imagination's working overtime.

In no time at all, they crossed over the Skykomish River and turned onto the deserted dirt road leading to Garland Mineral Springs. Their journey through the small towns between Monroe and Skykomish was absolutely uneventful, and she'd seen any number of places where they could have fueled up or purchased provisions. Lara felt the same sense of peace she always did when the ancient old-growth forest closed around her. She set her odometer to clock the twenty miles before the side road that turned off to Raven's.

Her thoughts were a kaleidoscope of contrasting issues as she mourned losses from the life she was leaving. Even the incredibly banal things, like her early morning runs and the hours sitting in her therapy chair, called out to her. She knew at a bone deep level how much she'd miss everything.

The other side of her mind filled with uncertainties about whether they'd be able to transition to an agrarian existence. Somewhere around mile twelve, she made a concerted effort to stop thinking. Her innate tendency to be wary of the unknown was fucking with her head, and she pushed the button that would bring Maria Callas's voice back into her car. Lara relaxed into love scenes from La Bohème.

She switched off her cell phone—one modern device she wouldn't miss at all—after verifying it was beyond the reach of any tower. Before she knew it, she turned onto the short road to the farm, following Trevor's tail lights. Pulling to a stop in front of the log house, she was momentarily nonplussed to see Raven and Lillian come through the front door, lanterns in hand and broad smiles on their faces. Lara stepped out of the BMW a bit tentatively. *I don't suppose they'll still be smiling when they see all our groceries.*

"You made it." Raven's ageless face radiated relief. "Thank the goddess." He scooped Lara up in a bear hug. Letting go of her, he pumped Trevor's hand.

"Yes, when you stopped in Monroe, we really held our breaths." Lillian laughed, sounding like a schoolgirl. "And Raven, well he—"

"Silence, woman," Raven growled, shooting Lillian a stern look.

Good. They already know. Saves a bunch of explanations.

Lara stepped into Lillian's outstretched arms, grateful for the warmth of another hug. Gunter jumped and barked, wanting to be in Lillian's arms as well. Looking over Lillian's shoulder, Lara saw that Raven had draped an avuncular arm about Trevor's shoulders. The two men talked animatedly.

When the greetings died down, Raven asked, "Do you want to bring things in tonight, or would you rather wait until tomorrow? I know the groceries need to be unpacked, but..."

Lara looked at Trevor, who shrugged. "I'd like to do a spot of unpacking," he said finally. "Especially since Raven's already tended to all the critters. It'd get the kinks out from the drive, and a few other things too."

Turning to Raven, he asked, "If you know about Monroe, do you also know what happened before we left Seattle?"

"No," the mage replied. He scrunched his brows together, looking concerned. "You'll have to tell me. I do know that someone tried to follow you here, though."

"Yes," Lillian concurred. "Stopping in Monroe actually turned out to be a good thing, since it gave us time to employ diversionary measures."

CHAPTER 17

"So there *was* someone there," Lara exclaimed, telling them about the dark-colored car she'd seen skulking about Monroe. "Why on earth would anybody want to know where we were going?" And then she thought about the nameless stranger who'd tried to break into her car in the middle of Mercer Street. "Guess they wouldn't have to know anything about us," she said thoughtfully, as she pulled grocery sacks out of the back of the BMW. "Just the fact we've got cars with gasoline in them—that are obviously stuffed to the gunnels—would be enough to attract attention."

"Why do you think I've been dogging the two of you to wrap things up and get out here?" Sounding beleaguered, Raven grabbed armloads of grocery and clothing sacks. "Other than the food, you can sort things out later," he called over his shoulder as he loped up the broad front steps. "I'm just going to drop your belongings in the living room."

"Merciful it's a good-sized space," Trevor mumbled, pushing past her with an armload of his own. The resurgence of his dry humor heartened Lara. It had been a while since she'd heard him joke about anything.

Lillian came over with her hands extended, and Lara pointed to the remaining grocery sacks. "Mmm." Lillian breathed appreciatively. "Basil and chives. And avocados." Poking at them, she said, "We'll need to eat that one right away. Maybe I'll get something going in the kitchen while the three of you haul things in. We'll just end up tripping over one another otherwise."

"Can you take him with you?" Lara asked, gesturing toward Gunter who was tearing about like a mad thing, barking and biting at the air.

"Certainly, child." Lillian made a clicking noise and the exuberant dog fell in at her heels.

Lara watched them go, before turning to drag more things out. Rather than picking and choosing what to take first, she decided to work her way from back to front. She rather liked Raven's philosophy about sorting through things later. After all, it'd be easier when they had something other than kerosene lanterns providing illumination.

An almost-full moon peeked from behind some clouds, streaking the grassy yard with a luminescent glow. Lara decided it was a good omen and shuffled toward the steps with a box of books balanced between her outstretched arms. Trevor and Raven had made several trips while she lollygagged next to her car. When she passed the Ford, she saw they'd made quite a dent in its contents. *Maybe this won't take so long after all,* she mused, chucked her box, and went back for another.

True to her word, Lillian took over the kitchen. Long before they were done unpacking the vehicles, a rich aroma filled the old lodge, making Lara's mouth water. Someone had lit a fire as well. Seeing the blaze in the stone hearth, Lara blushed as she remembered the last time she'd lain in front of that fireplace. Pausing for a heartbeat, she laid a hand over her midsection and smiled softly.

Lillian moved to her side. She placed a hand over Lara's and searched her eyes. "The conception was sweet. I can tell. That means a hearty babe. It's propitious it happened here. That means this is where you're meant to be." Lara felt Lillian dig deep enough to inspect her soul before she chuckled and moved her hand. "Run along, dear. Supper's all set whenever the lot of you are ready to come eat it."

"How do you do that?" Lara asked, still feeling Lillian's presence within her. "It's sort of like my aura-reading, but ever so much more."

The other woman just smiled. "Hurry," she admonished. "Wouldn't want to have to heat everything up again."

On her way back out the door, Lara stepped to the side to avoid running into Raven and Trevor. "You don't need to go back out there," Trevor panted. "This is the last of it."

"Okay, I'll just close everything up," she offered, sprinting down the steps. She felt light-hearted, the anxiety and stress of the past few days fading into a far corner of her mind. As she plucked the keys from both vehicles, pushed the truck's tailgate back up and shut her car doors, she was amazed by how buoyant she felt.

I should be exhausted. Must be this place or Raven and Lillian. Or maybe it's the combination that's so invigorating.

The early part of dinner was quiet with everyone eating eagerly. Lillian had sautéed fresh vegetables together with herbs, made a pan-fried version of cornbread, and grilled the lamb chops from Buster's Market. "A veritable feast," Lara beamed. "My favorite meals are those I don't have to cook."

"Yes, those are everyone else's favorites as well," Trevor commented *sotto voce*.

Elbowing him, Lara glanced at Raven. "What did you mean about a window closing?" she asked curiously, taking another bite of vegetables.

"First, why don't you tell me what happened when you were leaving Seattle?" Raven said. "Maybe it'll shed light on what we sensed in Monroe."

"How far away can you sense things?" Trevor looked up from his meal, interest flaring from his eyes.

"It depends," Raven answered. Lara waited, since she was fascinated by the mage's magic, but he didn't say anything further.

"On what?" Trevor asked after chewing and swallowing another mouthful.

Lillian snorted. "You humans are just so literal. Even if he answered your question, you'd find it difficult to understand. Basically, the practitioner's level of power interacts with Earth energy and astrological forces. If we have enemies about, things become far more difficult." A wry expression turned one corner of her mouth downward. "The fear-fueled passion from widespread unrest—like what you just fled from—often gives us an additional boost."

"You feed off civil disorder?" Trevor sounded incredulous as he reached for a mug to take a hefty swallow of wine. "Just like the Demons?"

"We can," Lillian corrected sternly. "Just because we can doesn't mean we always do. In fact," she smiled benignly, "we're rarely so crass. Unlike dark practitioners, who welcome such events."

Raven pounded the butt of his knife on the wooden table top, startling the puppy. He whined sleepily from a braided rug in front of the stove. "None of this is relevant," Raven snapped. "You have yet to answer my question." He glared at Trevor. "Worse, you haven't been shy about asking a bevy of your own."

"Okay. Okay." Trevor sounded mildly defensive. "I was just making conversation. Is that a lost art among you?" Pinned by Raven's gray gaze, Trevor studied his lap and stammered, "The problem happened just before we got to the freeway. Lara was stopped at a light and this guy in sweats raced to her car. I couldn't see his face because he had his hood up and he was facing away from me, but he was big. Tall and broad, built like a linebacker.

"If her door hadn't been locked, I'm sure he would've yanked her out of her seat, jumped in, and taken off. Oh yeah, and he had accomplices. They were a goodly way behind him, but they would've gotten there soon enough. Looked like they had baseball bats."

Lara winced. He hadn't told her about the bats. Had she been only seconds away from having her windows smashed out? A wave of nausea battered her, and she dropped her head onto her chest and shut her eyes, willing it to pass so she could finish her meal.

"So the light changed in time?" Raven asked, looking at Lara, an odd note in his tone.

"No, not exactly." Heat rose in her face. "Trev called me and told me to step on it. He was right," she hurried on. "There weren't any other cars. I was just so scared I wasn't thinking."

"Humph." The mage made a noise between a snort and a grunt.

"Where were you when that was happening?" Trevor asked, still focused on Raven.

"We'd probably not even left your house yet," Lillian answered.

"Then you were certainly close enough. Why didn't you—?" Trevor began.

"It's not a matter of distance, but of attention," Raven growled. "We were setting wards about your house. I considered it a waste of time, but she," he pointed at Lillian, "thought it might be a deterrent the next time that detective shows up. When we're working on one task, the odds of another snaring our attention go down."

"I need to learn more about what I can do," Lara announced. The surge of vertigo was short-lived and she began eating again.

"That you do," Raven concurred. "When would you like to begin?"

"How about now?" she countered. "Just as soon as I'm done with the rest of what's on my plate." Glancing at Trevor, she added, "He'll kill me if I don't eat better. I've already gotten the first and second lectures in that series."

"But Lara," he protested, looking injured, "you've got to think of—" He broke off with a hangdog grin "Och aye," he said, aping Elidora's accent. "And ye were but teasin' me, eh lassie?"

Lara raised a hand to her lips and blew a kiss his way.

"What happened to the book you were supposed to be reading?" Lillian gathered dishes, carrying them to the sink. She pumped the handle for water, said, "Brrr," and rummaged in a stack of cookware for a pot. As Lara watched, the Sidhe stirred the pot with an index finger before dumping dishes into it.

"Did you make it warm?" Lara asked, fascinated. "If that's what you were doing, it's the first thing I want to learn." She hesitated, and then turned to Raven. "Didn't you say there was some sort of heating mechanism in the spring house?"

"I did," he concurred. "It needs repairs. Runs off solar, and several of the panels are broken. Once upon a time, there was electricity out here—"

"The book, child?" Lillian broke in, shooting Raven an exasperated look.

"I suppose it's in there somewhere." Lara waved expansively toward the other end of the large room spanning the entire first floor.

"Mmph," Raven muttered and stood. Hands outspread, he wandered among the stacks of belongings, stopping to pull the volume in question out from under bags stuffed with clothing. He dropped it in front of Lara with a *splat*.

"I want to learn to do that too," she said, smiling at him. "It's like a dowsing rod for lost things. It certainly would save a lot of time."

"Are you sure you're not too tired for magic practice?" Trevor asked, his face scrunched into concerned lines. "There's always tomorrow."

"Actually, I'm feeling better than I did when we left our house," she said. "How about you?"

Trevor shut his eyes, as if he were taking an internal inventory. "I do too," he admitted, sounding surprised. "Of course I felt perfectly wretched when we finally left the house, so anything would be an improvement." He grinned at her, and a ghost of his boyish good looks resurfaced. "I was certain I'd fall on my face the second we got here, but I've actually got enough starch left to do a few more things."

"Excellent." Raven nodded. "You can go to work out there." He hooked a thumb at the piles in the living room. "I'll light some lanterns so you can see what you're doing. While you're about that, Lillian and I will give Lara her first lesson. The pregnancy will ease things. It's one of those boosts Lillian referred to earlier."

"You won't do anything that might harm our child." A frown

creased Trevor's forehead, and he shoved too-long blond curls out of his face.

Raven shook his head. "We want that child too," he said. "In many ways, as much as you." Air whistled through his pursed lips. "Sometimes unexpected things happen, without direct intervention from us. I never would've thought to tell you to dredge up Elidora's love charm, yet you thought of it on your own. Or perhaps the goddess guided your hand. Regardless of how it came about, the child who's been waiting in the wings, and for years, mind you, saw her opportunity and heeded the call."

Guiltily, Lara thought about all the variations of birth control she'd used. Pills, intrauterine devices, cervical caps. She'd only stopped using her diaphragm about the time Lillian warded their house after one of her earliest visits.

"What's past is past." Raven laid a hand over hers. "Looks as if Lillian's about finished with most of the dishes. Are you ready?"

Well, am I?

She reminded herself that she'd asked for this. "Yes," she replied. "I've been ready for a long time. I just didn't know it."

Trevor walked over and bent to kiss her. "I'll be in there, trying to make sense out of what we brought. If they warded our house, there's at least the possibility of retrieving things we left behind."

"Possibility," Raven cautioned. "That doesn't mean it'd be either easy or advisable. As I warned you before, your safest course is to remain here. Come." He crooked a finger at Lara. "We'll begin by drawing a power circle."

Remembering the pentagram woven into the rug in Lillian's tree house, Lara wasn't surprised when Raven sketched the same geometric form onto the wood of the kitchen floor with a piece of charcoal he plucked from the stove.

Lillian dried her hands on an apron and joined them. She looked at the pentagram, raised an eyebrow at Raven, and asked, "First magic or second?"

Raven cocked his head to one side from where he knelt on the ground. "First, I think," he said at last. "If we have difficulty, we can switch." Glancing up at Lara, whose mouth was open to ask a question, he held up a hand. "This is a time for you to absorb what we have to say and follow instructions," he advised sternly. "Questions can come later. If we choose not to answer, you must learn to accept that."

Lara closed her eyes; her stomach knotted with anxiety. This was the real deal, just like her wedding had been, a door that once kicked open, would never fully close again.

"Are you sure, child?" Lillian looked hard at her, reading her mind easily. At Lara's sharp nod, the Sidhe intoned, "We shall begin. Grasp the amulet in your right hand."

A surge of energy shot through Lara—quite different from her normal experience with the spelled moonstone. Apparently, the amulet was more multifaceted than she'd thought.

"Breathe," Raven said. "Focus on your breaths. Breathe in power and knowledge. Exhale anything standing between you and your magic."

I can do this. It's a lot like structured relaxation. As she yielded to the process, her world shifted. Instead of the homey kitchen, pathways opened before her in four directions. Lillian and Raven exhorted her to pick one.

Twirling in a slow circle, Lara peered closely at her choices. One led into a grassy, sunlit glade, another to the shores of a rushing creek. The third led downward into the earth and the fourth upward toward unseen heights.

Always drawn to growing things, she picked the glade. As she wandered through a wildflower-strewn meadow, Lillian instructed her to bow to the goddess and make a request. Not knowing where the impulse came from, Lara knelt and laid a hand on the grass as she asked for heat from the Earth's core. The response was instantaneous, and she pulled her hand away, startled by blisters on her fingertips.

"Gently," Raven laughed. "Gently. Only ask for as much as you need. If you squander resources, the goddess will stop answering your requests. Try it again."

The grass, which had grown uncomfortably warm under her, cooled quickly. She tried again, this time requesting just enough heat to warm a pan of water. She felt something like a small jolt. Lillian told her to close her eyes, grasp the energy, and visualize pulling it into her body.

When Lara opened her eyes, she was back in the kitchen in the center of Raven's crude rendition of a five-pointed star. Walking determinedly to the pot of water in the sink, she dropped a fist into it. "Nothing's happening," she murmured after a few seconds.

"Open your hand," Raven said patiently.

Feeling foolish, Lara stretched out her fingers and sure enough, the dishwater got warmer. Not warm enough to do much with, but definitely a few shades better than it had been. "Takes some practice," she noted wryly.

Lillian laughed. "Yes, child, lots of practice. Nonetheless, this is a good start."

"What are the other three pathways?" Lara asked, before remembering Raven's moratorium on questions. "Never mind," she mumbled.

"It's understandable you'd want to know." Lillian shot Raven a *told you so* look. "I, for one, appreciate curiosity in my acolytes. Raven is more old school."

"Seen and not heard, huh?" Lara quirked a brow at him.

"Where did that come from?" he asked, looking puzzled.

"It's a leftover from the eighteen and early nineteen hundreds," Lara replied. "That's how we used to say children ought to be."

"Each of the pathways offers something particular." Lillian answered Lara's earlier question. "After a while, you'll learn where to seek what you need. And you'll be able to do it with the amulet alone, rather than needing a power circle to boost its effects." She cleared her throat. "You'll find you have more of an affinity for some pathways than others. The magic can become unwieldy when you must enter one of the less comfortable quadrants, because none of the others hold what you need. Now go back and try again to get sufficient heat to warm the water in that pot."

It took two more tries, but Lara finally stood over the dirty wash water with a broad grin on her face. "Yes," she mumbled. "I could do this again, now that I know how. Trev will be happy. Means we can have a bath in the upstairs tub without hauling buckets and buckets of water."

"Lillian!" Raven turned away to stare fixedly at something. "That intruder. Goddess blast it. He's trying again."

"Are you certain?" Lillian asked, frowning.

"Of course I'm certain," he muttered and strode purposefully out the kitchen door.

"Scrub the circle off the floor," Lillian called over her shoulder as she followed Raven out of the house, long red braids in disarray and her skirts flapping about her.

Using her newly-warmed water and a cloth, Lara cleaned the floor. When she was done, she wandered to the kitchen door, surprised to see the sky lightening in the east. She started down the steps with the intention of helping Raven and Lillian, but Lillian's voice rang in her mind. *Do not interfere. You are not yet strong enough to be other than a hindrance.*

Lara retreated inside. As she pulled the door closed, sudden weariness washed over her. Maybe Lillian had done something to ensure she didn't hinder whatever she and Raven were up to.

Hunting for Trevor with the intention of telling him it was time to go to bed, she found him curled up on the sofa snoring softly.

What a good idea, especially since we'll be going after Adriana in just a few hours. Snuggling down half on top of him, Lara pulled a blanket over them both and was asleep so quickly she barely had time to wonder whether Lillian and Raven found anything sinister out in the farmhouse yard.

CHAPTER 18

Trevor woke to a weak winter sun dribbling into the living room. When he tried to move, it took his sleep-fuddled brain a few moments to realize Lara had jammed herself in next to him on the couch. He didn't want to disturb her, but his overfull bladder won out and he moved her as gently as he could. Untangling his limbs, he stood, and let himself quietly out the front door.

It was a glorious day with a grayish, cloud-filled sky. Pale pink streaks played among the clouds as they raced along in the jet stream. Inhaling deeply, he filled his lungs with pure mountain air. At a nagging twinge from his nether regions, he walked down the steps and moved about fifty yards off to the side to pee. Clawing and yipping at the door drew him back up the steps to let Gunter out. The dog's sensitive nose found Trevor's urine immediately and he squatted right over it.

"Got to be top dog, eh?" Trevor laughed and ruffled the puppy's ears. He glanced skyward and guessed it wasn't yet noon since the sun was still on the eastern side of the sky. He waited for the puppy to finish, and then clucked to him. Trying to be quiet, he shepherded the dog back inside.

"You can let go of him. I'm awake." Lara was still prone, but her eyes were open.

"Did we bother you, love?" Trevor perched on the edge of their impromptu bed.

She shook her head. "No. It's time for us to be up and about, anyway. Have you seen Raven or Lillian?"

"No, but I didn't really look for them. I've only been betwixt here and the front yard. Why?"

"They interrupted my lesson last night because they thought whoever tried to follow us was closing in."

Trevor's guts tightened. At least he knew where the shotgun was. He'd taken care to place it upright, next to one of the downstairs bookcases, the ammunition stacked on a nearby shelf. That was something they'd need more of. He'd loaded his own shells as a boy, but he'd need some sort of manual if he was going to start doing so again, not to mention the black powder, shot, and casings.

"I'll just run upstairs to the bathroom." Lara got to her feet. "Should be done in a jiffy. How about if you work on breakfast?"

"Sure. It'll be interesting to see if I can make a decent cup of coffee with a percolator on top of the woodstove."

"Well, you've got to get a fire going in it first." Lara scrunched her nose at him. "Got to pee. Back down soon. 'Sides, while I'm upstairs, I can check for Raven and Lillian. If I don't find them inside, maybe I'll see them if I look out the windows."

Trevor didn't bother telling her he was close-to-sure the Sidhe and mage weren't in the house. There was a feel about them he'd come to recognize, and it was conspicuously absent. Sort of a warmth that permeated things. Whistling bits of an Irish folk song, he went into the kitchen, pulled open the door of the stove, and glanced at a still-glowing bed of coals. "Hah! Got lucky," he muttered as he tossed small chips of kindling in, following them with bigger pieces of wood. By the time Lara joined him, he had a decent fire going and the coffee was just beginning to pop into the glass bubble of the old-fashioned percolator.

"Anything I can do to help?" she asked.

"Didn't find 'em, huh?"

"No, but you probably knew I wouldn't. The house has a different ambiance about it when they're here."

"Funny, I was just thinking the same thing. He caught her in a hug. When she turned her face upward, he kissed her and was delighted by the enthusiasm with which she kissed him back. They were still standing in the kitchen, pawing and groping at one another, when Trevor heard Raven cough discreetly.

"One baby's likely enough for now," the mage said, chuckling.

"Does your kind stop once there's no more need for lovemaking?" Letting go of Lara, Trevor turned to face Raven, a crooked grin on his face.

"Ah, son, now that would be a closely guarded secret." Raven's mouth was set in serious lines, but his eyes glittered mischievously above his dark beard.

Lillian glided into the kitchen and latched an arm around Raven.

Trevor wondered about the extent of their relationship. It seemed platonic on the surface, but there was something else there too, a close companionship that bordered on the romantic. Thinking, *Oh, what the hell?* he asked, "Are the two of you—?"

Raven held up a peremptory hand. "That would be one of those questions that will *not* receive an answer, so I don't need to hear the rest of it."

"How about this one?" Lara jumped into the fray. "Did you find anything out there?"

"Unfortunately, no." Lillian sounded vexed. She'd re-braided her hair at some point during the hours Lara had been asleep. The new braiding schema pulled her hair back from her face, making her appear stern. "Someone was out there, perhaps as close as a mile away, because he triggered the markers we set. Yet, when we searched we didn't find anything significant."

"Did you look for footprints?" Trevor asked. "The dirt's soft enough. If anyone had been there, you'd likely have noticed."

"No, the way we search is more esoteric," Raven replied, turning toward the stove. "Is the coffee ready?"

"Yes, it should be. How about if I look for clues after breakfast?" Trevor suggested. "I can walk along the road and probably tell if anyone's been there—besides the two of you, that is—since we drove in here last night."

"Maybe that's not such a good idea," Lara said, looking worried. "If there is someone out there—"

"I'll accompany him," Raven announced.

"Splendid," Trevor said. "Done. Now, if you'll all move a bit, I'll get some oatmeal in that pot." The truth of it was, he preferred being out and about doing something, rather than sitting behind closed doors hoping for the best. Some aspects of modern life had chafed at him for years. No one knew better than him that his job with KLM was fairly pointless—unless something drastic occurred and a plane was in trouble. He'd only been in two crash situations. Both had left him feeling wonderfully alive. He'd tried to hold onto the sensation after he was safely on the ground, but it faded quickly, despite his best efforts.

Deftly stirring oatmeal and dried fruit into boiling water he called out, "Anyone milk the goats this morning?"

"Nope, but that's remediable," Raven said and clapped Trevor on the arm on his way out of the kitchen.

Sipping at his coffee, empty oatmeal dish in front of him, Trevor frowned, and then took another swallow, swishing the coffee around in his mouth. "Think I ground the beans too fine," he muttered. "Coffee's bitter and I suppose it's because the water washes up over the grounds again and again, rather than just once like it does in a drip machine." He brightened and cast a significant glance at Raven and Lillian. "I didn't think of it before we left, but might either of you know where I could find a French Press? It would be useful—until we run out of coffee beans. Crikey." He snapped his fingers. "Maybe you could find some more of them too."

"How about a gramophone with some records while you're at it?" Lara looked up from her cereal, smiling hopefully.

Raven mumbled something unintelligible in a language Trevor wasn't familiar with. Lillian poked him, and he rolled his eyes. "Yes, yes, I realize I'm the one who told them they shouldn't leave here." The mage eyed Trevor. "Make a list over the next week or two. That way you'll not be sending me on constant errands."

"It would probably be easier if we hunted for things ourselves," Trevor offered. He started to expound on the advisability of such a plan, but closed his mouth when he saw the expression on Raven's face.

Trevor cleared his throat and asked, "Ready to go?" Placing his palms on the table, he pushed himself up from his seat. The table and chairs were heavily carved oak, the chairs generous enough for Lara to curl up in. Trevor, who'd always liked old furniture, stroked the grain of the wood in the tabletop as he waited for some indication from the mage.

"How about if you keep the pup in here," he suggested to Lara. "That way he'll be safe, and he won't obliterate clues that might be important."

"Sure thing, dear." Lara scraped the last of the food off her plate.

Raven drained his mug. "We should be back in a couple hours," he told Lillian as he got to his feet and started toward the kitchen door.

"Should I bring the shotgun?" Trevor looked quizzically at Raven, but the big, bearlike man just snorted. "Guess not." Trevor answered his own question, bent to kiss the top of Lara's head, and followed the mage out the door. Once outside, he glanced at a sky that threatened rain, the delicate pastel coloration from earlier having faded. "I'm going to run back in for a jacket," he said. "I'll come round by the front door and meet you on that side of the house."

"Fine by me," Raven replied.

He waited near the bridge, and Trevor fell into step with him as they crossed it and headed down the road. "Tell me where you and Lillian looked." Trevor glanced at Raven.

"That isn't exactly how we do things." The mage cleared his throat. "Lillian and I didn't go far from the house. We have other methods of determining things such as this."

"Scrying?"

"Something like that." Raven quirked an eyebrow. "I keep forgetting you were raised by Druids."

"Speaking of which, how are Elidora and Gren going to get here in time to help with Adriana?"

"They'll be here. Everything's been arranged." The set of Raven's mouth told Trevor the subject was closed.

"Okay, so how about you take that side of the road, and I'll take this one?" he suggested. "Look for obvious things like footprints and less evident clues like small branches that have broken off." Responding to Raven's expression, which intimated he was far more used to giving orders than taking them, Trevor added, "I used to hunt as a boy. Sometimes it was the only meat we had."

When Raven didn't respond, standing rooted to the road with a scowl on his face, Trevor stopped walking and turned to face the mage. He folded his arms across his chest and tried to keep irritation out of his voice as he said, "If you've got a better suggestion, I'm certainly willing to hear it. Don't you want to find out for sure if someone was here?"

"We already know they were," the mage pointed out, his tone mildly patronizing. "It is not a matter of *if*, but *who*."

"I already said I'm open to ideas. Have you any that might be more effective than the strategy I suggested?" After a short pause, Raven shrugged, and Trevor bent forward to begin an inspection of his side of the dirt road, pulling up his collar against rain that was worsening.

As he walked, Trevor embraced being surrounded by a forest again. The smell of the pine trees mingled with rain-wet earth and the odors of other growing things. He identified anise, mint, and wild onions along his path.

Trevor turned his head to scan for something that flickered at the edges of his vision. And then he saw it. Making his way carefully over to a large fir tree, he pointed at a place beneath its spreading boughs where the needles had been scooped away. "Someone made this," he said, pointing grimly, "and not so long ago. You can tell by the color of the needles that they were covered until quite recently. Actually, whoever it was could even have slept here. It's a big enough space."

Raven moved silently to his side, peering at the place beneath the tree. Closing his eyes, the mage extended his hands, chanting in Celtic Gaelic. After a time, he met Trevor's eyes. "I believe you're correct," he said, his lips set in a thin line. "Yet, they're no longer anywhere close by. What are you doing? We should return to the women."

"Looking for footprints," Trevor answered over his shoulder. "If someone really was here, they walked in here and back out. I want to see if I can find anything."

The forest floor was thickly carpeted with evergreen needles, and the person had apparently been extremely cautious. Between those two problems, Trevor only found half a footprint moving away from the farmhouse. Shaking his head in frustration, he asked Raven, "Can you tell anything?"

"I sense energy," the mage replied, "but it's dim, which is why I know they've left the immediate area. The part I don't like is there's magic involved. Not with whoever stayed there," he gestured toward the cozy nest under the tree, "but with another who also passed this way."

"You mean like Gradoxst?" Trevor paled; his heart thudded harder in his chest as he grappled with sudden fear. Human intruders were one thing. Demons quite another.

Raven jerked his head forward. "He or another of them. There's a characteristic miasma. It's faint enough, but it's thickened as we've moved farther from the house."

"Do you suppose they're working together?" Trevor sniffed the air, trying to identify what alerted Raven.

"Unlikely, but possible." Raven's tone was curt. "Demons will use humans, but they rarely travel in tandem with them." Trevor felt the mage's gaze on him. "You can stop that snoffling, son. It's not my nose that tells me evil was here."

Trevor studied Raven speculatively through narrowed eyes. "Is there some way you could set a trap? Since they stopped here before, odds might be good they'll return to the same place, what with the nice dry nest under this tree and all."

"Good thinking!" Raven clapped a hand on Trevor's shoulder. "Of course I can do that. Step back to the road to give me room to work. We actually need two traps. One for the human and one for the... other. I won't be able to complete the second snare until I have access to Lillian's power, though."

At first, Trevor watched discreetly, but when lights began flashing around Raven, he turned and stared. *Sodding hell, if he doesn't look like an Old Testament prophet with all that hair swirling round him.* Raven stood at the center of a vortex with blues, greens, and violets streaming out from him until the colors disappeared into the trunk of the fir tree.

After a time, the lights winked out. Raven dropped his outstretched hands, wiped them one against the other, and walked carefully back to the road, turning a time or two to obliterate his tracks. "Our fellow was awfully wary," he noted. "It wouldn't be wise to alert him that we were here."

"You mean the Demon?"

Raven laughed. "Nay, son. I was talking about the human. No matter what I do, any Demon worth his salt could figure out we were here. I have something else in mind for him. Remember, I need Lillian for that."

"Yes, of course," Trevor agreed absently, as he turned toward the house, feeling flustered by Raven's nonchalant analysis of supernatural creatures. *Oh for God's sake,* he chided himself. *That's what he is. I can accept his presence. Why's it so deucedly difficult to get my brain around the Demon aspect of things?*

With his thoughts chasing one another, like a cat after its own tail,

Trevor finally dragged his mind back to more familiar territory. "Raven?"

The mage turned and looked at him. It seemed he too, had been deep in thought. "Yes?"

"That person who holed up under the tree— It's almost like he's had some sort of paramilitary training. It's uncanny he was able to make it to that bed of fir needles without leaving more than the half boot print I found." Trevor paused. "Are you certain he's not a magical creature too?"

"Most certain."

"Any possibility you might be wrong?" Raven's visage darkened, and the line of his jaw tightened. "Ah, never mind," Trevor inserted hurriedly. "Didn't mean anything by that. It's just it seems strange someone would go to all the trouble of getting this close and not do anything else."

"I am never wrong." Raven bit off the words, enunciating each painfully clearly. "Occasionally, I may miss things, but—"

"Yes, yes, I get that. Look, sorry old chap. Truce?" Trevor stopped long enough to hold out his right hand.

Raven's face cleared, and he threw back his head and laughed, the rich sound booming off ancient tree boles. "So that's how you humans do things? You malign another's character, say you're sorry, and offer to shake hands?"

Trevor considered telling Raven he hadn't meant to denigrate him, but decided against that approach. "I may have been raised among Druids, but I spent precious little time with them. I was trying to assess how certain you were about… Well, about the human intruder being just that. I didn't mean to imply you didn't know what you were talking about."

Raven shrugged. "Ach, never mind. I'm often too quick to judge."

"Truce, then?" Trevor repeated and smiled.

Raven started to say something, but held up a hand for silence. Trevor froze, waiting. The mage's nostrils flared, and his gaze locked on the horizon. Even his hair appeared more alert; the ends of the long strands curled in the direction he faced. After long moments, he drew in a deep breath, blew it out in a whoosh, and Trevor, understanding the need for silence had passed, did likewise.

Though he was burning up with curiosity, Trevor held his tongue. There was no way to dredge information out of Raven. Either he told you, or he didn't. Begging or pleading wouldn't help things along. He shot the mage a questioning glance, and gestured toward the house. At Raven's nod, he turned and began walking slowly, hoping the other man would catch him up and talk with him.

For a time, Trevor walked by himself. Hooking his hands together behind his back, he thought about what just happened. And then his thoughts ranged farther: to Lara and their child. The fact that there wouldn't be a hospital nearby didn't bother him. He had faith in Elidora, since she'd birthed most of the bairns in the countryside outside the town of Carlisle.

Something nagged at him though, as he considered the prospect of fatherhood. Once he understood what it was, his spirits sank. He was terrified he'd be a wretchedly inadequate father. That was one of the worst problems with having shitty parents. You never got a blueprint for what decent parenting looked like.

Lara never had much in the way of parents, either.

Yes, but at least she studied psychology.

Raven caught up with him. "What was that about psychology?" The mage sounded mildly interested.

"But I didn't say anything," Trevor protested.

"Doesn't matter." Raven's gray eyes nailed him.

Trevor snorted. "I don't suppose it would. I was worrying about how Lara and I would manage as parents, since our own were so deficient."

"It's a natural process, son." Raven waved a dismissive hand. "We have greater things to concern us than a future event that has yet to occur," he said firmly. "I felt the Demon's presence again, but it was far away. I need Lillian to tack it down with more precision. Certain magics require masculine and feminine energies to function. I was able to ascertain that he's headed this way again."

He glanced at the sky. "Elidora and Gren will be here by nightfall. We have some preparations to make, and then we shall leave. You'll be alone for a few hours. It's important you stay within the house."

"Why might that be?" Trevor phrased the question as gently as he could, because he felt gun shy of Raven's temper. "Not that I'm thinking of doing something different, mind you," he added quickly. "I'm simply curious."

"You humans and your curiosity. Look where it's gotten you." Raven chuckled, but the sound didn't have much warmth. "The farmhouse will protect you because Lillian and I have spelled it to do so," he explained patiently. "If the forces of evil knocking around out here choose tonight to try something, it'll be safer for you to be within the walls of the house."

"I have my gun," Trevor muttered. And then he remembered the three young hoodlums he'd killed and closed his mouth abruptly. Besides, would something as ordinary as a shotgun have even the slightest effect on someone like Gradoxst?

"The taking of life is serious business," Raven said gently. "It's good you're prepared to kill, yet each soul who dies by your hand is linked to you forever. You'll always remember watching the life flicker out in their eyes. It's the goddess's way of keeping you honest in your dealings with others."

"Do you mean Brigid?"

"Not necessarily. I'm referring to all that's both sacred and feminine. Pick whomever resonates for you. It could be Brigid or Cailleach or one of the Greco-Romans like Artemis."

Raven's eyes drilled into him like gray zephyrs. A vision of himself at fifteen rose with shocking immediacy, and he was back in the barn behind his house, pitchfork clutched in his hands. It was slick with blood, and he watched himself shove it into his father's body one more time before he ran howling out into the night. "Bloody hell," he muttered, still holding Raven's gaze. "Those things never go away, do they?"

"Nor should they." Raven pulled Trevor against him for a fast, hard hug. "You grew up in a battle zone. Your bastard of a father deserved to die. You were the goddess's instrument that night. Never regret your actions. They were the only ones you could have taken. Now come on." He pushed Trevor toward the turnoff to the house. "Coming out here was an excellent idea. I give you full credit."

Trevor blinked away the desolation scouring his soul and loped toward the old guesthouse that was imbued with Raven's magic.

CHAPTER 19

*L*ara had been expecting Trevor to return for at least an hour before she heard the front door slam. *Thank God he's back.* She rushed down from the upstairs bedroom where she'd been putting things away.

The puppy made a dash for Trevor too, barking accusingly as he chided his master for having the audacity to leave without German Shepherd guidance and protection. "When you get bigger," Trevor said, petting the puppy, "never fear, I'll take you everywhere."

"I'm glad you're back," Lara murmured, moving in close for a kiss. "I was getting worried. Did you find anything?"

"Uh-huh." He tugged his nearly-soaked jacket off and shook it briskly over the stone hearth, before hanging it on a nearby peg. "I'm going to have to get some more wood chopped. If we have to keep at least one of these stoves going full time to heat the place, it'll require a lot more than what's stacked out by the barn."

"What did you find?" Lara pressed, trying to quell her anxiety, as she sat down on one of the upholstered chairs close to the hearth.

"Someone had definitely been here. They dug themselves out a place underneath a big tree to keep dry. It was odd, though," he said, settling on the arm of her chair. "Whoever was there must've been a pro because, other than those scruffled fir needles, there was scarcely any evidence of their presence."

"Could Raven tell anything?"

"Yeah, he could sense someone had been there."

Lara peered closely at him. "There's something you're not telling me."

A half-smile made the edges of Trevor's mouth twitch. "I suppose this perspicacity of yours will only get worse as your magic strengthens," he mumbled and grasped one of her hands.

"Well?"

"Raven said there was a Demon somewhere in the mix. And that he—or maybe it—was moving toward us."

Biting her lower lip, Lara frowned. "So there are two things out there following us? One human, and one not?"

He nodded, still uncomfortable with the idea that evil could take on corporeal form.

"That means you could very well be in danger tonight while we're gone, doesn't it?" Her stomach tightened, not liking the direction this was going at all.

"Not exactly." Trevor smiled reassuringly. "Raven says so long as I stay in the house, it'll protect me."

"Okay," she said in measured tones, her dark gaze fixed on him. Extricating her hand, she pointed a finger at him. "So that means you'll do just that. No heroics, no matter what you hear outside."

"Promise." He raised an index finger to his lips, and then touched her mouth.

"Thanks," she said softly, capturing his hand. In spite of his promise, she was still worried. Trevor had a way of marching to his own drummer. It was one of the things she'd always loved about him. For half a heartbeat though, she wished he was a shade more predictable.

"What have you been up to?" he asked lightly, looking at the still over-crowded living room.

"Mostly unpacking and finding places for things. I thought I'd try to cook something and was hoping for a bit of advice, but when I hunted for Lillian, I couldn't find her, so I went back to putting things away."

"Do you have any idea where she is?"

Lara shook her head. "She did say she needed more preparation than she'd thought for trying to rescue Adriana tonight, but she also said she'd be around if I needed her."

"Mmph. I'd be glad to help cook. It's been quite a while since breakfast." Trevor glanced hopefully toward the kitchen end of the house.

"I boiled some rice and mixed in butter and cheese, but we need way more than that."

"Sounds lovely. I'll add some vegetables and cook up more of the meat we bought yesterday, since it won't keep. Stove still going?" At her nod, he got up and walked into the kitchen.

Trailing after him, with the puppy third in line, she said, "One of the reasons it looks as if I haven't gotten much done is because I was taking stock of the books in the library upstairs. It's intriguing," she noted with a grin. "There are first editions on everything from magic to organic farming, except they didn't call it that back then, and a little cast iron stove keeps it nice and toasty."

"Even more reason we'll need more wood," he groaned, tossing ingredients into the pot that held the rice mixture. He bent to retrieve a couple sticks from the bin next to the stove and added them to the firebox, saying, "See, wood, wood, and more wood. I miss natural gas already."

"Is there anything to eat?" Raven's gruff voice preceded him through the kitchen door. Lara thought he looked more out-of-sorts than usual and figured it might be because Lillian was gone.

"About twenty minutes," Trevor said, adding, "What's wrong?"

"I told her not to go anywhere, and she's not here. There are things we must do."

"So we're not the only ones who don't do as they're told." Lara furled her brows at the mage, but he just snarled at her.

The air next to Raven flickered. It had to be Lillian returning, or else Elidora and Gren. "I heard that." Lillian laughed, as she became progressively more corporeal. "Come on," she said, still chortling, as she tugged on Raven's arm. "We can talk while the youngsters finish cooking." Heads bent together, the pair walked out of the kitchen.

"I know you're worried about me," Trevor murmured, looking up from his pot, "but I'm more than a little nattered about you. Have you had any visits from Gradoxst of late?"

Shaking her head, she said, "Not since my last trip to the beach. That wasn't really all that long ago, though. Only a couple days."

"I thought you only saw him the first time you ended up there."

"Technically, that would be true. I didn't actually see him when I was trying to comfort Adriana, but I could feel him hovering."

Trevor lapsed into silence, as he stirred their makeshift supper. Lara eyed his familiar form, faded Levis still damp from his earlier trek, and attempted to quiet all the *what ifs* scuttling about in her mind.

At least one of the reasons they were going after Adriana was because she'd insisted. The Old Ones inhabited a different world, where a certain number of losses were expected. She didn't know if she'd shamed them into acquiescence, or if they would've eventually come to the same conclusion about tonight's action being the proper one without any pressure from her.

"Lara." Trevor's voice broke into her thoughts.

"Um-hum?" She walked to where he stood by the stove.

"Dinner's ready. I've told you a couple times, but you were just off somewhere. I was worried it might be another of those bloody visions, except you weren't twitching or moaning. And you were on your feet instead of sitting."

"I was thinking," she said and coaxed a smile she wasn't feeling. "I'll hunt down the others." She clucked to the puppy to give him a chance to go outside, and let herself out the kitchen door.

～

THEY WERE JUST SCRAPING the last of supper out of the cook pot, when Lara felt something nearby shift oddly. Unlike Lillian's earlier arrival, a doorway opened off to one side of the kitchen, and Elidora and Gren stepped through. Gren barked a command, and the glittering rectangle winked out of existence.

"Och! We missed supper?"

Elidora sounded so disappointed, Trevor jumped up and said, "I can make more. Won't take half an hour, since the stove's still hot." With an impish grin, he added, "That food we bought in Monroe's come in quite handily. Looked pretty quiet in Skykomish. Maybe I could wander into town tomorrow and pick up a bit more."

"In your dreams." Raven shot Trevor an unmistakable look.

"We have sufficient time for everyone to eat," Lillian interrupted soothingly, making a chopping motion with her hand in Raven's direction. "Feed the body first, then the soul finds its own way."

"I still an on ween 'at we'll want for anither." Gren looked hard at Raven. "We s' hae five, whit's an ackwart nummer; cat-wittit if thoo fang my meanin'. Unless thoo's myntit Adriana wad be th' saxt."

"Aye, an' 'at wad be th' plan," Elidora echoed. "Tae hae th' lassie bring us tae th' number we shall need t' get oursel' oot o' 'at horrid place."

Lara struggled to piece the conversation together. She looked at Elidora through narrowed eyes. "You just said we need six for us to be successful." At the Sidhe's nod, Lara went on, "Jungians talk about the power of numbers also. For example, three is the number of transformation, four of completion. The odd numbers always seem to be begging for something to happen."

"'Tis similar then." Gren nodded. "Sud th' lass no lang bide i' th' atween, backlins comin'll be a sair pech."

Lara looked helplessly at Trevor, who said, "Gren's worried that if Adriana's not there any longer it'll be difficult for the five of you to get yourselves out. I'm not sure I like this, Lara. Not even a little bit." Frowning, he turned back to his cooking project, stirring with a vengeance.

"Raven and Lillian managed to pull me out of there." Lara bit at her lower lip as a combination of worry and confusion swept through her. "We were three, so I don't understand."

"All numbers have different possibilities imbued within them," Lillian began in what Lara was coming to think of as her teacher's voice. "A significant difference was you spent mere minutes there, while this other child has been there for days."

"Did you ask the goddess for help?" Lara mumbled, feeling supremely out of her element. Even as she asked the question, she wondered how one might go about raising a goddess to ask for anything. And then she reminded herself that Raven was a god.

There's a whole new rulebook in play here. And I understand very little of it.

"What do you think I was doing all afternoon," Lillian inquired dryly, "entertaining myself? I engaged in our ritual purification by immersion in water to invoke Artemis. She'll assist with sufficient light, but she mirrored what Brigid said, which is that our time will be short."

"How much is a turn of the glass?" Lara asked. "I wondered about that in the *Dreaming*."

"Just shy of an hour," Raven answered. "We must complete our task in half of that."

"So long as we're chatting," Trevor said in a strained voice as he placed the cook pot and two clean bowls on the table. "What happened at that gathering you went to in the Old Country? The one where you were going to take stock of other hybrids like Lara."

Lillian shot a penetrating glance his way. "How would you know anything about that?" she asked brusquely.

"Because I told him," Raven said, holding up a hand. The expression on his face was enough to forestall further commentary, even from Lillian. "We haven't the time to go into that now. All our efforts must focus on planning how tonight shall unfold. We will leave just before midnight to take advantage of the power the night has to offer."

"It's a full moon," Lara objected. "It'll have risen and moved past the horizon by then."

"Not where we're going, lassie," Elidora said, spooning the ground meat and rice concoction into her dish.

Telling herself to listen more and stop broadcasting opinions, Lara sat back in her chair, pulled up her legs, and tucked them beneath her.

"Hae thoo a gibble wi' tae sned th' chyne?" Gren looked from Lillian to Raven, who shook his head tersely. Gren opened his mouth, and then shut it firmly, looking troubled.

After listening for another half hour while Elidora and Gren finished their meal, Lara felt befuddled. Much of the discussion, though conducted in English, might as well have been in Gaelic for all she'd been able to dredge out of it. Finally, she asked in a small voice, "What will I be doing?"

"I will ensure we come out in the proper place on the beach," Raven said. "You'll find the girl."

"That took much longer than thirty minutes last time," Lara protested, fighting down panic. "It felt as if it took hours—and there's no guarantee she'll be in the same spot. In fact, I'm still not sure how I managed to come across her last time. That whole shoreline looks a lot alike."

And then she remembered driving home and looking at the car's clock after her last trip to the beach. Finding Adriana hadn't taken hours, not really. It only seemed that way.

"Time flows differently there," Elidora said gently, mirroring the conclusion Lara had just drawn out of her memories. "Ye might have a greater chance than ye see sittin' here."

"In any event," Raven broke in, "as I said, you'll show us where Adriana can be found. We shall attempt to free her and translocate ourselves back here."

"Why can't you find her without Lara?" Trevor asked, walking to the back of Lara's chair and placing protective hands on her shoulders. "I still don't understand why she has to go. Besides, that would help with that number thing you were grousing about earlier."

"For reasons that aren't entirely clear to us," Lillian said and steepled her fingers under her chin, "Lara is linked to Adriana. That bond was forged when the Demon conscripted Adriana's father into trying to trap her. Raven and I have discussed this," she went on, shooting a pointed glance at the mage, "but we haven't untangled it."

Raven held Trevor's eyes. "It's unusual that Lara was not only able to find Adriana, but to engage her in conversation. When humans spend as long in that arena betwixt the worlds as Adriana has, their sentience is almost always eroded, generally beyond salvation."

"So," Lillian continued, "even if we find the human child, she may be beyond our ability to reclaim."

And then she must be sacrificed, rang through Lara's mind. Swallowing hard, she wondered if she'd be able to stand by while the innocent young girl was murdered.

"We do not kill unnecessarily." Raven shifted his intense gaze from Trevor to her. "Would you rather she lived the half-life of the damned for all eternity?"

"But her only offense, and it's really not one at all, was her father knew me, and I managed to piss off Gradoxst," Lara protested, feeling the hot bite of tears behind her lids.

"An' have ye not yet figured out life is seendle fair, lass?" Elidora asked. She pushed her empty bowl away and dug deep into Lara's being with her dark eyes.

Lara locked gazes with the old wise woman. "Is there anything I need to do to get ready?" she asked.

"Lillian's the only one close to ready to leave," Raven muttered. "We must all purify ourselves and pray to Artemis for safe passage under Her moon."

"You'll have to show me what to do." Lara pulled her feet out from under her, set them firmly on the floor, and stood. Turning to Trevor, still standing behind her chair, she offered him a weak approximation of a smile. "It'll be all right," she murmured. "It has to be."

"Believing in one's cause is, indeed, half the battle," Lillian said, rising from her place. "Come, child, you'll not find this pleasant, but you must follow me out-of-doors for this rite."

Half an hour later, Lara stood naked and shivering by the banks of the creek cascading down from Troublesome Mountain several thousand feet above. Her clothing was scattered about and her goose flesh glimmered in the accommodating light of the moon.

Lillian had guided her to a place above the house where the stream fell into a rocky cauldron, creating a waist-deep pool. Following the Sidhe's instructions, Lara stepped into the pool, and then dunked herself so that even the top of her head was under the frigid water, while opening herself to the presence of the goddess. She fought a closely held battle to maintain control of her thoughts, and was at least holding her own, until she stepped out of the cold water and a brisk breeze attacked her wet body. After that, the needles of cold lacerating her flesh obliterated her concentration.

"Breathe, child," Lillian hissed. "Breathe. Do not give in to discomfort, or we shall have to begin all over again."

Drawing one shuddering breath after another through chattering teeth, Lara called on every deity she knew to give her strength. *Why stop at Artemis?* her cold-numbed brain demanded. *Maybe there's power in numbers.*

She rattled off goddess names as they came to her, and her strategy worked because she did start feeling warmer. *Hell, maybe I'm just doing a better job ignoring being cold. Or the wind died down.* The phrase *victory has a thousand parents* ran through her mind, and she suppressed an urge to giggle. That was a quote she'd used often enough with her patients.

"You may get dressed," Lillian said after what felt like a very long time. "You're dry." She paused, and then added, albeit a bit grudgingly, "You did well. Better than I would've expected for a mortal raised to comfort."

"Ah, but I wasn't," Lara said snugging gratefully into her sweats. Balancing on one foot, she pulled on a thick sock and then stuffed her right foot into a boot.

"Perhaps that explains things. You'll have to tell me more about the aunt who took you in once your parents died, but not tonight. Now is the time to think exclusively of the task ahead."

Nodding, Lara tugged on her other sock and boot, before dragging her jacket over her sweatshirt. Reveling in the feel of warm fabric against her skin, she followed Lillian back to the farmhouse. Before they got there, they passed Elidora, Raven, and Gren heading for the same pool. Following a hunch, she asked Raven, "Did you build that pool?"

"Of course I did," he said as he swept past her. "Perceptive of you, though."

"Well," she said to his retreating back, "I made a career out of being observant."

"So you did, child." Lillian laughed. The sound, like pealing crystal bells, filled Lara with hope.

All too soon, the evening hours pushed toward midnight. At quarter to twelve, everyone was standing in the living room. Trevor held Lara tightly against him. "Now do exactly what they tell you," he said, a catch in his voice betraying his deep worry. "Take care of her," he begged, his sea-blue eyes moving from Raven to Lillian to Elidora to Gren. "Do not come back without her."

Moving out of the circle of his arms, Lara faced the others. "I'm ready," she said resolutely and raised her chin a notch.

"Dinna fash, laddie. Only a tumshie would not be afeart by what we do," Elidora murmured, walking to Trevor to give him a quick hug.

"Yes, son, pray for us. We'll return before dawn," Raven said. He'd just swept his arms upward in a motion Lara recognized, for it presaged departure, when he lowered them and looked intently at Trevor. "Remember, stay well within these walls. When I began to open the portal, I felt…"

The mage's forehead creased into fine lines, and he dropped his gaze, as if he were struggling with something. "How can I say this so you'll understand?" he muttered half under his breath. When he looked up, his gray eyes were troubled, and his voice held a somber note. "That person who slept under the fir tree is close, but evil is closer. Mayhap the two of them are entwined in some way I have not yet ascertained.

"Yet, we must leave. We have prepared for this, and our path is clearly marked. This is another gateway that will close should we not go through it."

"I understand." Trevor nodded solemnly. "I'll do as you say."

Brusquely drawing his hands up once again, Raven began to chant, followed at proscribed intervals by Lillian, Elidora, and Gren. Lara's last glimpse of Trevor, before the living room swirled away to nothingness, was of a stern-faced, tight-lipped man gripping his hands together. Worried as she was about the role she was about to play, she sent up a prayer to the goddess to watch over Trevor. And then she wrenched her mind to full attention for the task at hand. She'd heard enough from Lillian to understand that anything less than her best effort could only end in disaster.

CHAPTER 20

Trevor stood stock still as he watched everyone vanish before his eyes. Oh, they'd shimmered a bit, and then dimmed, but the long and short of it was they'd left in a way that addled his brain. For the briefest of moments, he wondered what it would feel like to wander through the space between the worlds. Then he recalled Lara's badly depleted mental and physical state after her last sojourn and ground his teeth together.

The full import of Raven's last words hit home, and he sprinted to lock the front door, and then the one off the kitchen. It was apparent long years had passed since either of the locks were engaged; they screeched a hearty protest at being turned. He really had to put his back into the effort to get the rusty parts to move.

"There," he said to the puppy, who looked up at him expectantly, small pink tongue lolling. "That's about all Daddy can do just now. Sorry I didn't get to take you out again. Not sure just what we'll do about that."

Trevor thought about the last time the group had gone off, and a vision of the three young men—scarcely more than boys, really— who'd broken into his house rose to mock him. Especially the Jenkins lad. Sitting down heavily in a straight-backed chair near the fire, he dropped his head into his hands. His heart was beating too fast, and his breath stuck thickly in his throat.

"Stop it," he chided himself, voice muted by his hands. "Chances of there being young hoodlums all the way out here are nil. That person who hid himself was some sort of pro." The puppy whined, and Trevor jumped.

The fire cast some light, but not nearly enough for his taste, given his current mood. Staring nervously at the dark shadows, he hefted a kerosene lantern, lifted the globe and the chimney, and lit it with one of the long matches from off the mantle. As he rolled the wick back a bit and resettled the glass pieces on the old lantern, he felt slightly heartened by the soft rose-colored light it shed.

Not much to do now except wait.

The puppy growled low in the back of his throat, small hackles rising.

Straining to hear whatever had upset Gunter, Trevor came up dry. After a few moments, the puppy stood down. *Bollocks! I'm not going to sit here cowering like some old biddy.* Springing to his feet, Trevor caught up the lantern and walked to the kitchen. Once there he stoked up the fire in the wood cook stove and heated water to get the dinner dishes done. Carefully spooning what was left of the evening meal—which wasn't much—onto one of the dirty dishes, he set it in front of Gunter to finish. Somewhere between waiting for the water to heat, starting the dishes, and setting down his dishtowel an hour later, Trevor recovered a bit of his usual equanimity. By then the puppy was standing by the back door whining.

Not wanting to jeopardize all the work that had gone into housebreaking the young dog, Trevor grabbed a lantern with a bale from a hook next to the door, lit it with a scrap of kindling, and turned the old-fashioned key. It objected just as loudly as it had going the other way, and the squeal of metal on metal scoured his nerves. Deciding it wouldn't be all that risky, because he wouldn't go any distance at all from the house, Trevor pushed the door open just far enough for him and the puppy to squeeze through.

Rethinking things, he shoved it wide open. *If the house is supposed to protect me, maybe its circle of influence will stretch a bit if I open things up.* He laughed at the idiocy of his reasoning. Gunter, having no such inner dialogue to get in his way, was already at the bottom of the steps squatting. When the dog started sniffing around, Trevor knew he wasn't done.

"Since the puppy doesn't seem to think there's anything threatening out here anymore," Trevor murmured, shining the lantern in a wide circle to illuminate the back of the house, "maybe there never was." Using the vantage point of the raised porch, he peered closely at the surrounding trees and bushes cloaked in night shadows. Though he ventured as far as the bottom step, he still didn't hear or see anything.

When the pup scampered up the steps, still awkward with paws he was growing into, Trevor blew out a tense breath and followed Gunter back inside, locking the door behind them. The bale of the lantern slipped in his sweat-slicked hand as he brought it close to his mouth to blow out, and he understood how frightened he'd been.

"And of nothing," he snapped irritably. "Being careful is one thing, but I'm turning into a superstitious fool. Too much time with those blasted Sidhe." He debated going upstairs to try to sleep, and then decided he'd rather stay on the couch where he'd spent the previous night. With the help of a penlight, he rustled through one of the many boxes of books they'd brought, selecting a volume of nineteenth century English poetry. Returning to the kitchen, he retrieved the kerosene lamp with the rose-colored shade.

Trevor yawned as he slipped out of his boots and lay down. When the puppy began pawing and yipping softly, Trevor hoisted him up onto the sofa. The only thing left was to drag the blanket down off the back of the couch. When he did, a scrap of paper rustled and fell to the floor. Curious, Trevor scooped it up, unfolded it, and saw Lara's scrawling handwriting.

Somehow I knew you'd sleep down here. Even though I'm not there to hold you, my heart is with you. Always has been, always will be. The fact that you're reading this means you're inside where Raven told you to stay. Thanks for doing what you can to keep yourself safe. I don't know what I'd do if I came back and something had happened to you. As it is, it's hard enough to forgive myself for leaving you alone, especially after what happened with those three boys who broke into our house. Hold the puppy, close your eyes, and travel to where Psyche can give you dreams. I'll be back before you wake. All my love, Lara.

Fighting waves of guilt at his unauthorized trip out the back door, Trevor held the note close to his heart and thought about Lara. He'd never quite understood what motivated him to flirt with her on that long-ago flight. He'd made a point of being efficient and reserved with the passengers on all of his planes. He'd never even come close to inviting one to tea, much less...

His face heated as he remembered how he'd come on to Lara, smiling suggestively as he touched her shoulder. No one had been more surprised than he to end up in her bed a few hours later. Yet there'd been a rightness to it that etched itself into his soul. Once within the circle of the magic the two of them made together, he'd stayed, growing more attached with each passing day.

The edges of his mouth curved into a gentle smile; the apprehension dogging him since Lara and the others left dissipated. Unexpectedly, he felt his eyes grow heavy. He blew out the lantern, rolled half onto one side, and gave himself up to sleep.

True to Lara's prediction, dreams came. Gentle, nonsensical ones at first, and then he slid into a variant of the dream that had upset Lara so much. The dream so many of her patients and students had shared. Except this time, the tree was old and gnarled instead of green and verdant. As he gazed at the immense trunk, he saw it was riddled with rot. When the crone came for him, she wasn't beautiful and terrible, but old and wasted with the bones in her face showing through. Tugging at him with skeletal fingers, she shoved him so hard down the stairwell under the tree that he tumbled all the way to the bottom. Panic-stricken, Trevor tried to crawl back up the stairs, but they crumbled to dust as he mounted them, and he knew, with a desperate certainty, that he was stuck, that the Tree of Life had transmogrified into a Tree of Death.

Where the illumination beneath the tree had been a golden glow in the first dream, it now held a putrid, greenish cast with streaks of orange. When he looked down the long corridor, it was littered with the bodies of small dead animals. The same animals he'd gathered up to save the last time. Trevor moaned, a high, thin sound shot through with fear. And then he was clawing through something that felt like molasses, certain he was going to suffocate. He understood with painful clarity that if he couldn't escape the dream, he'd be a dead man.

He didn't know if it was falling onto the floor, or the dog's frantic tongue licking his face, that brought him back from that nightmarish landscape. He pried his eyes open, and found himself tangled in the blanket on the floor between the sofa and coffee table, gasping for breath.

"Ach, Mary mother of Jesus," he panted. "What the bloody fuck just happened?" The fire had died down to embers, and the room was dark as a crypt—or a grave. When he closed his arms around Gunter, Trevor realized he was shaking. He heard his teeth rattling against themselves, and he clenched his jaws together to quiet them. It took several minutes, and a concerted effort, to get his breathing under of control.

He staggered to the woodbin and tossed some kindling into the stone fireplace. As it caught, he followed it with larger pieces of wood. Still fighting against a chill that emanated from his core, Trevor pulled on a jacket and wondered what time it was.

Uncomfortably aware of a more-than-full bladder, he went toward the door, *en route* to his front yard pissing spot. He'd begun to turn the key when he came to an abrupt halt and slapped a palm against his forehead. *Bollocks! What am I doing? I can't go out there.* Fighting disorientation from his nightmare, he turned and felt his way up the dark stairs, heading for the upstairs bathroom. He banged a shin on one of the risers, stumbling over the puppy who'd insisted on coming with him.

As he stood over the old-fashioned toilet, urine splattering into the water, something caught his attention out of the corner of one eye. Instinctively, he moved away from the window, losing himself in the shadows between the bathroom and the hall. A convenient curtain provided just the right camouflage for him to peek through one of the hall windows, but he didn't see anything unusual.

Trevor was on the verge of deciding it was foolish to continue staring into the darkened yard, when a flash of red floated by, moving from one large evergreen to the next just beyond the barn. Eyes widening, he pressed himself closer to the window. In a few seconds, there it was again, about twenty feet farther on. Though still a distance from the house, the light was definitely moving closer.

His blood froze in his veins as realization dawned that he was seeing a night vision lamp. The nest they'd found in the woods had been made by a professional used to covering his tracks. The military used night vision devices. He assumed mercenaries would as well. Heart pounding, he tried to tie the clues into a cohesive whole, but there weren't quite enough puzzle pieces to click into place. Who the hell was in their yard? And why?

After only a moment's hesitation, Trevor started down the stairs. Whoever it was needed to use illumination, so they must be human. He didn't mind the thought of a confrontation with another person. It was just Demons and magic that unnerved him. Reaching for the shotgun and some shells scattered on a nearby shelf, he loaded the gun quickly. The puppy milled around his feet, whining softly. "Guess you need out again, huh?" Trevor said, bending to scratch Gunter's ears.

Did I leave those shells out there loose? Damned sloppy of me.

He didn't want to risk taking the puppy outside into danger. He remembered Lara had told him the basement floor was dirt. Trading the gun for his penlight, he led the way to the top of the basement steps, picked up the puppy, and carried him down to a patch of earth off to one side of the bottom step. Gunter looked up, a confused expression on his young face, but Trevor clucked approvingly and said, "Good puppy."

Seemingly satisfied this part of the house was an acceptable potty spot, the young dog squatted. When he was done, he placed his paws on the first step and looked over one shoulder at Trevor before starting up them.

Once they were back upstairs, he picked up the gun and moved to the sofa, boosting the dog onto a cushion with his free hand. "Daddy has to go outside for a bit," he told the puppy. "You're going to want to come, but you have to stay here." Bending, he kissed the top of Gunter's soft head. Almost as if he understood what Trevor had said, the dog curled up in a ball, tail over his nose.

Trevor pulled on a wool watch cap to cover his bright hair, tucking the ends up under the cap. He slipped on a pair of black gloves, picked up the shotgun, and then moved silently to one of the front windows. Unfortunately, unlike the clear panes upstairs, the glass was too thick and wavy to afford him much of a view. "Nothing for it but to go see," he muttered, teeth clenched tightly.

I don't have to do this. In fact, I promised I wouldn't.

"Shut up," he growled. "Yes, I do need to see who the bloody hell is out there, or Lara and I will never have a moment's peace. If our magical cronies were here, they could take care of this, but it's just me. If I don't do this, whoever's out there might leave, and then I'll never know who it was. Best to take the bull by the horns and face this straight on."

He started to unlock the front door, then decided to go out the back so he'd have the house between himself and where he'd last seen the light. Muscles tight as rocks and breath hissing as he exhaled, Trevor stopped at the bottom of the back steps to calm himself.

Scanning the darkness for threats, he willed his eyes to greater sharpness as he sucked down some air, and then some more. When the tremor in his hands lessened, he thought hard about the wisest course of action and finally decided to make a broad circle at the edge of the clearing where the trees would partially mask his presence.

Moving fast before he could change his mind, he trotted rapidly across the open yard to where the trees grew thick, stopping in the shadows of a large blue fir. Slowly and deliberately, he crept from tree to tree. It wasn't long before he saw the flare of the night vision lamp again. It was definitely inching closer to the front porch. Whoever it was would have to leave the treed perimeter soon if their objective was the house.

It pretty much has to be. No one would come all the way out here to examine a bunch of evergreens and a few chickens and goats in the dark.

Sure enough, the figure slid across the clearing to the base of the front steps and looked up at the door. A rifle of some kind was slung over his shoulder, and Trevor swallowed hard as he wondered if it was something ultra-lethal to match the night vision glasses.

Jaw clenched, teeth set in a hard line to keep them from knocking against one another, Trevor felt disgusted with himself. *Sodding hell. Stop trying to think the situation to death.* Just then, another figure sprinted out of the nearby woods, catapulting toward the man at the bottom of the porch steps. Trevor shrank back, trying to make himself invisible in the night shadows. Nausea rose in his gorge, and he felt like someone just punched him in the guts.

Two of them. There's two. The one without a weapon must be a Demon.

Trevor looked longingly toward the house. He understood too late he never should have left its four walls. He was estimating his chances of sneaking back to the wraparound porch, when the new arrival sprang, pulling the first man to the ground. As they wrestled, odd lights illuminated the pair, and Trevor's breath congealed in his chest.

Jesus fucking bloody Christ, what have I stumbled into here? Eerie green and fluorescent orange lit the night, the colors gloomily reminiscent of the nightmare he'd barely had the luck to escape from. The colored light seemed to be coming from the Demon, but it was hard to tell.

The two intruders grunted as they rolled about on the ground. For a time, it seemed the first man was getting the worst of things, and then he managed to swing the butt of his rifle. There was a sickening crunch as it connected with the other creature's head. Quick as lightning, the first man was on his feet, gun cocked, and the rattle of automatic weapon fire cut through the night like an alien arpeggio of death and destruction.

Thinking this might be his opportunity to run for safety, Trevor had just gathered his legs beneath him for a quick sprint, when the unthinkable happened. The second uninvited visitor, who must've taken twenty rounds of direct hits, rose slowly to his feet. Maniacal, twisted laughter poured from the creature, along with blood that spouted everywhere.

Except the thing wasn't dying. Far from it. As Trevor watched, horrorstruck, it raised gore-streaked hands and began to chant in a guttural language. The first man fired one more time before the weapon fell from his hands. He clutched at his throat, cried out once, and crumpled to the earth.

Ach, no! Nothing human ever sounded like that. Or took point blank gunfire and got back up.

With his margin of safety shrinking by the moment, Trevor wracked his brain for a strategy. The Demon wasn't aware of him— yet. Once it figured out he was there, Trevor didn't suppose he'd fare any better than the man on the ground, who groaned piteously in little gaspy pants that sounded as if he were strangling.

A good fifty yards lay between him and the house, the last part of it open ground. He'd never make it back there without alerting the Demon. Trevor sucked in a desperate breath and strode forward briskly before his nerve failed him. With the shotgun pointed at the creature, he shouted in Celtic Gaelic, hoping against hope the magical quality of the language would aid him.

"You will leave," he screamed. "In the name of the goddess and all that's sacred, leave these grounds." At the sound of his master's voice, the puppy started barking frantically from inside the house.

The thing pivoted toward Trevor, still laughing like a mad thing. A sudden swath of moonlight bathed the abomination in an eerie glow.

As Trevor stared in macabre fascination, he saw red-rimmed eyes gleaming wildly from a bony, grime-crusted face. Black hair stuck out in clumps, and a stringy beard fell partway down the thing's chest. It shouted something in a language Trevor didn't know. With its cracked and broken teeth bared in a parody of a grin, it raised its clawed hands.

His hands shook, but Trevor fired, pumped the shotgun, and fired again, praying to every deity he could think of for aid. After the first shot, the moonlight disappeared abruptly, as if someone had dropped a chiaroscuro curtain over it.

If an automatic weapon didn't kill the bloody blighter, there's no way my little shotgun will do anything.

Contrary to all his expectations, the creature stopped in its tracks, grappling at its chest, a surprised look on its mask-like features. The orange and green light began to fade.

"S—silver," the thing gasped in heavily accented English. "Sssilverrrr." A brackish glow oozed from the center of its chest, obliterating what was left of the orange and green. Strands of its body peeled off one by one, bursting into noxious smelling flames. A few cinders floated down, but most of the burning material winked out of existence shortly after it caught fire. In minutes, the place where the Demon had stood was empty.

Trevor gaped at the impossible. His legs buckled under him, depositing him on the rain-soaked earth. For a time, the world spun crazily, and he shut his eyes, struggling for both consciousness and control. "Don't lose it now, old man," he muttered, his brain feeling slow and muddled as he processed what had just happened. "What the sodding hell? How did I get silver-laced shells for this shotgun?" And then he thought he understood.

"Raven," he spat. "That old bastard knew I wouldn't follow his orders. Thank Christ. He saved me from myself." *That's why those shells were sprinkled about on the bookshelf. He gambled I'd load them first, rather than opening an ammo box.*

Trevor didn't know how long he sat there, reveling in the fact he was still breathing. From time to time, he glanced anxiously at the other intruder, but the man wasn't moving. *Wonder if he's dead?*

The chill damp from the earth became more and more uncomfortable where it seeped into his pants. Deciding he was cold enough for one night—both inside and out—Trevor struggled to his feet. He was considering what to do about the stranger when he heard a gagging sound, and the man rolled into a sitting position, coughing.

Looking up slowly, the man said, "Trevor. It's me."

"Bloody bollocks!" Trevor peered at him as recognition flared. "Archer? Your face is all blacked out. What in God's name are you doing here? Why are you stalking us? What's your connection to that thing that just went poof?" Trevor tossed both his hands in the air, before bending to pick up his shotgun.

Brad Archer cradled his head in his hands, rubbing his temples. "I never saw that abomination until it jumped me," he mumbled. "Jesus Christ, it damn near killed me. By strangulation from ten paces away. What the fuck was it?"

Trevor stared intently at the detective, gun at the ready just in case. "Something evil. Look, Detective, I know you're used to asking the questions, but I need to know why you followed us out here."

"I'm here," Brad spoke with an earnest dignity, "because Lara's my only connection to Adriana." He eyed Trevor across the twenty feet separating them. "Your gun's trained on me. Could you at least engage the safety?"

"Not until you tell me more," Trevor growled. Until he understood why the detective had trailed them all the way from Seattle, he wasn't taking any chances.

Brad nodded tightly. "It's simple enough," he began. "One of the times I was at your house, I figured you were on your way to somewhere. Sensed it. After I pulled out, I went round by your alleyway. Noticed all the work you'd done next to the gate. It was obvious those bushes had been freshly cut, so I pulled them apart to look through the slats in the fence. I saw the Ford all piled up like something out of a dustbowl Okie migration, and that pretty much clinched it."

"You spied on us," Trevor said coldly, not feeling any better about Brad Archer.

"I'm a detective, for chrissakes. Spying is what I do for a living," Brad spat back. "Put the goddamned gun down, Trevor, before you shoot me by mistake. What's already happened out here tonight is unnerving enough."

"Not until I understand why it was so bloody important for you to keep tabs on us."

"I already told you that." Brad sounded exasperated. "Lara's my best hope of getting Adie back. No one else knows anything."

"That doesn't explain why you were creeping toward our porch with a gun. What were you planning on doing? Shooting us?"

"I'd have brought my service revolver if I had that in mind," Brad replied, an edge in his voice. "Less messy. These woods are full of mountain lions and bears. Brought the rifle to protect myself, not to hurt you."

The detective rolled over onto his hands and knees and then lurched to his feet. "Think, man. If I hurt Lara, it'd be like shooting myself. She's my only link to my daughter." Brad sucked in a deep, ragged breath and took a step toward Trevor. Just then, the moon emerged from behind a bank of clouds, and Trevor saw the detective's strong-boned face clearly beneath its coating of greasepaint. It was haggard and drawn, the face of a man who'd lost everything he ever valued and didn't much care one way or the other about his own life anymore.

Trevor slowly lowered the gun and clicked on the safety. *Artemis's moon. Raven and Lillian were waiting for it, and it seems to be helping me too.* "How about if you come inside?" he suggested gruffly. "We could brew a nice cuppa and clean up a bit."

The gratitude washing over the detective's wan features was painful to see. "Sure," he replied. "I'd like that. Lara's probably sleeping, but maybe I could wait in the living room or something until she wakes up." Cocking his head to one side, he listened to Gunter yapping. "Think your dog—or all that gunfire—might've wakened her?" he asked hopefully as he bent to retrieve his weapon, engaging the safety with an audible click.

Trevor wondered if he should tell Brad that Lara wasn't there, then thought better of it. "Probably not," he murmured. "She sleeps like the dead."

So long as he thinks she's asleep, I've bought a few hours. They should all be back by dawn.

He envisioned Raven's wrath at finding anyone other than himself in the house and shuddered. *Well, nothing to be done about it. Or about how furious he'll be when he figures out I used his conveniently-placed silver shells.* Grimacing at the thought, Trevor led the way up the front steps, remembered the front door was locked, and headed for the one off the kitchen.

As he wove in and out of the furniture littering the wraparound veranda, Raven's voice rumbled through his head. *Silver is a mortal poison to us.*

Bloody hell, Trevor thought. *If it wasn't Raven, then who swapped out those shells?*

"I answered your questions," Brad said, trailing behind Trevor into the house. "I only have one. What was that thing that attacked me? And how the hell did you manage to finish it off with a shotgun when my Heckler and Koch couldn't do the job?"

"That's two," Trevor noted, leaning the shotgun against a corner of the wall as he bent to pet Gunter, but the young dog raced past both men through the open door and down the steps.

"Okay, so it's two," Brad agreed, sounding exhausted. "Here's a third. Why did he hiss *silver* just before he vanished? Surely it wasn't some sort of vampire..." His voice trailed off, and a sick understanding dawned on his face. "Aw, shit," he muttered.

Aw, shit, indeed. Trevor whistled, and Gunter bounded back up the steps. Once the puppy was inside, Trevor locked the door almost as an afterthought. Fighting an urge to break into hysterical laughter, he understood just how fine a line he'd trod out in the yard. And how close he'd come to being killed.

"It's a long story," he said, looking hard at Brad. "I'm not even sure I know enough of it for it to make sense." Stepping to the sink, Trevor pumped water into the kettle. "I'm going to heat some water for tea, and so you can get that black crud off your face. Whilst we're waiting for it to get hot, you can listen." He plonked the kettle onto the stove, tossed some wood into the firebox, and fell wearily into a kitchen chair, gesturing for Brad to take the one next to him.

After hesitating for a moment, the detective propped his weapon next to Trevor's and folded his tall body into a chair.

"Evil feeds off chaos," Trevor began. "All the shortages and riots and such seem to have opened a gateway so that dark forces can enter our world…"

CHAPTER 21

The mist that had surrounded them on their journey parted slowly, and Lara found herself back on the beach where she'd last seen Adriana. Everyone else shimmered out of a numinous fog that dissipated gradually once they'd all arrived. Just as the beach had been different the second time she'd seen it, it had changed once again and she looked out on a Kafkaesque world. The moon hung low in a violet sky, and the beach was coppery with a pale green ocean lapping against its sands. Lara looked at Lillian. "What should I do?" she asked. "I don't have time to make any mistakes."

"Indeed," Lillian replied, exchanging a pointed glance with Raven.

The mage shook his head. "No," he said. "'It's best if Lara finds her. We might unearth many things and never locate the girl. It's Lara who has the link."

"G'on," Elidora urged in her soft brogue. "Ye'll no' be wantin' t' stand still here. 'Tis akin to death."

"Parteecular sin we're sae mony," Gren agreed.

No hints from them. Lara glanced from side to side as she sought clues about where the keepers of this bizarre place might have sequestered Brad Archer's daughter. She began walking, still scanning the sand from beach to trees. Since she'd last found Adriana among the trees, she cut diagonally across the damp sand, her booted feet making squelching noises as they sank in.

"Do you always come out the same place here?" she asked Raven.

"What do you mean?"

"That spot on the beach where we materialized. Is it the same location as when I was here the last two times? There aren't any landmarks, so I can't tell."

"No," he said, after a lengthy pause. "Probably not, but that doesn't matter. This isn't like the world you came from. Things shift and change from moment to moment. That's why the colors are always different."

She opened her mouth to ask another question. Raven held up a hand. "You don't have to understand everything," he said kindly. "Or even anything at all. Save your energies for the girl. You're the reason we're here. The goddess will give you what you need if you trust in her."

Lara closed her eyes trying to feel something, anything, that might tip her off. Since the others weren't making a point of whispering, she cupped her hands around her mouth and called, "Adriana. Adie, where are you?"

She'd taken a few more steps when she thought she heard the faintest of whimpers off to her right. *Is that her? Or is it a trap?* Lara tried to send her sixth sense out, but crashed back at her the second she released it. Staggering slightly, she muttered, "Guess that doesn't work here."

Lillian laid a hand on her shoulder. "No, dearie, it doesn't."

"I thought I heard—" Lara began.

"Follae't," Gren urged without waiting for her to finish.

Lara raked the darkness and made out a pair of reddish eyes glowing within the trees. A second pair winked into being. Once she knew what to look for, she caught her breath. Hundreds of eyes, glaring and malevolent, glittered. Her amulet began emitting its warning vibration.

She looked mutely at Lillian for guidance, but the Sidhe made shooing motions with her hands. "Surely you didn't think those holding the girl would let us waltz in and snatch her up," she commented with an unexpected return of her dry humor. "Keep moving. Elidora is correct. Remaining still is unwise."

A dry cawing rose from the trees, and before Lara had a chance to do anything, the red-eyed creatures were upon them. With bodies like marmot-sized rodents and wings like bats, the hideous dark brown animals emitted a hissing snarl that was a cross between a growl and a bird's hunting cry.

"At least it means we're close." Raven scowled, raising his hands. "Get behind me," he snapped at Lara, "so we don't hit you by mistake."

She moved with alacrity as she scuttled behind the mage. Bolts of energy flew from his big hands. The others opened magical fire too. As she watched, horrified, the strange animals dropped to the ground, twitching and moaning. Black blood spewed from them, until the coppery sand was slick with it.

Magic flared around her hot, and so bright the white light hurt her eyes. Soon at least a hundred of the misshapen creatures lay either dead or dying. The smell was so atrocious Lara caught at her midsection, bent, and vomited onto the sand.

"What the hell are they?" she asked, swiping a sleeve across her mouth.

"Yon be curaets. Wirricowes' dauties," Gren said curtly. "Whit mean thair maisters canna be hyne away."

Curaets. Demons' spawn.

While Lara was trying to decipher the rest of what Gren had just said, she heard that small whimpering again. Picking her way between the curaets' bodies, she sensed she wasn't moving quickly enough and ran toward the noise she hoped desperately was Adriana. As her boots trampled the dead animals, she felt their bones crunch under her heels, and a shudder coursed through her. Her stomach clenched, but she kept going, not bothering to glance over her shoulder for the others.

Either they were behind her, or they weren't. It didn't matter. The only important thing was rescuing the innocent girl who'd been hauled to this miserable place because of her.

Coming around the trunk of an unusually large tree with red leaves, Lara cried out, "She's here. Hurry!" Leaping forward, she knelt in the dirt next to Adriana who was lashed to two stakes driven into the ground. The girl's blonde head lolled to one side, and her complexion was so pasty Lara wondered if she was already dead.

Reaching fingers forward to feel for a pulse, she stopped dead when Raven thundered, "Do not touch her."

Startled, Lara looked over one shoulder. "Why not?" she demanded. "We can't get her out of here if we can't lay hands on her. Besides, I want to check to see if she's still alive."

"Because it might not actually be her," he replied grimly, his mouth set in a hard line as he strode forward. "It could be an illusion, controlled by those who sent the curaets."

Lara pulled her hand back as if stung. *There's a whole hell of a lot I don't know,* she thought, biting at the insides of her cheeks in frustration.

Raven and Lillian were on opposite sides of the thing that might be Adriana, hands extended. Chanting, they lowered their hands until they were scant inches above the comatose figure. After a few moments, Lillian inclined her head. "It's her," she said, exhaling sharply. "Much remains to do, and time grows short."

"We must not touch the stakes," Raven informed the group. "They've been spelled to trigger a trap."

Lara eyed the chains wrapped around Adriana's emaciated body. "How the hell are we going to free her?" she demanded. "We have to touch the chains and they're connected to the stakes. It'll be impossible to disturb one without the other."

"Carefully," Elidora said grimly, a deep frown on her face as she surveyed the problem.

"Is she alive?" Lara asked anxiously, still wondering if they'd come too late. She'd been watching the girl closely, and hadn't seen any evidence of life within the emaciated form.

"Aye, she leeves still an on," Gren murmured. "Poustit ere lang, an we staund here bletherin'. Hers be a haundy pith tae haud this place. Sae thay needna breuk their ain."

"What?" Try as she might, Gren was well-nigh impossible to understand.

"The girl still lives—barely," Raven said shortly, not bothering to look at her. "The Goblins are draining her energy to maintain this place."

Raven and Lillian had their heads together, conversing in Celtic Gaelic. Lara stared with dismay at the welter of thick chains traversing the young girl's slim body. Her hands were manacled and attached to metal rings in the tops of the stakes. Chains fell downward from there, wrapped three times round her torso, and were tacked back against the stakes.

"Now that we know it's her, can I touch her?" Lara asked.

"So long as you do not disturb either chains or stakes," Lillian said tersely.

Kneeling next to the wasted form of Brad Archer's daughter, Lara reached out a none-too-steady hand and stroked her filthy cheek. The girl's face was streaked with blood and dirt, and her white-blonde hair hung in greasy, matted tangles. Tenderly, Lara pushed the hair away from Adie's face. "It'll be all right," she crooned softly. "We'll get you out of this horrid place. Truly we will. Your father loves you. He's been worried half to death.'

"Lara!" Raven's voice held a peremptory edge. "I've told you twice to move aside."

"Sorry," she muttered, scootching out of reach of the chains.

"We are the first focus for you," Lillian growled. Now and always. Get back farther."

Lara pushed to her feet and moved about ten feet away. As she watched, Lillian and Raven joined hands on one side of Adriana while Gren and Elidora did likewise on the other. On what she assumed was the Gaelic count of three, power blazed from each of the pairs of magic wielders. When the flashing lights cleared and Lara could see again, the chains that had been holding Adriana's wrists to the stakes lay shattered on the ground.

"Humph," Raven snorted. "That worked." Moving forward quickly, he shoved Adriana's hands behind her body.

"You weren't sure—" Lara began.

"Silence," Raven bellowed. "Stay back and keep your mouth shut."

He resumed his position across from Lillian, and another blast of energy lit the night with white light. Adriana began whimpering. Lara started forward, but Raven shouted at her to stay put. When the aftershocks cleared, two of the three lengths of chain securing Adriana's torso lay on the ground, and Lara began to feel hopeful, despite the amulet tolling what sounded like a death knell.

"Ane mair," Gren breathed, batting at a place where Adriana's rags had caught fire.

"Hoot aye," Elidora agreed. "Then we must away."

A high-pitched, unearthly shriek from far up the beach commanded Lara's attention. Peering through the thick trees, she couldn't see a thing.

"Goblins," Lillian hissed. "We must've hit one of those goddess-damned stakes. Quickly now." The next flash of power rocked the ground beneath Lara. She tried desperately to clear her vision, but all she saw were stars.

Raven urged her to grasp his hand so they could leave. The Goblins' cries were coming closer, and she felt the pounding of hundreds feet running toward them. Metal clanked against metal. Lara cringed, helpless and blind.

"I can't see," she moaned, trying to figure out where Raven was by the sound of his voice. She felt his hand on her wrist pulling her roughly against his bulk, and her sight finally returned.

Mist rose about them as the first Goblin lurched into their clearing, howling his rage that their prisoner had escaped. Lara gasped in disbelief at the lumbering monster, almost like a Cyclops with a single eye above a rhinoceros-like tusk. Battered armor covered his trunk, and a vicious-looking axe was clasped in one ungainly hand. His bald, mottled head glistened in moonlight filtering through the trees, and he sneered right at her through a mouthful of stained, crooked teeth.

"Think of home," Raven said, urgently, his breath hot against her ear. "Else we shall be stuck here."

Lara wrenched her mind to the rambling log house in the clearing. Afraid it wouldn't be good enough, she yanked a vision of Trevor front and center, and forced herself to think about him waiting for her. The gloom-and-doom vibrations from the amulet dimmed slightly. The mist thickened, and the swirling sensation intensified. Her relief that they were truly going to escape was so intense she felt weak. The odd, vertiginous feeling she experienced when traveling between worlds assailed her senses, and she clung to Raven.

It seemed to take longer than usual, but finally the mist receded, and the familiar furniture in the parlor came into view. She looked around anxiously for Trevor and felt his arms close around her from behind.

"Thank bloody God," he muttered. "It's an hour past dawn. I was terrified I'd never see you again."

She turned in his arms and drank in his wonderfully familiar face, but his expression shifted rapidly from joy at seeing her to horror at something behind her back. Spinning rapidly, she shrieked as she saw Goblins tumbling through a multihued vortex whirling above them.

Elidora screamed something in Gaelic, and Raven and Lillian unleashed bolt after bolt of power. The air in the room fairly crackled with it. Gren, hampered by the burden in his arms, bent to lay Adriana tenderly on the sofa, then turned and added his magic to the mix, a resolute expression on his face.

"What's Elidora saying?" Lara shrank back against Trevor.

"Close the gate," he gasped.

The roar of gunfire filled the house as Brad Archer shouldered his assault rifle and fired at the Goblins. As their misshapen bodies fell, dark blood sizzled, making smoking holes in everything it touched. The amulet thrummed its approval, and Lara watched in horrified amazement as their lifeless bodies folded in upon themselves and disappeared.

"Stap!" Gren shouted at Brad. "Thoo gar't sair difeecult tae sneck th' portal. See efter thy dochter." He gestured to where Adriana lay on the sofa, her eyes shut, barely breathing.

"What?" Brad's gaze flew to where Gren pointed. Dropping his rifle, he raced to Adriana's side. "You found her? Jesus Christ, I didn't even notice I was so focused on those things coming through the ceiling." Cradling his daughter against him, Brad called to her. "Adie, Adie, it's Poppa. Oh my God. My sweet babe, what sort of bastard did this to you?"

Elidora shouted something in Gaelic that sounded like *no*. Gren went to the Sidhe and hugged her hard. He told her something, the ancient Gaelic rich as a fine wine, and then he jumped into the void above them. In seconds, the airy whirlpool stopped pulsating and vanished, leaving nothing but a fine vapor in its wake.

Feeling shell-shocked, staring at the ruins of the living room, Lara tried to absorb what had just happened. There were bullet holes in the walls, burnt places where Goblin blood had dripped on things, two shattered lanterns, and the reek of spilled kerosene hung heavy in the air.

Elidora wailed piteously, tearing at her long hair, and Lillian took the other Sidhe into her arms, crooning low.

"What just happened?" Lara looked at Trevor.

"Gren told her she was his one true love, his only love," Trevor said, looking wretched. "Ach, Lara. This is so bloody sad. I didn't realize it until just now, but I remember him from my village. He was a traveling blacksmith then. At least that's what he pretended to be. He used to come round to stay with Elidora."

"He may yet survive," Lillian murmured soothingly.

"Not standin' alone agin' so many," Elidora moaned. "Ach, whatever shall I do without him by my side?"

"If he calls upon the gods…" Lillian's face twisted with pain for her friend. Holding Elidora close, she spoke low and urgently, "You must not give up hope. Come, let us lend him our strength." In her husky, mellifluous voice, Lillian began to chant. Straightening her spine, Elidora joined in.

Raven, looking as if he were stretched taut as piano wire, said, "No, this one," and began a different incantation.

Lara sagged against Trevor, her mind racing. How had the goblins managed to follow them? And what had Gren done to close off the gateway? She tripped over the puppy who'd inserted himself between her and Trevor, clearly frightened half out of his young wits by the gunshots.

"Can any of you help my daughter?" Brad asked, white-faced, from where he knelt on the floor next to Adriana. "She's dying." When no one answered him, the detective rose to his feet, picked up his daughter, and started for the door.

Raven blocked his path. "You cannot leave," he said.

Brad narrowed his eyes and stared at Raven. "Why not?" he demanded. "Adie will probably die *en route*, but I have to at least try to get her to a hospital."

"Think, man," Raven growled. "They'll ask you where you found your daughter. How she got injured. What will you tell them?"

A confused look washed over Brad's face. "Uh, I— Well, I'd come up with something," he sputtered, trying to push past Raven.

The mage extended a hand. "Do not make me hurt you," he said. "I must help the women, and you need to tend to your daughter as best you can. No one can know about this place—or about us."

Energy flowed from Raven's hand, circled Brad, and disappeared into the detective. Moving like an automaton, he retraced his steps and carried Adriana back to the sofa.

CHAPTER 22

"*P*oppa." The voice was thin, raspy, and so faint, Lara wasn't sure she'd even heard the word until Brad responded to it.

"Yes, heart of mine," he murmured, from where he sat on the couch holding Adie's head and shoulders in his lap. Lara came closer to see if she could help. The girl's eyes were open, and they were the same clear blue as her father's. Her skin was so pale, Lara could see the faint tracery of veins and arteries just beneath the surface.

Trevor came up next to Lara with a glass of water in one hand and a full pitcher in the other. "Maybe she could drink something." Reaching out wordlessly, Brad took the glass, raised Adriana's shoulders, and held the liquid to her bloodless lips. She swallowed obediently, once, twice, and then her head fell backward.

"T—too hard," she whispered, as some of the liquid dribbled down her chin.

"Do you think we might try to transport her to Skykomish?" Trevor asked. "There's probably a small clinic there."

Lara elbowed him. She'd just opened her mouth to remind him of Raven's warning when Brad said, "She'll never make it. It'd take too long on that dirt road."

Relieved that Raven's spell seemed to be intact, Lara stroked Adriana's hands, murmuring encouragement to the girl. When Raven had barred the detective's egress, she'd thought it unreasonable. Now that she'd had a chance to think about it, she'd come to a reluctant understanding that Brad and Adriana's appearance at any hospital might well lead a bevy of authorities right to their doorstep.

"Is there anything we can do to help her?" Trevor asked.

Brad looked up out of grief-stricken eyes. "Before I was a cop, I was an Army medic. Adie needs fluids. IV fluids. She's desperately dehydrated. She must've lost a lot of blood somehow, and I think she has internal injuries and an infection since she's burning up with fever. She needs to be airlifted to a level one trauma center, and that's not going to happen. Not from out here."

"Does your Chief know where you are?" Lara asked carefully, still concerned the secret of their location might be breached. If it would be anyway, there was no reason not to try to get the girl to some sort of assistance.

Brad shook his head. "No. I'm not on duty. Didn't want anyone to know where I was going after I checked out, so I have my own car. If I had my cruiser, it would have radio equipment and a comprehensive first aid kit, not that it would help much." He set the glass on the floor.

"I'm not sure I understand how Adriana got this way, but since you seem to have extricated her from some sort of magical place, do you suppose any of them," he waved an arm at the trio who were still chanting earnestly, "could help her?"

"I don't know," Lara replied, feeling utterly helpless. "They've got their own set of problems right now. What they're doing is Gren's only hedge against a Goblin horde. Here, let's try to get some more water into her."

Adie took another drink when her father retrieved the glass and held it to her lips. Opening her eyes again, the barest ghost of a smile crept across her face. "It's okay, Poppa," she said softly. "I was just so scared I was going to die all alone in that awful place. Even if I die here, at least I'm with you now." Her voice trailed off, and her eyes closed again.

Brad's blue eyes filled with tears, and Lara saw him fighting for control. "My wife—" he said in a voice so low it seemed he was talking to himself. "She blames me for this. Hasn't said three words to me since Adie disappeared. We never did have much of a marriage. Only reason we stayed together was because of our daughter."

As his words hung in the air between them, Lara gathered herself to say something supportive, and then reminded herself she wasn't his therapist.

Glancing over at the others, she knew Raven and Lillian well enough to see signs of exhaustion tugging at them. She debated breaking into what they were doing, then looked at Elidora's pinched face and the anguish reflected in the woman's clear, dark eyes, and rejected the idea.

Likely, they knew Adriana was dying. They'd said she had almost no chance, even before they risked so much to rescue her. Lara knew they'd do what they could for the girl once they were through with their prayers on Gren's behalf.

"Would you like me to get some of that filth off her?" Lara asked softly. At Brad's nod, she started for the kitchen to get a basin and sent Trevor upstairs for clean cloths and towels. By the time she returned, Brad had tossed fresh wood into the fireplace and the room was perceptibly warmer. As they stripped the pathetic rags off Adriana's skeletal form, Lara had to bite her lower lip to keep from crying out. The girl had bruises over much of her body and long lacerations that did, indeed, look infected, the skin puffy and purulent.

"Bloody hell," Trevor fumed. "Whoever did this should be horsewhipped."

"Yes," Brad growled through clenched teeth. "If I ever get my hands on those bastards, I'll tear them to pieces. Even if it was one of those unholy monsters that fell out of the sky and into this house."

Adie moaned as they worked on her, treading the surface of consciousness, and then dropping beyond their reach. About the time

Brad and Lara were wrapping her in one of Lara's soft robes, Raven, Lillian, and Elidora lowered their hands and fell silent. A low moan escaped Elidora just before she dropped her head into her hands and began to weep.

Looking up from what felt like the hundredth basin of dirty water, Lara met Lillian's clear, green eyes. Questions bubbled to her lips, but the Sidhe shook her head as she blinked back tears. "Gren is in the *Dreaming*," she said after a long pause. "He will never leave there."

"My poor laddie, he is between th' wind an' th' waw, an' wounded beyond reckonin'." Elidora raised her tear streaked face to look at Lara. "Mayhap 'twould hae been better had he been granted succor in th' Summerlands." Another tear gathered in the corner of one eye and rolled down her pale, haggard face as she spoke.

"That was not the will of the other gods," Raven reminded her sternly. "Gren may yet find an end to his long life, but now is not his time."

"If he's in the *Dreaming*, you'll be able to go to him, won't you?" Lara asked, hopefully. The amulet's emanations suggested otherwise.

"No, child." Elidora smiled sadly. "His body was decimated by Goblins. Only his spirit remains, and it inhabits a part o' th' *Dreamin'* tha's closed t' those o' us with corporeal form."

"Lara," Trevor's voice was tinged with urgency. "Please."

"Could you help Adriana?" she asked, looking from Raven to Lillian to Elidora.

"We can make a potion to keep her comfortable." Raven spoke gently, holding Lara's gaze with somber eyes. "Yet I fear she too, is in the hands of the gods. I could feel her life trickling away even as we were trying to assist Gren."

"Anything you could do," Brad said in a broken voice. "I know she's in pain, and I don't have anything to give her."

Crossing to where Adriana lay, Lillian placed a hand on the girl's forehead. "Fever," she muttered as she opened the robe to inspect Adie's body. Though the Sidhe didn't say anything, Lara saw her eyes narrow as she took in the teenager's ravaged flesh. Culling through pockets, Lillian drew out some pieces of what looked like bark.

"White willow," she said, pulling out her pocket knife and stripping the inside of the pieces into a small pile. Selecting a few scrapings, she tucked them into the girl's slack-jawed mouth. "Make sure she drinks whenever she's conscious. I will make a poultice of onion, garlic, and mustard seed—if I can find any—to draw heat off the putrid places where her flesh is rotting."

"I'll help," Elidora, who'd been hovering just behind Lillian, offered. "'Twould be a blessin' t' hae somethin' t' do just now."

"While they're about that." Raven settled his bulk heavily into a chair, steepled his fingers under his chin, and stared at Trevor. "Perhaps you could tell me how Detective Archer got inside this house."

Trevor looked so miserable that Lara went to stand beside him, draping a protective arm around his shoulders.

"I guess you would've already figured out I disobeyed your directive," Trevor said stiffly, his gaze fixed on the ground. "You see, I had this dream…"

As she listened to the latest version of Psyche's prophecy, panic raced along Lara's nerve endings. "Could he have died in that dream?" she demanded, moving swiftly to stand before Raven, hands on her hips.

"Yes." Raven nodded. "He could have."

Though she waited, it soon became clear he wasn't going to say anything more, at least about Trevor's dream.

"You're not done." The mage looked hard at Trevor. "I still don't know why you left the protection of these walls." As the story eked out in fits and starts, Raven listened intently, asking for clarification at one or two junctures. When there was no more to be told, the mage drew in a thoughtful breath and exhaled through his teeth. "I think I understand," he said after a long silence.

"Well, I don't." Trevor sounded less cowed than he had at the beginning of his recitation. "The Goblin seemed to think I'd shot it with silver. You just told me you never touched the shells on the bookshelf. They're lead shot, not silver. So, how in the hell did I end up with silver bullets?"

"Artemis's moon," Raven said, a tired ghost of a smile lighting his face. "She sent Her energy to finish off the intruder. And to save you from harm. You told me the moon cast its light on the Goblin just before you fired. Artemis's power guided your hand and lent strength to your efforts."

"I, uh, t—that is…" Trevor stammered and raked both hands through his curls. "None of this seems real. Goddesses lending a hand to mortals. It's like something out of mythology."

"Where do you think the old tales came from, son?" Raven eyed him, quirking an eyebrow. "After all, *I* am helping you. Why would you view Artemis's aid as odder, or more numinous, than my own?"

"It's easy to forget you turning into Wôden on Halloween," Trevor mumbled. "I am sorry I didn't do a better job of staying in the house, though."

Raven shook his head. "You did nothing wrong. I do not always see the future as clearly as I might. We brought the girl. She's dying. It's good her father is here to ease her way to the Summerlands."

"Lillian and Elidora," Lara protested. "Maybe…" The words died on her lips as she saw the truth in Raven's eyes, heard it in Adriana's uneven breathing, and felt it from the sad, slow thrum of the amulet.

"More water." Brad held out the empty glass.

"Certainly." Trevor snatched up the glass, filling it from the pitcher.

"And more towels, please," Brad said, rolling his daughter so he could pull the damp ones out from beneath her. They'd tucked thick towels between Adriana and the warm bathrobe. As Lara helped, she saw that the soiled ones were tinged with blood mingled with the girl's urine.

∼

"COULD you please tell me what happened after that Goblin stumbled into the clearing where we found Adriana?" Lara asked Raven once they'd done all they could for the comatose girl. "Did we touch those stakes, and that's why the Goblins came? How were they able to follow us here?" With her gaze searching Raven's face, she dredged up one last question. "Why can't we save Adie? Gren gave up his life for her."

"No!" Raven shook his great head so hard his beard bounced on his chest. "Gren gave up his life for all of us. Ach, child, there's so much you don't know, it's difficult to figure where to begin." He opened his mouth and then shut it again. "I must have sustenance if I'm to follow that path," he muttered, as he pushed himself wearily to his feet.

"I'll get something for you," Trevor offered, walking briskly toward the kitchen. "Does anyone else want food?" he called over one shoulder.

Lara thought about it and realized it had been so long since she'd eaten her midsection felt dead. "I do," she said, before getting up to help. A few minutes later, she helped Trevor carry a plate with cheese and crackers, and a six pack of ale, to the living room. Just before she got there, the amulet began a dirge she'd not yet felt from it, and she looked up in surprise, seeking the source of its angst.

"Please, Adie, just a little more," Brad whispered from his spot on the couch. "Don't go yet. I'm so sorry."

"You have nothing to be sorry for, Poppa," the girl said, her voice clearer than it had been since her rescue. "They're calling and I have to go. There's a light…a beautiful light. Try not to be sad for me. Tell Momma I love her." Adriana's voice was weakening, but she struggled to add, "I love you too, Poppa."

Food forgotten, Lara and Trevor sprang to Brad's side. Her throat thick with tears, Lara hunkered down and reached out to touch Adriana, saying, "Your father's right, dear. Just a bit more. Lillian and Elidora will be back soon. They'll have—"

With an inarticulate, impatient sound, Raven pushed in front of Lara and sank to the floor to grasp Adriana's hands in his. The Celtic

Gaelic that flowed from him was so eloquent Lara didn't need Trevor to translate. Tears flowed down the mage's face as he urged the desperately ill child to reach for the light. He told her not to be afraid, that her loved ones would find her in the Summerlands, and that she was truly safe from her tormentors and would soon find surcease from her pain.

Adriana's slight chest rose, quivered, fell, and rose one last time before the last of her life fled. Her head, cradled in her father's hands, drooped to one side, and a radiant smile appeared on her bruised and battered face.

"What did you do?" Brad asked Raven in a voice so ravaged by sorrow Lara had to struggle to make out the words.

"Brought her home," the mage replied, his voice gruff with emotion as he wiped tears from his face. "She couldn't have survived in this world, since she spent far too long in the other."

"But..." Lara was having a hard time talking; her tongue felt thick, and words were elusive. "Brigid told us we had to wait."

Raven smiled sadly. "Yes, this was a fool's errand from its inception. We knew the child could not endure after so long in that realm. Had we gone after her afore the full of the moon, we'd not have had Artemis's help, and even the slenderest of hopes would've crumbled. Our gamble was she'd live long enough to return her to her proper place."

With a sadly practiced gesture, Brad placed fingers on his daughter's lids, closing her eyes for the last time. "I'd like to sit with my Adie," he managed, "before we bury her." Letting his head fall back against the couch, a low, wailing lamentation escaped him, and the detective sobbed helplessly as he held his lifeless child to his chest.

Laying a hand on one of Brad's, Raven said, "May the goddess assuage your pain, human." He rocked back, got to his feet, and crooked a finger toward Lara and Trevor. The puppy, still frightened from the Goblins, crept out from under a chair and padded after them as they went out the front door, leaving it ajar.

"Oh my." Lara's hand flew to her mouth as the brilliant colors of the morning sky sparkled against her tired eyes. Pastel tones played among the clouds, and the sun was just cresting the eastern horizon atop the tall evergreens. "It's beautiful." Groping, she caught one of Trevor's hands.

"Never been one for religion," he murmured, "but it's almost as if someone's welcoming that poor child."

"The Summerlands did welcome her," Raven said, sitting heavily on one of the porch steps. "I saw to it. When she started talking about lights, I had to make certain they weren't the wrong ones. After all our effort, I did *not* want her to end up back with those unspeakable Demons."

Lillian and Elidora came out of the woods, their arms laden with plants.

Lara thought she should tell them the herbs and things were no longer needed. Raven shook his head, reading her mind easily. "They already know, child," he murmured. "It was good for Elidora to be out in the forest. And for Lillian as well. Trees are her natural element, as herbs are Elidora's. They knew before they left there was little enough to be done. Between those two," he spread his hands wide, "they've helped hundreds, if not thousands, of souls into and out of this life."

Lara settled next to Raven with Trevor on her other side. "What did you mean about Gren forfeiting himself for the rest of us?" she asked.

Lillian exchanged a glance with Raven and laid her bundle of roots and vines on the bottom step. "It's critical the boundaries betwixt the worlds remain in place," she said, holding Lara's gaze. "We were a shade too slow leaving the in-between. That gap allowed the Goblins to hold the portal so they too, could use it. They don't belong in this world. For them to remain here in such numbers would've been the true death knell for Earth. We had to shut the gateway, just as we closed the conduit they'd opened to your office. Not just for us, but for every creature inhabiting this planet."

"It dinna help 'at they follaed yon snoot here." Elidora's soft brogue was fuzzy with her grief, and she gestured vaguely toward the house.

Placing an arm around her friend, Lillian continued talking. "Gradoxst has been furious ever since we severed the working that linked Brad to him." She made a sign against evil and spat in the dirt. "I've felt him pushing at me—hissing and threatening—whenever I've cast even the smallest of spells. He's been trailing after the detective too, trying to lure him back. Because he was keeping a close eye on Archer, Gradoxst knew we'd left here and surmised it was to extricate the daughter."

Lillian looked hard at Lara, as if assessing just how much truth she could tolerate. Nodding, she went on, "That's why the Goblins found us so easily in the in-between. They knew when to look. It's possible we didn't jostle either of those damned stakes at all."

"So was it Gradoxst that Artemis helped me kill?" Trevor cocked his head to one side looking hopeful.

"Would that it were that easy," Lillian replied ruefully as Elidora slid from under her embrace. "Nay, that one always sends others to do his work. He was here, though. I can still sense traces of his presence. Bah!" She shuddered.

"How can he—or any of them—be here and not disturb that balance point you were taking about?" Lara looked at Raven, her eyebrows furled into question marks.

"There are always some of the Demon spawn here," he replied slowly. "Those who were born human or Sidhe—and Gradoxst began his life as one of us afore he was seduced by evil—have an easier time traveling betwixt their world and our own. It's more a matter of how many and for how long that creates problems."

"Gradoxst started out as a Sidhe?" Trevor sounded skeptical.

"Och aye, laddie. And a dowie day t'was for us all when he chose the path o' the damned," Elidora muttered, shaking her head dolefully. Silence stretched among them after her words died away.

"Gren knew the true meaning of courage," Trevor said at last, looking at Elidora.

"Aye, laddie, that he did," she said sadly. "Dae ye hae mynd o' him?"

"He was the blacksmith." Trevor smiled softly. "Of course I remember him. He used to ruffle my hair and give me hard candies."

"Aye, and he did love all th' bairns," Elidora murmured. "He and I, we couldna geet our own, so all children became his."

Lillian wrapped her arms around Elidora again, pulling both her and her armful of herbs close. "We were talking, while we were gathering," she said to Lara and Trevor, fixing them with her green gaze over Elidora's shoulder. "Elidora shouldn't be alone for a while. Since I shall be here often, it would be good were she to be here as well."

"You'd be more than welcome, especially with our own bairn soon to come." Trevor pushed to his feet, descended to where the two women stood and closed his arms about them both. "There's no way I can ever repay—" he began, his voice choked with emotion.

"Hush," Elidora said. "'Tis no' a matter o' owin'."

"No, it's not," Trevor agreed, "but a matter of wanting. And I want you here with us."

"Yes, we'd be honored," Lara chimed in, smiling, but her smile faded.

'What are we going to do about Adriana?" she asked in a low voice. "Brad said something about burying her, but shouldn't we take her to the local coroner first?"

"That probably wouldn't be a very good idea," Trevor said. Letting go of the two Sidhe, he returned to his place next to Lara. "They'd just ask a whole lot of questions, like what was she doing here in the first place. And how she got so banged up." He reached out a hand and grasped one of hers. "Lara, it's the same reasons Brad couldn't take her to a hospital."

"I suppose you're right." She shrugged helplessly. "Even after all that's happened, there's a big part of me that's still stuck in twenty-first century America."

"It's good you're beginning to recognize that as a problem," Raven said with a touch of his caustic wit. "Do you suppose you might rescue that food and bring it out here?" He looked hopefully at Trevor.

"I'd rather not disturb Brad," Trevor replied, looking uncomfortable, "but I can get more from the kitchen. Back in a moment."

The five of them shared sharp cheddar and crackers, washed down with dark ale as the sun climbed higher in the sky. Gunter, as if sensing that now wasn't the time for play, lay quietly in the yard, chewing on a stick.

"Those groceries we got the other night have been a godsend," Lara noted, turning to shoot a hopeful glance at Raven. "Do you suppose we might risk another trip?"

The mage shook his head. "Nothing's changed," he said shortly. "The fewer who see you, the less likely anyone will discover your presence here."

"You've come and gone for years," she pointed out.

He began to laugh. "Yes, but scarcely through the local town," he managed around a mouthful of crackers.

"Well," Brad's pained voice jutted into the conversation. "I'm glad you're all having such a good time."

Stricken, Lara jumped to her feet and ran to where the detective stood, framed in the open front door of the house. "We're not," she protested. "Not really."

Brad held up a hand. "Don't mind me," he said. "Shouldn't have said that. I've been around death enough. Survivors try to normalize things." He took a deep, shuddery breath, and then dropped his hand. "Door's been open. I've heard most of what you've been saying, but I'm not together enough right now to talk about any of it. What I need to know," he said, looking at Raven, "is where I can bury my daughter."

"I'll show you." The mage rose in a fluid, graceful motion. "Here, man." He thrust a bottle of ale toward Brad. "Take this and follow me."

CHAPTER 23

The day moved on toward sunset. Trevor and Raven constructed a casket from wood they found in the shop. Lara, Lillian, and Elidora helped Brad dig the girl's grave. After those tasks were done, the women prepared the body, leaving Brad to find the other men. When Lara realized they were planning to bathe the corpse, she said, "I just washed her," assuming her earlier labors would be adequate to their purpose.

"'Tis a ritual," Elidora murmured, as she worked in tandem with Lillian to lay Adriana across the kitchen table. "Besides, her hair is still clotted with filth from those infernal wirricowes."

Understanding surfaced and Lara bent to help as they smoothed stove-warmed water lovingly over Adriana, consecrating her to the goddess in an ancient rite. "Wait," Lara told the two Sidhe, who'd begun to wrap Adriana in the fleece robe. "I have a dress for her."

Back a few minutes later from the front room where she'd been rummaging through boxes, Lara held up a sky-blue sheath made of soft wool. "Don't know why I packed any dresses at all," she mumbled, sheepishly. "Trev told me to leave all of them, but there were a few I couldn't part with."

"Aye, and th' goddess works in inexplicable ways, She does," Elidora said with a broad wink and snatched the soft fabric out of Lara's hands. Holding it up, she nodded approvingly. "Should fit th' lass perfectly," she pronounced as she and Lillian drew it over Adriana's head. The girl's newly-washed hair was just beginning to dry and it lay fair and shimmery against her translucent skin.

While they completed their ministrations, Lara went to find the men. It took her some time to locate them. Finally, in frustration, she called to the puppy. Following his yips led her to the pool above the house where she and Lillian had prepared for their journey to the otherworldly beach. While not exactly drunk, it was obvious the men had been sharing the bottle she saw balanced atop a rock. "That looks like Gren's," she said, remembering the mead the Arch Druid had brought to her wedding.

"It is," Raven concurred. "We are toasting him, as well as Adriana."

"Seemed only right." Trevor smiled at her, from his half-submerged spot in the pool.

"Brrr," she intoned. "Don't know how you can sit in that."

"Oh, I made it a touch warmer." Raven smiled knowingly as he settled himself lower in the water.

Wondering why Lillian had practically let her freeze to death in the same pool, Lara just said, "We're ready," before turning to walk back to the house. Gunter followed along at her heels, seemingly glad to have something to do.

When the men crowded into the kitchen, Brad gasped as he saw his daughter. "She's beautiful," he managed at last. "Thank you." He bowed slightly, first to Elidora, then to Lillian. It was an old-fashioned gesture with a poignancy and simple stateliness that tugged at Lara's tender heart. Gathering Adriana into his arms as if she weighed nothing, he walked toward the grave they'd dug, talking softly to his daughter.

Lara started to follow along behind, then a thought struck her and she dashed back into the house for a blanket from the upstairs linen cabinets. A bit breathless as she caught up to everyone else, she laid the blanket in the bottom of the casket that stood open next to the grave. Brad placed Adriana oh-so-gently atop it, before taking a reverent step back.

"May she find peace," Lara murmured.

She opened her mouth to say more, but Raven waved her to silence. "You'll tell us of her life," he told Brad. "And then we shall lower her to her rest."

Over the next hour, Lara listened to Brad recount his memories of Adriana's short life. She was an accomplished actress, among other things, as well as a singer, who'd been hoping for acceptance at Julliard. She'd excelled at sports, loving soccer and softball. The girl had adored animals, volunteering at a veterinary clinic in one of the poorer sections of Seattle. She'd also urged her parents to take in foster children, but Brad said he'd always demurred, not wanting the extra responsibility on top of his demanding job. Another mead bottle circulated among them as he spoke.

"That's all I can think of," he said at last, his gaze seeking Raven's.

Lara realized Brad had figured out who held power here without being told. She wondered why that should surprise her. He was used to wielding command. Of course he'd recognize it in others. She surfaced from her thoughts as Raven captured her attention. He sang in Celtic Gaelic, joined at intervals by Lillian and Elidora. Trevor, apparently recognizing the song, raised his fine baritone and joined in, harmonizing with the haunting melody.

Once the casket's lid settled into place, the men lowered Adriana into the ground. Everyone took turns with the shovel, covering the pine box with dirt. At first Gunter saw it as a game, but after the second time he jumped into the grave, intent on chasing the dirt, Lillian scooped him up, talking earnestly to the puppy. After that, he lay off to one side and went to sleep, tail curved around his body.

Once they'd finished heaping dirt over the grave, they sat in a circle as daylight faded from the western sky. "I don't know how to thank all of you," Brad said, looking from one to the other out of swollen eyes. "You didn't exactly tell me where you found my girl, likely because I couldn't have gotten my mind around the reality of it, but I don't think it's the sort of place she'd have rested easy."

Turning her unsettling gaze on him, Lillian tilted her head to one side. "It would've been a living death, extending mindlessly through eons," she concurred. "You have no idea."

She continued to skewer Brad with her unyielding eyes, staring appraisingly at him. "You must not disclose our existence to anyone," she said after a lengthy silence. "Nor the fact that Lara and Trevor are living here."

"'Twould be best if ye said nothin' about the last twenty-four hours," Elidora joined Lillian in staring at the detective. "If ye will find that difficult, there are things we could do t' ensure thy silence."

"That sounded ominous," Lara muttered, turning to face Elidora. "Whatever did you mean? I, for one, have had quite enough of death for a while."

"Och, modern verbiage." Elidora threw up her hands. "I merely meant we could alter th' lad's memories a wee bit."

"That won't be necessary." Brad sat straighter. "If there's one thing I learned in twenty years of police work, it's how to keep my mouth shut."

"Where do they think you are?" Raven asked curiously. "Doesn't law enforcement keep close tabs on all their officers, even when they're off duty? In case they need you for an emergency."

"Normally, yes," Brad replied. "I, ah," he colored, and cleared his throat, obviously embarrassed, "suppose you could say I went AWOL." Hastening on, he added, "See, I knew you two," he pointed at Lara and Trevor, "were leaving. Didn't know where, but I knew if I didn't track you from the moment you left, I'd be dead in the water. You'd just disappear, and I'd never find you or my Adie again. So I told the Chief I was going to spend some time with my wife. If they call down to Wenatchee, they'll figure out quick enough I lied to them."

"Where's your car?" Trevor asked.

"Down the road a piece." Brad jerked a hand over one shoulder.

"Can't they track it?"

"You've watched too much television." Brad smiled sadly. "Or maybe you haven't. It's my car, not one of theirs. There was no reason for them to put a tracking device in my personal vehicle."

Bending forward from where he was seated on the ground next to Adriana's grave, he kissed the earth above her. "Farewell, my sweet," he murmured. "May the angels watch over you, since I can't anymore."

Moved by the deep tenderness in his words, Lara felt the quick bite of tears. Leaning against Trevor, who sat next to her, she said, "Maybe we should all go in." As she shifted position, the chill from the ground seeped into her body, and she shivered.

"Yes, we should," Lillian said, folding her legs under her so she could stand. "There's been precious little in the way of food today and you of all people," she glanced at Lara, "need to eat."

"Yes, and one of us needs to milk those goats and check on the horses," Trevor said as he got to his feet.

"I'll do that," Raven said, reaching out to lay a hand on the grave. Once he'd said a few words in Celtic Gaelic, he rose. "It'll be my contribution to the meal, since cooking isn't one of my strongest attributes. I'll see if there are any eggs while I'm about it."

Making another dent in what was left of the food from Busters, Trevor fired up the wood cook stove and grilled ham slices with canned vegetables. *Tsking* at him as he opened cans, Elidora rummaged through Raven's stocks and came up with some sort of flour she coaxed into biscuits. She and Lillian sliced up the bounty they'd found in the woods, so they had fresh sautéed vegetables alongside the canned ones. Raven provided more mead, and by the time the meal was close to being ready, everyone was decidedly tipsy.

"Are you sure," Lara demanded, placing a companionable arm around Lillian, "that it's okay for me to drink?"

The Sidhe just rolled her eyes. "That's the third time you've asked me the same question," she pointed out. "If mead was going to hurt your child, I'd be the first to tell you."

"As would I." Elidora bustled by, her floury hands leaving white splotches on everything she touched.

Mollified, Lara reached for the bottle again. The alcohol created just enough of a haze that the worst of the day moved off to the side, far enough away she didn't have to think about it. "You'll have to show me where you found all those vegetables," she motioned to the pan Elidora was stirring.

"Just wild ingans and ramps with a curn yerbs," the Carlisle witch-woman said. "Easy eneu' since t'aw grows near aboots. O' course I'll be ashowin' you if ye want."

"Hey, Lara," Trevor called to her. "Get a couple serving dishes. Most everything's ready here."

Lara was relieved that dinner felt somewhat normal. The crushing sadness from the losses of Gren and Adriana receded enough to allow her to enjoy the goodhearted banter flowing around the table.

"Why'd the two of you leave?" Brad pushed himself away from the table a foot or so, crossed his legs, and folded his arms across his mid-section. "Do you have some sort of inside information?"

"Not exactly." Lara looked across at Lillian and saw the Sidhe shake her head. "We were just tired of living in the city."

"Excuse me, Doctor, but that's bullshit." Brad met her eyes. "I know a lie when I hear one."

"Guess that means I can't tell you," she said, spreading her hands in front of her.

"What if I asked if I could stay here with you?" he said. "If you're doing what I think you are, you'll need all the extra hands you can gin up."

Eyes widening, Lara exchanged glances with Trevor.

"That would be a discussion you would not be part of," Raven said firmly, looking at Brad. "Tell me, human, why you made that offer. Is this something you're sure of, or was it one of those hastily-crafted decisions your kind are famous for?"

"I—I'm not sure," Brad stammered, color rising to stain his fair skin. "You're pretty direct, aren't you? I thought I didn't have much in the way of tact, since being a cop sort of drums it out of you, but I'm a piker by comparison."

"Oh, yes." Lara began to giggle. "Those little social niceties that lubricate everything aren't much of a consideration with the Sidhe." Nonplussed, she clamped a hand over her mouth. "Ah, whoops," she blurted. "Sorry, sorry. Guess I'm drunker than I thought."

"The what?" Brad looked confused.

"Never mind," Lara said quickly, relieved her faux pas hadn't been as bad as she feared. *Of course he'd never have heard of the Sidhe—or demigods like Raven. Not unless he studied Celtic mythology.*

"It grows late," Raven said abruptly. Lara, who'd gotten better at reading him, knew he didn't sound pleased. "You," he said pointedly to Brad, "will go now to sit with your daughter. Your presence this night will comfort the both of you."

"Okay," Brad agreed. "I'll leave in a minute. You asked why I want to stay here." He looked at Raven, hesitated, and then began talking again, his voice low. "When I was sitting with Adie, and all of you were outside, Elidora said the one who suckered me into setting Lara up was still following me. And then Lillian said that him tracking me —and the fact I was here—somehow foiled your attempt to rescue Adie."

Brad swallowed hard. "So it seems I'm responsible for my daughter's death. If I'd just ignored those emails and phone calls right after she disappeared..." He took an uneven breath, before sighing heavily. "I've done this long enough. I should've known better than to be duped." His face crumpled, a sob escaped him, and he buried his face in his large-boned hands.

"It's encouraging that you see your part in this," Raven said. "Now, go sit with your daughter. We must ensure her spirit remains in the Summerlands and doesn't wander. This first night is the most critical."

Just as Trevor had lost himself in Lillian's trees at her command, so Brad raised his tear-streaked face, pushed back his chair, rose, and left the room. Waiting edgily, Lara girded herself for a lecture over her loose tongue. It never came.

"So," Raven said, after taking his time finishing his meal, "what do the two of you wish to do about your latest house guest?"

Lara looked at Trevor who shrugged noncommittally. "It's not like we know the bloke very well," he said. "Once he's here, we're likely stuck with him, since he won't be able to leave, either."

"Is that true?" Lara looked at Raven for confirmation.

"Why would it be any different for him than for you?" Lillian demanded with an irritated edge to her voice. "Or are you simply hoping for someone who can run back and forth willy-nilly to that world you still cherish so much?"

"You'd love it if I saw everything just like you," Lara snarled back, feeling a quick, brittle rush of anger shoot from her guts, "but I don't. And guess what? I don't even want to. While we're at it, why didn't you tell Brad his daughter was as good as dead after a couple days in that hellhole? He's blaming himself and—"

"He *should* examine the consequences of his actions," Lillian interrupted heatedly.

"We all need to sleep," Raven broke in, looking meaningfully at both women. "The rest of this discussion can wait for morning. If we continue it tonight, we'll be at one another's throats."

"We already are. Come with me." On his feet, Trevor held out a hand to Lara. As she rose to meet him, she thought she'd never felt quite so weary.

Lying under the quilts in their second floor bedroom, she rearranged her body so she faced him. "What do you think about Brad living here?" she asked abruptly, too exhausted to add any nuances to her question.

"Probably better for us to come to some consensus," Trevor agreed, pulling her against him. "I don't know, Lara. It's one thing having Elidora here. I know her from my childhood. Archer's sort of a wildcard, if you get my drift. On the other hand, it'd be a big help to have another man around to do the heavy stuff. What do you think?"

Well, what do I think?

"Seems like a risk on one side of things," she murmured. "On the other, if Raven and the Sidhe banish him, or whatever they do to people they want to get rid of, he'll never be able to sit next to his daughter's gravesite and mourn her. And he has helped us."

"Except for when he sold you out to Gradoxst," Trevor reminded her.

"Shit, haven't thought about that for a while." She blew out a breath. "Thanks for the reminder. I like to think I've seen the last of Gradoxst, but that's wishful thinking—particularly since he apparently knows we're here."

"Maybe not," Trevor replied thoughtfully. "He's known where to find you ever since you called the Institute for a consultation about that dream, so the fact he knows you're here doesn't seem all that significant. If you do a good job studying those things they gave you and let Elidora help—"

"You trust her," Lara cut in. "I barely know her. It's hard enough to keep my mouth shut when Lillian and Raven push me around like I'm still a child."

"To them you are," he mumbled against her hair.

"Back to Brad," she said, sleepily. "Your instincts about people tend to be better than mine. Do you think it would be all right if he were here? If we send him away, it's going to be a death sentence for him, and I think he knows it. If he doesn't get killed in one of those riots, something else will get him."

"Those are good reasons for him staying," Trevor agreed. "Let me think on it for a bit here."

As she listened to the steady beat of Trevor's heart under her ear, Lara felt the tight places inside her shaking themselves out. The horrors of the last day and night dropped away, and sleep crept closer, sending wisps of something soothing into her heart.

"I think we should let him stay," she murmured. "If that's what he really wants. He needs to understand what it means, though. That he can't ever leave."

"I agree with you," Trevor replied, after a pause so long she thought he'd fallen asleep. "What made you swallow your ambivalence?"

"Your dream," she said simply. "Psyche's telling us there's not much time left."

CHAPTER 24

The first rays of dawn were just peeking through their window when Trevor opened his eyes to the new day and glanced over at Lara. She lay on her side, making the little half-snoring sounds she did whenever she was truly exhausted. Careful not to disturb her, he slid out of bed and gathered his clothes.

Gunter hadn't slept with them. The last place Trevor had seen the dog was on Lillian's lap, so he assumed the puppy was with one of the Sidhe. After he pulled the door closed, he dumped his clothes on the floor, sorting through them. It was chilly in the upstairs hall. Gooseflesh rose on his torso as he stood there half naked, pulling on his sweater and trousers. Socks and boots followed, along with a down vest he zipped up to his chin.

A cursory examination of the downstairs yielded nothing but empty space, and Trevor wondered where everyone else had sequestered themselves. He remembered Raven's curt comment about preferring to sleep outdoors and shrugged, figuring he'd see them when they were ready to be seen. Pulling open the front door, he trod heavily down the steps to what was becoming his customary outdoor latrine and pissed. He was just stuffing himself back into his pants when he heard, "No indoor plumbing?"

Brad Archer strode toward him, a wan smile on his face.

"Yes and no," Trevor replied, elaborating. "There's only one bathroom and it's on the upper floor. Didn't want to wake Lara. She was fairly knackered."

"Maybe we could rig something on the first floor," Brad said, sounding as if he'd welcome a project to get his teeth into.

"Funny, I'd thought about the same thing myself. Water to the upstairs is hit or miss since it's reliant on a gravity feed system from the creek. Pressure's pretty puny a lot of the time."

"Bet it'll freeze come winter," Brad said. "Place I grew up had the same problem. Some days there wasn't any water at all unless we melted snow on the stove."

Not wanting to get sucked into a conversation about the future until some other things were tacked down, Trevor faced Brad. "So you really want to stay?" When the detective nodded, Trevor asked, "Why? It'd mean no one will know where you are. You'll lose access to your buddies on the police force, your wife, any other family you might have."

"I thought a lot about it last night," Brad said. "And I discussed it with Adie, though I know how strange that must sound."

Not strange at all, Trevor thought wryly. *Not after what I've lived through recently.* "Come on," he said. "You can tell me all about it whilst I get some coffee going."

Brad settled himself at the kitchen table and rested his chin on fingers that were woven together. "What are you going to do when you run out of coffee beans?" he asked.

"Guess we'll drink tea made from the local supply of roots and berries." Trevor looked askance at Brad. "That's not what you were going to talk with me about, though."

"No," the detective admitted a bit sheepishly. "It's not." Blowing out a breath through compressed lips, he added, "Okay, here goes. Hope you're patient, because it may take a few minutes."

Putting on his Lara-face, Trevor mimicked her way of encouraging disclosures, infusing as much compassion as he could into his nod toward Brad.

Jesus, he looks trashed. Hope this isn't as hard to hear as I think it's going to be.

"I grew up on a cattle ranch in Colorado," Brad began. "Left when I was sixteen to join the Army. Things at home weren't good. Served in the Middle East, and when I got out I went to college on the GI Bill. Never found it easy to get close to much of anyone, so I mostly kept to myself in the service and at the University of Southern California too."

Trevor pulled up a chair so he sat across from Brad. His ears had perked up when the man mentioned a less-than-optimal childhood. He'd almost asked for more detail, but decided that was more Lara's bailiwick than his. *I might get more than I bargained for if I start asking questions,* he told himself and returned his attention to Brad.

"...majored in Police Science and joined the Seattle Police Department when I was just shy of thirty. Since I didn't have any particularly bad habits, I rose through the ranks fairly quickly." Looking up, Brad asked, "Say, is that coffee done yet? It smells mighty good."

"Should be." Trevor rose to check, returning with two mugs and the percolator. "Best give it a couple minutes for the grounds to settle out. Basket doesn't catch all of them."

"Somewhere along the line," Brad picked up the pieces of his tale, "I met Barbara. She worked as a dispatcher. By then, I was closing on thirty-five and thought I ought to get married. Didn't exactly love her, but I guess I deluded myself it wouldn't matter."

Coloring, he reached for the coffee pot and poured himself a cup, adding honey from a container on the table. "Maybe it was because of that mess in my house growing up, but I wasn't able to give her what she needed. She always complained, and I don't suppose I blame her. I wasn't around much, and when I was, I was always working on cases. That's how I made detective in record time." He took a sip from his mug. "Wow, that's strong."

"It's the percolator," Trevor explained. "Go on, the quicker you get through this, the easier it'll be."

"How true," Lara called from the middle of the house. Walking slowly into the kitchen wrapped in a warm robe, she looked around and asked, "Where's the dog?"

"With Lillian or Elidora," Trevor replied. "Have a seat and some coffee, love, and let Brad get back to what he was saying."

Coming up behind Trevor, she wound her arms around his neck and gave him a quick kiss. "You've picked up some useful therapy skills over the years. Nice work!" Turning to Brad, she said, "Sorry for interrupting. Mind if I listen?"

"Not at all," he murmured. "Barbara had other men from time to time. She didn't tell me directly, but I knew. We were close to divorce, and then one of the pregnancies stuck."

Looking at Lara, he added, "One thing I told you was partially true, about us trying and trying to have kids. Anyhow," he sighed, "I had one foot out the door when they did amniocentesis, and I found out it was my baby. So I stayed and Adriana became the true love of my life. I doted on that girl. My marriage never really got any better. In fact, it got worse. Barbara was jealous of every minute I spent doing things with Adie, and she got lots more blatant about her affairs.

"I finally sat her down one night and told her if she brought one more guy home, I'd file for divorce and go for sole custody. That seemed to get through to her. She didn't stop fucking... Uh, sorry, Doc." He glanced contritely at Lara.

"No worries." Lara smiled gently. "I've heard much worse."

A corner of his mouth turned down as he said, "Yeah, I suppose you have. At least Barbara stopped hauling her men home after that. We were planning to split up as soon as Adriana was out of high school, which was fine by me. I couldn't stand to touch her. Hadn't even kissed her for years, not since I knew for sure about all her lovers. When I sent her to Wenatchee after the riots started, she as much as told me she wasn't coming back.

"Reason I told you all that," he splayed his long-fingered hands on the table, "is so you'd understand I don't really have anything to go back to. Haven't been back to Colorado since I left. Don't have any friends on the force, just lots of acquaintances. They're men I'd trust my life to, but somehow we never found any common ground outside police work.

"Adie's here, and I think that means I should be too. So," he looked from Trevor to Lara and back again, "if you'll have me, I'd like to stay. I didn't bring anything with me to help out, but that's only because I didn't understand."

Trevor exchanged a glance with Lara, who nodded at him. With the knowledge born of long familiarity with one another, he felt certain of her support when he reached over, hand extended, to shake one of Brad's. "It's fine with us if you want to be here," he said. "There's lots I don't know about subsistence farming, and it'll be good to have another pair of hands."

"Yes." Lara smiled at the detective. "Trevor and I talked about it last night. We pretty much decided you'd be far safer here than going back."

Raven, Lillian, and Elidora pushed through the back door with Gunter at their heels. Glancing at them, Trevor was appalled by how worn down they looked. Trying not to stare at their gaunt faces, he wondered what the three had been up to, since it didn't appear they'd slept at all.

While he was considering what might have kept them awake, Gunter ran hard for him demanding attention, detouring along the way so Lara could pet him too.

"There you are, snookums," she cooed. "Did you miss me? Because I sure missed you. It was lonely with just Daddy and me in the bed." Looking solemnly at her, the small Shepherd licked her before heading for his food dish.

"I heard some of that conversation," Raven informed them stiffly. "I don't mean the one you just had with the dog," he looked at Lara, "but the words that came before. Our decision was somewhat different. After discussing the matter for much of the night, we think yon human," he pointed at Brad, "must leave. We will tease out the memories associated with him being here and erase them. After that, he will return to whatever it is he did in his world."

Trevor looked from Raven to Lara, since he had a feeling what was going to happen next. He laid a hand on Lara's arm, but she shook it off. "Watch it," he said softly. "If you irritate him, it's hard to say what might happen." Trevor pushed his chair back, wincing in anticipation of Lara's temper.

She leaped to her feet and swung to face the mage. "Oh, so you *decided*, did you?" she inquired acerbically. "Well when you *decided* Elidora should be here, Trevor and I agreed. Not because I know her very well, but to support her, since she just lost her husband. Brad's lost his daughter. If you get a vote in terms of who's to be here, I say we get one as well."

Standing ramrod straight in front of the mage, she balled her hands into fists. A clump of hair fell across one eye, and she shook out of the way.

Elidora's soft laughter broke the tension. "Och aye, my laddie, ye've got yoursel' a bit o' a spitfire."

"Yes, she is a tad on the temperamental side," Lillian agreed wryly. "Found that out early on. My trees tried to correct her, and she didn't take well to their opinions."

Oh, what the bloody hell, Trevor thought, just before he opened his mouth. "When you were trying to convince us to move here," he said to Raven, "one of the issues I brought to the table was what would happen if we did something you didn't care for. As I recall, you sloughed it off, calling such an occurrence inconsequential. If we're going to be here, we can't be your puppets. Lara and I are our own people. We don't always agree, but we do make our own decisions."

"And our decision was Brad could stay," Lara said firmly, still planted about six inches from Raven as she glared at him, defiance blazing from her dark eyes.

The corners of Raven's mouth twitched above his beard. His gray eyes twinkled, and he threw back his head and roared until tears rolled down his face. Wiping them away, he finally stopped laughing long enough to pull Lara into an embrace. "Well said, human. Sometimes I need reminding I'm not omniscient." Releasing her, he swung her toward Trevor, smacked her playfully on the rump, and said, "Go."

"I told you they've gotten presumptuous in the past few hundred years." Lillian smirked complacently. "You haven't spent much time with them. I have."

"Och, the two o' you." Elidora threw her hands in the air. "I have been far closer t' yon humans than either o' you, and they always had a good bit o' nerve mixed in with plain horse sense."

"Now that's settled, could we scare up something to eat?" Lara asked, looking around at everyone. "There are things we need to talk about."

"Like who's going to milk the goats this morning?" Trevor asked, smiling.

"Already taken care of," Lillian informed him. "Left the pail on the porch along with half a dozen eggs."

"Brilliant!" Trevor stood and culled through some open bins. Straightening, he said, "Think I've got what I need for French toast, or, more accurately, French biscuits." He turned back to Brad, who'd shrunk to near invisibility while Lara and Raven haggled over him.

Apparently noticing Trevor's gaze, Brad mumbled an embarrassed, "Thank you." He pushed to his feet with a forthright gravity and bowed slightly, first to Lara, then to Trevor. "That's the first time in my life anyone's ever stood up for me. I like how it feels."

"Your daughter would've," Lara said softly, "if she'd been able to finish growing up."

"Yes." Brad nodded. His eyes glistened with tears that he brushed away. "I'm sure that's the truth of things." Walking over to Raven, he stuck out a hand. "You won't be sorry," he said with conviction. "I wouldn't do anything to jeopardize this location. Not now. Not ever."

After a pause long enough that Brad's hand began to droop, the mage reached out and clasped it. "I am sorry," he said, and sincerity underscored his words. "It wasn't your fault my friend and companion, Gren, is no longer with us. Yet, I wanted to blame someone, and so I blamed you. That was wrong. Please forgive me."

"Nothing to forgive," Brad stammered slightly. "I forced my way in here. I'm just grateful to be allowed to stay. Should I move my car?" Brad still held the mage's gray gaze.

"Where is it?"

"A mile down on a logging road under some trees."

"Aye, ye'll be wantin' t' do that. There are natural protections here to ensure it willna be found," Elidora answered. Walking over to Brad, she patted one of his hands. "We have both lost someone we loved more than all th' world," she continued in her soft brogue. "If ye'll have me, I would walk with you. Th' silent spaces in our grief will be a comfort t' us."

The detective stiffened at Elidora's touch. Her tender words must have struck a chord though, because after a moment or two he offered her his arm, and the two of them walked slowly from the room.

"Lara." Trevor walked to her side and touched her with flour-coated fingers. "Feel like helping out?"

"Sure you want me to?" She looked at him, her dark eyes luminous and happy. "You've always seen me as a jinx in your kitchen."

"Yes," he said and tugged her into an embrace, heedless of getting flour on her robe. "I am."

Raven, who'd detoured into the living room, returned and plunked the Sidhe book on the kitchen table. "When you've finished helping with breakfast," he extricated Lara from Trevor's arms, took her hand, and laid it atop the thick volume, "You can settle in with this."

She smiled broadly at him, "I'm not sure quite why, but I really want to read it now. It's not like the other times when I felt as if I *had* to, and a part of me rebelled." The moonstone amulet thrummed warmly against her skin, adding its endorsement to the conversation.

"That's because you're here, daughter." Lillian moved close and drew her into a hug. "While not quite as powerful as my tree house, this place has its own style of magic. If you let it, it'll heal some of the wounding from the past few days." Kissing Lara tenderly on the cheek, the Sidhe let her go.

"What do you want me to do?" Lara asked and walked to Trevor's side.

He was busy whipping eggs and milk together in a stoneware mixing bowl. "There's butter from the market over there," he pointed, "and a skillet beneath the counter."

"I get the picture." She laughed. "Melt fat for you to fry those biscuits in, once you've soaked them in eggs and milk."

"Yes, love." As he smiled back at her, the apprehension that had dogged him ever since the night his car had spun out of control began to recede. *Maybe this will work out better than I think. Even though the Sidhe can be difficult, it's quite the stroke of luck that Lara found Lillian in the first place.*

Maybe not luck, a different inner voice intruded. *Perhaps things were meant to happen just as they have.* He tossed more wood into the stove and whistled a merry Gaelic tune as he dunked the biscuits into his bowl, and then dropped them into the waiting skillet to cook.

Gunter yapped happily from his spot on the braided rug next to the woodstove. Getting up to make the rounds, he solicited pets from everybody.

"It's almost as if you know there'll be a happy ending," Lara murmured, stroking his puppy fluff that was giving way to a rough outer coat.

"That, my dear, will depend on you." Lillian clucked to the dog as she looked meaningfully at Lara.

Smiling at the Sidhe, Lara reached for the book that would teach her about her magic, flipped it open, and began to read.

YOU'VE REACHED the end of *Dark Pursuit*. Read on for a sample from *Dark Promise*, last of the Soul Storm books.

ABOUT THE AUTHOR

Ann Gimpel is a USA Today bestselling author. A lifelong aficionado of the unusual, she began writing speculative fiction a few years ago. Since then her short fiction has appeared in a number of webzines and anthologies. Her longer books run the gamut from urban fantasy to paranormal romance. Once upon a time, she nurtured clients, now she nurtures dark, gritty fantasy stories that push hard against reality. When she's not writing, she's in the backcountry getting down and dirty with her camera. She's published over 50 books to date, with several more planned for 2018 and beyond. A husband, grown children, grandchildren and wolf hybrids round out her family.

Keep up with her at www.anngimpel.com or http://anngimpel.blogspot.com

If you enjoyed what you read, get in line for special offers and pre-release special reads. Sign up for Ann's newsletter on her website or her blog.

This series concludes in *Dark Promise*, Book Three of the Soul Storm Series. An excerpt follows:

DARK PROMISE—PROLOGUE

Gradoxst slipped away from the festivities. His Goblin commanders were so drunk they could barely stand; they'd never notice his absence. Once he'd put some distance between himself and the revelry, he allowed his lips to draw back in a sneer. He needed his Goblin cohorts, at least right now, but their coarse ways disgusted him. They reeked of dead meat, and the dirtier they were, the more they liked it.

He knew better than to let them know how he truly felt. Gradoxst wasn't under any illusions. The Goblins would turn on him in a trice if they could see into his mind. A muted laugh bubbled past his lips. Not much danger on that front. Mind reading was a Sidhe skill. As far as he knew, he was the only Sidhe who'd embraced darkness in millennia.

As he walked toward the castle in the *Dreaming*, Gradoxst recalled the day long ago when the gods picked Raven over him. Even now, thousands of years later, anger ate at his guts like acid at the memory. To be sure, he'd waited his turn, but the gods had passed him over many times. Finally, sick of waiting for the recognition he deserved, Gradoxst had taken matters in hand. The gods weren't the only ones who could augment his power.

He walked beneath an impressive stone archway that curved fifteen feet above his head. The castle was made of flat gray stones so cunningly arranged it was hard to see where one block ended and the next began. A sense of pride in Sidhe workmanship filled him, but he pushed it aside.

Gradoxst needed to hurry. The stones would recognize his Sidhe blood and allow him entrance. But they'd sense soon enough he'd parlayed with Demons. By then he needed to be well ensconced in the lowest level of the castle for his plan to succeed. He grinned, pleased with himself. To be sure, he and the Goblins were gradually wresting the *Dreaming* from the Sidhe. If he was successful, today would hasten things dramatically.

He trotted down curving stone staircases ever deeper into the earth. His mage light bobbed along beside him, adding a crimson tinge to things. A shudder ran through the rock. He knew he'd been discovered and broke into a run, sucking air like a bellows. He cursed his ancient bones. Every step made something ache.

What he wouldn't give to be young again. Truly young, before he'd traded sidestepping the aging process to enhance his magic. He still remembered the lascivious grin on the Demon lord's face as he'd asked if Gradoxst was quite sure he was willing to relinquish the *appearance of youth.* The second he'd nodded, his body had felt as if it were on fire. When he'd staggered to a mirror, he'd been shocked to see a seamed face and rheumy eyes staring back at him.

He breathed a calming spell as he ran, aiming it at the rocks. They were always slow to react. He might still make it in time—but only if he gave it everything he had.

Pushing open a heavy door, he raced into a subterranean chamber and immediately placed his hands on two adjacent walls. The incantation he'd readied spilled out almost before his hands were in the proper juxtaposition. He sent his will into the stones, along with a curse that would separate the full-blooded Sidhe fighting him from the roots of their power. Careful to maintain his own link, he concentrated on the Sidhe he'd met in battle over the past month. One by one, he clipped the strands.

The stones trembled. A high, wild sound filled the air. It took a second before Gradoxst realized he was laughing. "Yesssss," he muttered. "It's working. Once I have control of the castle, it's only a matter of time before the rest of the *Dreaming* belongs to me."

He hadn't quite figured out how he'd manage to send the Goblins packing after he no longer needed them. But he was certain he'd think of something. It was possible the stones themselves would undo his handiwork. He just hoped they couldn't work fast enough to sabotage his plans.

"You do not belong here!" echoed through the chamber.

"You're absolutely correct," Gradoxst answered the sentient rocks. "And there's not a damned thing you can do about it now."

DARK PROMISE, CHAPTER ONE

*L*ara McInnis sat at an old-fashioned foot treadle sewing machine, working her way through a stack of ripped and worn clothing. As she pulled another pair of Trevor's work pants from under the presser foot, she shook her head and shoved a few long strands of coppery hair out of her eyes with an absentminded gesture.

"I don't see why it's so hard to keep things decent out here," she muttered, pulling thread through the built-in cutter behind the needle holder. Sitting straighter, she rotated her shoulder blades. As soon as she moved, Gunter, a seven-month-old German Shepherd, rose from where he'd been lying in a corner of the room and came to her, shoving his nose against her leg. His rough outer coat was still damp from an earlier romp outdoors.

"You're right," she announced to the dog. "I've been sitting here way too long. Bet you'd like to go outside and stretch those legs." The dog whined, tossed his head, and trotted to the door, looking over his shoulder as if to say, *aren't you coming?* He shook himself from stem to stern, black fur flying. Lara eyed the dust bunnies in the corners of the room and started to laugh. Cleaning was a pretty low priority when you had to hunt down your food before you could cook it—with no friendly neighborhood store to bail you out.

It hadn't seemed safe to venture as far as Skykomish, let alone a larger city, to replenish their supplies. Her thoughts turned to the riots and food shortages that had driven them out of Seattle and she shivered.

She wondered what time it was. She'd stopped glancing at her wrist for the watch that wasn't there a couple months before. Getting to her feet, she strode briskly to the window and craned her neck to see if she could determine the juxtaposition of the sun in the sky.

Aw crap! It can't be that late. Apparently, she'd been sitting at the sewing machine for hours since it was closing on late afternoon.

A sudden chill ran through her. Maybe she'd imagined it, but it felt as is if someone just walked over her grave. Lara shook her head to clear the uneasiness. Her pregnancy made her hypersensitive. That was probably it.

"Come on." She clucked to Gunter as she clattered down the stairs of the rustic, turn-of-the-century lodge that had become her home four months before. Pushing the front door open so the dog could go outside, she scanned the empty yard. Trevor and Brad had left that morning to go hunting. She didn't understand why they hadn't returned yet.

"Brrr." She shivered, pulling the door shut. Lara wasn't worried about the dog. He never ranged far from home. As she paced through the one large room that comprised the bottom floor of the house to the kitchen end of things—passing assorted soft furniture and overflowing bookshelves along the way—she was more than a little worried about her menfolk, though.

She'd joined her life to Trevor's well over twenty years before. Brad was a much newer addition to their household. He'd become part of their family after she'd helped rescue his daughter from Goblins that had kidnapped her. Her usual sadness whenever she thought about Adriana surfaced, and Lara offered a silent prayer to the goddess for the lovely, blonde seventeen-year-old buried behind their barn.

Brad had been a cop. A detective actually. She and Trevor first met him when he'd apprehended the violent husband of one of her patients, who'd been intent on murdering her. Fortune had thrown them together, and he'd been a part of their lives—in one way or another—ever since.

Lara lifted the lid on the cast iron soup pot she'd begun tossing ingredients into hours before. A fetching smell rose to greet her. Snapping up a spoon, she first stirred, then tasted, the bean and canned vegetable mélange, flavored with the last of a chicken they'd killed two days before. "Not bad," she murmured, wishing for more salt. They'd run out of that last week.

The dog scratched at the back door and she went to let him in. He ran to her and shook himself, water droplets going every which way. "Okay, okay," she laughed. "I get that it's still raining out there." *February. Or is it March by now? Has it done anything but rain this entire winter?*

She shrugged a wool cloak over her shoulders, pushed her long braids under its hood and looked at the dog, eyebrows raised. "Do you want to come?" she asked. "I have to milk the goats and look for eggs."

She'd just walked out onto the wide porch that wrapped all around the house, dog prancing before her, when she felt something curious. Laying a hand on her gently swelling stomach, she stopped, heart filling with wonder as she willed the sensation to return. Yes, there it was again. Like the gentlest of fish tails, brushing against her insides. Sudden tears pricked behind her lids, threatening to overflow.

"Elizabeth," she breathed. "You really are in there." And then she felt foolish. Lara was old to be having a child, and a first child at that. But joy at the life quickening within her brimmed over, and she hummed a tuneless song as she picked up the milking pail and trudged across the muddy yard to the barn. Her boots squished in the ever-present muck. It had rained so much—and snowed when it wasn't raining—nothing ever had a chance to dry out. She shook back her hood and bent to the first goat. The animal stared accusingly at her out of its rectangular eyes.

"I know I'm late," she told it. "The way today has gone, you're lucky I got here at all." But the goat just made goat noises, and Lara stopped talking to it. Eggs in the basket and milk in the pail, she started for the house, noticing light was fading from the day. Her thoughts turned to Trevor and Brad again.

Where the hell are they?

She poured half the milk into a bowl to sour and split the rest between two bottles. As she worked, she thought about Trevor with his blond good looks and his devastating past. She'd been a psychologist before fate had plunked her down at this remote farm. And he'd been a flight attendant. They'd had a pretty posh life. Especially compared with the way things were now.

The dog whined. Her head came up sharply, wondering if it was the men coming back. She rushed to the window, peering out into the gloom-shrouded yard, but it was tough to make out much of anything through the wavy, fin-de-siècle glass.

Reaching for her cloak, she realized she'd never taken it off, and she ran out the back door shouting, "Trevor? Trev, that you?" The slightest of echoes rolled off nearby canyon walls, muted by evergreens growing thickly around the clearing that held the three-story log house. Gunter rubbed up next to her, wet fur against wet wool. He whined again.

"What is it, boy?" she asked anxiously as she scanned the darkening yard. Just as she was about to go back inside, her moonstone amulet began what she'd come to recognize as its warning dirge. It was a magic moonstone, and its assessment of danger was never wrong. Lara laid a hand over her heart; suddenly it was beating far too fast.

"Trevor," she gasped. "Something's happened. I know it has, or else he'd be back by now." Kicking herself for not being more vigilant about the time, Lara knew she had to look for him. That was what the amulet was trying to tell her. It was only half an hour from full dark, and she didn't have any idea what direction he and Brad had taken.

She stood there for half a minute, flummoxed, trying to figure out what to do. It would've been helpful to confer with Lillian, Raven, or Elidora, but they'd left yesterday. In contrast to previous leave-takings, Raven wasn't sure just when they'd be back.

"Yeah, I could really use their magic right about now," she muttered as she thought about the three Sidhe—well, Raven was actually more of a mage and a god—who'd taught her everything she knew about how to summon and control her own magical abilities. She'd been late learning about them too, just like she was late becoming a mother.

Sometimes she felt like Alice in Wonderland because nothing was like it seemed. Turned out Baen Sidhe meant *woman of the Sidhe*. Though both Lillian and Elidora had introduced themselves that way, their magical ability extended far beyond knowing who was to die and wailing over corpses.

Lillian's voice filled her mind. *I have been many things in my lifetime. It was a wee bit early for psychology, but I did spend years as a local wise-woman, handing out advice.*

Wishing for some of that advice now, Lara trooped back into the house for warm gloves, a flashlight, and a few bandages. Stuffing things into a backpack, she poured some mead into a flask, tucking that in as well. The dog milled about as she ran this way and that, gathering things.

By the time she was finally as prepared as she could be, it was almost totally dark. She considered taking one of the two horses, but decided it would be too risky. She didn't ride well as it was; a journey in the dark, where she couldn't see to guide the animal, seemed particularly unwise. If the horse threw her, she might lose the baby. Besides, she'd never tried mixing her magic with horseback riding before, and this didn't seem like a good time to start.

Damn! She realized she hadn't eaten since breakfast. Before letting herself and Gunter out the door, she damped the fire under her soup and grabbed some leftover cornbread. Out in the yard, she stuffed crumbs into her mouth, chewing hastily. Then she stood still, quieted her mind like Lillian had taught her, and grasped the moonstone. Nothing happened. It took her a minute or two to understand and, fuming with irritation at the delay, she tugged off one of her gloves, placing her hand on the magical gem, flesh to stone.

The familiar jolt of power rocked her. Four paths opened: one leading up, one down, one to a grassy glade, and another to a babbling brook. "Tell me," she spoke harshly. "Which passageway should I take?" The moonstone just thrummed in her hand.

Her mind was in too much turmoil to sense anything. Lara forced herself to breathe as she stood in the bone-chilling rain. After what seemed like ages, the timbre of the amulet changed, and she understood she was to tread the road going down into the earth.

"All right," she said evenly, turned to Gunter, and sent him back onto the porch. She couldn't take the time to escort him. Once the magic took her, she didn't dare deviate from the path it set. She wasn't proficient enough yet, even with the boost from her pregnancy.

Lara started walking. She'd taken each of the paths at least a time or two, but this route was by far the hardest for her. The sensation of earth closing about her was claustrophobic. She fought terror as every step led her farther and farther from the familiar. Some of the spirit paths were kind, but not this one. Lara trusted the amulet, though. She gripped it so hard the edges of the gold setting cut into her hand. As her blood dribbled out, the amulet's song intensified. Lillian's voice rang in her mind. *Blood consecrates all.*

She worried about Gunter, but even a minor shift in her concentration caused the dirt walls about her to waver, moving even closer. She wrenched her attention back to the moonstone and her missing love.

Lara's breath was ragged. Her steps felt leaden—each one a struggle—when the earth beneath her feet shifted, leading her upward. For the briefest of moments she was afraid she'd collapse and die in this magical realm, with millions of tons of dirt as her crypt, but the amulet pricked her hand and she pulled herself together.

Just keep walking. Yes, that's right. One step in front of the other. If I think about this, I'll be lost. Her body ached. The hand glued to the amulet was cramping. As the slope under her boots steepened, she wondered how much longer she could keep going before her legs refused to obey.

Suddenly, as always happened when she trod the magic-imbued ways, the dirt fell away like a curtain pulled open by an unseen puppeteer. She was back in the forest, and it was completely dark. Disoriented, she had no idea how far she'd traveled or where home might be. Cupping her hands around her mouth, she cried out for Trevor, understanding this was where the goddess had led her. Her voice, barely there after her minutes—or had it been hours?—underground cracked, so she dropped her pack to retrieve a water bottle, took a slug, and tried again.

"Trevor? Trevor?"

"Lara!" His oh-so-welcome voice reverberated off to her left.

"Yes, it's me. I'm coming." Heart hammering in her chest like a frightened bird, she sent hasty prayers to Brigid and Artemis for keeping him safe. At least she thought he was safe. He could still talk. Why hadn't he come home? Had he gotten lost? She shook her head. *Not possible. He's always had the bearings of an Indian scout.*

"This way. Hurry, Lara!" His voice spurred her into action. Pulling out the flashlight she'd carefully conserved for emergencies, she shouldered her pack and moved toward the sound, using her light to avoid tripping over the thick, wet undergrowth. *Good thing I didn't bring one of the horses. They'd have caught a hoof in that mess and gone down for sure. Besides, then I wouldn't have had magic to help me, and I'd probably still be wandering about in the forest screaming my brains out.*

The two men came into sight quickly. Trevor knelt on the ground next to Brad, who was propped against a tree. Scrambling to his feet as soon as he saw her, Trevor opened his arms, drawing her close.

"Blimey, love, but you're a sight for sore eyes." His British accent, pronounced as ever, cheered her, and she hugged him hard.

"What happened?" she asked, inhaling Trevor's enticing scent that mingled with the wet wool he wore.

"Someone else has been out here," Trevor said, a hard edge in his voice. "Must've been, because Brad stepped into a trap. Lucky it was just for mountain lions or coyotes. If it'd been a bear trap, he would've lost his foot. As it is, he's lost a lot of blood. We tried walking a few times, but he always started bleeding so badly, I worried he'd pass out. And I can't carry him."

Lifting her head from Trevor's shoulder, Lara looked about nervously. What if someone was watching them? Her hand snaked to the amulet in search of clues, but it lay passively in her grasp.

"Nicked an artery. Or maybe a vein." Brad's weary voice rose from his bed on the ground. "Kept thinking if we just rested it a bit and bandaged it tight, it'd let up. But it never did. Maybe because we didn't have much in the way of bandages." He hesitated, then added, "Trap was rusty, so it might've been here for a long time."

"How far are we from home?" Worries about the trap's owner lurking somewhere in the darkness nagged at Lara.

"But you just found us," Trevor said and then shook his head. "Sorry. Wasn't thinking. Guess you couldn't have tracked us. It's dark. Must've used your magic." He was still hanging onto her for all he was worth.

She pushed back to look at him. Wet, blond curls clung to his skull, but his ever-so-blue eyes shone with happiness that she'd found them. She hunkered down, playing her light over Brad. His normally pale complexion was even whiter than usual. A wool cap covered his shaggy, white-blond hair, and his bearded face was pinched with pain. She patted his hand, and then rocked back on her heels and pushed to her feet.

"By the time I knew you weren't coming back," she explained to both of them, "it was well toward twilight. I asked the goddess for help, which is why I have no idea where the farmhouse is." She shucked her pack and pulled out the flask. "Here." She handed it to Brad. "Drink some of this. It should help. I'll take a look at your leg and try to get it better wrapped. I brought bandages."

Brad extended a hand for the flask, uncapped it, and took a deep draught. And then one more. She dragged her pack over next to him and twisted around, handing Trevor her flashlight. "Don't know what the hell we're going to do when we run out of batteries. Maybe by then I'll have mastered that mage light thing Lillian keeps trying to teach me.

"Anyway, hold the light steady."

Branches made squelching sounds as Trevor repositioned himself. When she got a good look at the lower part of Brad's pant leg, she gasped, and then clapped a hand over her mouth. "Sorry," she mumbled.

"Yeah, I know. It's pretty bad." Brad's voice was weak. "Remember, I was an Army medic before I was a cop."

"Okay." She drew in a breath. "I hadn't actually forgotten that, but it wasn't front and center, either. Since you've had that training, what would you do with a wound like this?"

"Cut the pant leg away, clean it, stitch it, and put a tourniquet higher up if it wouldn't stop bleeding."

She rummaged through her pack for what she'd brought. "With all this water," she waved a hand at the falling rain, "you'd think there'd be a brook somewhere nearby. Is there?"

"Yes. About fifty feet to the north," Trevor replied. "If I go for water, I can't hold the light."

"I'll manage," she said tersely, already using a multi-faceted pocketknife with a small pair of scissors to cut through the blood-soaked denim of Brad's jeans. "Rain'll help some. But it would be good to sluice a decent stream of water over what's under here. How long ago did this happen?"

"A few hours," Trevor said sheepishly. "Kept trying to tell him we needed to stop and tend to it, but he wanted to keep going. And then he got so weak we had to stop."

She turned her attention back to Brad's leg. "There. Just a little more."

Trevor handed her the light and she balanced it in her lap. "Back directly," he said.

Lara snipped at the thick fabric. It didn't help that the scissor blades were only an inch long. At least they were sharp. When the fabric finally fell away, her eyes widened. "Jesus Christ," she breathed. "It's down to the bone in one spot here. No wonder it wouldn't stop bleeding."

He's going to get an infection unless we can get this clean and keep it that way.

"Need antibiotics." He spoke in a remarkably matter-of-fact tone. Almost as if he were discussing someone else's injury.

"Uh-huh. When was your last tetanus shot?"

"Not sure. But it's up-to-date. Had to be for the police force."

Thank God. One less thing to worry about. She heard Trevor's boots trampling through wet vegetation. For a moment, she thought maybe they should boil the water, then she stifled a sour laugh. Odds of getting a fire going out here were practically nil.

Trevor bent over her and a long, low whistle escaped him.

"Never mind that," she said tersely. "Just pour." Once he finished, she added, "Sorry. Haven't had nearly enough to eat today. So I'm grumpy."

"I noticed," he replied, with a touch of understated humor.

She dredged bandage material out of her pack. Working quickly, she wound layers of gauze from Brad's ankle halfway to his knee, following it up with a good-sized Ace wrap.

"That should do it," she said. "It really didn't bleed much while I was dressing it." The corners of her mouth turned downward. "Should've gone to medical school. Too bad I wasn't a shade more prescient about the future."

She picked up her flashlight, moving it to illuminate Brad Archer's gaunt face. "If both of us help you," she asked, "do you think you could walk?"

"I have to," he said, reaching both hands toward Trevor. "Come on," he urged. "Don't worry about hurting me. Just help me up." A muted yelp escaped the normally taciturn detective as Trevor pulled him to his feet.

Lara threw everything in her pack and hoisted it onto her back. "You never did tell me. How far are we from home?" She walked to Brad's side and looped an arm around his waist to help support him. Trevor took the other side, placing his arm just below Lara's.

"About an hour, I think," Trevor replied. "There's a game trail just over there." He pointed with his free hand. "But they're only helpful if you're traveling single file. We'll put Brad in the middle. That way he'll have an easier time walking."

They made slow progress since the ground on either side of the trail was uneven and choked with plants and vines. Lara's flashlight got dimmer and dimmer. "Damn!" she swore. "It's about to die. Not that it'll be much worse than what we've had for the past while. The light's been so weak, it hasn't been any good at all. How much farther do you think?"

"Not sure," Trevor murmured. "Part of me thinks we should have been there by now."

A chill ran down Lara's spine. The Goblins and Demons were far from gone. Gradoxst, sort of a Demon who'd started out as a Sidhe, had it in for her. He'd been hounding her for months. Eyes widening in horror, she wondered if he'd laid the trap. Things rusted quickly in the ever-damp Pacific Northwest. It could've been set last month—or last week—for all she knew. Lara shifted her gaze from side to side, trying to see.

Was Gradoxst out there somewhere, watching them?

"Hang on," she said, slowing so she could reach for the amulet with her free hand. It had been strangely silent since leading her to Brad. Usually it maintained a soothing hum.

Closing her Earth eyes, she reached for the place where she could see things through her third eye. Brad's fading energy and Trevor's warm concern pulsed against her, but she didn't sense Goblins anywhere near. Breath whooshed out of her, and she knew how tense she'd been.

Lara was fairly certain the amulet could lead them home, except she'd never used it as a dowsing rod before. She was just contemplating what to do next and how to bend the amulet to her will, when a gibbous moon slid from behind a cloud, shedding a greenish glow on the damp landscape.

"Artemis and her moon," Trevor cried and blew an enthusiastic kiss skyward. "Things are looking better, love."

Startled out of a half trance, Lara thought about the goddess who'd saved Trevor from certain death at the hands of a Goblin and smiled to herself. *Who knows? Perhaps things are getting better.* "Hush, dear. I'm trying to concentrate."

He shook his head. "Lara, I know where we are now. I can see some landmarks. I got a bit off course is all. We're only about a quarter mile from home. It's just off to our left."

She stared at the thick, evergreen forest. *Landmarks? Shit, it all looks the same to me.* "Are you sure?"

He nodded, then asked, "How you doing, Brad? Can you make it another ten minutes or so?"

An almost imperceptible moan was followed by, "Yes. Lara did a good job. I don't think I'm bleeding anymore."

True to Trevor's uncanny sense of direction, even Lara knew they were close to home after five more minutes of walking. They came to the brook bubbling down from Troublesome Mountain. Tonight it was more like a raging torrent, so they followed the bank until they reached the bridge. Water lapped over its rough log planks. Gunter's excited barks rang out, and the young Shepherd raced out of the shadows of the yard to dance around them, nipping and yapping shamelessly.

"Enough." Trevor reached down to calm the over-excited dog. "Yes, we're home. We wouldn't leave you here by yourself, silly."

The porch steps weren't as difficult as Lara feared they might be. Brad had obviously spent time on crutches and he leaned on both of them in lieu of putting weight on his injured leg. As they passed through the door and into the farmhouse, Trevor said, "I'll get the fire going."

"And I'll heat some water to do a better job cleaning your leg," Lara told Brad once they'd settled him on one of the sofas in the living room. She dropped her pack and hustled toward her soup pot, stumbling with weariness as she shucked her sodden wool cloak and draped it over a peg in the kitchen.

Wonder if I can coax a fire with magic or if I'm too done in. Peering into the woodstove's firebox, she was pleasantly surprised to see coals. She tossed in more wood, scooped a mug of lukewarm soup out of her pot, and slurped it down greedily. She'd just started on a second mug, when both soup and water seemed warm enough for Brad.

"Trev?"

He was by her side in an instant. "I'll take some for Brad and me." He ladled soup into two more mugs.

"Great, I'll run upstairs for clean linen and get a basin of hot water."

"You sure?" He put down the mugs and spun her to face him, hands on her shoulders. "You look knackered, love. Sure you don't want me to get those towels?"

"I'd say we're about equal in the knackered department." She tried to copy his accent and failed miserably.

"I'm not pregnant," he pointed out, lowering one hand to place it protectively over her midsection.

"It's not a disease," she countered. "Just go give Brad his soup. He needs liquids since he lost so much blood. There's some leftover cornbread too, if he feels like it."

"Well, even if he doesn't, I do. I'm so hungry, the nosh could be boiled Goblins, and I'd suck it down anyway."

When Lara came into the living room, towels draped over one arm, balancing a basin of steaming water, she was heartened to see the men eating and finishing off the mead from the flask in her pack. Brad's color looked a smidge better too.

"Nurse Nancy, at your service," she quipped, settling herself at the end of the sofa. Brad's boots were already off, and Trevor had removed the detective's soaking wet socks. The fire had warmed the room nicely, and the socks were steaming on the ornamental grate in front of the open fireplace.

"If your feet are as wet as his," she looked hard at Trevor, "maybe you should get your boots off too."

She unwound the Ace wrap. Brad had been correct that his wound had finally quit bleeding. When she got all the bandages off, she surveyed the damage in light from a kerosene lamp. "There's only this one place that looks really bad to me," she said. "The rest of it is just a series of puncture wounds from the jaws of the trap."

"Those are the worst kind," Brad noted as he craned his neck to assess his injuries. "Because they're deep, they're really prone to infection."

"I brought iodine with me from upstairs." She drew a bottle of Betadine from a pocket. "That should help."

"Maybe." Brad sounded dubious. "Antibiotics would be better. Do we have any here?"

"I don't think so." Trevor scratched at his wet curls.

"We left in such a hurry," Lara added, "we weren't as thorough as we should have been." She rolled her eyes. "Raven predicted gloom and doom if we didn't drop everything and skedaddle. Does it hurt?" She tucked towels under his leg, pouring hot water over the wound to finish cleaning dirt and debris out of it.

"Some. But it's not bad. Let me help." He took the cloth from her and scrubbed his leg far more vigorously than she'd been doing. "I know what I can tolerate," he explained, wincing. "Give me another one." He held out his hand for a fresh towel.

Once the wound was as clean as Lara thought it was going to get, she furled her brows at Brad and asked, "What do you think? Do we saturate it with iodine and leave it open?" The detective nodded. She dribbled disinfectant over each place the skin was torn.

Straightening, she picked up the mead flask. "Is there any left?" Without waiting for an answer, she upended it, licking droplets off the neck of the bottle when she was done swallowing. "Why don't you sack out here?" she suggested to Brad.

Despite all the empty bedrooms on the second and third floors, Brad had settled in one of the outbuildings. The arrangement offered all of them privacy. If things got worse, though, she thought it would be easier if they didn't have to drag him back into the house.

He didn't answer. When she looked at him, his eyes were already closed.

Trevor touched her arm. Placing a finger over his lips, he gathered the blood-soaked towels and cooling basin of water, gesturing for her to follow him. "Water still hot?" he asked as they reached the kitchen.

"Should be," she replied wearily. Falling into a chair, she supported her head on an upraised hand.

"Great. I'll just brew us up a nice cuppa. Do you want any more to eat?" At her nod, he ladled soup into a mug and cut her a generous slice of cornbread before selecting tealeaves and pouring water over them. Gunter, who'd been asleep, lurched muzzily to Lara's side, probably hoping she'd drop something.

"Feel like talking?" she asked between bites.

"Sure." Trevor ate like a starving person, chewing and swallowing as fast as he could manage.

"If that wound gets infected..." Her voice trailed off.

"I've already thought about that," he broke in. "We did have antibiotics back at home. Lots of them. We were twits not to bring any. They wouldn't have taken up any space at all."

"So?" She blew out a tired breath. "They may as well be on Mars for all the good they'll do Brad. Tomorrow I'll hunt for wild onions and garlic and try to make a poultice. Maybe Elidora and Lillian will be back by then. I'm sure they know how to treat infections."

"Do you know where they went?"

Lara shook her head. "They were even more close-mouthed about their plans than usual this time."

"Humph." Trevor sipped his tea. He looked across at Lara, a touch of defiance in his expression. "Hear me out before you say anything."

Cocking her head to one side, she gestured with the hand not holding her fork. "Whatever it is, Trev, out with it. I'm so tired I'm starting to wonder if I'll be able to climb the stairs to our bed."

"If Brad gets worse, and Raven and them don't come back in time, I'll take one of the cars and go find him some medicine. I probably won't have to go all the way to Seattle—"

"*What?*" she screeched, incredulous. Her eyes flew open in spite of her exhaustion. "You can't do that. Raven said we can't leave. That it's too dangerous. They've left here these last four months, so they know what it's like out there. We haven't. They said—"

"I don't care what they said." Trevor's voice had the mulish tone it got whenever he was determined to do something. "I'm not going to stand by and let Brad die." He hesitated. "Look, Lara. It's late and we're both shattered beyond measure. Let's let this percolate, and we can talk about it more in the morning."

She drained her tea, stood, and clumped toward the stairs, too stunned by his pronouncement—and far too worn out—to attempt anything further in the way of conversation.